P9-BIU-862

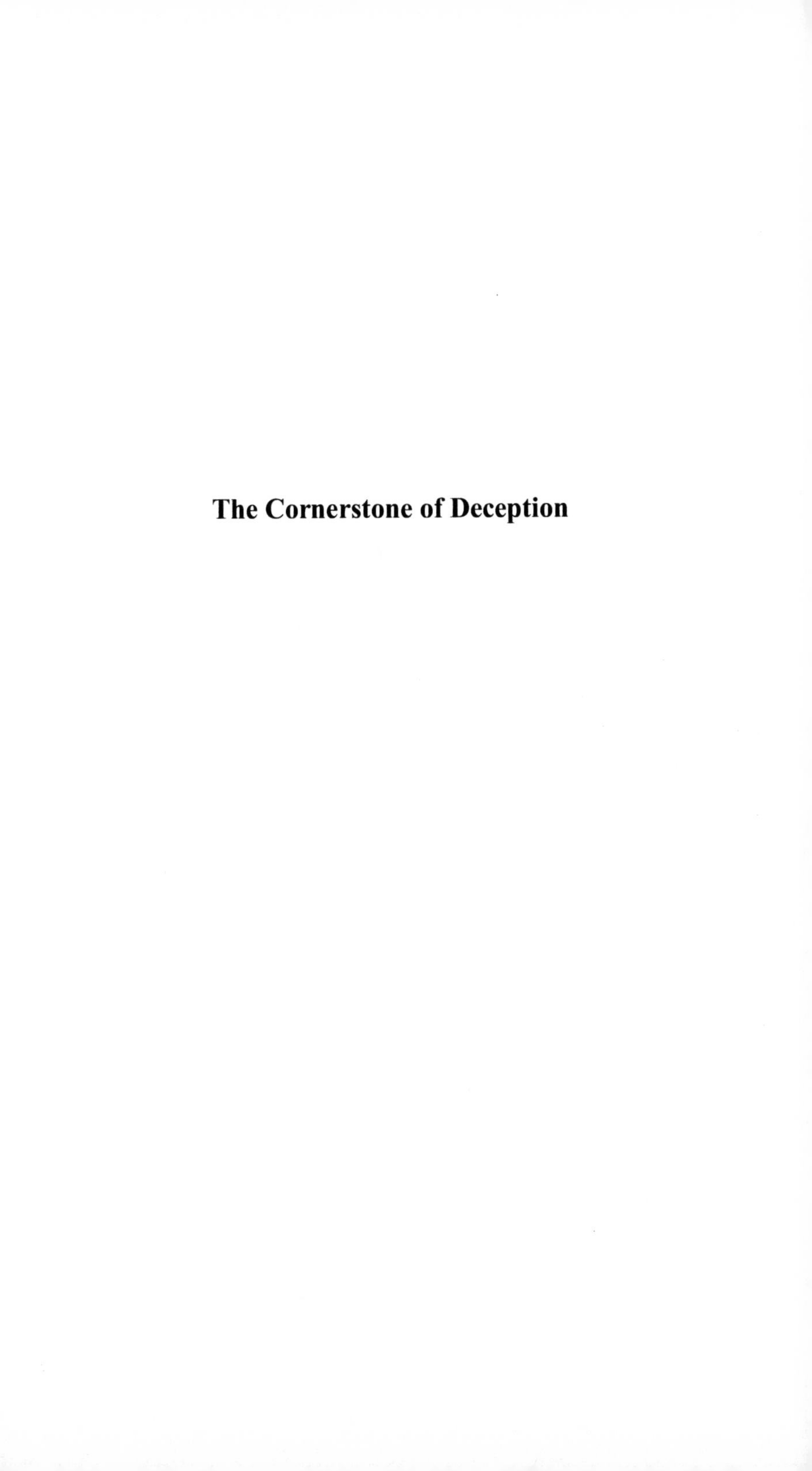

The Cornerstone of Deception

The Cornerstone of Deception

A Novel

by

Cheryl Simani

© Cheryl Simani 2011-03-31
All rights reserved.
No part of this publication may be reproduced or transmitted in any form or by any means, electronic or mechanical, including photocopying, recording or any information storage or retrieval system, except for the inclusion of brief quotation in review, without prior permission in writing from the author.

Library of Congress Cataloguing-in-Publication Data
A catalogue record for this book is available from the Library of Congress 1-585010406.

ISBN-13: 978-1461052814
ISBN-10: 1461052815

Published by The Third House
in the United States of America.

Dedicated to:

David and Masha Fink,
who first encouraged me to rewrite my
research as a "conspiracy theory" novel.

Then God designated a worm at the dawn of the next day, and it attacked the garden plant so that it withered. (Jonah 4:7)

The Cornerstone of Deception

ACKNOWLEDGMENTS

It is essential to express my immense gratitude for the professionalism, patience, and kind assistance of archivists at University of Oxford and the Oxford Dictionary of National Biography. I would also like to thank the librarian at the Royal Asiatic Society, the staff in the Middle East Department at the British Museum, and Manuscript Collections and Enquiries at the British Library. Additional thanks go to the Département Philosophie de l'homme and the Département de la reproduction at the Bibliothèque nationale de France, who provided essential research material and information.

I am deeply indebted to Selina Bichard for her diligent editing of the manuscript and enhancing its British character.

A very special thanks is due to my family and friends for all the encouragement, proofing, and suggestions:
Mark Ephron, Mendi Slodowitz, Dov Liberman, Mark Krezner, Lloyd Kleiman, Suzan Wikoff, Steve Rosenblatt, Della and John Wing, Bill, Tammy and Steve Smith, Mary Schustereit, and Nancy Martinez. I must express my gratefulness to our children – Guy, Sarah Malkah, Opher Ron, and Simon David; but more than any other, to my dear Israel, who patiently endures a wife who is always researching and writing.

INTRODUCTION

During the Enlightenment Era, the "pursuit of truth" was established as the foundation of modern science. For most early scientists, however, the Bible fell on the flat-world side of the debate and scientific methodology became synonymous with discovering evidence that refuted or disparaged the "Holy Writ."

As an alternative historic perspective, *The Cornerstone of Deception* seeks to restore voice to those who protested the hubristic and despotic tactics of Sir Henry C. Rawlinson and George Smith, but whose voices were silenced more than a century ago. By modern, professional standards, their discoveries are suspicious, for they had the motivation, opportunity, and technical skills needed to perpetuate a fraud.

The Cornerstone of Deception explores a crime against history and the lives of those who wittingly or not played a role.

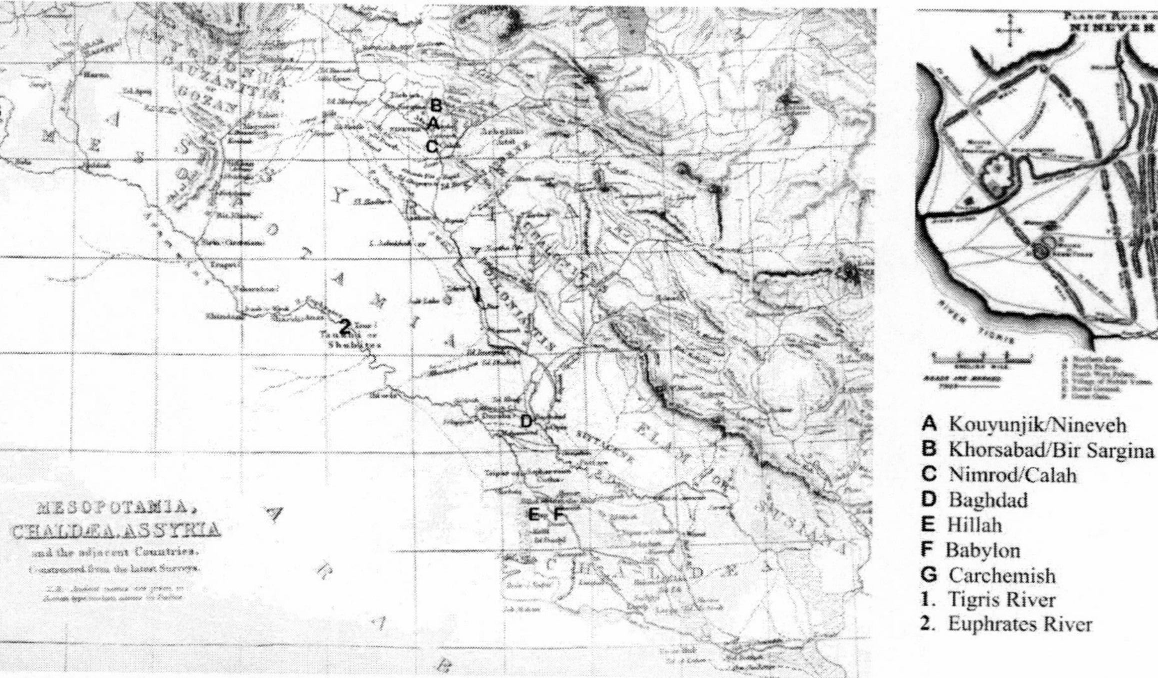

A Kouyunjik/Nineveh
B Khorsabad/Bir Sargina
C Nimrod/Calah
D Baghdad
E Hillah
F Babylon
G Carchemish
1. Tigris River
2. Euphrates River

Map of Mesopotamia: George Rawlinson, *Seven Great Monarchies of the Ancient Eastern World, Vol. I.* New York: John B. Alden, Publisher, 1885.
Map of Nineveh: George Smith, *Assyrian Discoveries: an Account of the Explorations and Discoveries on the Site of Nineveh, during 1873 and 1874.* New York: Scribner, Armstrong Co., 1875.

CHAPTER 1

In Search of Nineveh

Monday, 29 October 1849
Tel Kouyunjik, Turkish Arabia (Iraq)

"That's odd–what have we here?"

Another sniff of the cool, dry air confirmed the faint scent of horse sweat blended with the familiar mustiness. When Austen Layard raised the lantern above his head, the shadows shifted just enough for him to make out the shape of a boot near the entrance to the hewn chamber ahead. He did not proceed until he felt the reassuring heft of the pistol concealed beneath the folds of his robes.

Moving over the high gloss of the sleek riding boots, the light fell on a heavy, black coat covering the sleeping intruder. A mass of dark curls rested on the dull lustre of a saddle. Enough of the sleeper's features were exposed beneath the tilted military cap for a positive identification. Layard grunted and gently kicked his uninvited guest.

In one smooth manouvre, the heavy coat was flung open and a pistol, cocked and ready, was aimed at Layard's chest.

"Easy Rawlinson," Layard soothed. "When did you arrive?"

"I wish you would stop impersonating the native sheiks," Rawlinson muttered sleepily. Propping himself up on his elbow, he added, "That damned *thawb* nearly got you killed."

"It is *you* who should be grateful to be alive, major!" Layard retorted, returning his weapon to its shoulder holster. "You sneak into my realm in the middle of the night, and then have the nerve to insult my lovely gown."

"We arrived just after midnight," Rawlinson said, allowing Layard to pull him to his feet. "I did not wish to disturb your dreams." Finding his canteen near the saddle, he rinsed his dry mouth and quenched his thirst.

"Has the sun risen yet?"

"No. It rises later and later this time of year." Layard brushed his thick, dark hair back from his forehead. "What could be important enough to prompt the British Consul to ride from the comforts of Baghdad to God-cursed Nineveh?"

"Before, you swore that your beloved Nimrod was Nineveh." Rawlinson said, as he massaged his stiff shoulder. "Now, it's this pile of debris."

"Well it is a lady's prerogative to change her mind, isn't it?" joked Layard, holding the side of his robe. Rawlinson chuckled and shook his head. A horse snorted in the dark of an adjacent tunnel.

"Sahib, is it time to go?" asked a sleepy voice in Hindi.

"Yes, Sunil," replied Rawlinson. "Take the mounts out for water and grazing."

The horses skittered back as a lamp illuminated their subterranean stall. A dark, slender man adjusted his turban and silently began gathering the gear. Layard was not surprised. The sepoy had been at Major Rawlinson's side since his early years in India.

"We've ridden for three days. Do you mind if we rest with you before continuing?"

"Consider yourselves my guests," Layard said, bowing slightly. "But where are you going?"

"I'll get to that in a minute," said Rawlinson, taking the lantern from Layard's hand. He held it close to a partially exposed, pitted limestone slab and read aloud, "I, Sennecherib, king of Assyria, servant of the great god Asshur."

"Then you have done it?" exclaimed Layard as he moved nearer. "You have deciphered the script?"

"Did you ever doubt me?" Rawlinson asked, watching Layard's expression.

"No…no… I knew that you would, but I must admit that I am surprised by your speed," Layard stated and nodded, as the servant retrieved Rawlinson's saddle.

"Good morning, Sunil," he greeted. The Indian's black eyes sparkled in the lamplight and a disarming smile flashed beneath his thick moustache. Sunil bowed respectfully before continuing. Layard watched him pause near the junction of the two tunnels, but did not interfere as the man determined which way was correct. The air in one was deathly stagnant, while a slight breeze beckoned to him from the other.

"I look forward to a tour of your latest discoveries," Rawlinson said, retrieving his riding crop from the dust.

"You will be pleased. They are magnificent. This wall in particular is very promising."

As they spoke, a deadly desert scorpion pulled its armoured body from the crevice behind the slab. The movement caught Layard's eye and he reached down for one of the fragments of brick strewn on the uneven floor. Just as the scorpion stretched out against the marred wall, the ancient clay shattered against the slab. The scorpion curled its venomous tail in defiance, but only a quick retreat saved it from the next missile.

"Damned vermin!"

"You were away too long." teased Rawlinson as Layard dusted his hands together.

"It was worth it. Green fields and the smell of sweet, fertile soil, it is as different from this place as Heaven is from Hell," Layard sighed, taking the lantern from Rawlinson. The sound of shouts in Arabic drifted down from the tunnel entrance. His workers were ready to begin digging.

"Come on," said Layard, "I must give my foreman orders, or the morning will be wasted."

The lantern cast deep shadows on the uneven walls as the men made their way through the ruins. Rawlinson ran his hand over the engraved feathered shoulder of a great winged lion that had been partially excavated from the grey dirt wall. At the entrance to the tunnel, Layard assumed a posture of authority as they stepped into the large, irregular trench.

The workers squatted on their haunches at the foot of the ramp used to haul statues to the surface, smoking crude, hand-rolled cigarettes. Their shadows loomed in monstrous proportions against the walls of the excavation. At the sight of the Bey, their lord and benefactor, they jumped to their feet. A tall, stout young man stepped forward.

"Good morning, Toma," greeted Layard in Arabic.

"Good morning, Layard Bey," replied Toma, bowing so low that the sides of the *keffiyeh* covered his face. "The sun will be very hot again today."

"Yes, so it seems," replied Layard, glancing up at cloudless sky. The glimmering stars were fading away one by one, as the inky darkness grew lighter and more translucent.

"Divide the men into two groups. Have one continue clearing this area," Layard pointed to a large section of engraved slabs still shrouded in darkness, "and the other will begin working on the wall we discovered yesterday. You will need to dig an airshaft at the end of the tunnel. It's a foul as a tomb down there. I shall return in two hours to inspect your progress."

"Yes, O Bey, but the men will need more tools."

"We have plenty of tools, Toma," stated Layard with a slight irritation in his tone.

"Before, we had many, O Bey." The palms of Toma's great hands turned upward and his large dark eyes joined them in his plea to the vast mercy of Allah. "But, they have disappeared and cannot be found."

"Find them!" snapped Layard as he started up the ramp.

Toma was disappointed that his ploy was unsuccessful, but recovered quickly and barked a command to the diggers. He glanced warily toward the two crazy infidels.

"Come on, old man," Layard said, turning to Rawlinson. "I am sure we can find you a good cup of Turkish coffee and a bite to eat."

"That man's a thief," stated Rawlinson. "Why do you keep him?"

"My usual foreman did not return this year. Toma lives just across the river in Mosul, and the workers respect the man for his great size."

They climbed up from the great hole, where the labourers prepared to tear the intricately inscribed slabs from the exposed walls beneath the hard gaze of long abandoned stone deities, impotent to prevent them.

On the plateau, the two Englishmen were greeted by a rose-tinted horizon rapidly giving way to a pale, grey blue sky and a near full moon setting low in the west. Layard stood silent while Rawlinson excused himself and entered the only building on the parched and barren plateau—a small mud hut with a reed roof used by his Chaldean workers.

The morning breeze was cool and refreshing, but Layard could not shake off an uneasy feeling that something was odd about the ease with which his friend had deciphered the inscription. There was no question that Rawlinson was a clever and resourceful man. One does not rise through the ranks of the East India Company without possessing those qualities.

The Company had long since abandoned the textiles trade for the more interesting pursuit of military and administrative control of India and the Orient conducted in the name of the Crown. Over the years, it had become a repository for wayward British youths, provided that a family friend or relative had the connections to arrange their appointment. Rawlinson had joined the company as at the age of seventeen. The young cadet had quickly mastered Hindustani and the Mahratti dialect of India. As a young lieutenant, he added the Pharsi of Persia. His labours had been rewarded with a transfer to Teheran. During the Afghan War, a promotion to Major had accompanied his command post at Kandahar.

When stability had returned, Rawlinson had requested the posting to Baghdad because it was closest to the cryptic inscriptions at Behistun that loomed 300 feet above the passing travelers. At whose command had men dangled from the steep mountain face to engrave it, and what message was of such import as to justify the danger? He had been determined to be the first to decipher it and to answer these questions; however, that remarkable feat had taken him ten years to complete. Unfortunately, Rawlinson's knowledge of the Indo-European languages of Hindi and Pharsi, which had aided him with the Old Persian portion of the inscription, were useless for decoding the remaining two sections. These were in Semitic dialects, and thus, based on a completely different linguistic system. This fact troubled Layard.

"Have you found the Assyrians' latrines?" Rawlinson grinned as he emerged from the crude service hut, clearing his nostrils of the foul odour.

"Latrines?" queried Layard.

"They must have had them," smiled Rawlinson.

"Oh certainly - but can you image the sensation the arrival of such a shipment of artefacts would create in London!" Layard laughed.

The dun plain stretched before them, waiting for the relief of the winter rains. Millennia of exposure to the harsh desert winds had rendered it dull and barren.

"I am curious. How did you manage to decipher the symbols?" Layard said.

"Following some good advice I received in a letter last winter, I redirected my energies from Arabic to Hebrew. I found a competent tutor in the good Reverend Strong, under whose instruction I toiled through June. I then locked myself in my study, emerging only to deal with the most urgent business of my office."

Layard was puzzled. Rawlinson had only begun to study Arabic a few months before they met in 1846. Though he could converse reasonably well with common words and redundant-phrases, he was far from bilingual and relied heavily on his secretary for important correspondence. How could he have mastered the long-dead Assyrian tongue with only six months of tutoring in Hebrew? It just did not make sense.

"From whom was the letter?" asked Layard.

"Edwin Norris. He's a translator at the Foreign Office and an assistant secretary to the Royal Asiatic Society," Rawlinson smiled.

"Yes, I've met him. He's a rather timid fellow," Layard said glancing at his companion.

"He has been helpful in editing my articles on deciphering the Old Persian of Behistun," continued Rawlinson, "and also supervised their publication. He even developed a typeface for the symbols."

"Yes, we used it in the publication of my *Nineveh and Its Remains,*" Layard added in a cheerful tone. "I just received my copy. I would like your opinion of it. I mentioned your discoveries."

"I look forward to reviewing it," responded Rawlinson, as they arrived at the edge of the mound. Layard led the way to the incline, which served as the primary access from the village below. They turned their backs to the sun, which was growing more oppressive by the moment, although the morning mist still clung to the strips of green bordering the dark waters of the Tigris. From their high viewpoint, Rawlinson easily spied his servant sitting near the river with his horses.

"So tell me more about why you have changed your mind about the location of Nineveh?"

"Shortly after arriving in London," said Layard, "I met the Irish scholar, Edward Hincks, at the Museum. He convinced me that none of the mounds taken alone fit the biblical or classic historians' descriptions of Nineveh. But if we view these four great mounds as a series of royal palaces connected by a grand, sprawling city complex, the archaeological evidence complements the textual descriptions of Assyrian capital. I am now convinced that the northern boundary was Khorsabad, which was the grand palace of Sargon. Here at Kouyunjik, we are standing in the palace of Sennecherib and perhaps the later kings. Nimrod, to the south, was actually the earliest Assyrian settlement, called Calah. At Karamles, the palace of Shalmaneser formed the southern boundary."

Rawlinson was distracted by movement at the base of the mound.

"Aren't those the pack mules that I left to help with the excavations?" he frowned.

Layard followed his companion's gaze to a group of women and girls struggling to keep large skins of water on the backs of the two animals as they made their way from the river towards the ramp.

"Why yes, they are. I lent them to the women who fetch the water."

"You pamper your workers too much. Those animals were intended to assist the men with the heavier work."

"I see no reason why they should have to haul those heavy water skins on their backs up this steep slope every morning. After all, they are women, not pack animals. Their lives are miserable enough, and it does no harm to the animals. Considering their poverty and the maltreatment they so often endure from husbands, this is a small help."

"But that is the work for which they are paid," insisted Rawlinson.

This meddling in his affairs was irritating, and Layard sought to change the subject.

"After all your intensive studying, I hope that your labours at deciphering weren't in vain," "Why do you say that?" Rawlinson lashed the air to free his crop of the dust.

"At my request, the Trustees have commissioned Reverend Hincks to organise the British Museum's Mesopotamian collection, which I shipped earlier, and to translate the more important relics. He has greatly advanced our knowledge in Assyrian studies."

This was nothing new to Rawlinson. In his frequent letters to the Major, Norris had not only explained the connection between Hebrew and Akkadian, but also sent a full account of Hincks' groundbreaking work.

"Who else is working on the decipherment?"

"In France, there is a young linguist, Jules Oppert."

"Oppert?" queried Rawlinson.

"Yes, he accompanied a group of French scholars to see my London exhibit. At that time, he boasted of mastering Old Persian and having published a paper on the Behistun Inscription. On my way back here, I visited the Musée du Louvre and met him again. Our collection had inspired him to take up Assyrian studies. I was impressed by how much progress he had made in such a short time."

"Do you know of anyone else working on these translations?" probed Rawlinson.

"As you know, my paymaster, Hormuzd Rassam, accompanied me to England. While there, he spent eighteen months studying at Oxford. He has worked on his Assyrian, but he is young and, I fear, lacks the self-discipline that such an endeavour requires."

"You should have known better," Rawlinson said. He felt vindicated. "A native is not suited to a gentleman's occupation."

"It was worth trying. He is a clever fellow and a direct descendant of this great civilisation." Layard noted the tension in the older man's jaw. He took the Major's arm, forcing him to stop midway on the ramp.

"Listen old man," he said. "The great universities in England and on the continent are producing top scholars. You, Hormuzd, and I cannot possibly compete with them. Such men are both well-educated and well connected. Hincks' father was a professor of Hebrew and Oriental languages. Fox Talbot, who collaborates with him, can afford the finest training and has had the leisure to press his studies forward at a remarkable pace. Oppert is Jewish and studied Hebrew and Aramaic from his childhood. If Norris were not so timid, he too would be a major player as well. He has already mastered a dozen languages."

Rawlinson stood at ease, with the expression of one sizing up the other riders and horses before a race.

"Twenty-four to date," he corrected. Noting Layard's confused expression, he added, "But, should he actually master the Assyrian and Babylonian, then Norris will surpass his famous uncle by two languages."

Layard pitied the old chap. All of this must be terribly frustrating for him. He placed his hand on Rawlinson's shoulder.

"The fact that you are self-taught accentuates the greatness of your accomplishments, yet the reality is that you are here, and they are there," Layard stated as they resumed their descent. "I shall write to Canning later today," he offered. "He is still at Constantinople and has great influence. I am certain that he can be persuaded to arrange a posting for you to the Shah's court in Tehran. After all, your publications have firmly established your pre-eminence in the field of Persian language and culture."

"And you?" Rawlinson had tired of Layard's patronising. "What are you plans?"

"I imagine that it will take me at least another four years to clear all the mounds along the rivers and glean enough to retire."

"So before you reach my age, you can re-enter British society in style — perhaps even gain a seat in Parliament?"

"Perhaps, it would be better for you to drop the Assyrian." Layard didn't like Rawlinson's tone, but tried not to take offence. "If you want to collect artefacts, then take a few of my men and start excavating one of the Persian sites." His companion made no response.

'So generous of you,' thought Rawlinson. His head was pounding. 'The great Austen Layard will graciously toss me a few scraps while he basks in the honour and wealth of his amazing discoveries. The demand is for finds that can be linked to the Bible. That is what sells books and packs lecture halls. But, what is it to you if I spend the remainder of my life as an obscure officer, eating dirt in some God-forsaken, cholera-infested hole?'

"It is good of you to offer your men to assist me, Layard," Rawlinson said, smiling. "But I will not be here long enough to engage them. I have been granted a leave of absence and am on my way home now."

"Really?!"

"Well, it has been twenty-two years since I left England. It is about time that I visited my family. Don't you agree?"

"Why, yes…yes, of course. Is your mother still alive? I recall that your father passed away a few years ago."

"My mother is well, thank you for asking."

The water-bearing women had made their way up the ramp and were approaching the two men. They were a ragged group. Layard greeted each by name as she passed, and paused as the last of the group reached him.

"Maryam?" he inquired of the short, round woman. "Is it you?"

"Yes, Layard Bey," She cast her mournful eyes to the ground, "it is I."

"But where is your husband? I did not see him among my workmen."

A piteous wail escaped from the woman's lips. Her arms waved in the air as if trying in vain to take flight. She fell to her knees, beating first her chest and then the sides of her head, imploring the Almighty for mercy. From the occasional intelligible word, he gathered that his old foreman had died suddenly a few weeks ago. Some of the women ran to her side, trying to comfort and lift her from the dust. A graceful young girl with a long, black braid whipping behind her ran from the lead mule to Maryam, knelt before her, and joined in her wails and cascading tears.

Ten years in the Middle East had conditioned Layard to such emotional out-bursts. Though he appreciated that the widow's suffering was sincere, he also understood that emotions in this region, like any other weapon, were used in the most efficient manner and only at the most advantageous time.

Rawlinson rolled his eyes at the spectacle, which was certainly staged to extract the greatest amount of sympathy — both verbal and monetary — from the woman's employer. Judging by Layard's expression, it seemed to have accomplished its goal. 'He is so pathetically gullible to their incessant flattery of Lord Layard,' Rawlinson thought. 'With such a weakness, he should never have been entrusted with a position of authority.'

With considerable effort, the women managed to raise the widow to her feet. A tin cup of water helped to soothe her pain. As the wave of grief subsided, the young girl approached Layard and kissed his hand. Wishing upon him every form of blessing from above, she thanked him for permitting her and her mother the comfort of his protection. He had always been enchanted by the green lights in those soft, almond eyes when as a child she would stop playing with her friends and run to kiss his hand. But the girl was no longer a child, and the touch of her moist lips aroused more than she intended.

"Could this be little Hadla?" Layard spoke his thoughts out loud.

"Yes, O great Bey," she whispered, and the green light of her eyes was veiled by thick, black lashes. When she straightened to full height, her head barely reached his shoulder. He was befuddled by her transformation from a thin child –into a young woman with well-rounded curves. Knowing the danger of showing too much interest in a female worker, Layard turned abruptly from Hadla and addressed her mother.

"Peace be upon you and your daughter. Your husband will always be remembered as an honourable man and a righteous Christian. I am pleased that you have chosen to rejoin my workers, good Maryam."

"Thank you, O Bey," Maryam kissed his hand "my Hadla and I will work hard and eat little."

"Go now, and help with the water. The men are thirsty." From the corner of his eye, Layard savoured the vision of the girl.

"I believe that I promised you breakfast," he said, turning his full attention to his guest.

"And I'm looking forward to your fulfilling that promise, my friend," smiled Rawlinson.

"You see, my daughter," Maryam whispered reassuringly as the men walked away. "I was right. All will be well now. He will protect you."

The smell of a wood fire, hot pitta bread and coffee drew the men towards the simple house that Layard had had built just outside the workers' tent village. It served both as his residence and his office, since he rarely set his notes and drawings aside before midnight.

☙❧

Rawlinson did not intend to remain long in Layard's crude abode. He was too accustomed to the spacious diplomatic compound in Baghdad. He found the home of the British Consul at Mosul, Charles Rassam, more amenable accommodation.

After a long day at the excavation site, the two men returned to Layard's house. The long table had been cleared of the stack of sketches, meticulously copied the characters, and papier-mâché cast squeezes of the larger monumental inscriptions that usually covered it. Now suitably attired as befits an English gentleman, and with his good friend and bodyguard, Ibrahim the Bairakdar, nearby, Layard hosted the evening meal, which had been prepared by the women of the village. The Englishmen sat at the table while their companions sat on plush cushions and ate from a low round table of hammered brass.

"I must congratulate you on a most remarkable discovery today," stated Rawlinson, finishing his wine.

"It was rewarding. Too many days are spent in mindless labour, and then suddenly, as today, we stumble upon a real treasure, one that is truly priceless."

"The details of a siege and fall of an ancient city are simply stunning, and most of the slabs seem in excellent condition."

"It is exceptional," replied Layard.

"What city do you think it might be?" asked Rawlinson.

"Perhaps, you will be able to answer that question," responded Layard, slicing the last of his meat, "when you have had the time to study the inscription farther."

"I am not certain that I'll have the time at present," responded Rawlinson, thoughtfully. "If it is possible, I would like to take squeezes of the more impressive slabs with me to London."

"I'm sure that that can be arranged," reassured Layard as he reached for the bottle of wine, Sunil rose from his seat.

"Sit down, man and enjoy your meal," Layard insisted, "Are you accompanying Major Rawlinson to London?" asked Layard as he refilled his glass.

"Yes, sir," the Indian replied with a smile, "I have family, my mother's cousin and his children, there; but, I do not remember them. They left India many years ago, when I was very small."

"It is good that you are traveling with the Major." Turning to Rawlinson, Layard added, "By the way, thank you for handling the crating and shipping of my artefacts after I left. It was an onerous task, and I want you to know how much I appreciate it."

"It was my pleasure." Rawlinson smiled at his friend's naivety. "My office is always available to assist in the advancement of knowledge, especially when it enhances the glory of Britain and the Crown."

"I only wish that the governor's office in Bombay had been as conscientious," Layard sighed, as he refilled heir glasses.

"Why, what happened?" asked Rawlinson.

"They lost several of the most valuable pieces," Layard snorted in disgust. "They actually displayed them to the public! Of course, the officials claimed innocence. They swore that the items I described were not among those displayed. It is so very disheartening to know that even those of the higher castes cannot be trusted." His features appeared severe in the sharp lamplight as he muttered, "I still lament their loss, especially those lovely terracotta figurines."

"Mr. Kemball has assumed all of my duties during my absence," Rawlinson reassured him. "I am certain that he will be happy to render any assistance that you may need in transporting your new discoveries to London."

"Layard Bey."

"Yes, Ibrahim?"

"Tell me, why are your countrymen so eager to worship these ancient idols that you take such care with them?"

Rawlinson roared with laughter. Layard looked at his friend with an indulgent smile.

"We do not worship them, Ibrahim. We place them in a great house of study in order to increase our knowledge of a once great civilisation."

As a true believer, Ibrahim had difficulty accepting this answer.

"How can studying idols increase a man's wisdom?" he wondered aloud. "If you truly wish to increase wisdom in your land, O Layard Bey, then you should teach your countrymen the glorious Quran, instead of sending them evil images."

Suddenly, the door burst open. Hadla ran across the room and threw herself at Layard's feet.

"Save me, O mighty Bey!" she screamed in terror. Crouching with her forehead only inches from his feet, she trembled beneath a veil of jet-black hair.

Outside the doorway, a man was pushing Maryam and shouting curses at her as she beat at him with a hairbrush. The last blow slowed his progress enough for her to rush inside before him. She joined her daughter on the floor, pleading for the merciful protection of the great Lord Layard.

The man followed, but stopped suddenly when he saw that the Englishmen were flanked by Sunil and Ibrahim whose pistols were held high, waiting only the command to fire. The intruder put on his most pathetic face and began to whine.

"Please pardon, if you will, O Bey, the foolishness of these mindless women. As you see, I tried to prevent them from disturbing you, but they lack the manners of a goat." Glancing nervously back and forth between Sunil and Ibrahim, he continued. "This is a domestic matter. You should not be troubled by a quarrel between a husband and his wife."

Hadla's grip tightened around Layard's ankle. His body flushed with fire. It took enormous effort to maintain his detached expression.

"This pig is not my husband!" Hadla shouted. She proudly tossed her head back, locked her palms together in prayer on the altar of Layard's knees, and pleaded, "Save me, O Bey, for if you cannot, I swear that I shall throw myself into the river and drown before submitting to him!"

"I have paid the bride price. The girl is mine. Restore her to me, and I shall amply punish her for disturbing your meal."

"Is this true, Maryam?"

"No," protested the old woman. "He has not paid in full. He will take my child and abuse her. And I shall die of grief, alone and wretched."

"I shall judge the case," announced Layard. "The women may sit there."

Hadla helped her mother up, and they seated themselves on the heap of pillows next to the low brass table. Rawlinson nodded to Sunil, who slipped his pistol back into its holster and brought a pitcher of water and basin to Layard. He held out his hands, and Sunil poured water over them. Watching the water trickle into the basin, Layard wondered if he would be able to save Hadla. If the bride price has been paid, he will be powerless to annul a marriage agreement.

With swift, skilled hands, Maryam began brushing and braiding her daughter's hair. It was not proper that her beauty should be so blatantly flaunted before strange men. The mother closed her eyes and muttered a prayer under her breath.

The man stood as near to them as he dared, ready to grab the girl as soon as this annoyance was over. His brownish robes emitted a foul odour. His beard was dusty from lying in wait for hapless travellers on twisting back roads.

"Search him for weapons," said Layard.

In a matter of moments, Ibrahim produced a knife and a pistol. Sunil cleared a space for the weapons on the table next to Rawlinson, who found the drama immensely entertaining. Taking a cigar from his jacket pocket, he settled back to enjoy the show.

As the trial began, Hadla sat rigidly, clutching her mother's hand. All eyes turned towards her. Even barefoot and clad in faded striped robe, she was beautiful.

"What is your name? Are you also of the Jebour tribe?" Layard asked the man.

"My name is Musa," came the reply. He did not disguise his irritation. "No, I am not from any of the branches of the Jebour."

"What is your occupation?"

"I am a humble merchant, O Bey."

"Then state your claim."

"It is as I have said. I entered into an agreement with the girl's father, and now her mother is trying to prevent me from taking what is rightfully mine."

"Why did you not take her when you paid the price?"

"It was not possible," Musa said, shrugging. "I had business to attend to first."

"And you, Maryam. What do you have to say?"

"What does she have to say?" Musa grunted incredulously. "She is nothing but a woman. What can she have to say?"

"In my court, a woman's voice is also heard," snapped Layard. Musa's face darkened and twisted. Maryam rose and stepped forward.

"It is true that, in desperation, my poor husband agreed to give him our daughter for two sheep, a donkey, and few measures of wheat." She stood before them straight and proud. "A few days later, he returned with a donkey, and asked for more time to deliver the rest. But, the donkey was sick and too weak to work, for just a week later it dropped dead while carrying our few possessions to my brother's village," Maryam said. "And now, hearing that my husband is no longer here to protect us, this thief has come to steal from me my only living child."

"The woman is lying! I paid the full price, and the girl is mine!" Musa screamed and lunged towards Hadla. Before he could reach her, Ibrahim's thick arm coiled around Musa's throat. Dragging the foul creature from the house and threw him to the ground outside. Musa retrieved the dingy coil of fabric that served as his turban and wrapped it over his bald-head.

"Wait here until the Bey has rendered justice," Ibrahim said, slamming the door.

Layard thought for a moment. He believed the mother. He knew that the girl would die, by her own hand or by Musa's, if he did not intervene. He went to the adjacent room and returned with a generous sum of coins.

"Maryam, take this and use it to pay the settlement," He instructed, handing her the coins. Tears of joy trailed down the older woman's face. Layard motioned to Ibrahim, who opened the door and addressed Musa.

"If now you have remembered how to behave in the presence of the Bey, you may enter," he said. The old Arab toyed with his beard as he resumed his previous position.

"I have reached a decision that best serves the truth and justice in this case," Layard said. "I order the widow Maryam, mother of the girl Hadla, to replace the donkey paid by Musa and to give an additional two sheep to repay the service that they benefitted from it. The girl Hadla will remain under the protection of my roof until the transactions have been fulfilled. To safeguard her honour and good name her mother, Maryam, will remain with her. Musa, your weapons will be returned to you only if you agree to these terms and leave this region immediately afterwards."

"What is this?! This is not justice!" screeched Musa, but he fell silent when Ibrahim and Sunil raised their pistols. After a quick calculation, he agreed to the arrangement and left.

"I shall go to the market early in the morning," Maryam whispered, "and settle with this miserable man." She embraced her daughter and added, "Now that we are protected by the Bey, Musa will not dare to return." She kissed her daughter on the cheek. "Here, hold the money. I must go to the tent and bring our things." Maryam held the kind hands of the Bey to her forehead and thanked him profusely before leaving.

The moon was shining brightly, and her step was light for the first time since her husband's death. It was amazing how fast news travelled, for the short walk to her tent on the outskirts of the village was slowed by a constant flow of questions and well wishes from the other workers.

Maryam knew exactly where to lay her hands on the things she wanted. In another few minutes, she would be resting in the comfort of the Bey's house. She crawled into the small, dark enclosure of her tent and grabbed the bundles. She backed out of the tent, dragging the bundles carefully, so as not to lose anything. When she emerged from the narrow opening, a hand jerked her head back sharply by her long braids. The violent motion sent a sharp, throbbing pain down her neck and back. Her scream for help was muffled to a squeak by a filthy hand clasped over her mouth. A burning pain deep in her chest was followed by a sickening sucking sound. The cruel, thin blade struck twice more. Maryam gasped for breath, but none came. A flash of light and the pounding in her temples ceased, and all was silent.

ঌ

Please, Hadla have something to eat" offered Layard.

"You are very kind, Layard Bey," she replied, watching the door. "But I must wait for my mother to return."

She disliked sitting idle, and began clearing the dirty dishes from the table.

Layard glanced at Ibrahim, who swallowed the last of his coffee. He took a lantern from the wall and left the house. A few minutes later, he opened the door.

"You are needed out here, Bey." When Layard reached the door, Ibrahim whispered, "Perhaps the Major and his man should also come."

"Rawlinson, would you and Sunil come with us, please." Before the words were spoken, Hadla was at his side, ready to join them. "No, you will remain here." Layard insisted.

The hard ground under Maryam's contorted body was stained a deep brown. Her clothing was twisted, torn, and covered with the bloody handprints of the murderer, who had searched her for the money. The men grimly followed his footprints to where he had mounted his horse. By now, a small group of village men had joined them.

"Ibrahim," Layard sighed, "have one of the village women tell the girl what has happened. There is nothing more we can do tonight. At first light we will begin the search."

"I'll tell Rassam tonight." said Rawlinson. "He'll inform the Turkish authorities for you. What will you do with the girl?"

"She must remain under my protection for now. She will not be safe until we have caught the bastard. Perhaps we can locate some relatives who will care for her afterwards."

Layard and Ibrahim searched every crevice of the desert until the murderer was captured. They turned him over to the authorities in Mosul for punishment, but the wily character escaped.

ઙ80

For many weeks, Hadla took refuge in Layard's house, not daring to leave while her mother's murderer was still at large. She cleaned the house, shared Layard's food and slept in the corner of the main room on the pile of cushions that she and her mother had shared on that last, fateful night. Each day when Layard left the house to supervise the excavations, Hadla barred the door. When word arrived that a man fitting Musa's description had·been spotted in the mountains, Layard gathered his men and rode after him. One week stretched into another.

Late one night, when Hadla had settling herself to sleep in her corner of the room, she heard a sound at the door. She sat up and listened intently. Then the door shook from the pounding. She nearly upset the short table as she sprang up. Wrapping a blanket about her, she crept to the door.

"Open the door, Hadla. It is I," called Layard.

The blanket fell to the floor as she struggled to lift the heavy bar from the metal hooks mounted on either side in the wall. A cold gust of wind rushed in and the coals in the fireplace spluttered and sparked into flame. Layard pushed the door closed. Hadla blushed as the Bey's gaze fell upon her. She retrieved the blanket and pulled it tightly around her until her nightgown was completely covered. He had been away so long that she had forgotten how tall the Bey was.

As Layard replaced the bar, his smothering passion for the girl flared again. He could not remember ever feeling so exhausted; and yet, being alone with her caused his heart to pound and his body to flush hot. He dropped his saddlebags beside the table and threw his long coat and hat on a chair. From the corner of his eye, he saw Hadla rush to the cabinet where the food was stored.

"Do not bother, Hadla," Layard's voice was thick and rough, "I am much too tired to eat."

"But, you should have something, O Bey."

"Just water please," he said, staggering to the washbasin. He removed his shirt and shoes, and poured water from the pitcher onto a fresh towel. Slowly he washed his face, arms, and torso. Hadla had never seen him like this. She dragged her eyes away from him and went to fetch a large metal cup and fill it with fresh water.

He sat down at the table and took a long drink. She watched the tiny beads of water dancing down his dark beard.

"Thank you," said Layard, setting the cup down. The girl turned away towards her makeshift bed on the large Persian rug.

"Hadla, wait," he said. She stopped but lowered her eyes to the floor at his feet.

He reached into his bag and took out a sprig of almond blossom. She smiled with delight and a fugitive hand reached out from beneath the blanket to accept the gift. When she was a child, her mother had always taken her to seek this first sign of spring in the mountains beyond their village. The blossoms disappeared under the blanket only to re-emerge above, near her nose. Most were crushed from the harsh journey, but to her they were the most beautiful sight in the world.

Again, Layard reached into his bag. This time he held out to her a dirty, tattered turban. There was a huge hole, singed and blackened with gunpowder. All that held the rag together was a large ugly stain of caked blood. Slowly Hadla's small hand reached out from under the blanket. It smelled like some dead, wild creature. She stared at the turban for a moment, then walked to the fireplace and threw it onto the coals. Tears rolled down her cheeks, but she held her head high, knowing that now her mother could rest in peace.

She heard Layard's chair scrape against the floor. From the corner of her eye, she watched him walk over to his bedroom door. He paused and looked at her with a strange intensity before he pushed the door open and disappeared into the darkness. She couldn't say for how long she stood there, staring back at her cold corner at the other end of the room. Without understanding why, she walked the other way. She shivered as her blanket dropped to the floor next to his great bed. When she slipped quietly under his blanket, she found that he was still awake.

Musa was never seen again.

☙❧

CHAPTER 2

Fate

Sunday, 27 January 1850
7 rue Trudon, Paris

Jules filled his lungs with the chilly air. He wanted to leap and shout "I love Paris!" but that would be foolhardy. Icy puddles and snow drifts threatened a nasty fall if he dared to try. Fresh snow settled on the brim of his hat and on the fur collar of his heavy, wool coat. He had lost track of time, but had no desire to check his pocket watch. The late morning sun slipped from behind silvery clouds to congratulate him. He tipped his hat in return.

Blowing steamy clouds of breath, a team of haughty dark horses appeared, pulling a beautifully carved carriage. They turned down the narrow street in front of Jules, bringing his triumphal march to a temporary halt. His gaze followed it into a picturesque scene of elegant, snow-trimmed homes and ice-laced branches. Enough time remained before luncheon to investigate this charming, quiet side street. The way seemed smooth and level, but soon his boots were sinking ankle-deep in soft snow. He kicked a new path down the pavement.

A sunbeam escaped the clouds and illuminated the richly coloured stained glass of an Eastern-style cupola on top of a stately three-story home. A warmly dressed child scampered down the front steps. Two other young boys holding snowballs called to the lad from further down the narrow street. With his arms whirling like a rickety windmill, the boy ran towards them. Before he reached them, the war was on. Snowballs flew in all directions, but few hit their intended targets.

A movement caught the corner of Jules' eye. At first, he mistook the infant for a small dog sitting on the last step of the boy's house, until the toddler managed to stand up on unsteady legs. He had neither hat nor coat, but seemed determined to join the winter warriors. The thud of hooves and clatter of a carriage pulled Jules' attention to the large, menacing shape racing recklessly towards the children from the end of the avenue. His jaw tightened when he realised that the small child was moving directly into the path of the black hooves and wheels.

Jules' heel skidded as it landed on the icy cobbles. He managed to regain his balance before scooping the child into his arms. He was not so fortunate in the dash to safety, as his right ankle suddenly twisted on the treacherous snow. Protecting the child as they fell, Jules hit his back hard against the kerbstone. The child recovered his breath before Jules and let out a piercing scream. It was only when he paused for breath that Jules heard the cries of women.

"Gabriel!"

"Merciful God! Gabriel!"

Jules was thankful when the shrieking child was pulled from his arms, and even more so when two strong hands lifted him from the icy stream of the gutter. A sharp pain shot straight up his leg when he tried to stand. His back ached and his head throbbed. The boys, drawn to the greater drama, abandoned their battle and followed the flurry into the house.

Jules was uncomfortably aware of leaving solitary, dirty footprints on the thick oriental carpet. His rescuer, who was obviously the butler, left him grasping the curved banister as he closed the door. Jules glanced dizzily up the graceful stairway. Soft hues dappled the walls from the stained glass cupola above. The boys slid across the marble floor of the vestibule. The butler helped Jules to remove his overcoat as one of the boys brought him his hat.

Ungrateful for the risk Jules had taken, Gabriel was still screaming. His mouth drooled blood, and nothing the three ladies said or did could console the child.

"Sarah, where is Rose?" cried the petite, dark-haired women holding the child.

"In her room," replied the taller blonde.

"Well, call her!" the other demanded and to the butler she said, "Escort the gentleman into the salon, please, Maurice." Turning to Jules, she added, "Pardon me, sir, for my son's sake." Her voice seemed familiar. The women spirited Gabriel away, with two maids close on their heels.

"You should be comfortable here, sir," the butler said, easing Jules down onto a red damask sofa, and offered a matching, well-padded footstool. "Please permit me to remove your boot," he added, straddling Jules' injured leg. After an excruciating tug or two, the swollen ankle was free. Maurice's hands, as sure as any physician's, examined Jules' injury.

"It is only a sprain. You should rest it for a few days."

"Are you sure that it is not broken?" Jules said.

"Yes, sir," Maurice smiled, "I have seen many such injuries. If you will excuse me, sir, I shall bring a bandage."

Jules ran his finger over the fine lace that draped the arm of the sofa. The salon was large, with white walls accented in gold. Colorful rugs warmed the white marble floors. Between him and the large ornate fireplace lay a huge white bearskin. Above his head, well-executed paintings of the nine Muses graced the walls, with the name of each sprite of artistic genius inscribed below in golden, Greek letters. Magnificent vases filled with fresh flowers created the allusion of spring. He found the decor charming, but he knew that his mother would not approve. The rustle of satin skirts rubbing caught his attention.

"Monsieur..." The mistress of the house announced her presence.

"Jules, Madame." He attempted to rise, but she motioned him to stay. "Julius Jules Oppert."

"Monsieur Oppert, what can I say? To thank you is impossible!"

Jules knew that he had seen her before. He stared into her dark, beguiling eyes, set deep beneath a serious brow. The resemblance was amazing. Perhaps, if her dark hair was free, instead of parted and pulled tightly back into a plaited bun, he could be certain. The lady sat next to him on the sofa.

"Excuse me, Madame, but has anyone ever mentioned that you bear a strong resemblance to the great tragedienne, Mademoiselle Rachel?"

For a moment, she gazed blankly into his demure, hazel-green eyes. Then she laughed—a soft, controlled laugh that became progressively freer. Twice she tried to regain her composure, but each time his befuddled expression dissipated her resolve.

"What is it?" inquired a soft voice. They had not noticed the two other young ladies seating themselves in the room.

"Oh, come now, do stop laughing and tell us what he said," added the other.

"Nothing, nothing..." She took a lace handkerchief from the cuff of her chemisette and dabbed the corners of her eyes.

"Only that Monsieur thinks I resemble Mademoiselle Rachel."

The women giggled together.

"I meant no offence, Madame," Jules said. He brushed a stray lock of chestnut hair back from his forehead. Gabriel's mother cleared her throat.

"Monsieur Oppert, these are my sisters—Sarah and Rebecca."

"Monsieur Oppert," the ladies chimed sweetly.

"Dear sir," smiled Rebecca, "we only laughed because my sister *is* Mademoiselle Rachel."

"Mademoiselle…?" Jules' surprised expression nearly caused more laughter. "But just last week, I had the pleasure of attending your performance of Mademoiselle de Belle-Isle at the Comédie Française. A mesmerising performance, Madame! Simply mesmerising!"

By this time, Rachel's composure had returned, and she had time for a quick tally. Jules' overcoat, gloves, and hat were expensive; his suit was fashionably tailored, and his boots were of the finest German leather. His hands were slender, soft, and well groomed. He spoke impeccable French, but with a charming German accent. Even with his leg awkwardly supported by the footstool, his demeanour was relaxed and confident. The opulence of her house, even her fame, did not seem to intimidate him. Rachel smelled money – inherited wealth.

"I am so pleased that you enjoyed the play. I trust that you had a good seat."

"It was excellent," replied Jules, beaming. "My friends and I were in a balcony box." Jules paused. "Mademoiselle Rachel…truly this is an amazing twist of fate."

"For us, it has been a most fortunate one. Monsieur Oppert. Your steps were most certainly divinely guided, that you might protect our beloved Gabriel." She paused, and with a coy smile, added, "Please do not deny me the pleasure of rewarding your heroism and compensating you for your injury."

"Oh, no, no, Madame. None is needed. None is desired. It was my privilege. As you said yourself, the place and time were, most assuredly, divinely ordained."

Rachel's older son skipped into the room and sat cozily on the bearskin rug in front of the fire. A maid brought the younger child to sit beside him, and they began to play quietly with blocks and toy horses. Little Gabriel eyed Jules warily.

"Your accent, sir—is it German?"

"Yes. I am from Hamburg, Madame,"

Maurice had returned and Jules tried not to flinch as the butler bandaged his swollen ankle.

"Mademoiselle," corrected Rachel.

"For the past year, I have been Professor of German in Laval, though I have just accepted an appointment for the coming year at the university in Reims."

"Then you do not reside in Paris?"

"No, I was granted a short leave from the university in order to continue my research at the Louvre." Jules felt for his watch and was relieved to find it undamaged. "Pardon, Mademoiselle Rachel, but the hour grows late. I really must go. Surely, your husband will return home soon. I cannot impose upon your kind hospitality any longer."

"Husband?" Rachel's voice was lower, deeper, and its tone vibrated through him. "I have no husband, Monsieur Oppert."

"Jules," he corrected. "Please, call me Jules."

"Only if you will return the favour and call me Rachel," she said, extending her hand.

Jules marvelled at its delicacy and gracefulness, as refined as the gentle hand of a duchess. He could not resist bestowing it with a kiss.

The anxious trembling that so often exhausted and drained Rachel began to subside. The nearness of this strange young man calmed and soothed her. Sensing her sisters' stares, she reluctantly retrieved her hand. She held out her arms and the two boys jumped at the invitation.

"My little Gabriel you have already met," Rachel said, kissing the toddler's forehead and lifting him onto her lap. Drawing the older child closer to her, she added, "and this handsome, young gentleman is my darling Alexandre—the master of the house."

"Thank you, sir, for saving my brother today." The boy extended his hand and stood like a tiny soldier beside his mother.

"It was my pleasure, Alexandre," said Jules.

"Will you be here for Gabriel's birthday party?"

"What a wonderful suggestion, my dear Alex!"

"I could not think of intruding…" Jules tried to protest.

"Nonsense! You are our honoured guest," Rachel said. She stood up and spun around. Gabriel giggled and threw his head back. "After all, without your heroism, there would be no celebration tonight. No argument will be accepted. For that matter, you must stay with us until you have fully recovered." Rachel handed Gabriel to Rebecca and motioned to the servants.

"It is snowing again. Maurice, prepare a guest room for Monsieur Oppert. He will remain with us for a few days—perhaps a week." Turning to Jules, she added, "Maurice will provide for all of your needs. Are you hungry? But of course, you must be. Marie, arrange a tray. Maurice, Monsieur Oppert's belongs must be fetched from his lodgings."

"But, Mademoiselle Rachel, I really cannot stay here!"

"There is still so much to be done," she said, ignoring his protests. "You must excuse us, Jules." With that, she was off, declaring the hour too late for further conversation.

"Monsieur Oppert," said Sarah, "do not be alarmed by my sister's abruptness. She is an artist and acts by inspirations that others do not always understand."

"When Rachel becomes animated like this, it is best simply to follow instructions," reassured soft-eyed Rebecca. "You will become accustomed to her in time. Please excuse us, Monsieur."

They left the salon in search of their sister.

Jules settled back into the comfort of the cushions and studied his lame leg. If he must be incapacitated for a few days, he could not imagine more pleasant surroundings. The young man rested his head on the intricate lace cover, savoring the fragrance of Rachel's perfume and dreaming of her lips.

cgɛo

The hour was late when Maurice assisted Jules' limping descent of the stairs, aided by a walking cane. His head felt heavy and he longed to return to the comfort of the soft pillows on his bed. His throbbing ankle set him on edge. He cursed to himself that he had been persuaded to remain. His lodgings were simple, yet comfortable. He could have taken his dinner in his room and rested his leg in peaceful solitude.

As he stood in the doorway, the buzz of chatter grated on his nerves. How would he make it through the evening? The dinner had advanced to the soup. He wished it were dessert, for then he could ask their forgiveness and return to his bed.

"Ah, here he is!" Rachel sprang to her feet. The brief, refreshing moment of silence that followed only intensified Jules' longing to leave.

"Dear family and friends, may I present the heroic young man who this very day rescued our darling Gabriel from certain death - Monsieur Julius Jules Oppert of Hamburg!"

Jules smiled through clinched teeth at the applause. Leaning on the cane and with painful, limping steps, Jules attempted to enter unassisted. The cane slipped on the glossy parquet floor, but Maurice's trusty grip braced him and guided him to a seat to the right of his hostess.

"Shall I bring you soup, sir?"

"No thank you, Maurice, just wine please." The smooth red Bordeaux soothed his nerves and helped dull the pain. Maurice refilled his glass as the maids cleared the table of bowls. After Jules' glass was filled, all echoed Rachel's toast: "To Jules!"

"Do you intend to introduce us?" a stately gentleman whispered in Rachel's ear.

"Soon, Louis," she replied, placing her hand on his. "We should wait until he is more awake. The physician gave a sedative to ease his discomfort."

"Do not tell me that you fancy this queer little fellow?"

"Perhaps I do. Are you jealous?"

"I would be, if it were not such a supreme waste of time," he laughed. "Didn't you tell me after Hector that you were finished with the scholarly Jewish type?"

"Yes, I remember." Rachel sipped her wine and smiled. "But, this one is Jewish, scholarly, and heroic. An interesting blend, don't you agree?"

The room was a blur of colour and sound. Jules' head was not yet clear enough to distinguish facial features. Velvet and satin gowns, silk shawls over tight, embroidered basquine bodices, and hair styled back from a center parting—some with clusters of ringlets secured by pastel ribbons—alternated round the table with black dinner jackets, stiff white shirts and immaculate bow ties. Hidden by a cloak of social invisibility, the staff served slices of fried cod with an anchovy sauce.

"It is good to see you again, Jules," stated a broad shouldered man seated on his right. Jules studied him for a moment.

"Count Van Nieuwerkerke?" Jules asked, with some hesitation.

"You must remember Princess Mathilde Laetitia Wilhelmine Bonaparte," announced the count, leaning back to reveal the haughty, beautiful woman next to him.

"It is good to see you again, Jules," she said.

"Oh, of course, Princess Bonaparte," Jules responded, inclining his head.

"You know each other?" asked Rachel.

"Berlin, was it not? At one of Émilien's art exhibits," suggested Princess Mathilde.

"I saw your mother just last month, Jules." added Nieuwerkerke, "A friend of hers purchased one of my sculptures."

"I am envious of you, sir," Jules said, "For I have not had that pleasure since the early autumn."

There were not as many guests as he had originally thought. The table could easily have seated twenty, but tonight it accommodated only fourteen. The china was trimmed in gold, with a single golden 'R' framed by a buckled belt in the centre. The heavy silver was marked with the same ornate 'R' for Rachel. 'How ostentatious,' thought Jules. 'Mother would never approve.'

"Such an interesting crest," he complimented, as he took another sip of wine.

"Yes, it is. Rachel had the design drawn up herself," smiled Sarah.

"Please, Émilien, tell us more about this brave young man," cooed Rachel as Maurice served the fricasseed chicken, "What do you know of his background?"

"Since the young man is too modest to tell you, I accept that pleasant responsibility. The story you told us earlier, Rachel, does not surprise me now that I know the identity of your benefactor." He paused to permit Maurice easier access to his plate.

"Honorable deeds come naturally to men of noble families," he continued. "Jules' lineage is of courtiers going back at least as far as the Holy Roman Emperor Leopold I, king of Hungary and Bohemia. When the Turks attacked Vienna in 1683, it was Jules' ancestor, Samuel Oppenheimer, who financed the emperor's army, thus enabling a Habsburg victory. And I believe that your mother's lineage is also illustrious, although you must forgive me for not remembering the particulars."

"Her father was a descendant of Rabbi Isaac ben Judah Abrabanel," explained Jules.

"The Abrabanel," responded the elderly man at the end of the table "was a direct descendant of the royal house of King David."

'Jewish royalty', thought Rachel

'Financiers', thought the stately gentlemen seated on her left.

"Thank you, Count van Nieuwerkerke, for painting such a glowing picture," replied Jules, "I see that your artistic talents are by no means restricted to marble."

"Jules, permit me to introduce to you my other guests," said Rachel, who smiled mischievously to her most distinguished guest. Ignoring protocol, she continued, "The gentleman sharing the end of table with Alex is my father, Jacques Felix. Seated to his right is my dear mama, Theresa."

All of Europe knew Mademoiselle Rachel's rags-to-riches story, but when faced with the reality behind the legend, the mind needs a moment to adjust. No amount of silk and satin could disguise the generations of ghetto poverty so apparent in the demeanour of old pedlars such as Rachel's parents. Jules greeted them in Yiddish.

"Rachel tells us that you are a teacher. How does a German financier find himself teaching in France?" demanded the mother.

"My father is in business, Madame," replied Jules. "I fear that I was a disappointment to him in that I abandoned the study of law and economics for linguistics."

"Mama," said Rachel gently, "I have not finished introducing the guests."

Maurice entered, bringing the *remove* of boiled tongue garnished with Brussels sprouts. Rachel nodded her approval, and they proceeded to serve the guest.

"To my father's left is my brother, Raphael. Next to Mama is our youngest sister, Melanie, and with her is our sister, Adelaide. Beside Raphael is Rebecca, whom you met earlier." Rachel paused.

"Monsieur." responded the siblings.

"Next to Adelaide is Gabriel's father, Count Arthur Bertrand, whose own father was Emperor Napoleon's Grand Maréchal, Maurice-Gratien Bertrand."

"Congratulations, sir, on your son's birthday."

"Merci, Monsieur Oppert," Bertrand said. He finished the wine in his glass and held it above his head to be refilled. "My little wife and I are eternally grateful for your unselfish heroism."

"Believe me, Arthur," replied Rachel, "*not* marrying you was one of my better decisions."

"Yet, I shall always love you, my dearest Rachel, above all women." Bertrand saluted her with his glass. "But we must not forget the others," he said with a slightly sarcastic tone, adding, "Please, continue with your introductions, my beloved."

Rachel's eyes narrowed.

"The gentleman holding Gabriel, who is seated between Rebecca and my dear friend Princess Mathilde, is her brother, Prince Napoléon Joseph Charles Paul Bonaparte. Across from Émilien is my sister, Sarah, whom you also met earlier." Rachel paused. "Now, of course, the best is always reserved for last." She gently touched the shoulder of the gentleman seated next to her. "Jules, may I present Louis-Napoléon Bonaparte, President of the Republic of France."

"Sir, this is a great honour," said Jules.

"We are in your debt, Monsieur Oppert. Little Gabriel is very dear to us," stated Louis-Napoléon. Jules was just about to reply when Bertrand interrupted.

"It is a shame, dear Rachel, that Duke Colonna-Walewski could not join us," he said, maliciously. "His presence would have completed this touching familial circle."

"One more word, dear Arthur, and I shall have you thrown from the house," Rachel responded sweetly.

"*My* papa came for my birthday!" shouted Alex.

"Yes, of course, Alex," reassured Louis-Napoléon, "and I promise you that you will see him again very soon and that he will bring you another wonderful gift."

Maurice offered him the *rôti* —roast pheasant—and he nodded.

The remainder of the meal was cordial. Maurice served the *entremets*. The conversation was light as all enjoyed their choice of meringues à la crème, soufflé, and apple fritters. Gabriel and Alex were delighted when chocolate petit fours decorated with a stylistic letter "G" were served as the dessert.

"Maurice," called Rachel.

"Yes Madame," he replied.

"Please serve our drinks in the salon."

Jules was glad to return to the comfort of the sofa and the soft footrest. Prince Napoléon offered him a cigar.

"I must go," announced Raphael, staring at the tall clock in the corner. "I made plans to meet with friends this evening. Please excuse me, gentlemen, Princess."

"Raphael, do not be out late!" his mother shouted after him.

"So you are a linguist, young man? What languages do you speak?" inquired the elder Felix. Gabriel's sat on his grandfather's lap, engrossed in removing the icing from his petit fours.

"In addition to French and German, I speak English, Hebrew, Persian, Turkish, and Arabic," Jules replied. "I also read Ancient Greek, Latin, Aramaic, and Sanskrit. However, for the last few years, I have applied myself to deciphering the inscriptions of the Persian king, Darius the Great. In 1848, the year I left Germany, I published a series of articles on the Achaemenid inscriptions concerning the idioms of the ancient Persians. This research was well-received by the French Academy of Inscriptions."

"Is that why you chose to leave Germany and come to Paris?" asked Adelaide.

"No, Mademoiselle, it was for the climate," responded Jules. "Berlin is a very cold environ for ambitious young men, so I have journeyed to the warmer fields of France in the hope of a more fruitful career."

"Cold for all young men, or is it perhaps colder for young Jewish men?" asked Rachel.

"From my experience, it seems to be cold only for Jewish scholars who refuse to convert," explained Jules. "This is a requirement with which I never shall comply. Happily, in France we live under the gracious, enlightened rule of the Bonapartes, and thus, it is not an issue here."

"I was a young child when our great emperor opened the gates to the ghetto," stated Papa Felix, "and I shall never forget the excitement and confusion. My father mistrusted this most magnanimous decree, but when I came of age, I embraced the new freedom. My good wife and I travelled throughout Europe and learned to adapt. Not a day goes by that we do not bless the name of Napoléon Bonaparte."

"It was my uncle's firm conviction that Jews should be treated the same as any other citizen in our country," added Louis-Napoléon.

"Do not forget that his greatest opposition came from the religious establishment," interjected Prince Napoléon. "He was formally condemned by the Russian Orthodox Church as the Antichrist and an enemy of God for this and other humanitarian acts."

A round-faced matron appeared in the doorway with her hands on her hips and a huge smile on her face. She stretched out her arms towards the children.

"Alex, Gabriel, Rose has come to take you to bed," announced Sarah. Without a word of protest, the boys ran into Rose's arms. The nursemaid usher the boys and their younger aunts upstairs.

"Your recent studies sound most interesting," said the Prince to Jules. "Were the artefacts that Paul-Émile Botta brought back Persian?"

"No, those were Assyrian," Jules replied. "He partially excavated the mounds of Kouyunjik and Khorsabad, near the village of Mosul in Turkish Arabia." He paused to accept a brandy from Maurice.

"Have not the British taken over those sites since Botta left?" asked Louis-Napoléon.

"Yes. Austen Layard has been very fortunate in the region. Did you visit his exhibit in London a couple of years back?" asked Jules. Louis-Napoléon nodded.

"It is regrettable that this rich collection is in the British Museum instead of the Louvre," said Mathilde.

"But you say that your interest is in the Persian inscriptions, not the Assyrian," said Nieuwerkerke, turning to Jules.

"One leads to the other. The Behistun inscription is a proclamation by King Darius I, giving thanks to his god, Ahurah Mazdah, for establishing him as king of kings over a great empire. The inscription is trilingual. It consists of three parallel texts. In this respect it is similar to the Rosetta Stone, which was discovered during Emperor Napoléon's Egyptian campaign."

"So, you are another Jean-François Champollion, the decipherer the cryptic Egyptian hieroglyphs," announced Rachel.

"Hardly, Mademoiselle," replied Jules. "The Egyptian on the Rosetta Stone contains a parallel text in Ancient Greek—a language still taught in schools today. The languages of the Behistun inscription—ancient Persian, Median, and Babylonian—are in a script composed of wedge-shaped characters from whence its Latin name, 'cunei-form,' is derived. When its inscriptions were first transcribed, these three archaic languages were still a mystery.

"The deciphering of the first, the Old Persian, was an international effort begun by a German linguist Georg Grotefend in 1802. Since then, many have added to our knowledge, including the Danish philologist Rasmus Rask in 1826, the Englishman Henry Rawlinson, the Irishman Edward Hincks, and the Norwegian Christian Lassen in the 1830s. As far as the Persian is concerned, I simply followed in the footsteps of these great men." Jules tapped the ash from the end of his cigar and continued.

"Reverend Hincks and Edwin Norris have made excellent progress on the second section. Last summer, my interest shifted to deciphering the third language, the Babylonian, which proved very difficult since only its right-hand side has survived. However, this morning, I made an exciting discovery while examining some terracotta tablets in Botta's collection at the Louvre."

"Which is…?" asked Rachel.

"I found that certain cuneiform characters correspond to known Hebrew root characters, and thus was able to translate those words. It has been known for some time that Babylonian, the dominate language of Mesopotamia, was a Semitic dialect akin to Biblical Hebrew and Talmudic Aramaic. In the ancient city of Nineveh to the north, a similar dialect was spoken by the Assyrians. It is a delightfully cryptic script!" Jules beamed with pride while the others sat in polite bemused silence.

"But why waste time on such studies?" asked Prince Napoléon, who seemed more interested in a painting of his famous uncle than in the conversation. "All enlightened minds know that the Bible is only a collection of useless legends."

"That would depend on the purpose of the study," argued Jules. "Methodological empiricism, the foundation of our scientific knowledge, does serve as a vanguard against conclusions based on *a priori* reasoning, irrational intuition, or unverifiable revelations. On the other hand, the quality of a scientific discovery is directly related to the quality of the methodology employed by the discoverer. Though the scientific mind might maintain a skeptic's opinion of the miraculous, it does not necessarily negate the value of the Biblical text as an historical record or a literary masterpiece. Besides, scholarly interest in the ancient Near East is not restricted to its relativity to the scriptures."

"Are you saying that you do not believe in the truth of our sacred scriptures, young man?" asked Jacques Felix. Theresa yawned and motioned to her husband to follow her.

"Sir, what one believes, or does not believe, is a personal matter," replied Jules gingerly. "We live in a modern world, a world based on reason. Faith has it place, but truth can only be established by tangible evidence."

"And you believe that you can find the truth by digging in the ground?" grunted Felix. He stood up slowly and puffed the last of his cigar. "It is late; gentlemen," he said, "and I admit that this conversation is not for me." With that, he headed for the stairs a few steps behind his wife.

"I do not see the worthiness of this proposal to send an expedition to resume Botta's excavations," snapped Prince Napoléon. Jules sat his glass down. He had not heard of a French return to Nineveh.

"There are many who feel the same as my cousin," Louis said, circling the mouth of his brandy glass with his finger. "They say that another expedition would be a waste of public funds." Louis stared directed at Jules with the word *financiers* echoing in his mind. "I would be interested in your opinion, Monsieur Oppert."

The room was silent. For years, Jules had dreamed of being part of an expedition to excavate the splendours of those lost empires. He saw his opportunity and seized it.

"A renewal of French excavations in the Tigris and Euphrates region is, in my opinion, imperative for a number of reasons," announced Jules with confidence. "First, knowledge of our ancient history must be preserved. Second, such an expedition would recover for the people of France the aesthetic and artistic expressions of the long-lost cultures of the Ancient Near East. Third, the British have taken advantage of earlier French explorations and are now sending shiploads of ancient treasure back to the British Museum, whose collection already dwarfs ours at the Louvre. Each day, France is falling farther behind the British in antiquarian knowledge. And fourth, it should be noted that the tighter their monopoly over these rare artefacts and inscriptions, the more our scholars will be at their mercy for future research."

"Yes, but the British have taken over Botta's excavations," stated Prince Napoléon. "I doubt that they will simply step aside and permit us to resume work there."

"How do you suggest that we re-establish our claim to these sites?" asked Louis, added with a wink, "Outside of military action."

"We have a sound claim that is based on prior excavations to continue explorations at Kouyunjik, Khorsabad, and Babylon." Jules said. "With effective diplomacy, sufficient funding, and professional staffing, the mission would most certainly be successful." He took another sip of his brandy.

"Nap, what do you say?" said Louis, smoothing his long, waxed moustache and turning to his cousin.

Prince Napoléon seemed to be engrossed in the last of his brandy, but actually, he was watching Rachel. His heart sank a little lower. He knew that expression far too well.

She was watching Jules from a chair near the window. Her dark eyes glowed as she absorbed his every gesture. She sensed passions as others felt the warmth of the sun. Louis had compared Jules to Hector, but sensed that they were very different.

"I must admit that an expedition to Babylon could prove intriguing," Prince Napoléon replied. He placed his brandy glass on the mantlepiece. He would gladly support the expedition if it would rid him of this new rival for Rachel's affections.

The butler set a tray down on the white marble table. He held a sugar cube over the mouth of a slender, long stemmed glass and slowly poured a bright green liqueur over the sweetener. Louis-Napoléon was served first, followed by the others in accordance to their dignity.

"Ah, thank you, Maurice," Rachel said, as she received the last glass.

"What is this?" asked Jules.

"Absinthe," answered Rachel. "Taste it. Not only is it delicious, but it renews the mind, expands the consciousness, and inspires imaginative and noble works."

"The flavor is anise," Jules said. He took another sip. "But I seem to remember reading a report by a prominent physician who denounced it as dangerous."

Prince Napoléon, eager to dull his desire for Rachel, drank his fast and returned his attention to the painting.

"If we left all decisions to physicians, life would be unbearably dull," said Mathilde.

"Actually," sighed Rachel, "I do not simply amuse myself with absinthe. For me it is a medicinal elixir prescribed by my dear friend and adviser Doctor Louis Véron."

"From here we should go to the casino," Bertrand suggested, then paused to take another sip of the bitter digestif. "I met someone very special there the other night. This girl was marvellous and, for the services rendered, very reasonably priced."

"Thank you for the offer, Arthur," replied Prince Napoléon, "but I promised Mademoiselle Judith that I would see her home after her performance this evening." He glanced at the clock and then at Rachel. To his disappointment, not the slightest hint of jealousy darkened her expression.

"I think that you have had enough, Arthur," observed Louis-Napoléon. "Maurice, have my carriage brought around. I am afraid that it is time that we leave you, dear Rachel."

"Well, I suppose I should not keep you from your gambling and women," Rachel opined as she rose from her seat. Louis-Napoléon met her as she crossed the room and kissed her hand. Rachel drew him near and whispered something. He smiled and kissed her hand again.

"Arthur, please be mindful of your health," she said with a motherly tone, as she kissed him lightly on the cheek. It irritated him that such a rich purse as hers was so tightly secured from his needs. Before he could respond, she had moved on to Prince Napoléon.

"The rumours about the theater are that Mademoiselle Judith is enamoured with you, Nap. She speaks of nothing but your praise. Enjoy you evening, my dearest." He too received a familial kissing on the cheek, which he returned with pleasure.

At this point, the effects of the absinthe hit Jules. The dinner wine and brandy had dulled the pain of his ankle and raised his spirits. Absinthe was many times stronger. The voices of the Bonapartes faded. The nine muses shimmered on the walls above him and began an enchanting dance. Jules leaned his head back to watch them. They swirled and kicked their dainty feet toward the ornate ceiling. He marvelled that they managed to avoid entangling their arms in the myriad pendant prisms of the crystal chandelier.

Arthur was the first to notice him. Jules' mouth had fallen open and his wide eyes were making small, circular motions. The laughter at his intoxication was long and loud, but Jules heard only the tingling song of the muses. At last, Rachel decided that the only way to end the hysteria was to remove its source. She called Maurice and had Jules taken upstairs.

☙❧

CHAPTER 3

The Great Exhibition

Friday, 22 August 1851
Crystal Palace Exhibition, London

The reproductions of the great Assyrian winged bulls were magnificent. The colours were so vivid and the features of the braided heads were so realistic, that the visitors would not have been surprised had they bellowed a command to clear the great Syndenham Exhibition hall. The Four plaster sphinxes, each measuring eighteen feet tall, flanked the arched entrance.

Inside the hall, next to the treasures of the Near Eastern exhibit, Henry Rawlinson paused for a sip of water and surveyed his audience. The enthralled crowd waited impatiently for him to continue his lecture.

"My knowledge of Greek, Latin, Hindi, and Persian facilitated my earlier success with the Old Persian cuneiform. However, the Assyrian inscriptions, which are not among the noble Indo-European and Aryan languages, remained an elusive enigma. Fortunately, the monument at Behistun is trilingual. I isolated geographic and personal names in all three and, with a moderate knowledge of Hebrew, rendered the whole inscription intelligible. Thus it is that, by a design that defies reason, I have been blessed with this honour." he smiled with satisfaction.

"There is no more humbling experience for any scholar than when he obtains, as a gift from the Divine hand, the key to some great and lost knowledge. In that moment, the years of strenuous study and sleepless nights are all forgotten. The fog lifts, and the solution becomes clear." The turnout was much larger than he had anticipated—he doubted that another body could have been squeezed into the hall.

"As the deeds of the bloody, idolatrous Assyrians unfolded before my eyes," he continued, "my thoughts turned to my trusted comrade, good Layard, labouring by the sweat of his brow in those desolate ruins. Overcome by a burning desire to share my discovery with my friend, I ignored the late hour and rode hard throughout the night.

"Those who know us well understand the advantages that our complementary strengths bring to antiquarian research. Layard is the hard-working excavator, totally dedicated to the tasks at hand, while I delight in the writings of the classical scholars, linguistics, and the wisdom of historians. Perhaps, on occasion, we have clashed in opinion, and at times, we maintain opposing views on the subject. However, these differences have never led to rancour or jealousy, such is the mutual esteem and respect we have for each other. We are each ready at all times to assist the other. But I digress..." Rawlinson took another sip of water as the crowd waited reverently.

"The fatigue of the journey began to overwhelm me as I reached Layard's camp shortly before dawn. Not wishing to alarm his party at such an ungodly hour, I found shelter in the labyrinth of tunnels that he had burrowed into the mound. You can imagine his surprise, when, at dawn—it is his custom to begin work at first light early—he found me lost in dreams of ancient warriors. I told him that I had now deciphered the Semitic script, as I had previously done with the Persian.

He was beside himself with joy. My ribs nearly broke under the force of his fraternal embrace as the great man lifted me effortlessly from the floor. Later, over a light breakfast and strong coffee, Layard heard for the first time the adventures and superstitions of the lost people of Mesopotamia as I translated for him the cryptic cuneiform script. I remember him sitting with his great head cradled in his calloused hands with an expression of wonderment. To see the joy my reading gave him warmed my heart and relieved the fatigue of my exhausted limbs.

"Unfortunately, it was beyond the cognition of the methodical Frenchman, Botta, or Layard, my dear friend and colleague, to identify with certainty the palaces that they had discovered. Regardless of how astute their faculties or how painstaking their preparatory pedagogy, access to that crucial knowledge was hidden until that fortunate day when I deciphered the cryptic scripts. When I first revealed to Layard that his hasty identification of Nineveh was in error, he was incredulous and profoundly disturbed. However, after I spread before him the evidence of my calculations, anchored as they were on the authority of the Holy Writ, he had no alternative but to concede that these ruins, called Kouyunjik by the locals, were no other than the heart of ancient Nineveh.

"Early the next morning, I suggested that he began digging at the very site abandoned by Botta, which until then he had ignored. The richness of the site provided immediate gratification. Within a few days, a long courtyard was unearthed, lined with carved slabs depicting an enormous battle scene. Then I read those long forgotten words: "Sennecherib, king of the country of Assyria, sitting on the throne of judgment before the city of Lachish. I give permission for its slaughter."

We had discovered the 'palace without rival' of Sennecherib, the oppressor of good King Hezekiah. No further proof was necessary to establish beyond doubt that Kouyunjik is, in fact, the ruins of Nineveh, the capital city of the mighty Assyrian Empire.

Upon my return to the barren lands of the Near East, I shall personally dispatch to The British Museum these awe-inspiring relics for you to examine with your own eyes." Rawlinson paused and was gratified by the silence.

"To our Lord alone do I owe gratitude for the many favours showered upon me since my happy homecoming –from the gracious invitation to dine with the royal family at Buckingham Palace, *to* the kind attention of London's literary societies. God save Queen Victoria and Prince Albert!" There was an instant uproar of patriotic cheering. When tranquillity was restored, Rawlinson continued.

"However, the greatest of all and dearest to my heart has been this warm reception by you, the good people of London. I am overwhelmed by your enthusiasm, and only pray that I can live up to your lofty regard.

"Her Majesty's government has determined that it is in the interest of our glorious nation to increase my burden, and has therefore laid upon my shoulders the responsibility of Ambassador to Turkish Arabia. Thus, duty calls me back to the savagery of the parched shores of Mesopotamia." His voice broke with emotion. "Soon, I must once again leave my loving family," Rawlinson turned and held out a hand to the members of his family, seated strategically between paintings of hunting scenes taken from the stone slabs of Nimrod. "Thank you for coming to hear me this evening," he said, "and may God bless!"

The crowd applauded loudly and many cheered. "God bless you, Colonel Rawlinson!"

Samuel Birch, of the British Museum's Department of Antiquities, recognised his cue. He quickly moved centre stage and shook Rawlinson's white-gloved hand. Even the pragmatic Birch was impressed. Colonel Rawlinson was a commanding figure in his full military uniform: his red coat glittered with rank and war decorations.

"Ladies and gentlemen, please, be quiet…a word, please!" pleaded Birch. "On behalf of the organisers of the Great Exhibition, I would like to thank Colonel Henry Rawlinson for interrupting his studies and graciously agreeing to speak to us here tonight. For those of you who are interested, the Colonel has consented to sign copies of his pamphlet purchased this evening. The proceeds from the sale will help augment the British Museum's building fund. Also, remember that the judges will present the prizes for the best Foreign Nations exhibits before the close of the Exhibition tomorrow. Those of you who are purchasing a pamphlet, please, move to the side and form an orderly line."

଴

"The man is a marvel," remarked Lord Russell, the Prime Minister of Britain, as he and his company enjoyed the spectacle from the balcony.

"I could not agree more," added Lord Stanley, the Earl of Derby. "He began the year by presenting not one but two papers before The Royal Asiatic Society on his studies of the Near Eastern inscriptions. He has to his credit more than a dozen publications in the past eighteen months, seven of them in the *Athenæum.*

"I knew by his performance during the Afghan War that he would go far," added Lord Ellenborough, First Lord of the Admiralty.

"A young reporter from the *Daily Telegraph* informed me that whenever they print a story on Rawlinson, they publish an extra edition to meet demand," added Anthony Panizzi of the British Museum.

"Well, it is obvious that much thought went into planning his stay in London. His social calendar has been nearly as demanding as mine," noted Russell.

"Gentlemen, I want you to know that Rawlinson has my full support," stated Ellenborough.

"I wager that, if he ran for Prime Minister tomorrow, he would carry London." teased Lord Stanley, glancing at Russell.

Panizzi caught the eye of Duncombe as he glanced up at the balcony from the crowded hall below, and beckoned him to join them.

"Mr. Duncombe, after the crowd has dispersed, will you ask Colonel Rawlinson if he could spare us some of his time?" asked Panizzi. "I should like to talk to him. Please bring him to Mr. Vaux's office at the Museum."

"Yes, of course, sir," responded Duncombe. "Does this mean that the trustees have reached a decision?"

Lord Stanley nodded.

"Well, gentlemen, I see that we are done here. We have another engagement tonight," said Lord Russell. "Good evening, Mr. Panizzi." Donning their top hats and capes, the Government ministers sought an inconspicuous exit.

ꕥ

Rawlinson embraced his mother and sister and spoke briefly to his younger brother before settling behind the table for the signing. He was pleased to see that the first in line was Edwin Norris. Rawlinson rose gallantly to greet the unassuming, middle-aged man and vigorously shook his small, delicate hand. Dazzled by the uniform and military metals, Norris' face shone with delight to be honoured publicly by such a distinguished man of action; a man so adventuresome and heroic.

"Mr. Norris, I am pleased to see you again," Rawlinson said. "I still do not feel that enough has been done to express my undying gratitude for your enlightening and encouraging correspondence over the years."

"Oh, Colonel Rawlinson, you exaggerate. The marvellous inscription that you troubled to bring back for me as a gift is more precious than any other memento that I possess."

"You are too modest, sir," added Rawlinson. "Your assistance with decoding the squeezes I brought back is deserving of international praise."

"No, no, sir. I seek neither honour nor glory in this world," blushed Norris. "But if I may, Colonel, I would like to present to you my family. This is my wife, Ann." The fair matron at his side curtseyed, but said nothing. "And this is our son, Henry, an attendant at the Museum."

"It is always a pleasure to meet another Henry," said Rawlinson, shaking the young man's hand. The smiles on the family's faces broadened.

"And these are our two daughters, Isabella and Emily."

"Such charming young ladies, Mr. Norris, you are truly blessed! By the way, if you can spare a few minutes, I should like to speak to you in private. Not tonight, of course—I would not want to take you away from your family."

"Any time you wish, Colonel Rawlinson. I am your most devoted servant."

ঔ৪০

Jules Oppert watched Rawlinson chatting with Norris. He turned to Rachel, who was shielding as much of her face as possible behind a lace fan. She was wearing a plain gown of pale blue and lavender and a modest muslin and lace bonnet so as not to draw attention to herself.

"The line is already so long, and it's still growing," he said.

"Jules, I really cannot queue up for an hour just so that you can exchange a few words with this man. If I am recognised, you will see how quickly a crowd can form. We would never make it back to the hotel."

"You are right. My purpose in bringing you here was to afford you a break from the public. Come, I shall show you the collection while waiting for the crowd to disperse."

They walked down the hall and admired the artefacts in the many glass cases.

"I cannot believe that anyone can read such tiny, odd marks."

"I can understand some of it, though apparently not as much as the colonel. The man must be one of the greatest geniuses of the age to have reached such proficiency in so short a time."

"Why do you say that?"

"The first steps in deciphering the cuneiform were made by Hincks. He recognised the name 'Nebuchadnezzar' on some baked bricks. Next, he identified the place name 'Babylon' and then deciphered 'king of.' He also differentiated between cursive script, which they used for clay tablets, and lapidary signs, which we find on stone inscriptions. Most recently, he established a table of Assyrian numerals. However, it took him five years to progress this far. Using the inscriptions brought back by Botta, I have also managed to identify a few words. However, Rawlinson has mastered entire sentences."

"Perhaps," responded Rachel.

"What do you mean by that?"

"I have always taken pride in being a good judge of character. Oh, these are lovely!" Rachel pointed to a collection of ivory artefacts. Two were of Assyrian women, one with an intricate headdress and the other with her hair braided down her back. A fragment of an ivory panel showed an Assyrian deity holding an ankh, the Egyptian symbol of life.

"Yes, they are Assyrian ivory decorative pieces excavated by Austen Layard," Jules said.

"What is this one, Jules?" Rachel was pointing to the larger of the panels.

"It is an ivory carving in low relief. The upper part is a royal figure. Below is a bearded warrior with a shield, killing a lion. The lion probably symbolises savagery, which threatens civilisation and must therefore be destroyed. But what were you saying about Rawlinson?"

"You say that no other scholars can read entire sentences?"

"Very little of it can be read at this point."

"There is a saying, my dear Jules, 'In the kingdom of the blind, the one-eyed man is king.'"

"What do you mean?"

"If no one reads it very well, then who is to contradict him? Besides, he does not strike me as the type of man who could accomplish what he says he did. That's all."

"And what type of man is he, Mademoiselle Rachel?" When Jules whispered in her ear like this, it always sent a shiver down her back. Blocking the gaze of any curious passerby with the wide wing of her fan, Rachel leaned forward as if to tell him a secret, but instead licked the lobe of his ear.

"Mademoiselle is incorrigible," Jules gasped. Rachel stepped away, and he followed.

"Now, take the colonel back there. He is exactly what you see—a military commander." She permitted Jules to catch her long enough to place his hand for a moment on the small of her back, before walking to another exhibit case. "Commanders direct wars, they do not fight them." She waved her lace fan to cool Jules' face. He ached to kiss her, but there was no place to hide.

"If we were having a wager," Rachel said, "I would stake that he pays or tricks others to do the work, while he takes the glory."

"You are too cynical," Jules said. He laced his fingers in hers and leaned toward her lips. "And what, then, am I, O wise one?"

"You," She ran her index finger along his solid jaw line. "You are my treasure, my own secret refuge from the madness," she said.

"Is that all?" He moved back. "You make me sound like a country cottage." He sounded hurt. She laughed at him.

It must have been the laugh. All heads turned toward them.

"Mademoiselle Rachel!" someone cried, and a crowd began to gather and move towards them.

Two bold young men pushed past the others. Jules began looking for the nearest escape. He had been with Rachel often enough after performances in Paris and on tour to know what would happen next.

"By Jove, it is her!" stated the taller young man. "Mademoiselle Rachel," he said, bowing, "This is such an unexpected pleasure."

"I am sorry, sir, but you mistake me for another," she replied. Jules had had enough.

"You are mistaken, sir," he said, taking Rachel by the hand and marching off with her in tow.

ಌ

Rawlinson looked up from signing a pamphlet. The crowd was thinning. To one side, a boy was pulling at his mother's hand. As the last gentleman left, the woman took a deep breath and stepped boldly forward. Rawlinson opened and closed his hand to relieve a cramp. Their clothes, probably the finest that they owned, were worn but clean. At first glance, the woman reminded him of his mother—exhausted more from worry than from work. Her simple bonnet covered neat auburn hair, but when he saw her eyes, they were strong, proud, and a shade of blue that could rival the clearest summer day. He set his fountain pen down and greeted her with his best smile.

"Please excuse us, Colonel Rawlinson, but my son talks of nothing but you and your adventures."

Rawlinson leaned over the desk and extended his hand to the boy with uneven sandy hair. "I am pleased to meet you…"

"George," the boy mumbled shyly, shaking his hand.

"So, you are interested in ancient civilisations?"

"Not arf! I – I – I mean, yes, guv! Yes sir!" replied the boy.

"How old are you, George?"

"Eleven, guv, I mean, sir."

"Where do you live?" Rawlinson asked, as he picked up a copy of his pamphlet.

"Britten Street, sir, dahn in Chelsea."

"Well, George, here is a copy of my pamphlet just for you."

The mother took her change bag from her dress pocket.

"No need, Mistress…?"

"Smith, sir."

"Mistress Smith, this is a gift," Rawlinson stated, signing a copy. The boy stared in amazement at the words written on the pamphlet:

"A gift to the young scholar,
Master George Smith.
Colonel Henry C. Rawlinson
August 22, 1851"

George's mother smiled wistfully as she read the inscription. 'Is it right to encourage the boy?' she pondered. 'What chance did a carpenter's son have of becoming a scholar?'

"Excuse me, Colonel," interrupted Duncombe, "but once you are done here, Mr. Vaux and Mr. Panizzi request a word with you."

"Are they here?" asked Rawlinson.

"They left a little earlier. A carriage is waiting to take us to the Museum."

"Of course," replied Rawlinson, rising from the chair. He shook hands with the boy. "Good evening, Master Smith," he said, and bowed to his mother. "Pardon me, Madam."

ଔଌ

Rachel jerked her hand free when Jules finally stopped near the entrance.

"How dare you embarrass me like that? No one has ever dragged me from a room. Never do it again!" Rachel stormed at him.

"I shall not stand by and watch those young hounds drool over you," Jules retorted between clenched teeth.

"You are impossible," Rachel said. She walked away, but inside, her heart was sinking. She knew that look too well: it always foreshadowed a break-up. Jules hesitated, but then followed her. She paused near the great Assyrian bulls, seemingly to study their craftsmanship. He stood just behind her.

"What can I say, Rachel? Sometimes it is more than I can endure. These people constantly place demands on you, as if you owe them something. The men behave as if you are only waiting for their request to fulfil their every fantasy."

From the corner of his eye, Jules caught the flash of a red military uniform. Rawlinson was leaving with a discreetly dressed gentleman.

"*Oy Vey,*" exclaimed Jules.

"What is it?" asked Rachel.

"Rawlinson, he just left!"

"Come, Jules, we need to find Rose and the children. I am afraid that the day has been too much for me," Rachel said.

ଓଃ

Duncombe ushered Rawlinson into the office of the Director of the Department of Antiquities. Behind the locked glass door of a mahogany armoire was an impressive collection of ancient coins. Rawlinson admired these as well as Vaux's extensive library. The man had excellent taste, especially since several of Rawlinson's own works were among the books.

"Colonel Rawlinson," stated Duncombe, "this is Mr. William Vaux."

"Yes, yes of course," smiled Rawlinson, "It is a pleasure to meet the author of *Nineveh and Persepolis.*"

"Thank you, Colonel Rawlinson. It is good of you to come at such short notice. Have you met Mr. Anthony Panizzi, the Keeper of Printed Books?"

"I had the pleasure of meeting the colonel after his lecture at the Royal Literary Society earlier in the year," Panizzi said in his smooth Italian accent.

"Please, have a seat," Vaux said, offering Rawlinson a cigar that he accepted with a smile as he settled into a sturdy leather chair.

Rawlinson needed to cultivate a friendship with both men. He studied Vaux. He had a weak chin, thin features, a sensitive mouth, and emotional eyes. He would not have survived a week in Rawlinson's military unit. Panizzi, on the other hand, was harder; more calculating.

"I understand that you will return to Baghdad soon," Vaux said. He was busy filling his pipe.

"Yes, I have already extended my leave by a year, and I must reassume my diplomatic duties."

"We shall come directly to the point, Colonel," stated Panizzi. "Perhaps you have heard that the French Assemblée Nationale has granted seventy thousand francs to renew Botta's excavations at Nineveh and Bertrand's excavations at the site of ancient Babylon?"

"Yes," said Rawlinson, "I had heard of the plan, but not of the sum committed."

"Victor Place has already taken over as the French Consul at Mosul. His primary mission is to resume the excavations at Khorsabad and Kouyunjik. Their Babylonian excavations are to be reopened under the direction of Fulgence Fresnel," Vaux said.

"The French have no scruples," said Rawlinson flatly, as a cloud of mellow smoke floated about his head.

"An understatement, Colonel," injected Vaux. "Louis-Napoléon may have been elected president of France, but he is still the nephew of the dictator. The return of the Bonapartistes to power is an ominous sign."

"How would you evaluate Dr. Layard's work, sir?"

"Regarding Austen Layard, I have serious reservations as to his fitness for the position entrusted to him. He fraternises with the natives, at times going so far as to discard the attire of an English gentleman and adopting the mannerisms and robes of a local sheik. His laxity and inconsistent discipline encourages the indolence that is innate in the oriental."

"Members of the trustees have expressed similar concerns," Panizzi said. "With the return of the French, the complexion of the region has changed. It is felt that the interests of the Crown and the British Museum will be better served by appointing a seasoned diplomat to take charge of the excavations. Your superior knowledge of the history and culture of that hostile land, as well as your proven valour as an officer and gentleman and your unquestionable loyalty to the Crown, have convinced the trustees that you are the man most capable of protecting our interests in the region. They wish me to convey to you their offer of a commission to direct all excavations in the vicinities of ancient Assyria, Babylonia, and Susiana."

"What of Layard?" Rawlinson asked.

"Mr. Layard will be recalled."

"And what of remuneration?" asked Rawlinson. A thick cloud of smoke lingered above his head.

"Of course," continued Vaux, "we appreciate that you must be properly compensated. A line of credit consisting of several thousand pounds—the final sum as yet to be determined—will be established to cover the expedition's expenses."

Rawlinson nodded his approval.

"I assure you that, under my guidance, productivity will more than double, since the lazy rascals will have proper discipline. I feel that I can say with confidence that this will result in the museum's collection doubling in size.

"However, should I accept the trustees' offer; I shall find myself burdened with increased responsibilities. In addition to my duties as Ambassador to Turkish Arabia, which encompass running the daily affairs of the Baghdad embassy and an endless flow of correspondences, I shall be taking on the additional burdens of explorer and excavator, as well as decipherer and interpreter of those extinct languages. My staff would need to be increased and reorganised."

"These complications were anticipated," Panizzi replied. "An additional five hundred pounds has been generously offered by the Prime Minister to lighten your burdens. In addition, but on the condition that the harvest of artefacts is plentiful, you will be permitted to retain as your personal collection one half of the artefacts retrieved."

"A most generous offer;" replied Rawlinson, "however, I must insist on one condition."

"Which is?"

"Upon the conclusion of the excavations, I shall be given a special contract to supervise the official publications of the cuneiform inscriptions by the British Museum."

"That is the position held by Reverend Hincks," stated Panizzi.

"I would value your evaluation of the work of Reverend Hincks, Colonel Rawlinson," injected Vaux.

"I have reviewed Hincks' publication, *On the Khorsabad Inscription*, and I consider it almost as wild and unintelligible as his previous contributions. He has perhaps a few fortunate hits. My own investigations have revealed that the cuneiform character originated in Assyria; however, the system of writing was most certainly borrowed from old Egyptian or Aethiopic. The alphabet is partly ideographic and partly phonetic. Phonetic signs are, in some cases, syllables, and in others, literal depictions. Where a sign represents a syllable, I conjecture that the syllable in question any have been the specific name of the object which the sign was supposed to depict."

The men were properly impressed. Glancing at the clock on the wall, Rawlinson stood up and extinguished his cigar.

"The hour is late, gentlemen," he commented, "Please notify me of the trustees' response to my condition."

"I shall inform the trustees of your very reasonable condition," added Mr. Panizzi. "Thank you again, Colonel Rawlinson, for coming at such short notice.

"Thank you, Mr. Vaux, Mr. Panizzi. Good evening, gentlemen."

Rawlinson smiled to himself as he descended the grand staircase. Layard was such a fool. He deserved to be removed. He, on the other hand, would never be so irresponsible as to allow another man access to his crates of priceless artefacts. The time he had invested in inspecting and packing the shipment had afforded him the most marvellous opportunity to select choice pieces for his private collection. They had proven most useful for currying the favour of London's most influential families.

When he left the Museum, Rawlinson stood under the Greek façade with his back to the carriages on Great Russell

Street. He considered each carefully orchestrated strategy of the past two years. The night was clear, with a gentle breeze. The stresses of the past waned under the thin summer moon. He savoured the deep peacefulness that came over him. 'Yes', he thought,' the taste of victory is sweet'. With the step of a lad of twenty, he descended the granite stairs. Suddenly, he stopped, turned and stood for several minutes appreciating the magnificent Ionic columns. He took a deep breath.

"Nothing will deter me from accomplishing my goals," he whispered and added, "nor will anyone stand in my way."

ଓଃ

CHAPTER 4

Sweet Hadla

Wednesday, 10 December 1851
Mosul, Turkish Arabia (Iraq)

The dark liquid began to boil. Brown, frothy bubbles raced upward. Just as they reached the brass rim, Hadla removed the *finjan* from the flame and poured the thick, sweet brew into two small, blue and white porcelain cups. The rich aroma confirmed that it was morning. A distant flash of lightning revealed an eerie glimpse of the world hidden behind the pre-dawn shroud.

She examined the streaked faces of the windowpanes. They need to be cleaned again, Hadla thought. As she carried the tray, she examined the room for any breach of the strict order that she imposed on the house and noted that the floors were dusty again.

After placing the tray on the short table, Hadla pulled her multi-coloured woollen wrap around her shoulders. The heat from the tiny wood stove had not yet overcome the damp chill in their small house. Layard, sitting cross-legged on the thick Persian rug, had just finished his last bite of feta-filled pitta. His great hands reached up and encircled Hadla's tiny waist, pulling her onto his lap.

"Are you cold?" he muttered, enveloping her in the warmth of his arms.

"A little," she whispered, wiggling deeper into his embrace.

"We cannot resume work until this downpour ends," he said. "What have you planned for today?" He inhaled her enticing fragrance and buried his face in the black forest of her hair. Her body swayed gently as he kissed the back of her neck. She was sweeter and more stimulating than a hundred cups of coffee.

"Visiting Lida," she giggled. Then she laid her head back against his shoulder, "but perhaps the sun will not rise, and we can remain like this forever."

"The thought is too happy. Life would never permit it," Layard sighed.

"Are you happy with me, my beloved Bey?"

"In all of my life, I have never been as happy as I am with you."

He cradled her back against the cushions and straightened her hair. She was perfect, and he had the pleasure of protecting and pampering her. The wind howled through the balcony shutters like a lost soul begging for mercy and with it came the return of torrential rain. Hadla quivered at his touch as a peal of thunder rattled the glass panels of balcony doors.

"Your coffee will be cold," Hadla cautioned.

"You'll make another," Layard replied. He lifted her slight form as he rose from the carpet, and carried her back into the bedroom.

❧

An hour slipped by, and then another. The rain slowed. Then it stopped altogether. The sun struggled through the racing clouds, but the biting north wind drained all its warmth. No longer restricted by the shutters, a meagre morning light seeped into the room through the narrow doors to the balcony.

The couple had just settled down to savour freshly brewed coffee when there was a knock at the door. Hadla looked at Layard. He shrugged. Hadla jumped up from her cushion, draped her long scarf over her head, and opened the door. The tall, foreign man looked familiar, so she meekly stepped aside, permitting him to enter.

"Rawlinson, you old dog!" shouted Layard, rushing across the room to embrace his old friend. "Come in. Please, have a coffee with us." Noting the new insignias on Rawlinson's coat, Layard laughed. "Hadla, prepare the *Colonel* a cup of coffee," he commanded.

"You look well-attended to, Layard." Rawlinson watched the enticing girl disappear through the door. He hung his wet overcoat on a brass rack, the only western furnishing in the room.

"When did you return?" Layard asked. "Do you have accommodations for the night? You are welcome to stay with us; we have enough room here. Did you have an opportunity to visit my uncle? What news do you bring from London?"

"One question at a time, please," Rawlinson said. He raised his hands to stem the barrage of questions. Layard sat down and motioned his friend to do the same.

"It was necessary that I report first to my Baghdad office," Rawlinson continued. "So the answer to the first question is 'about a fortnight ago.' Thank you for the invitation, but when we arrived at the Consulate yesterday evening, Charles Rassam arranged accommodation for us in his house. Your uncle received me warmly; he sends not only his best wishes, but also letters from himself and your brother, Edgar." Rawlinson placed a bundle of letters on the table.

"Excellent!" Layard's eyes sparkled like a boy's on Christmas morning.

"So, what is going on here?" asked Rawlinson, tilting his head toward the kitchen and lowering his voice. "I trust that you haven't done anything foolish?"

"No, no," Layard said. He raised his eyebrows and lowered his voice. "After her mother's death, I employed her as a servant to cook and clean for me, but you know how these things are. We kept the secret well enough until a few months back, when the local Chaldean priest, a Father Nathan, showed up at my old cabin near the mound. He insisted that I free the girl from her shameful servitude or convert and marry her. Of course, all three demands were impossible. The religious issue seemed the best diversion, so I refused, stating that I was born a Protestant, and a Protestant I would die. He was incensed and stormed off in a huff. Afterwards, both the weather and gossip turned nasty, so I set her up in this house and dressed her like one of their queens. No one dares to confront us."

Both men fell silent when Hadla returned. She set the hot cup before their guest, and frowned at the mud he had tracked on the rug.

Rawlinson could understand Hadla's appeal. A man would have to be made of stone to resist such a beauty. Yet, he could also see the fatal flaw in the relationship. Not even the many years Layard had spent beneath the desert sun could darken his skin enough nor could hers ever be light enough for either of them to find acceptance in the other's world. "I shall look through these later," Layard said, setting the letters on the table. "Tell me about your trip, your family, and your adventures." Rawlinson settled back on his cushion and began relating the highlights of his visit home.

Hadla was bored. She took her cup into the kitchen and gathered the things that she had purchased in the market for Lida. Finishing the drink, she covered it with the saucer, flipped it upside down, and examined the patterns made by the thick deposit of fine coffee grounds against the white interior of the cup. A shiver went down her spine. She saw a sign that she did not quite understand. It seemed to indicate a great change. For some reason, this frightened her, and she rinsed it away. Immediately, she regretted destroying the omen. She should have studied it in more detail or taken it to Lida, who was wise about such things. Quickly, she cut a date and nut *gilacgi* into neat squares, made a pot of tea, and placed the items on the table before the men.

"The new French Consul to Mosul, Victor Place, arrived about a month ago," Layard was explaining. "He immediately laid claim to Botta's areas of excavation, both here and at Khorsabad, where he spends most of his time. When the duties of his office detain him in Mosul, he turns the work over to an excellent supervisor named Nahouchi."

From the corner of his eye, Layard watched Hadla tie the ends of her waist-length braids together with a bright cord. She folded and tucked the long triangular sleeves of a heavily embroidered, red silk gown, put on her winter coat and round fur hat, and headed for the door.

"Where are you going?" he asked.

"I told you. I need to visit Lida. Do not worry, I'll return in time to prepare your dinner," she replied.

CSED

Hadla was lost in thought as she rode her donkey across the bridge over the Tigris River. She hardly noticed how high the water level had risen.

Rawlinson's presence disturbed her. Perhaps it was because he had been there that terrible night when her mother was murdered. She hit the donkey with her stick to make him walk faster. Arriving at the base of the great mound, she tied him to a post where he could nibble the tender leaves of a droplet-laden bush near Lida's shack. The previous winter, the workmen had built a small shantytown to replace the tents. Hadla knocked softly before entering. Lida lay in her mat, covered with blankets.

"Lida, here, I have brought you some fresh bread, eggs, and a little meat. No, no, don't get up. I'll take care of everything. Here, I am making a soup for your dinner. Aren't these nice vegetables?"

"Thank you, Hadla. You are so kind to help me," Lida said. A tiny cry, like that of a trapped cat, came from under the blanket. Lida unbuttoned the front of her faded green shift and help her new-born son to find his meal.

"Let me see him," cooed Hadla. "Ah, he is so precious. Now, do not worry about anything. You just take care of this one."

Hadla was true to her word. Soon Lida was eating well and chatting gaily with her friend. The new mother suggested that they have coffee, and Hadla told of her ominous reading.

"Is a change so bad?" asked Lida.

"No, I suppose not, but it made me afraid. I don't know why."

"Here, I'll make us a cup and take a look," Lida announced with an air of authority. She handed the baby to Hadla, who held him close and gently kissed his soft head.

"Oh, how I wish I could have one like you, but one with beautiful blue eyes like my sweet Bey."

"Perhaps you will. Ah, that might be the change the coffee foretold," encouraged Lida. "The Bey would certainly marry you if you gave him a son."

"I fear, Lida," Hadla said, looking away, "that I am barren."

"No, no. Why do you say that?"

"Then why have I not conceived? We have been together for so long, and still, nothing." Tears rolled down the girl's cheeks. "Every morning when I wake, I thank the blessed Saviour that he permits me another day with my beloved. The Bey is so good to me. No other man would be so kind. Truly, Lida, I love him more than life, but why should he marry a barren woman?"

"Here, here, stop this sad talk. Finish your coffee now. Sometimes it just takes more time, but you will see—before you know it, you will fill the Bey's house with beautiful, blue-eyed sons."

Lida watched her friend dry her face with the hem of her shirt. Poor girl. Lida remembered when every man in the region had wanted to marry Hadla; but, since her mother's murder, they had been afraid to look at her. Then she had dishonoured her family by seducing the great Bey. It would not be surprising if Heaven had punished her with barrenness. What will be her end, Lida wondered. The Bey has refused the true faith, so even if he should be merciful to her and keep her, she is still condemned in the eyes of God and all righteous men.

Hadla finished her coffee and handed Lida the cup.

"Yes, yes, I do see a change," Lida said, "but look here, see? This is a sign of peacefulness. The shaping is odd, but I am certain that it will prove a good sign. Yes, yes, I am certain that you will soon conceive—perhaps even tonight."

"It is late. I must go now," Hadla said.

"Go in peace, dearest Hadla," Lida replied. She squeezed her friend's hand.

"I shall try to come again tomorrow," said Hadla. Lida could not help feeling envious as her friend put on her fine warm garments and left.

☙

The heavy, overcast sky added to Hadla's gloom. A light rain began to fall. She kicked the donkey hard and he did not slow down until they reached the *souq*. As she rode by, the eyes of all righteous men turned away. The others glared like hungry jackals, waiting for the lion to have his fill and walk away.

As she closed the door to the basement where her donkey and Layard's horse were stalled, Hadla heard footsteps running toward her. She darted for the stairs, but stopped when she recognized the dark features of Hormuzd Rassam. He looked very handsome wearing his finest turban.

Hormuzd had escorted Rawlinson from his brother's house. While waiting for him in the coffee shop, he had watched Hadla leave. Since Rawlinson had declined his assistance when he returned from his visit with Layard, Hormuzd had sat there, practising what he would say when she returned. This was the opportunity for which he had longed. Now she stood within arm's reach. The glisten of raindrops trapped in her fur hat created a saintly halo about her head. All of Hormuzd's fine words were forgotten.

"Dear Hadla," he began.

"Yes, Hormuzd? Do you want me to give a message to the Bey?" Hadla asked, removing her gloves. She was impatient to begin cooking the evening meal.

"No, I have no message for the Bey. I wanted to speak to you, Hadla."

"To me?!" She felt like laughing, but the pain in his large brown eyes restrained her. "I am sorry, good friend," she said, "but it is late, and I have much to do. We will have to speak another time."

She started up the stairs again. He could not let her go without telling her. She must know. He grabbed her hand and pulled her back. She was horrified. No man besides Layard had ever touched her.

"Stop this! What are you doing? Have you gone mad, Hormuzd?" she said. She tried in vain to free herself.

"If love is madness, then yes. Only if you stop fighting will I let go of you."

She dropped her hand. With forced calmness, Hormuzd continued, "I only want you to know that you have nothing to fear. I shall take care of you." He released her hand. "It does not matter what anyone says. I love you, and shall marry you."

Hadla was shocked.

"You are mad! How dare you speak to me like this?!" Her eyes were round with disbelief. "Go away!" she shouted, running upstairs. "Go away and never come back!"

Her heart was pounding when she closed the door on the cold, insane world. The room was warm, and she tore away the layers of protective clothing. Layard was where she had left him, but now he was alone, staring at the crack in the plaster on the wall. He sat so still that it was not until she was very near that she could see him breathing. His eyes were red and he did not greet her. Nervously, she broke the silence.

"Are you hungry, my love?"

Layard closed his eyes and slowly shook his head. She knelt down and caressed the cluster of dark curls at the base of his neck.

"Has your friend been gone long?" she asked. He clenched his fists, but still did not speak.

Then she saw that two of the letters on the table were open. She recognized the seal of his uncle. Layard had tried to teach her to read English several times, but since he worked until midnight each night, he rarely found time to help her with this boring task. She squinted at the handwriting. It was all so confusing. Sometimes the letters were made of straight and round lines, and at other times, they were swirled and wriggled like these. Besides, she had too many important things to do, caring for this fine house, to be bothered with it.

"What does your uncle say? Did he enjoy his visit to the village of Italy?"

"Idiot!" Layard's fist crashed down on the letter and the brass table clamoured at her. "Italy is a client state of France, but it is useless trying to explain the world to you." He swung around to do what he had dreaded most—face her.

"What is this seal?" he demanded, holding a letter up to her. She backed away.

"That of the British Museum?" Hadla muttered meekly.

"Good, at least you have learned something," he said. He felt sick for having frightened her. "If you could read, you would know what it says, and I would not have to tell you," he snapped.

She could not speak, but her eyes begged him to tell her. Layard's heart sank. It hurt too much to look at her, but he could not look away. Between clenched teeth, he managed to force out the words he dreaded to speak.

"The British Museum has withdrawn their support. I have lost my commission as director of the excavation of Nineveh. Do you know what that means?"

She shook her head.

"It means that I have nothing more to do here. I must turn everything, all of my work, over to Rawlinson and return to London at my earliest opportunity."

Hadla's face went pale.

"And here," he pointed at the other letter. "My uncle insists that I return home immediately." He rephrased it simply: "I must leave Mosul with no hope of returning."

"Take me with you," she said. Her eyes brimmed with tears.

"How can I? Where would I put you? I have no house of my own there. My uncle is a prominent solicitor and a respectable man. How could I introduce you to him? 'Dear Uncle, this is the illiterate native child who shares my bed.'"

In desperation, she fell at his feet.

"I will be your most obedient servant. I will work hard and eat little. If my being with you displeases your uncle, I will sleep far away, in a small corner of another room. You need not touch me ever again. Just, please, O Bey, please take me with you. Without you, I have no life."

The images that Hadla's pleading conjured in Layard's mind were each more ridiculous than the last. He loved her too much to treat her as a servant or see her in discomfort. She was ignorant of the gossip of English servants. Worst of all, his passion for her could tolerate no bridle. As much as he longed to hide her away in a discreet corner of London, he knew that the loneliness and gossip ultimately would destroy her simple soul.

"Let go of my leg, my sweet Hadla. I must go out."

It had always been inevitable that this day would come. He knew what must be done. He stood up and fetched his boots.

"Where are you going?" sniffed the girl. Tears streamed down her cheeks.

He leaned over and kissed her, relishing her dazzling eyes for one small slice of eternity. He had ended many affairs in his life; why did this one cause him such anguish?

"To talk to Consul Rassam," he replied. "I shall give you this house and as much money as I can afford. When I arrive in London, I'll send you more. Hormuzd will see to your protection."

Suddenly, Hadla remembered Hormuzd's strange proposal and the lack of confidence in his voice. Though he was Chaldean, like herself, the harsh question remained: would his brother and his English wife accept her into their family? She knew they would not.

Layard left without his coat or hat. He needed the cold air to clear his mind. He saw Hormuzd standing at the entrance of the coffee shop and called to him. The young man jumped to his side, but did not look up at his benefactor and friend. They walked through the souq in silence. Layard wondered if he knew.

Hadla sat on the floor, staring at the closed door. What was a house without him? It was nothing more than a shell. The walls seemed to crumble about her. She stood up. What was money? It was only the coins that he gave her each morning to buy useless things like food and trinkets. Without him, she had nothing—she was nothing. The thought of lying with another man was sickening. It made her feel dirty.

The distraught girl unthinkingly put on the fur hat and warm winter coat that he had given her and walked out of the house. Perhaps Lida could explain this. As she stumbled blindly along the path, rain mingled with her tears. Meaningless faces swirled around her. Their mouths moved, but they seemed to make no sound. All she heard was a strange buzzing. She walked aimlessly until she found herself in the middle of the bridge. She stopped and leaned against the parapet.

"He doesn't love me," she whimpered between clinched teeth. Shaking, nearly convulsing, she beat the wall with her fists and screamed his name.

The dark water below churned against the great stone pillars. The whispering of the brown, bubbling foam was comforting, like her mother's crooning lullaby of long ago. Grasping the cold, gritty stones, she pulled herself up onto the broad wet parapet. How inviting, how soothing, the water looked. A distant flash of lighting flickered across the grey, shrouded sky. She felt dirty and had an overwhelming longing to bathe. As the angry voice of heaven's fury shook the hills, she slipped over the parapet. In moments, the icy embrace of the turbulent waters of the Tigris below the bridge freed her from all confusion and shame.

ଓଃ

How much will she need to live comfortably?" asked Charles Rassam. "Or perhaps I should ask, how much are you willing to pay?"

"I have not had time to calculate the expenses," Layard said. A glowing log in the fireplace crackled and spluttered sparks against the fire screen. In another moment, it collapsed into glowing embers.

"The girl is an innocent, Rassam." Layard leaned forward in his chair, his elbows on his knees. "I was wrong to have taken her. Before I leave for London, a marriage must be arranged for her. I shall pay whatever the man demands to cover her shame."

Typical of most natives employed by the British, Rassam's office was a model of a civil servant's office – from the inkwell on his desk to the books on the shelves behind him. On days that Layard would relax in local attire, Rassam proudly suffered in a stiffly starched collar, shirt, waistcoat, tie and jacket.

"As far as the girl's future is concerned, the house will make a fine dowry," observed Rassam, "and, with a reasonable cash reserve, I am certain that a good marriage can be arranged for her."

"The news took me completely by surprise, and I have not yet had time to think through all the ramifications."

"I understand. Take your time," soothed Rassam.

The sound of voices could be heard through the study door, followed by a gentle knock.

"I instructed that we not be disturbed," called the Consul. The door opened a crack.

"The man says that it is of the greatest urgency, Mr. Rassam," explained his secretary. "He says that he must speak with Mr. Layard immediately."

"Who is it?" asked Layard.

"His name is Ibrahim, and he says that he is a friend of yours, sir."

Layard nodded, "Show him in."

"O Bey, you must come quickly," urged Ibrahim as he crossed the threshold.

"If it concerns the workmen or the excavations, you must speak to Colonel Rawlinson when he returns from the blacksmith."

"No, my friend, it concerns the girl, Hadla." Layard leapt from his chair. "It is said that she jumped from the bridge and disappeared beneath the water."

"They must be mistaken," protested Layard. The heat of the room was suddenly insufferable. "The girl is at home."

"I went first to your house, O Bey. No one answered the door. I suggest that we ride down river ." he added, "Hopefully, we can find her before dark."

"I tell you it is a mistake," Layard insisted as he raced from the room.

They found the witness in the *souq* near his house. Regardless of how Layard bullied him, the story did not vary. Layard raced to his house. The key jammed in the lock and Layard hammered on the door with his fists.

"Open the door, Hadla!" he shouted. Another attempt and it opened. He rushed through the house, but as Ibrahim had stated, it was empty.

"We are wasting time, Bey. We must search the river," urged Ibrahim, as he pulled Layard's coat over his shoulders and retrieved his broad brimmed hat.

"We will need rope to pull Hadla from the river," gasped Layard, still blind to the unthinkable truth, "and a blanket to warm her."

"Yes, my friend, I will bring them."

By the time they raced back down the courtyard stairs, Hormuzd was waiting with the horses.

Layard's heart sank when they did not find her clinging to the stones at the base of the bridge. They rode on. The turbulent water flooded over the riverbank, covering the brush and lapping over the edge of the river road. Hormuzd spotted Hadla's bedraggled fur hat, caught on the branch of a half-submerged willow. They rode at loop desperately, calling her name and praying to hear a cry for help, but only the river answered them. They all knew in their heart of hearts what their destination would be. The roar of the rapids could be heard for miles, and, at last, that is where they found her—lodged like a limp and lifeless doll between the massive stones of a long-forgotten monument.

In vain, Layard called to her. The swift water streamed over her head, washing away their final despairing hope. By the time they could ride back to town and arrange for men and boats to help, the dull light would fade into sunset. The thought of leaving her overnight was insufferable.

Layard leaped from his horse and tied the rope round his waist. Throwing the other end to Ibrahim, he waded into the icy pool. Twice he disappeared beneath the surface, only to re-appear nearer his goal. A lesser man would have succumbed to the force of the current; a lesser man would never have taken such a risk. Fighting against the relentless, powerful pull of the rapids and gripping the rocks with his fingernails was not nearly as difficult as the heart-breaking task of wrenching the girl's twisted leg free from the clutch of the boulders. Holding on to her lifeless form as the others pulled him to safety took more strength than he could have imagined.

Layard coughed and heaved the river water from his lungs as he dragged Hadla's dead weight onto the muddy bank. He tenderly held the nape of her neck and gently lifted her head. His heart was shattered. Although the pain of looking at her was unbearable, he could not look away. He cradled Hadla's limp form in his arms, pressed his lips against her cold forehead, and wept.

Unable to restrain his own tears, Hormuzd buried his face in the black mane of his mare. Only Ibrahim had enough grasp of his senses to know that time was short if they were to bury her before sundown.

Lida peeked out of her hut, puzzled by the strange procession passed through the workers' shanty town. Hormuzd led the way, followed by Ibrahim, who held the reins of the Bey's horse. The Bey himself slumped in his saddle, affectionately holding an odd bundle wrapped in soaked blanket. He was murmuring to it, like a mother to an injured child. Only when they had passed her and turned towards the small graveyard did she see the grotesquely twisted leg hanging outside the cover.

"Hadla!" Lida wailed.

Layard was unaware of the noise and bustle of the workers digging the grave. His head was clouded with memories of her. His feet and hands were numb and each breath burned his chest as the men lowered her into the dark, muddy hole. His only solace was that she was now resting beside her devoted mother. Faceless people urged him to come inside and warm himself by the fire, but he look through them as if they did not exist. Layard turned his face to heaven for a little comfort, but the waning moon hid its face behind a cloud.

ଓଃ

CHAPTER 5

Sweltering in Baghdad

Wednesday, 2 June 1852
Baghdad, Turkish Arabia (Iraq)

They could easily have walked the distance to the British Embassy from the French expedition's headquarters, but the blistering heat made it out of the question. Fresnel had had the good sense to arrange the appointment for as early in the morning as possible.

The guard at the gate moved so slowly that Jules Oppert could have shouted a few choice words at him, if the annoying fly buzzing about his head would only choose some other victim for few moments. Fortunately, Fresnel handled the process with the natural ease of a seasoned diplomat.

"It is only eight in the morning, and I am already sweating like a pig," complained the architect and artist, Felix Thomas, as they guided their horses into the shade of the tall palms that lined the cobbled driveway to the mansion.

"We will just have to adjust to the climate, gentlemen," stated Fresnel.

"If I had known how stifling it is in Baghdad," added Thomas, "I would not have been so eager to leave Mosul."

"March is a pleasant month, but now that summer has set in, it is just as hot in Mosul," said Fresnel as he reined in and dismounted near the back entrance to the house. The others followed his example. Two stable grooms rushed forward and took the reins from the men. The horses' heads went up and their ears pricked forward as they were led into the deep shade of the cool, dry stables. A servant darted before the three Frenchmen and knocked on the thick wooden door in the high, baked-brick wall. A small flap opened, and the coal black eye of a guard peered out. Fresnel stepped forward.

"We have an appointment to speak with Ambassador Rawlinson."

"Your names, sir?" asked the Indian officer in English.

"Fulgence Fresnel, Jules Oppert, and Felix Thomas, from Paris."

After a quick check of his roster, the guard opened the door and allowed them to pass. Inside, the temperature dropped sharply. Three sepoy guards surveyed them, standing motionless with the barrels of their rifles pointing towards the stone floor. All wore khaki uniforms and laced leather leggings. A large pin bearing the insignia of the East India Company secured the front folds of their high, elaborate turbans.

"You may wait in the courtyard, sirs," the guard instructed, pointing to the light at the end of the high, arched corridor. Long before reaching the doorway, they heard rushing water. As they stepped into the courtyard, all three experienced the same reaction: envy. All affluent houses of the region had gardens, but few were as lush as this. The fountain cascaded over large stones into a crystal clear fishpond.

"Why is our garden only of paved stones and a few potted plants?"

There was a slight rustling under the glossy, green leaves of a blossoming orange tree.

"Fear of snakes and other vermin," answered Fresnel. "Not knowing what lurks in these bushes, I would not feel safe sleeping here, but I would be happy to exchange fountains with them."

☙❧

A dark, slender man wearing a white turban decorated with military medals appeared and bowed slightly.

"Ambassador Rawlinson will see you now," he said.

The men followed him through the wide, arched portal down a hallway inlaid with blue and green stones. Their guide opened doubled doors of carved wood.

"Pukka Sahib, the Frenchmen are here."

"Thank you, Sunil," Rawlinson said, stepping out from behind a great mahogany desk.

"Gentlemen, please come in and have a seat." He enthusiastically shook hands with each of them. "I apologise for not being here to greet you upon your arrival in Baghdad. In spring, I tour the countryside inspecting the progress of our excavations." Rawlinson returned to the comfort of his high-backed chair. The head of a huge animal nudged his leg and he reached under the desk to stroke his favourite pet. "No, no Fahad, you stay down."

Sunil returned with tea and a silver tray containing an assortment of sweetmeats. The guests thanked him as he poured tea into short glasses that were set in intricate, silver holders with handles shaped like birds' beaks.

"We were happy that you could see us so soon after your return, Ambassador," responded Fresnel.

"The pleasure is mine, Mr. Fresnel," reassured Rawlinson. "How was your journey from Paris?"

"The usual," answered Fresnel. "We endured months of choppy seas, freezing mountains, swollen rivers, and parched deserts." They sampled the sweets.

"And how are your excavations progressing? Victor Place strikes me as a very capable administrator."

"When we arrived at Mosul, we found that M. Place had been called to the ruins at Khorsabad. Our desire to see the excavations was so great that the next day we resolved to make the journey. Having little knowledge of the region, we did not realise how arduous our trek would be. We crossed the Tigris and, after riding between the ruins of Kouyunjik and Nebi Yunis, we learned that we still faced a four-hour ride to the northeast before we reached the mound of Khorsabad. However, it was exhilarating to see the progress that has been made."

"Mr. Rassam showed us your excavation at Kouyunjik, which is supervised by his brother," added Jules.

"We especially admired the bas-relief of Sennacherib seated on this throne, receiving the homage of the captive Jews of Lachish," added Felix Thomas. "The artistic details rank it among the greatest works of art of all time."

"Some of the finds were rather unexpected," said Jules, leaning forwards in his chair. "While digging trenches at the palace of Sennacherib, Rassam opened a woman's tomb, which contained jewellery and a gold plaque depicting a mask. These objects were interesting, but it was odd to find among them a beautiful gold medal of the Emperor Tiberius. These antiquities are obviously Roman Era, and not from Assyrian Nineveh. I wish there was a method to analyse the different layers of occupation," he mused.

"Unfortunately, we must work in haste to preserve these relics," Rawlinson said. "Circumstances demand that the excavations be accelerated. The harsh elements and irrational superstitions of the Arabs, which drive them to disfigure any image, make it impossible to leave the relics exposed for any length of time." Turning to Fresnel, Rawlinson added, "And when did you reach Baghdad?"

"On the twenty-seventh of March," replied Fresnel. "Our consul, Lysimachus Tavernier, met our boat immediately rented a house for us. We are fortunate to have a Consul in this remote corner of the world who is educated in so many branches of history. Of course, our consulate is relatively modest compared to the splendid accommodation enjoyed by your illustrious nation."

"Mr. Tavernier is a most conscientious man who conducts his duties in Baghdad with dignity and honour," responded Rawlinson.

A rapid clicking noise caused all heads to turn towards the doorway. A creature, its mouth clamped in a death grip at the base of the reptile's head, was dragging it across the room. At first, Jules thought that it was a cat trying to eat a snake. As the animal approached, Jules noticed that its nose too pointed and its head was too narrow. The underside of its fluffy, tawny coat was yellowish, while its face and tail were accented with dark red. Its claws clicked across the tiled floor as it struggled to deliver the twisting green viper to Rawlinson's feet.

"Excellent!" praised the Englishman, rising from his seat to inspect the trophy. "Sunil, bring Tick-Tack his reward."

"Immediately, Pukka Sahib," replied the sepoy.

"Very nicely done, old chum," praised Rawlinson, "you have caught a *dispholidus typus* this morning. Do you gentlemen keep a mongoose, Mr. Fresnel?"

"No, Colonel. I have not seen one at our house."

"You might consider acquiring one. They make useful pets, especially if rewarded with a nice fresh hen's egg." The mongoose dropped its prey and jumped on the desk. Rawlinson gingerly scratched the small, inquisitive animal behind its round, red-tipped ears.

The snake's large eyes were fixed in a death stare, but its body still squirmed and coiled beneath its broken neck. Its jaws were locked open and venom dripped from the menacing fangs.

"It is a beautiful colour. Look at the mosaic of greens in its markings," observed Thomas. "Is it deadly?"

"Quiet lethal," replied their host. "The venom causes severe bleeding in its victim. Rather unpleasant, I presume, since death may take several hours. The boomslang is not as common here as other vipers. They are native to Africa. This one probably arrived as a stowaway among some freight."

The snake's convulsions caught the attention of two large, yellow eyes under the desk. A sleek shape with black and golden-brown spots pounced on the writhing reptile. Rawlinson anticipated the great cat's movement and, grasping his collar, jerked the leopard back. It twisted and turned, eager to toy with the boomslang.

"No, no, Fahad, you may not play with this one. Unlike our cunning little friend there, you are not immune to its venom." The Englishman had to pull with both hands to restrain the beast.

"Sunil!" Rawlinson called, as the Indian returned to the room with Tick-Tack's reward.

"I am here, Sahib."

The mongoose scampered to the saucer of egg on the table. Sunil gingerly took the snake by its tail and carried it from the room. With the distraction removed, the great cat calmed down enough to be led into another room.

"You must forgive Fahad. He is young and still quite playful."

"Such a magnificent creature," was all that Fresnel could manage. Rawlinson, fully aware of the awe that his pets inspired, brushed the cat's hair from his beige trousers, straightened his brown waistcoat and returned to his seat.

"Now, where were we? Ah, yes, you had just made the acquaintance of Mr. Tavernier. So, how do you like our fair city?"

"It definitely has its charms, but the days are unbearably long and hot," said Jules. "We are forced to spend them in the cellar of our house. Not a drop of rain has fallen for more than three weeks. When will this drought end?"

"Usually in mid-October," answered Rawlinson. "Until then, all of Mesopotamia will be a furnace." He smiled, "Welcome to the Near East, gentlemen! Now, how can I be of assistance to you?"

"Since our arrival," Fresnel agreed that it was time to come to the purpose of their visit, "we have been preparing for our trip to Babylon, but we have met with continuous delays. Indeed, the Turkish regional Marshal Namik Pasha told us that the road to Babylon is completely impassable. He claims that the Wadi Arabs have rebelled against his authority, and that they control the roads to the southwest. He says that it would be very unwise to begin the journey now."

"Unfortunately, he is correct," Rawlinson replied. "I know that region very well, and it is not safe to travel to the ruins of Babylon at this time. Hopefully, the situation will resolve itself soon, but until then you must remain here in Baghdad, but I must forewarn you that life here is not without its intrigues."

The three men exchanged glances. So far, their mission had been a waste of time.

"Is there no possibility that the Pasha has overstated the danger?" asked Thomas.

"Namik Pasha, the regional Marshal for the Empire of Turkey, is a man of energy and undeniable will. He is the first to receive notice of trouble in his region," replied Rawlinson.

"We found him to be intelligent and well educated," said Fresnel slowly. "It seems that he lived for a while in Paris. He speaks French with purity and aristocratic slowness."

"Mr. Tavernier warned us to beware of him," Jules asserted. "He said that the Pasha is one of those on whom the progress that Turkey has made over the past thirty years is lost. He told us that, like many Muslims who have lived in Europe, the Pasha realises that Western civilisation is more advanced than Asian. This has given him a relentless hatred of the West. Many like him see the differences between the two civilisations as a mark of their inferiority."

"M. Tavernier explained," added Fresnel "that many have come to believe that reviving Muslim fanaticism is the only way to regain power for Turkey and to compensate for her failures. As much of a free thinker as he once was, Namik Pasha has adopted these fanatical views. For instance, it is known that he disguises himself and roams the streets during Ramadan. If he meets any poor Muslim who is not fasting, he is said to do away with him. He also showed evidence of his violent nature earlier, while living in Beirut. He had a man beaten for an utterance of some trivial statement."

"Yes," responded Rawlinson, "that is why I should caution you not to speak your mind freely in Baghdad. But I understand that you, Mr. Fresnel, were the French consul to the

Arabs in Jeddah for some time, so you must have experience of such delicate matters."

"Yes, Colonel, I am well aware of the ramifications of this issue," Fresnel conceded, with a knowing smile.

"If you should run into any difficulties, please do not hesitate to call upon my office for assistance."

"Thank you, Colonel," replied Fresnel with a warm smile for his host.

Rawlinson rather abruptly turned his attention to Jules.

"I understand, Mr. Oppert, that you and I share a fascination for deciphering Persian and Mesopotamian cuneiform."

"I am one of your greatest admirers, Colonel Rawlinson," responded Jules, "and I ask only for the privilege of studying under your guidance, sir."

"Are you familiar with the ongoing debate between Reverend Hincks and myself?" asked Rawlinson.

"Only regarding the earlier Persian inscriptions," replied Jules, rather sheepishly. "I embarked on my Assyrian studies in the summer of 1849 and chose to rely solely on my own ingenuity and a sound decryption method."

'Ah yes', thought Rawlinson, 'such arrogance is typical folly of young scholars.'

Fresnel turned to Thomas and motioned for him to follow to the other side of the room. They began inspecting the Colonel's library.

"Shouldn't we leave, M. Fresnel?" asked Thomas anxiously. "It is getting late and will be sweltering hot on our ride back to the house."

"I agree, but we need the Colonel's help if we are ever to get this expedition under way. Let the two scholars enjoy their conversation for another few minutes, then I shall ask that we be excused."

"And what conclusions have you reached from your solitary scholarship?" asked Rawlinson.

"Firstly, I recognised consonant-vowel and vowel-consonant signs that could combine to form a consonant-vowel-consonant configuration, which confirmed the Semitic origin of both the Babylonian and Assyrian dialects," Jules responded. "Later, I noted a double character in the writing in which a partly ideographic and partly phonetic system was employed."

"The first," smiled Rawlinson condescendingly, "was discovered by Hincks in June 1846. He accomplished this by identifying the proper name 'Nebuchadnezzar'. It seems that he also deduced the title, 'king of Babylon,' by using the same vowel-consonant signs tactic as you. Personally, I find much of the language unintelligible, except through the imperfect key of the Behistun translations and the faint analogies with other languages." Taking out a paper onto which cuneiform characters had been copied, Rawlinson continued, "What do you make of these?" He handed the paper to Jules, who studied it.

"The first is certainly Semitic," he said. It is the first person singular verb, *anaku.*"

"I consider it to be *anak* and derived from the Egyptian *anok,*" said Rawlinson.

"I do not see a connection to Egyptian," Jules said. "It is clearly related to ancient Hebrew. Its root is the same as that of the first word of the Ten Commandments: *anoki,* meaning 'I am.'" Jules was stunned. How could a scholar of Rawlinson's stature have made such a blatant error?

"But, you must agree that the original language of the cuneiform was Egyptian?" pressed Rawlinson. "Hincks believes it to be of an Indo-European origin, but you will surely agree that he is mistaken."

"I am convinced of neither an Egyptian nor an Indo-European root," said Jules thoughtfully. "I have not yet collected enough evidence. I am intrigued by the title 'King of Shu-mi-ri and Ak-ka-di' found in our Botta collection. It seems that Akkad was an early name of the mountain kingdom near Nineveh. Perhaps the Shumiri were an earlier civilisation in the region of Babylon?"

"And this?" asked Rawlinson, pointing to another.

"Kat-pa-tu-ka," sounded Jules, "It is the Assyrian for the region of Cappadocia in the Levant."

'So Oppert has arrived at the same conclusions as Hincks', thought Rawlinson. He saw the doubt in Jules' eyes and used the old military tactic of a defensive offence to save face. He began by redirecting the conversation to his own area of expertise: the Persian translations. From there, he could manoeuvre Jules back into the Assyrian and force him to admit his ignorance on an important point, thereby scoring victory in the debate.

"I read your recent paper, *Mémoire sur les Inscriptions Achéménides conçues dans l'Idiome des Anciens Perses,*" Rawlinson said. His voice was strained, as if trying to control his temper. "I was disappointed that you chose to ignore my contributions to the decipherment of Old Persian inscriptions. I find the audacity of your criticism of my life's work insulting in the extreme!"

"No offence was intended, sir," Jules said, "although I did indicate that certain points could, I felt, be improved upon. I thought that the criticism was within the bounds of scholarly dialogue."

"It most certainly was not! You completely ignored all of my more recent publications and focused your diatribe on my earlier works."

Fresnel was worried. The discussion had taken a dangerously negative turn. It was time to intervene.

"Pardon me, Colonel Rawlinson, but would you please explain to me what the problem seems to be?"

"I will tell you, sir, what the problem is. My work has suffered a grave injustice at the pen of your so-called 'scholar' here. He completely ignored all of my contributions to the field of cuneiform decipherment for the past two years!"

"The oversight was completely unintentional, I assure you, sir!" Jules said, defending himself. "As I mentioned earlier, I took little time away from my solitary studies during those years." Images of late parties, theatric tours, and endless nights with Rachel cascaded before him. "I should perhaps have realised that a scholar of your calibre would have published more on the subject, but at the time I lived in a remote province in Reims, and had access only to your work published before 1849."

"Colonel Rawlinson, M. Oppert speaks only with the greatest admiration for you," reassured Fresnel. "He considers your contributions to be unequalled by any other scholar, and has told me so on numerous occasions. I give you my personal guarantee that he will publish a retraction for any and all offensive remarks at the earliest opportunity."

"Most certainly I shall, Colonel Rawlinson," said Jules, reiterating Fresnel's plea. "I will publish it for all to read as soon as it can possibly be accomplished."

"Very well, perhaps I may have been a little sensitive," Rawlinson said, permitting himself to be appeased. "There is just one other point, Mr. Oppert. It concerns the Assyrian translation."

"And that is, sir?" Jules inquired. He was relieved that the worst was over.

"You seem to have overlooked the fact that the Assyrian signs are polyphonic."

"By polyphonic, do you mean that the symbols could have multiple sounds, Colonel?"

"You have understood correctly, sir. Not only do the clusters of symbols represent syllables and ideograms; they also represent distinctively different sounds."

"How could that be? If so, it would throw the deciphering into chaos. Like all others, this language must have linguistic rules," Jules protested, struggling with the concept while trying desperately not to create another rise in tension.

"Come here, and I shall demonstrate the conundrum to you," offered Rawlinson.

Fresnel relaxed a little as the two scholars sat down to examine the texts together. Jules conceded that he needed more time to explore the suggestion of polyphones. Rawlinson was impressed with the young man's love of precision and clarity of methodology. He was also relieved that he had gained the upper hand by playing on Jules' ignorance of polyphones. It was fortunate that Jules had not read Hincks' latest text.

Rawlinson invited Jules, Fresnel, and Thomas to stay for lunch, which they readily accepted. Afterwards, the members of the French mission endured the summer heat as they rode in silence back to their cool cellar.

Rawlinson was very pleased with the outcome of the interview. He had convinced his rivals to postpone their expedition. He had established his superior knowledge of cuneiform. By arranging for Jules to study under him, he would be able to draw on the knowledge and use the intelligence of this naive young scholar to advance his own reputation as the foremost expert in cuneiform research.

Jules awoke drenched in sweat. The sun had drained his strength, and he had overslept. He was the first up and was happy to have the washroom to himself. He filled a bucket with fresh water from the underground cistern and, returning to the washroom, secured it with a harness attached to a shelf. Standing over the drain in the tiled floor, Jules gently pulled on the cord attached to the harness. Water poured from the bucket through the perforations in the sieve beneath it. Fresh, cold water showered down on him and sent a shiver of relief through~~out~~ his body. Not a day went by that he did not feel grateful to Fresnel for having constructed the contraption. He tipped a little more water over the back of his neck and face, which stung from too much sun. By the time he had bathed and changed into clean clothes, the other two were up and fetching their own pails of water. Jules was surprised to note that the afternoon's heat had been so intense that the candles on the table had melted into a puddle of wax.

Their house was not as large or as well staffed as the British Embassy, but was still a mansion by local standards. The rooms surrounded a large square courtyard in which the mellow light of the setting sun glowed softly on the ornate panels and graceful columns. The lower floor of the building was dedicated to work and afforded a large, comfortable office for each of them. On the upper level were the bedrooms, with tall windows currently open to the evening breeze. They were comfortable here, and three servants were sufficient to care for their needs.

The sun had already set when they gathered in the central courtyard to enjoy a meal of tabbouleh salad, kebabs in a garlic and lemon sauce, a savoury lamb dish with almonds and raisins, and generous servings of rice. They had come to relish the fresh-baked, chewy, flat, oblong bread that the locals called *lafah*. Served with a tangy mango condiment and sesame spread, it was delicious. They were convinced that their cook was the best in Baghdad.

"How is your painting progressing, Felix?" asked Fresnel, breaking the silence.

"It is complete. I keep hoping the situation will improve, and that we shall leave for the excavations soon, so I hesitate to start another in oil. I shall just sketch until we leave."

"You might find the Shaf ve'Yativ Synagogue an interesting subject," suggested Jules.

"Are you going to go there again tonight?" enquired Fresnel.

"No, it's too late for evening prayers. I am going to the market to buy a gift for a friend in Paris. Do either of you want to come along?"

"Not tonight, I have some reading to do," replied Fresnel.

"Nor I, my head is still pounding from the sun today," added Thomas.

Jules was disappointed. He had wanted company.

"A person could die from boredom here," he complained.

"At least you will now have access to Rawlinson's inscriptions," encouraged Thomas.

"I know this waiting is difficult," said Fresnel, "but when we begin the excavation, you may look back on these days as a holiday. The nearest village to the ruins, Hillah, is very small and poor. Our accommodation will not be as pleasant as here. Between Baghdad and Hillah lies a scorching desert that we can only cross by night and to the south is a swamp, infested with scorpions and venomous vipers."

"At least we would be accomplishing something," opined Thomas.

"I had better go now," said Jules, "or the street will be empty when I return, and that could be dangerous. At times it is hard to decide which are worse: the slithering snakes or the two-footed ones." With that, he headed for the door.

ଓଃଃ

The night air was seductive. The river murmured through the reeds, whispering secrets to the tall palms, which passed on the gossip as it rustled in the night breeze. As Jules approached the main road, he could hear the chatter of conversation. During the day, the city baked in silence; but on nights like this, it came alive. Jules was glad that he had decided to go out. He found relief from his restlessness in the bustle of the crowd.

The ancient bazaar pulsed with life. The swirl of colours, smells, and chatter were timeless. The bazaar was solidly built and Jules marvelled at the skill of the craftsmen long ago. The high arched ceiling gave the air a freshness unknown in other parts of the city.

Piquant spices from India and glittering trinkets from Persia enticed Jules on every side. There were several booths offering European foods and goods. A youth, pushing a wooden barrow laden with the skinned quarters of a ram to a riverfront restaurant, *shouted* at a shopper in his path.

Jules realised that the bazaar hugged the banks of the river much as the rue de Rivoli follows the course of the Seine in Paris. The multicoloured booths meandered through much of the city for at least one and a half kilometres. The bridge that divided the city was crowded with people. Among the jostling crowd on the bridge, Jules found three familiar faces, smiling and sipping tea purchased from a street vendor. They were a colourful group, dressed in baggy striped trousers, richly embroidered waistcoats with woven sashes of scarlet, yellow, and blue, and tightly wound turbans. They greeted him like a long-lost brother.

"Monsieur Oppert, please come and sit with us," insisted Daveed Mageni.

Itzhak Simani waved to the tea vendor and pressed a coin into his hand. The vendor performed an amazing juggling act, manipulating the short glass, measuring out the tea, and pouring hot water from his great kettle into the glass. Jules was enchanted by the performance and the refreshing tea was very welcome. He tried in vain to repay his host's generosity.

The men were merchants from the mountain village of Saqqez, which could only be reached by a four-day trek through the rough Kurdish region of the Zargos Mountains. Jules was invited to sit down with them and to view their wares at leisure once he had finished his tea. They had found a convenient location, though not the best for those were already taken by the local merchants. Their corner was near enough to the flow of traffic to be noticed, but not so close as to excite jealousy. Here they had spread their mats and arranged their merchandise to the best advantage.

"We did not see you in the *bet hakeneset* for *Minha* and *Arbit* prayers," observed Eliyahu Aharoni.

"I was detained by business," explained Jules, happy for the chance to speak Aramaic.

"You missed a wonderful lecture by Hacham Yosef Hayyim," said Simani.

"That is unfortunate, but he will speak again soon," Jules replied. He remembered an incident that he felt these fellow Jews might find important. "Our French consul told me a sad story from Mosul yesterday."

"What happened?" asked Aharoni.

"A Jew there was accused of blaspheming against the Prophet Mohammed," said Jules. "M. Tavernier told me that only a death sentence would satisfy the Muslims for this offence. The people were rioting, demanding the man's execution."

"The *goyim* are always so quick to do us violence," grunted Mageni sadly.

"In France," Jules continued, "men have the freedom to speak their mind, but here, it seems to be very different. It required the intervention of both the French and English officials to save him."

"The Arabs are very easily excited by rumours," added Aharoni.

"Apparently they will put a person to death for blasphemy based on an accusation, even when there is no evidence," added Jules. "Fortunately, the consuls persuaded the Pasha to send the accused to Constantinople. The Pasha told the people that the Sultan would have him executed. This was the only way to end the riots."

"It was a wise move," Mageni nodded his approval. "The Ottomans in the capital know very well that such charges are rarely true."

"Usually," continued Simani, "they are the result of malice on the part of the accuser. After investigating and finding that there is no evidence against him, the Sultan will set him free."

"Yes, our consul M. Tavernier was very relieved that he was taken far enough away to save him from his enemies."

"Sadly," added Aharoni, "the Muslims will win anyway. As he may never return to his home, and women and children are not granted travel permits. The man may gain his life, but he has lose his family and business."

"M. Fresnel, the leader of our expedition, said that it was remarkable that their hostility remained limited to this one man and was not directed against the entire Jewish community."

"We live in peace with the Muslims most of the time, but they will attack us or one of the Christian villages, for the least reason," said Simani. "However, we fight back, and they are forced to respect us."

Jules turned his attention to their wares. There were silver amulets inscribed with kabalistic symbols, silk and wool rugs and blankets, and woven silk kerchiefs with geometric or floral designs in scarlet and gold. Mageni pulled out a soft leather pouch from his waistband. Motioning Jules to the side, he discreetly emptied the exquisitely worked gold earrings, some with pearls and others with lapis lazuli, into his hand. Jules selected a pair of earrings, an amulet, and a small woollen rug. Then he pointed to a piece of silk, intricately woven with an abstract pattern of goats against a geometric background.

"And this cloth, how much is it?"

"Ah," sighed Simani, "It is beautiful, is it not? Here, let me show it to you." They were happily haggling over the final price when a girl suddenly grabbed it from Jules' hand.

"You cannot sell this to a stupid foreigner," she insisted in Aramaic. "Tell him that you have already promised it to me, and I shall double his price." She thought that Jules could not understand her, as most Europeans were ignorant of their language.

"Go away! This one is mine," she demanded, in broken French. She hoped to intimidate Jules into walking away, but her tactic had the opposite effect. He stood up.

"Mademoiselle speaks French—how wonderful!" he said, bowing gallantly. "I am your humble servant, gracious lady, but I fear that I cannot relinquish this fine cloth, for I wish to present it to a good friend as gift."

She knew that she was caught. The girl had hardly understood a word Jules said, and she was red with embarrassment. She chose the easiest way out.

"These Kurdish peddlers," she said in Arabic, "are all thieves. I refuse to be cheated." And with that, she stormed away.

The three merchants saw that she was only the arrogant, selfish child of a wealthy family. However, none of them had ever been in love with Rachel. To Jules, she was a younger, purer version of his lover. It had been ten months since he had held her. Suddenly, he missed her painfully.

"Here, my friend," he said impatiently, "this should cover everything." He pushed currency many times the value of his purchases into the merchant's hand.

"But this is too much," protested Aharoni.

"I am happy with the price. Please, if you will, bring my purchase to the *bet hakeneset*. I shall meet you there at morning prayers. I must go now—I've just remembered that someone is waiting for me."

The merchants watched as Jules darted off after the girl.

"And he seemed like such an intelligent young man," said Mageni. The other two merchants shook their heads. One of them bundled Jules's purchases together, while the other counted their unexpectedly high profit.

༄༅

At first, Jules could not see her, but then he recognised her scarf. He followed her from a distance and saw her wave to a young man several booths down. Then someone stepped into his line of vision and she vanished. For some reason, he felt anxious. He pushed through the crowd to the spot where he had last seen her and heard a muffled sound coming from a narrow alleyway. He rushed into the alley on impulse and glimpsed two men, one holding the girl's legs–wrapped tightly in the folds of her skirt, and the other her body, as they emerged from the shadows into a streak of moonlight leaking through the roof.

The girl was struggling violently, slowing their progress. She bit the hand covering her mouth. The man cursed and snatched his hand away the girl screamed. Springing forward, Jules grabbed the shirt of the man holding her feet and flung him against the wall. The other man clung to the girl, dragging her towards another alley. The first man rebounded off the wall and hit Jules hard. Fury surged through him and he thought only of freeing the captive from her abductors. Jules struggled blindly, as in a nightmare, with his faceless foe in the dark, foul-smelling alley.

Suddenly, another figure rushed past them into the fray. The surprise was enough to throw Jules' opponent off-guard and Jules felled him with one lucky punch. Under a bright beam of moonlight, Jules witnessed a short struggle before a dark figure darted away as the young man from the bazaar gently picked up the girl and comforted her. Jules felt a strange surge of jealousy. As the remaining abductor struggled to his feet, the young man rushed at him and kicked him in the stomach. The man staggered to his feet and stumbled after his comrade.

"Lateef, tell Ahmed that if he tries to steal my sister again, I will cut his throat!" he shouted. He then turned on Jules with clenched fists. The girl forced herself between them.

"Who is this stranger?" he demanded.

"I do not know him," the girl insisted. "He is just some person from the bazaar," she added, pulling on his arm. "I do not even know his name."

"My name is Jules Oppert. I am an archeologist and part of an expedition to excavate the ruins of Babylon. We were sent here by the Emperor of France."

"I am Dawoud Shallal." He relaxed and shook Jules hand. "And this stubborn, wilful girl is my sister, Dinah." He took her hand and led them both out of the alley adding, "Come, it is not safe here. Ahmed might return with more friends."

Back in the crowded market, they did not stop until they reached a coffee shop in the Christian sector, where the two young people introduced Jules to their married sister, Umma, who was waiting for them. It was there, over hot tea and sweet cakes, that Dawoud enthusiastically told Jules about his grandiose plans to make his fortune in business, and Jules learned they were Chaldean Christians.

"My family is very concerned for Dinah's safety. She is not permitted to go out alone, and she is supposed to stay with us when in the shouq, but as you have seen, she is too stubborn and causes our parents much sorrow," Dawoud said with reprehension.

"This was not Ahmed's first attempt to abduct Dinah. Muslims consider it acceptable to abduct Christian and Jewish girls. Of course, they marry Muslim girls in proper religious ceremonies, but if they desire an outsider, they simply hold her captive, beating and starving the hapless victim into submission. Once she's pregnant, she's trapped for life. Their Shariah law permits this."

"The only solution is for Dinah to marry, and the sooner, the better. Only then will Ahmed lose interest in her. There are many who would be good husbands. A cousin has already agreed.

"I detest him almost as much as Ahmed," Dinah said. She glared at her sister. "He does not love me, and is only agreeing because our parents are pressuring him."

"It is getting late. We should return home," added Umma.

As they walked toward the exit from the bazaar that would lead to their street, Umma took Dinah's arm and pulled her out of earshot of the two men.

"What do you think you are doing?" she demanded.

"What am I doing?" asked Dinah defensively.

"I saw how you were looking at the foreigner. You are behaving shamelessly."

"I was only being polite to him; after all, he did save me."

"That was more than being nice."

"He is handsome, don't you think, Umma?" she said, locking her arm in her sister's. "And did you see how much money he has? He must be very wealthy. I can tell that he likes me."

"The way he was watching you was disgusting."

"I think that I could get him to marry me."

"How dare say such a wicked thing!" protested her sister, but it was too late. Dinah had made up her mind. As they reached the gates outside their large, comfortable home, Dinah stepped close to Jules.

"Thank you for rescuing me, Monsieur Oppert," she said with a coy glance. "I hope that we will meet again."

"I would like that very much, Mademoiselle Shallal," Jules replied. He turned to Dawoud. "Would you do me the honour of joining me for dinner? I should like to hear more about your business venture. It sounds like an excellent investment."

Dawoud was flattered. He did not want to ask his father for another loan.

'This is a good man,' thought Dawoud. 'He helped to save Dinah, and he might help to save my business. He may be a foreigner, but perhaps that can be overlooked.'

ঙ্গ

CHAPTER 6

Lost Treasures

Monday, 20 August 1855
Palais du Louvre, Paris

"Monsieur Oppert?" a familiar voice called from the doorway.

'Not another interruption,' thought Jules. He had hoped to find solitude here. The repository of Assyrian and Babylonian artefacts was full of crates. Some had been opened to examine their contents, but it would take months, perhaps years, to organise them all. It should have been the perfect hideaway.

"Yes?" Jules answered without looking up.

"He is in there somewhere, Monsieur," he heard the department secretary say.

"Thank you for your assistance," was the reply.

"For God's sake, Jules where are you?" The lanky, dark man zigzagged between the crates.

"Victor Place!" Jules shouted, "Is that you?"

"I believe so," Place replied, narrowing the distance between himself and Jules' voice. "Ah, there you are."

"When did you return from Baghdad?" Jules asked, extending his hand.

"I accompanied these treasures," Place explained. "Except for advising the committee of the Beaux-Arts exhibit at the Exposition Universelle, I have been at leisure to enjoy Paris. I asked after you when I arrived, and they said that you were in London."

"Yes. Last spring, the Minister of Public Instruction arranged for me to study the British Museum's collection," stated Jules. "I returned only last Friday to consult my notes from the expedition."

Place removed his top hat, revealing trimmed black curls and a well-groomed heavy moustache.

"You look quite dignified," observed Jules. "You must give me the name of your tailor."

"Thank you, I shall, but we have business to attend to now," replied Place with a pleased grin. "The Emperor requests our presence."

"And where might we find His Excellency?" Jules asked, carefully lifting up a delicate terracotta fragment for another quick inspection. He regretted having to set it aside.

"His Excellency and His Royal Highness Prince Albert are in the Salle du Manège at the Tuileries Palace," responded Place.

"I heard that the British royal family were here visiting the Exposition." Jules carefully rewrapped the fragile piece. "Permit me just a moment to leave this shard in my office."

Place followed Jules down the regal corridor of the Aile Richelieu, where a curator was arguing with a workman about the feasibility of altering the exhibit plans. They paused only momentarily in Jules' office.

"Have you any idea what His Excellency could want of us?" asked Jules slipping into his jacket and retrieving his tall hat.

"Something to do with the expedition would be a safe guess," answered Place, as Jules relocked the door.

It was still early. The seductive fragrance of roses floated under the lush greenery of the public garden.

"By the way, congratulations on being awarded French citizenship," stated Place as they started across the white stone parade ground that separated the Louvre from the Tuileries Palace.

"Thank you," smiled Jules briefly, then asked anxiously, "I heard that Fresnel was injured during the attack. How is he?"

"Very weak, I fear. Hopefully, he is improving. He gave me his surviving field notes and asked me to pass them on to you."

"To me? But why?"

"His injuries are severe." Place's wide, heavy brow creased into a frown over his bold features. His voice was hesitant. "His mind comes and goes. In one of his lucid moments, he said that he wanted you to publish the story of our Mesopotamian expedition."

"Nonsense. He led our expedition; therefore, he should publish the account," retorted Jules.

"He might not have that opportunity."

"Fresnel is one of the strongest men I have ever known," insisted Jules, "in body and mind. I am certain that he will recover."

"I hope that you are right." Place's tone was sombre. "Still, you should have the notes. Please tell me the best time to deliver them."

"You may bring them to my residence in the morning, if you like," said Jules. "It is not far—just across the river in St. Germain. I am not certain when I'll find the time to work on them. My stay in Paris will be short. I plan to return to London in another week or two." Then he added resolutely, "I shall hold them until Fresnel has fully recovered."

"How is your research progressing?"

"It's very exciting," Jules said flatly. "I have been studying the misappropriated Assyrian syllabary," his eyes narrowed and his jaw squared as he added, "which has proven to be the key to translating the cuneiform text."

Pausing in the shade of the ornate Arc de Triomphe du Carrousel, Jules added, "There was an incident that I found very interesting and somewhat disturbing."

"Where, here at the Louvre?" asked Place.

"No, at the British Museum," answered Jules, "and involved the distinguished Irish scholar, Edward Hincks. The Trustees of the Museum had commissioned him to examine the inscriptions and submit reports on their content. Shortly after I began last May, he noticed that I was copying the syllabary. He said that we should discuss it when he returned from a meeting. This was a great opportunity, so I waited for him. It was he who discovered the first fragments of the syllabary among these sent back by Layard.

"His meeting cannot have gone well, for he returned in a very irritable mood. He asked me a question, but spoke so abruptly and with such a heavy accent that I did not understand him. He shouted that if I could not answer, then I must understand nothing about the basic concept of polyphones. His tone was very condescending. It reminded me of my first conversation with Rawlinson in Baghdad. I was embarrassed, so I just waved him off and returned to my work," Jules concluded. The two men walked on toward the palace.

"Are you certain that was the best way of handling the situation?" Place inquired. "Wasn't there something that you could have said to soothe him?"

"What else could I have done? I did not want to risk the unpleasantness of a heated exchange. After all, I was only a guest. If our situations had been reversed, as it should have been, I would not have spoken so harshly to a scholar visiting the Louvre."

They arrived at the entrance to the Tuileries. The guard recognised Jules and held open the door to the grand vestibule. Great marble columns supported the arches of the ornate vaulted ceiling, which was crowned by its landmark squared, silver dome. The opulence was soothing, reassuring the visitor that all was well with the Empire. Leaving the hall by the door opposite, Jules continued with his account.

"I did not see Hincks again and became concerned, so I asked the department head, Dr. Birch, where I might find him. He said that Hincks had returned to Ireland. Birch was friendly but sparing with details. M. Layard had convinced the trustees to appoint Hincks. Later, it seems that the position was promised to Rawlinson, who returned a couple of weeks before Hinck's contract expired in May."

"I heard through diplomatic channels," added Place, "that Rawlinson tendered his request for retirement with full pension to both the India House and Foreign Office last October, so this move was planned far in advance."

"I regret missing the opportunity to speak with Hincks." Jules shook his head. "He has made great contributions to our field of study."

They turned down the northern lane that bordered the peaceful, private gardens and entered the long riding hall with its high arched ceiling. The morning sunlight flooded the hall through enormous windows flanking the upper walls.

"You are Messieurs Place and Oppert?" asked a servant.

"We are," answered Place.

"I shall inform His Excellency," assured the servant. "He is expecting you." He bowed and walked away.

Strategically seated halfway down the stable's exercise yard, two of the most powerful men in Europe were watching Queen Victoria and Prince Albert's two eldest children receiving riding tuition from France's most accomplished instructors. Jules and Place remained at a discreet distance.

Prince Albert beamed with pride as his daughter on a dapple-grey mare trotted past. The Princess Royal, wearing a full-skirted, riding habit and a small stylish hat, was gracefully riding sidesaddle. Albert Edward, the Prince of Wales, was more adventurous. Fortunately, his instructor was accustomed to handling high-spirited boys.

"This danger seems inseparable from the position," Prince Albert was saying.

"Yet, that assassination attempt was most unsettling," replied Louis-Napoléon. "Otherwise our visit to England last spring was delightful."

"The Queen and I have endured five such attempts," Prince Albert said, his eyes never moving from his children.

"Bertie!" Prince Albert raised his voice, "That is not correct. Follow the tutor's instructions." "The first was shortly after our marriage, can you imagine?" he continued, shaking his head. "Two years later, there were another two attempts, and incredibly, there were two more, in 1849 and 1850." The Prince Consort's jaw tightened. "In the last one, the deranged fellow struck my dear Queen with his cane, badly bruising her face. I find it unbelievable that any man could strike a woman, especially the gentle mother of young children."

"The world is filled with madmen," replied Louis-Napoléon. He turned to the hovering servant.

"Yes?" he asked.

"Messieurs Place and Oppert, sir."

"Ah yes. Please excuse me for a moment, Albert."

"Certainly," nodded the prince. Then he called to his eldest son, "Excellent, Bertie!"

Jules and Place bowed respectfully as the Emperor reached them. Louis-Napoléon motioned for them to follow to a place where he could see if anyone approached.

"Gentlemen, what can you tell me about this Colonel Rawlinson?" he asked.

"He is a very shrewd man in his mid-forties, who rose through the ranks in the East India military," Place said. "Before our expedition under M. Fresnel arrived in Baghdad, M. Layard was unexpectedly recalled. It seemed strange to me that the British Museum would dismiss an experienced archaeologist of Layard's calibre. My sources said that there was a heated exchange between him and Rawlinson shortly before he left Mosul.

"Unlike M. Layard, Rawlinson did not personally direct the excavations. Instead, he recruited men such as William Loftus, a geologist and John Taylor, the British Consul at Bussorah, as well as M. Hodder, Signor Antonetti, and others. To each of these he assigned a crew and an area to excavate. Generally, he remained in Baghdad, but from time to time, he toured the various sites.

"He was said to be a harsh taskmaster. It is said that he treated his men as little more than slaves. That of Loftus is a perfect example. Rawlinson assigned him the excavation of the Persian city, Susa. He complained of poor treatment, resign, and joined the newly established Assyrian Excavation Society in 1853. He took his entire crew with him to Uruk, an ancient site which he had discovered while working under Layard's direction. Early in 1854, Loftus made several very important discoveries.

"When Rawlinson received word that the British government had granted him an extension, he demanded that Loftus should leave Uruk and turn all the artefacts he had excavated over to him. When Loftus refused, Rawlinson wrote letters claiming that he had only given Loftus temporary charge and that he was now encroaching on Rawlinson's areas of excavation and inhibiting him from securing artefacts for the British Museum. Political pressure was exerted in London, and the Assyrian Excavation Society's funds were transferred to the British Museum. From that point on, Rawlinson moved in to take control of every site Loftus discovered and claimed the artefacts."

"When I assumed the responsibility of reopening the excavations of Botta," added Place, "Colonel Rawlinson agreed to a settlement in which the contested site at Kouyunjik would be divided into British and French sectors. But in December 1853, he instructed Hormuzd Rassam, who was simply a paymaster under Layard, and Lateef Agha to conduct illegal, clandestine excavations in our sector. I was outraged and immediately protested to the Colonel and through diplomatic channels. His response was to surround the site with soldiers and the pillaging continued."

"Interesting, isn't it," remarked Louis-Napoléon, "how quickly the English responded to Rawlinson's claim against Loftus, while French protests were ignored? But, are you certain," continued the Emperor, "that the native diggers were following his orders? Is it not possible that these excavations could have been conducted on their own initiative?"

"It is possible, Your Excellency." conceded Place. "However, it was by this tactic that they stole the priceless treasures of the great Library of Ashurbanipal from us."

"If I might add something here, sir," interrupted Jules.

Louis-Napoléon nodded.

"Beside the fact that the contents of the Library of Ashurbanipal rightfully belong to France," Jules said, "it should have been retrieved with the greatest of care. I had an opportunity to observe the excavation techniques that Rawlinson encouraged. He emphasised speed and quantity. I was shocked at the haphazard excavation method Rassam employed. His workers just dumped shovelfuls of extremely friable tablets into felt-wrapped crates, causing irreparable damage to irreplaceable texts."

"There is another matter that I found very disturbing," Place continued. "As you know, when transporting our treasures down the Tigris River, we were attacked by what appeared to be Arab pirates. Though I could not see his face, one masked raider giving orders to his comrades strongly resembled Rawlinson in bearing and mannerisms. This man was shot in the shoulder just as a raft carrying a magnificent winged bull capsized and sank. The whole scene was chaotic. Monsieur Fresnel was seriously injured at the same time and, as soon as possible, we carried him back to Baghdad.

"I went to Rawlinson's house to report the incident and found him in bed. He claimed to have fallen from his horse a few weeks before, while hunting wild boar and broken his collarbone; and that since then, he had been incapacitated. Perhaps I am completely wrong, but I often wonder if his bandages were covering a bullet wound. Shortly afterwards, Rawlinson left for Bombay, where he was hosted by the governor, Lord Elphinstone, for three weeks.

"During this time, we shipped our remaining discoveries from the excavations. They were held over in the port at Bombay for several days. Rawlinson was seen at the docks. When our crates arrived in France, we discovered that some artefacts were missing." Place's face was hard as stone. "I had hoped that these concerns could be brought to the attention of Queen Victoria," Place concluded.

"You are making some very serious accusations," frowned Louis-Napoléon thoughtfully. "Have you any evidence to substantiate them?"

"Besides Rawlinson's chauvinism and his having full opportunity, no. They are only disturbing suspicions," Place replied.

"Put your mind at rest, M. Place. Your suspicions are nothing more than the imaginative by-product of an extremely stressful episode," Louis-Napoléon said.

"Your Excellency," pleaded Place, "we had hoped that you might present to the Queen our legitimate claim for the return of at least a portion of the artefacts pillaged from our sites?"

"Gentlemen, France and Britain are at war together against Russia in Crimea. France cannot risk the alienation of a powerful ally over the loss of some broken tablets. Her Majesty is most favourably impressed by the colonel's accomplishments." The emperor paused, "As I see it, and I am certain that the Queen will agree, it does not matter which institution has care of the artefacts—whether the Louvre or the British Museum—as long as they are accessible our scholars. Instead of pressing for their return, we shall negotiate for a congenial agreement between the museums. Thank you both for coming on such short notice. M. Place, please keep me posted on M. Fresnel's condition. I trust that we shall see you both at dinner this evening."

"Yes, thank you for the invitation, sir," said Jules, as he and Place bowed. Emperor Louis-Napoléon walked briskly back to Prince Albert.

"Well, at least we tried to right the wrong," said Place.

"Come, my friend," encouraged Jules. "I know a wonderful new restaurant."

☙❧

Seeing Louis-Napoléon return, Prince Albert called to the instructor.

"That will be all for today." Stable grooms stepped forward to hold the bridles while the children dismounted.

"Are we done here?" asked the Emperor.

"Yes," replied the Prince. "The children must return to their rooms for their lessons."

The two men walked back toward the entrance.

"The prosperity that your regime has brought to France is impressive," Prince Albert said.

"Considering the previous government's instability," replied Louis-Napoléon, "we have made remarkable progress—business investments, manufacturing, and mining interests are better than ever. Every day, new railway lines are connecting previously inaccessible regions to our industrial and cultural centres. Remind me to show you the designs for our latest iron steamship before you leave us."

The children joined them at the entrance. The princess, her face flushed from the exercise, removed her riding gloves. The Prince stooped to receive an affectionate kiss on the cheek. The two young people walked ahead, towards the lawn where Empress Eugénie and Queen Victoria were seated in the shade of a large tree.

"I am worried about Louis," confided Eugénie.

"And what cause for worry have I given you, my dear?" asked her husband, as they approached them unnoticed.

"Oh, there you are," she smiled, shading her light brown eyes from the sun. "I worry that you exhaust yourself with work."

"Your continued good health is our only concern," Louis-Napoléon replied. He lifted his wife's hand to his lips. Eugénie pressed her other hand gently on her still flat abdomen.

The Queen was touched by the unabashed tenderness radiating from the imperial couple. In their world, where strategically arranged alliances within small elite of royal and aristocratic families were the acceptable reason for marriage, it was pleasing to witness another marriage that appeared to be as loving as her own.

"The first pregnancy is always the most worrisome," reassured the Queen "yet, nothing is more rewarding than watching your children grow about you."

"How do you feel about becoming a father?" asked Prince Albert.

"My only concern is for my wife's well-being."

"Shall we go in?" Victoria added. "It is becoming uncomfortably warm."

The Empress Eugénie rose slowly from her seat. She was eager for the cool and quiet of her chambers.

"Bertie, Adelaide, you will need to change before your lessons. You may go to your rooms." their governess instructed. "With your permission, Ma'am," the governess said, curtseying to Queen Victoria, "I shall prepare the children for their lessons." The Queen nodded her approval.

"Albert is devoted to the children's education," said Victoria, taking Eugénie's arm in hers. "He is especially involved in Bertie's. He designed the curriculum himself. One day, the weight of our nation will fall upon his shoulders, so his instruction is of paramount importance."

The governess followed sedately after the Prince of Wales and the Princess Royal. Prince Albert and Louis-Napoléon walked several paces behind the others, engaged in a conversation.

"What has become of France's foremost tragedienne, Mademoiselle Rachel?" Victoria asked. "We had hoped for a performance during our visit."

"That is my surprise," Eugénie said, beaming. "Our national treasure will join us for dinner, and afterwards, she will perform for us."

"How wonderful!" responded the queen. "The performance will be here, and not at the theatre."

"Mlle Rachel has made few appearances at the Comédie Française this year, due to a series of personal tragedies."

"Why, what has happened?"

"Last year her younger sister, who was also an artist of the stage, died of consumption," Eugénie explained.

"That is sad indeed," said the Queen.

"Overcome by grief, Mlle also fell ill," Eugénie continued. "The physicians feared that she also had the deadly disease, but to the relief of all, the fatal symptoms did not appear. Unfortunately, this was not her only concern.

"During her sister's illness, the playwright Legouvé presented Mlle Rachel with his most recent work, *Médée,* and insisted that the title role had been written specially for her to play. Knowing the story, she rejected it without reading so much as the opening line. However, Legouvé was not to be discouraged. He continued to press her during her period of grief and illness until she relented and signed the contract.

"Last autumn, when Mlle Rachel finally read the script, she felt again that she could never play the role of a mother who mercilessly murders her innocent children. She was deeply upset by Legouvé's claim that the role was expressly written for her. She saw it as a travesty of her life and her art."

"Most understandably!" nodded the queen.

"Legouvé pressed his claim in the courts. Rachel pleaded that, as a devoted mother, she could not bring herself to play such an unnatural role. The court freed her of the contract but ordered her to pay him five thousand francs, which she gladly did."

"Has her health improved?"

"It was not until this spring that she finally recovered her strength, but only to be greeted by more trouble. During her absence, the young Italian actress, Adelaide Ristori, became the new darling of the Paris stage. Insulting articles in the press suggested that Rachel should 'come and study Ristori' and even stated that Rachel only had a quarter of the talent of this great new artist."

"How impertinent!" remarked the Queen. "Did she accept the challenge?"

"Yes," Eugénie continued with greater animation. "A competition of performances was arranged at the Comédie Française in which Rachel played *Phedre* and Ristori, *Myrrha.* Her performance was, of course, magnificent, as was that of Mme Ristori. However, the unpleasantness of the rivalry has left her restive.

"Her family pressed for another grand tour. Her friends have attempted to dissuade her. I pleaded with her not to leave France, but I fear that there is little that any of us can do to deter her from undertaking the arduous journey to New York. All arguments have fallen on deaf ears."

"We can only wish Mlle Rachel success," said Queen Victoria, more concerned for Eugénie than for Rachel, "and hope to see her perform again in London soon." She remembered her own admiration for the brilliant actress when she first performed in London nearly fifteen years ago.

"At least we shall have her for a few more days," pined Eugénie.

"Paris is beautiful. We are so enjoying our visit," Victoria said to Eugénie.

"This Saturday evening, we have arranged a grand ball at Versailles in your honour."

"It sounds lovely." replied Victoria as the guard held the doors open for them to enter.

ↂ

A select company sat enthralled in the Salon de Louis XIV as Rachel delivered her climactic monologue Empress Eugénie's flawless complexion was paler that usual, giving her the appearance of an elegant statue, as she mutely lost herself in the drama. Rachel was playing one of her favourite characters—Camille in *Horace*. She looked magnificent and was delivering a flawless performance. The gold and lapis lazuli earrings that Jules had brought her from Baghdad complemented her iconic robes. Her rich voice vibrated through the crowd as Camille rose in defiance against her brother:

"Rome, the only object of my resentment!
Rome, for whose sake your hand just slew my beloved!
Rome, who gave birth to you and whom you adore!
Rome, who honours you, finally I abhor!
May all her neighbours as conspirators
Defiantly undermine her foundations!
And if all Italy prove insufficient,
May the east to the west arise against her;

May a hundred peoples from the ends of the earth,
Pass mountains and the seas to destroy her berth!
And with their own hands rip her guts!
May with my eyes, I see Heaven's lightning flash,
On her mansions and your laurels turned to ash,
See the last Roman breathe out his last,
I alone being the cause of all shall into ecstatic death pass!"

At this, her brother Horace attacked her; they struggled and she fell, mortally wounded. Jules Oppert heard only her words; his thoughts were on the previous evening when, wrapped in a bed sheet, she had given him a private performance that he would never forget. Regrettably, the vision was interrupted by Victor Place's elbow in his side.

"By the way," whispered Place, "I saw your wife in Baghdad before departing."

"And how is she?" asked Jules, with a slight irritation in his voice.

"As beautiful as ever—even in a widow's garb." Place's dark eyes flashed with mischief. "You can imagine my shock to learn that you had died on your journey home."

"I should have sent you a telegram," Jules replied never taking his eyes from Rachel. "But I was at a loss for best choice of words."

"I probably would have done the same under similar circumstances."

"My untimely death seemed the only way to free her from me, and me from her," whispered Jules. "Now she can remarry." His tone went flat when he added, "Her love for me died with him."

"What about you, Jules?"

"Perhaps yes, perhaps no, I have no plans."

The play was ending. The elder Horace praised his son for defending the nation and advised him to rule Rome as a king should—keeping his own council and remaining unswayed by the mob.

The French elite applauded with the enthusiasm of an audience twice its size. Afterwards, Rachel and the other actors mingled with them while still in costume.

"A remarkable performance by Mlle Rachel, don't you agree?"

Jules and Place turned to find Prince Albert standing beside them.

"Yes, Your Highness," replied Place, "It was breathtaking."

"Most interpret Camille as a mad, pathetic creature," Albert said. "I was fascinated with Mlle's portrayal of her as a prophetess of doom, denouncing those who had robbed her of all that she loved. Every gesture was expertly executed, drawing one into the depths of her character's anguish."

"Your Majesty's assessment is most astute," agreed Place, "Mlle Rachel has no rival."

"Mr. Place, you were the French Consul at Mosul, I believe."

"Yes, Your Highness."

"We have heard briefly of your lost artefacts. How did it occur?"

"We were attacked by pirates, sir. Among the articles lost when our barge sank in the Tigris River were a magnificent winged bull and an irreplaceable relief depicting the sacking of the city of Musasir by the Assyrian King Sargon."

"The Emperor has informed me that certain crates containing artefacts from your expedition were inadvertently shipped to the British Museum instead of to the Louvre."

"Yes, Your Highness, That does seem to be the case," answered Place.

"This is most disturbing. Austen Layard, the recently elected Lord Rector of Aberdeen University, also said that valuable items he had collected went missing during shipment to England. It would seem that, despite the efforts of the East India Company, many parts of that region of the world are still unsafe. I suggest that you prepare a comprehensive list of all the missing items and send it to Colonel Rawlinson. I am certain that he will give it the highest priority."

"I am sure he will, Your Highness," replied Place.

"One trusts that your research at The British Museum is going well, Mr. Oppert?"

"Quite well, thank you, Your Highness."

"We are always eager to assist in the advancement of scientific inquiry," added the Prince.

"Before the Colonel left London to take charge of the recent excavations," he continued, "he presented the Prince of Wales with an exquisite terracotta relic from his private collection. We were so proud of our son—he showed a maturity far beyond his years when, upon request from the British Museum, he happily surrendered his treasure to their collection."

Queen Victoria joined her husband.

"We were just discussing Colonel Rawlinson," explained Prince Albert.

"Indeed!" smiled Victoria. "We wished to recognise Colonel Rawlinson for his long years of service. Lord Clarendon conveyed to him our desire to confer upon him the Order of the Bath, but the Colonel's modest and humble nature prevented him from accepting. It is our hope that he will reconsider. A man of his valour and acumen should not deny his Sovereign the pleasure of bestowing upon him the honour he has earned. We were comforted to learn that he agrees to direct the reorganisation our Near Eastern collections."

"Gentlemen, you will excuse us. It is time to retire," murmured Prince Albert.

"Of course, good evening, Your Majesty, Your Royal Highness," chimed Place and Jules. They bowed as the British royal couple joined their hosts, who accompanied them upstairs.

"Jules?"

He turned to find Rachel at his side.

"I must change out of my costume," she said. "I shouldn't be long. Will you escort me home afterwards?"

"Certainly," responded Jules.

"Are you researching the Comédie Française as well?" grinned Place.

"Mlle Rachel and I are old friends." Jules cleared his throat slightly.

"I see," said Place as they watched Rachel ascended the stairs. "Well, I must be gone as well. I shall see you in the morning to review Fresnel's notes?"

"Yes. Shall we say at about ten?" suggested Jules.

"Perhaps eleven would be more comfortable," smiled Place and with that he left.

"Jules, would you join me in one last drink?" asked Arthur Bertrand.

"Why not?"

⁂

Rachel had anticipated trouble when she spoke with Louis-Napoleon during dinner, but she was surprised by how intransigent Eugénie was being.

"Rachel, I cannot bear for you to leave; not now. Please reconsider," he pleaded.

"No, Louis." Rachel adjusted her full skirts over the wide crinoline. "By continuing to insist, you are only making the situation worse," she reprimanded. At which point Eugénie collapsed on Louis' bed, crying inconsolably. Rachel rolled her eyes.

"As my Emperor, I respect you. As my lover, I adore you. As my friend, I cherish you," she said. "However, I am a *free* Frenchwoman, and my mind is set. I shall leave for America.

"Here, Louis," she said, turning her back to him, "be a dear and fasten this for me." He fumbled with the hooks but was too distraught to complete the task. He leaned his head against hers.

"Please, Rachel," he whispered, "stay tonight."

For a moment Rachel's resolve weakened, but she quickly recovered. She must preserve her dignity.

"No Louis," she sighed. "You ask too much."

She stepped away and slipped her arms into her jacket. While buttoning the front, Rachel turned to his distraught wife.

"And you, dear Eugénie, please stop this childish sobbing. How many times must I repeat myself!" Rachel paused to check her hair in the mirror and grabbed her costume. "Understand this and understand it well—I shall not be dictated to. I shall sleep in whichever bed *I* choose, and with whomever *I* choose. No one, not even the Empress of France, will command or restrain me!"

Eugénie sat up, her eyes round with shock. No one had ever dared reproof her like this. Rachel took advantage of her silence, scooped her jewellery into her handbag, and made her escape.

As the door slammed shut, Louis-Napoléon turned to his devastated wife.

"Eugénie," he said, walking over to her. "What can I say? I tried to…"

"There is nothing that you can say that could ever correct this," she replied, slowly sliding to her feet. Tears flooding her eyes, she added, "There is nothing more to be said."

He reached out to take her hand. She jerked it back.

"Do not touch me!" she screamed. "You disgust me! You will never touch me again!" With that, Eugénie pulled her robe over her porcelain shoulders, concealing the thin lace that enhanced her perfect breast, and stormed from the room.

Louis-Napoléon sank onto the round cushion seat of a chair carved for his regal predecessor, and stared at his reflection in the gold framed mirror on the wall.

Rachel fled down the hall, with her head held high. Viewing her only from behind, a young officer called after her.

"Your Imperial Majesty!"

She did not stop.

"Empress Eugénie, please a moment," his companion added, "Her Majesty Queen Victoria has sent you this note."

Rachel paused at the head of the stairs, turned and glared at the two idiots. Embarrassed by their error the two young men fell silent. When she had floated far enough down the stairs and he was certain that she could not hear him, he turned to his companion.

"Did you see that look she gave me?"

"Yes, I did," replied the other. "One would think that any woman would be flattered to be mistaken for our beautiful empress. But oddly, this one took offense to it."

ᏣᏰᏇ

Rachel found Jules sitting with Arthur. He wore a similar disappointed expression as Louis.

"Ah, here is my beloved little wife," slurred Bertrand. "We were just speaking about you, my darling,"

"Arthur, I have no patience for your drunken babbling tonight," She replied fidgeting with her gloves. Taking Jules' glass, she finished the last of his brandy and placed it in Bertrand's free hand. "There, now you are set for the night."

"Rachel, you are heartless," Bertrand mumbled, with bleary eyes. She handed her cloak to Jules, who draped it round her shoulders.

"So I have been told already tonight."

Rachel pulled the satin hood over her hair and, taking Jules by the hand, led him out into the cool evening air. He had called for their carriage earlier, and it was there waiting for them. Each sat at a window and watched the familiar sights of Paris as they passed, but neither spoke during the ride to her house.

Rachel fought back tears. She had hated to disappoint Louis. As the scenes of this summer's drama replayed before her eyes, she struggled with panic to flee. She must get away from France – the further the better. She must not be sad, but must focus on the excitement of her coming tour to America. By the time she returned, Eugénie would have a new baby to love. Rachel comforted herself with the reassurance that by then she would be forgiven for this evening.

Jules had thought that he understood Rachel, but after his conversation with Bertrand, he no longer knew what to believe. But then, why should anything that he heard about Rachel and the Bonapartes surprise him? She had never hidden her past from him, but doubt now clouded his mind.

From her childhood, Rachel had been fascinated by the Bonapartes. Her parents' tales of the great Emperor liberating the Jews from the ghetto had a profound influence on her. It was this fascination to which Jules had attributed Rachel's infatuation with Napoleon's illegitimate son, Alexandre Colonna-Walewski. Alas, not even he could keep her from the stage, and the degenerate crowd of gamblers, profiteers, and demimondaines that inhabited it.

Walewski had loved Rachel passionately, but chose Lady Catherine Montague, daughter of the Earl of Sandwich, to be his wife. Rachel's fame and wealth might conceal her lowly origins, but could never purge them. Jules could understand why the count had attempted to keep her as his mistress—few women could rival her passion or technique. Jules smiled sadly. He knew that one day he too must succumb to the pressures of his own family and chose a 'proper' wife.

At the same time, he understood Rachel. It was inconceivable that anyone could hurt her and escape her fury. She had subdued her will for two years to conform to Walewski's every wish, but nothing she did was enough. Then he sneaked away and married another. Did he expect her to sit meekly waiting for his knock at the door when Paris was full of men eager to become Rachel's lover? When Walewski had confronted her with *her* infidelity, Rachel had ended their affair with her infamous retort: 'I am as I am; I prefer renters to owners.'

Foolishly, Walewski had taken their son, Alex, from her. She countered with a threat. If her child was not returned, she would make such a public spectacle of herself that he would never be able to show his face in polite society again. He knew that she was not bluffing and complied.

Yet, Jules could not understand why she had taken Bertrand as her next lover. How could a woman like Rachel tolerate his incessant drinking? He still begged money from her to support his expensive habits. However, she had soon tired of Bertrand, and left him for Louis-Napoléon. All of this Jules had known for some time. However, his conversation with Bertrand tonight troubled him.

Rachel was so absorbed in her own thoughts that it was not until they were climbing the stairs to her room that she noticed Jules' sullen silence. She tossed her costume and cloak across a chair, and Jules lounged into its mate. He was beginning to make her nervous as he sat there, studying the floor. When she asked him to unfasten her bodice, he noticed that it was hastily fastened and held by only two hooks. She changed into her robe, leaving her garments draped over the dome of the whalebone crinoline.

The room with it opulent furnishings was Rachel*'s* private domain for entertainment and conquest, but not for rest. On the cherry-coloured cover of her magnificent bed, with its carved and gilded woodwork lay her tattered copy of *Horace.* She had forgotten it after rehearsing her lines this afternoon. She opened the small, thin volume to the title page and read the fading ink – "To my darling Eliza-Rachel from Papa."

She carried it to the adjacent room. The light from the grand bedroom revealed a small, bare chamber, containing only a narrow pull-down bed, a simple chair, bed table, and a low shelf of well-worn books. The volume slipped comfortably into its place. Into this Spartan sanctuary, she withdrew from the chaotic world of Mademoiselle Rachel and found solace.

Had Arthur told Jules? Tears filled her eyes. She could not bear to lose his respect. Jules was the only man who stayed when she demanded that he leave and who left when she demanded that he stay. After Rebecca's death, he was the only one who had cared enough to console her. He had lain here with her for the entire night, cramped on the thin, hard mattress, holding not *Mademoiselle Rachel* but simple, grief-stricken Eliza.

Rachel returned to the large, luxurious bedroom and sat at her dressing table. The eyes staring back at her from the mirror were red and exhausted. She smeared her face with thick white cream.

"I am sorry if I am not the best company tonight," she said to break the silence. The stage makeup transferred easily to the cloth, revealing her features in a pale reflection of her dramatic heroine.

Jules did not respond. She turned on the cushioned stool and faced him.

"You seem very quiet. Is there something wrong?"

Jules sighed and without looking up, he asked, "Who is Gabriel's father?"

She turned back to the mirror. She could have killed Arthur Bertrand at that moment.

"Arthur, of course. You know that," she said, as if only half interested. She wiped off the remaining make-up. "Why do you ask?"

"I talked to Arthur tonight." Jules did not look up. "I told him that Gabriel is a wonderful boy, one that any man would be proud to call his son. I told him to stop wasting his life and try to be a better father."

"I can imagine what he answered," Rachel said. She was not in the mood for this, but knew that it could not be avoided.

Jules lifted his gaze from the floor and looked at Rachel. "He replied: 'Why should I? No one, not even his mother, can say with certainty who fathered him.'"

Jules watched Rachel wipe the lines of colour from her neck and from around her hairline.

"Is this true, Rachel? Surely you know who Gabriel's father is!"

"Of course I do—in general."

"In general? Is that the best you can do?" Jules was glaring at her now. "Any boy has the right to know his father, and any man should know without a doubt if a child is his or not. This is the foundation of social norms, of morality; of the Torah, for God's sake."

"I never claimed to be a good Jewess," Rachel examined the fine lines at the corner of her eyes. "When did I pretend to be of high moral character?"

"We are not discussing *high* moral character. This is about basic morality. I cannot believe that you do not comprehend the seriousness of this matter."

"Alex needed a brother. I gave him a brother."

"To the rest of the world, they are both considered bastards."

"My sons are not *mamzers*!"

"Oh, please, Rachel, don't be ridiculous!" Jules said. He stood up abruptly. "No one says that they are *mamzers*. Do not attempt to sidestep the issue by bringing Jewish law into it. Neither was born as the result of a forbidden relationship such as adultery or incest. You were not married, so you did not commit adultery."

"If the relationships were not forbidden, what does it matter?"

Jules' face reddened. "To bear a child out of wedlock is against all social norms, including those of Judaism. The boys must live in the real world and face the prejudices of common people."

"Who cares what the world thinks?"

"Perhaps *they* will care. You had a choice; they do not. Perhaps your choices will not seem so simple to them."

She did not answer him immediately, but instead vigorously rubbed lotion on her arms and legs. He watched her, noting the dark circles under her eyes and the unnatural paleness of her skin. She was losing weight again.

"You had absinthe tonight, didn't you?"

"Jules. I am neither your wife, nor your daughter, so do not lecture me. Besides, you saw the performance I gave tonight."

"Yes, it was brilliant—tonight, but absinthe can impair one's memory. Where will you be if you cannot remember your lines?"

"My memory is excellent," she stated with a forced calmness. "Besides, you know that my health is in the capable hands of Doctor Véron."

Jules clenched his teeth at the mention of that sleazy opportunist. Standing behind her, he placed his hands on her shoulders.

"Rachel? Who is Gabriel's father?" When she made no reply, he continued, "Let us apply the process of elimination. Now, who are the prime candidates?"

"Oh, good, a game," mocked Rachel sarcastically. "Humm...Gabriel was born on the twenty-seventh of January 1848. Arthur and I were lovers until April 1847, but I threw him out so many times during that last month, and he was so seldom sober, that he probably does not remember much about it. So, who could it have been?

"Ah, yes, I remember now. Early in May, I left for a tour of England. The day we arrived in London, I met Louis and Nap. As I said, Alex needed a brother, and it stands to reason that he should also be a Bonaparte, yes? I remember that I wrote to Sarah that I would not return from London until I was pregnant. You understand, of course, how I am always on a tight schedule. To ensure success, I seduced both of them. It was a most remarkable summer, the three of us touring England together."

"A *ménage à trois*?"

"Yes, my dear Jules. They joined our troupe, and we engaged in a ménage à trois. Therefore, in the final analysis, I suppose that the choice must be between Louis and Nap, although we cannot completely rule out Arthur."

Jules glared at her and walked quickly to the bed to retrieve his hat. Rachel began to tremble. She couldn't let him leave like this; the night would be unbearable without him. She rushed after him and took his arm.

"Don't leave, Jules," she pleaded. She pressed her body against him. "Why are we quarrelling over things that happened before we met? What is done is done. It cannot be changed."

He felt the trembling of her frail body. It was no longer proud, domineering Rachel standing before him, but simple, helpless Eliza. She took his hand.

"I have done things of which I am very ashamed," she admitted. "Think what you will of me, but please, stay with me tonight. Soon I shall leave, and it will be an eternity before we are together again."

Why did she always have this effect on him? Jules pushed her back onto the bed. He tossed his hat at the chair and flung his short cape after it. Propped on her elbows, she smiled as she watched him. He was so adorable when he threw his clothes about like this. When he pounced on her, Rachel asked with feigned fear, "What are you doing?"

"Paying my rent," he replied.

Ο3ΣΟ

CHAPTER 7

Guy Fawkes Day

Monday, 5 November 1855
Fleet Street, London

As soon as the young woman stepped from the doorway of the printing house, the dreary sky released yet another heavy shower of rain. At this time of the year, the London weather could change in an instant. The streets were packed with carts and people of every description rushing to get indoors away from the cold afternoon.

Mary struggled to open her large umbrella, but she had not gone more than twenty paces before the rain stopped as suddenly as it had started. Emerging from behind the lowering clouds, the sun slipped a little lower in the west. The puddles at her feet danced in the unanticipated light. She paused behind a large delivery wagon to close the umbrella and stole a moment to enjoy the sight of bustling Fleet Street washed in the afternoon glow.

A youth dodged his way down the crowded pavement. His hands were crammed deep in his jacket pockets in search of warmth. A shabby knitted cap pulled down over his ears and a black woollen scarf were his only protection from the cold. He was late leaving work—two of his colleagues were off sick, and his foreman had given their work to him. A quick meal and he must return to finish the day. He was trying to decide what to have when a gentleman in a heavy overcoat stepped in front of him. He jumped to avoid him, only to bump into someone else. On a reflex, he pulled the stranger back from falling against the rear wheel of a delivery wagon. He was rewarded by the flash of dazzling blue eyes and the unexpected pleasure of holding a young woman. She saw only his common cap and stained corduroy jacket. She felt a dozen heads turn in their direction. Strangers grinned or laughed outright at her embarrassment.

"Take your hands off of me!" she shouted.

"Sorry, miss," the youth replied, fumbling for his words, "I didn't see you." Obeying her command, he removed his hands, adding, "I didn't want yer to fall." He retrieved her umbrella from the wheel, and gave a slight bow as he presented it to her.

"Clumsy oaf," she said.

"I said I was sorry!" he stepped back, but that was as far as he could move. The sensation of her body pressed against his transfixed him, rooting his feet to the pavement. The sunlight gave her fair hair an angelic glow.

Recovering her dignity, the woman took her umbrella in one hand and her bag in the other. It was late. The errand had taken too long. Waiting in that drafty lobby was a perfect waste of precious time. After a quick check of its contents, she fastened her bag, and in a second, it was snatched away. All that could be seen of the thief was a grubby cap darting through the crowd. Her sudden dismay broke the spell on the youth and in a flash, he was on the heels of the thief. In wiliness and wit, they were well matched, but the advantages of the youth's longer legs and reach brought the chase to an end within fifty yards.

"Give it 'ere!" he demanded, snatching the lady's bag from the boy's hand.

"Oh, George, wotcha do that for?" whined the grimy street urchin. "E's goin' ter be mad, real mad." The boy wiped his runny nose on his worn and grubby cuff.

"I don't care wot 'e'll be," growled George. "Now be off with you, or I'll…" He didn't have time to finish the threat, for the boy vanished as if into thin air.

Stuffing the bag deep in his pocket, George worked his way back, occasionally jumping on the side of a cart, searching for the lady in the dark green hat with a white fur trim. He found her standing not far from where he had left her, looking as lost as a discarded kitten.

"'Ere," said George with a large grin, "you'd better 'ang on to this."

He pressed the bag into her hands. Her smile was like a glimpse of Paradise.

"Bless you, young man," she said. She was amazed when she discovered that none of her money had been lost. "This is all I brought for a little dinner and the fare home."

"You 'ungry?" said George. Taking a firm grip of her hand, he added, "I know a place." He guided her expertly through the crowd, but when he opened a creaking door to an old tavern, she pulled back.

"What is this?" she protested.

"The best dinner at the best price," George said matter-of-factly. "Don't fret!" Dropping her hand, he pulled the door open wide. "Come on then" he urged.

She stood back, cautiously peering into the room. When a young couple emerged and turned their collars against the afternoon chill, she relaxed and followed George inside. He led her to a long, thick wooden table that appeared to have been there since the founding of the city. The room was reasonably clean, but the day was still young. The woman carefully removed her warm grey cape, revealing a full-sleeved, modest dress matching the green material of the hat, with the white lace trim. The bodice was stylishly fitted with braided Basques.

"Wot'll it be, George, my lad?" asked a round-bellied man with a snaggle-toothed smile.

"Only yer best for the lady, Will," he said, settling into his favorite spot on the long bench. "Only yer best will do for us," he reasserted, assuming the air of a man in charge.

"We've a nice mutton stew and fresh bread," suggested the landlord. The young lady nodded, removing her gloves.

"And two ales," added George. The old man limped away.

"Why is that woman crying?" the young lady whispered, tilting her head slightly toward the far corner. The woman in question sat with her hands cupped over her face. She seemed intent on filling them with tears.

"Oh, that's Polly," whispered George, "poor thing. A smile's not crossed 'er lips since the day her old man fell down the docks an' broke 'is neck. Now she's workin' nights to feed the kids."

"Now, then," said the old man as he set the drinks on the table before them, "who's the lady friend, George?"

George looked confused for moment, but was saved by the quick reply of his companion.

"Mary, good sir," she answered with a sweet smile. "Mary Clifton."

"Well, you're in good 'ands, Miss Clifton. George here is as good a lad as you'll find anywhere." The old man gave him a wink and hobbled off to his kitchen. George's throat was parched. He reached for his mug.

"Merciful Lord!" exclaimed Mary, "Your hands are black with soot."

"That's not soot," retorted George indignantly. "It's ink."

"Ink?"

"My 'ands are clean as they can be, but the ink stains won't come off."

"So you work for one of the dailies?"

"No," answered George. "I'm an apprentice at Bradbury and Evans, the publishers, down Bouverie Street – between Fleet Street an' the river. This being my second year, I've started learning 'ow to set up the engraver, but I also mix the inks and clean the press. I gets ten shillings a week for a ten-hour day." The proud inflection he placed on the last statement brought a slight curve to Mary's rosy lips.

"Do they provide you with a place to sleep as well?"

"No," said George, watching the kitchen door. "I live with me mum and dad."

The old man returned, balancing a tray with two bowls of steaming stew. After arranging his burden on the table, he gave George another wink.

"An' what about you?" asked George. "What's a fine lady like yourself do all day?"

"Fine lady?" Mary said, blushing slightly. "I wish that I were a fine lady of leisure." She stirred her stew to cool it faster. "The truth is, I was born in Soho. My dad was a street merchant, and my mum was a seamstress. She was descended from the Huguenots, who came to London about a hundred years ago seeking freedom from oppression. His family has been here for as long as anyone can remember."

"Well, I must say, you fooled me. So you lost your parents, then?"

"Yes, to the cholera in '53," she said, taking a small bite of the food. "Mmm… It's good stew. You should eat some."

George followed her instruction.

"Me dad is from Gainsborough in Lincolnshire, but the rest of us was born 'ere in London," George said. "Me mum's from Marylebone." After a pause, he took another bite of the stew and continued, "Cissie Elizabeth and me was born in St. Giles, in Long Acre." He continued talking while chewing a chunk of meat. "We lived in Pimlico for a bit an' me brother, Jimmy, was born there. Then we moved to Chelsea. There's where me mum had Mary and Joseph." Chewing another bite, he added, "Pa is the best carpenter in London. Jimmy works with him now."

"Did you say Pimlico? That's where I live," Mary said.

"Yeah? We was off St. George's Mews back then." George wiped a drip from his chin with his cuff. "You're dressed every bit as nice as any fine lady, and you're twice as pretty," he said.

"Now you're flattering me," Mary said, her cheeks flushed again slightly. "I made it myself, as well as the cape. Do you like it?"

"I've never seen anything nicer," replied George.

"My mother taught me," Mary said. "I worked with her, but when they died, I couldn't pay the rent, so I went into service. To make extra money, I do alterations for their family and friends in the evenings."

"How do you like being in service. Do you 'ave others to help?"

"I work in a fine house on Belgrave Street," She broke off another piece from the loaf and added, "for Mr and Mrs Lindsey. Then there's Mrs. Pennyworth, the head housekeeper and Mrs. Lindsey's lady's maid. She's very strict, but I suppose she has to be. Then there's Mr. and Mrs. Watson, the butler and cook. They've been married forever but never had any children. They are really very kind to me. I'm first housemaid now and share an attic room with Annie, the second maid. Then there's Lucy, the scullery maid." Mary took a sip of her ale. "Oh yes," she nodded, "and there's the new man, Timothy Collins. He's the footman and groom. His wife is dead. He shares a room off the stables with his son James, who just turned eleven." Mary was more relaxed now.

"A package arrived today for Mr. Lindsey at the house that should have gone to his office. It was very important, so I was sent to deliver it."

"I know loads of people from Soho," said George, chewing a chunk of lamb, "an' they talk nothin' like you."

"That's because I don't want to sound like them," Mary replied. "I listen very carefully to the master and mistress, and when I'm alone, I practice speaking proper English."

"Why'd you want to do that?"

"Because I do not want to spend my whole life waiting on others," said Mary with a frown.

"What do you want to do then?"

"Perhaps I want to have my own dress shop," she mused, "or perhaps I'll find a nice gentleman, but I'll not live like my poor mother in a cramped, damp flat on a dirty, disease-infected street and watch my babies die one by one. No. I want to live in a good part of London." She took another sip of her ale. "A respectable husband doesn't want a wife who talks like a guttersnipe, so I practice gentle manners, I do. I read the books in Mr. Lindsey's library, and I make nice clothes for myself."

George nodded and smiled politely, but inside, his heart sank. Earlier she had called him an oaf, and she was right. With his black hands and worn, stained clothes, he must look like a tramp to her. Embarrassed by his coarse speech, he was reluctant to say anything more, so they sat in silence.

"George," Mary finally said. He took a large bite of the bread and nodded.

"How old are you?" she asked. She had been studying his handsome features and had noticed that his cheeks were smooth, with only a few new whiskers on his chin, but she couldn't place his exact age.

"Fifteen," he answered, washing the bread down with a large gulp of ale.

"Guess how old I am," challenged Mary. He shook his head. "No, really," she insisted, "how old do you think I am?"

"Oh, I dunno…eighteen?" he said, swallowing hard.

"I just turned twenty-one," she whispered, leaning a little closer to him. "It's not good. It's not good at all. Soon I'll be too old to marry." She stared towards the door contemplating her fate.

"You'll never be too old," George whispered.

At that, Mary blushed and laughed. "You are such a sweet boy," she said.

George smiled, but for some reason, he felt hurt.

They saw old Willie approaching them, and Mary sat up and greeted him with a proper nod.

"Oh, George, I nearly forgot to give you this," he said, handing him a copy of the *Daily Telegraph*. The old man cleared the dishes and wiped the table with a damp rag.

"Thanks, Will," George said. He began scanning and turning the pages.

"Are you looking for a particular article?" Mary inquired.

"I like to read the *Telegraph* with me dinner." George crossed one leg over the other knee and shook a fold from the newspaper. He cocked his head slightly to the side and studied the page. "Ol' Willie always saves one for me." He laid the paper on the table and covered the food stain at the lower corner with his hand. He hastily studied the page. He turned a couple more, then stopped and carefully tore out a column. "I keep all of these." He informed her.

"What's it about?" she asked.

"About?" George did not lift his eyes. "Why, only about the greatest man of our times, Colonel Henry Rawlinson," he announced. He turned in his seat to examine the small piece of paper by the dim light that found its way through the dirt-encrusted window.

"He's a patriot an' a hero," George said while scrutinising the tiny print. "He fought the infidels in the Afghan War. He's a true man of science, and a crusader against ignorance and superstition. He can read the long dead languages of the Ancient Persians and Assyrians. I've-collected loads of stories 'bout 'ow 'e risked death to discover those lost treasures and bring them home to England."

"That was beautiful, George," said Mary in amazement. "You spoke very well just now." When he turned to look at her, she saw something in his face—something hidden beneath the ink and the shaggy hair. It was the look of an intelligent, scholarly young man.

"What do you want to be, George?" she asked. "That is, if you could be anything in the world, what would you choose?"

"That's easy. I'd work with Colonel Rawlinson in the Museum. I'd learn to read and understand his ancient tablets."

George folded the cutting and, stuffing it deep into his pocket, he added, "I need to go. I'll be late for my work."

"Yes, of course. I must also be getting back." Mary turned and unfolded her cape. George quickly stepped forward and helped set it squarely on her slight shoulders. He turned and placed a couple of coins on the table.

"Please, let me pay. After all, you did rescue my bag from that little thief."

"No," George said. He pressed her hand back.

"Thank you, George. Thank you for everything. You've been so good and kind," Mary said, smiling warmly. Strange—he seemed older to her just then. They walked towards the door.

"Mary?"

"Yes, George?"

"Maybe you'd learn me..."

"'Maybe you would *teach* me,' she corrected, and completed his question: "to speak better?"

"Yeah."

"I would love to teach you," she replied, as George held the door for her. "Just now, I cannot think of anything I'd rather do."

It had started to rain again and George opened Mary's umbrella for her.

"What is the number of your work in Bouverie Street?" asked Mary, pulling on her gloves.

"Number 31. Why?"

"This is what I'll do," she said, taking the umbrella from him. "I'll ask Mr. Watson if you can come for lessons in the kitchen on some evenings after my work is done. If he agrees, I'll write to you at your work with the address."

George leaped into the air and laughed with delight. "I'll come wherever you say and do whatever you say, Mary. I'll be the best scholar you ever saw!"

A hackney cab had just dropped off a fare at the corner. Mary ran to catch it. George raced ahead and held it for her. "Thank you again, dear George. I'll write," she said. He watched until she was out of sight and whispered a little prayer that she would keep that promise.

7. Guy Fawkes Day

ꕥ

London was ablaze with a thousand bonfires. Smoke drifted up on a gentle breeze. From street to street, gangs of masked children marched in procession, escorting their ragged effigy to its fiery fate. As George neared home, he joined in the chant with a group of familiar young voices:

"Remember, remember, the fifth of November,
Gunpowder, treason and plot.
I see no reason why Gunpowder Treason
Should ever be forgot.
Guy Fawkes, Guy Fawkes,
'Twas his intent
To blow up the King and the Parliament.
Three score barrels of powder below,
Poor old England to overthrow.
By God's providence he was catch'd,
With a dark lantern and burning match.
Holloa boys, Holloa boys, let the bells ring.
Holloa boys, Holloa boys, God save the King!"

Lifting the guy high in the air, George led the others in shouting:

"Hip hip, Hoorah !
Hip hip, Hoorah !"

The march continued into a courtyard, where the flames were already leaping high. The children rushed about, picking up pieces of rags, papers, and wood to feed the bonfire.

Many of the children in their ragged clothes, broken shoes, and threadbare coats were not much better dressed than the guy.

"'Ere's to Guy Fawkes," toasted an old man, "the only man ever to enter Parliament wiv honest intents." Laughter followed, and everyone, children as well as adults, took swigs from the bottles that were being passed around. After George had his nip of the gin, he wrapped his scarf tighter about his neck and slipped back into the dark, dirty street.

Men and women staggered about the streets, laughing and swearing. Girls of his age, some that he had known from childhood, stood on the corners with scarlet lips and curled hair, wearing great overcoats and little else. An outsider would have deemed the place seedy, but George hardly noticed them. For him, these dark streets were home.

A brief break in the clouds revealed the last silvery sliver of the waning autumn moon. George wished that it were full, to better light his way. He slipped through the familiar darkness toward his flat. He was almost there, when he suddenly stopped in his tracks. He knew every inch of the place, and he could sense there was wrong. Someone was hiding in the dark alleyway in front of him. They came at him fast and pounded his thin body with fists and sticks. Strong hands grabbed him under his arms and dragged him into the alley. The sound of a lucifer scuffing across a rough surface, the scent of burning sulfur, and a dazzling light as oil-soaked rags burst into flames.

"Hullo, Georgie boy," snarled a large, square fellow with a flattened nose. "We ain't seen your ugly mug for more'n a fortnight."

"Hullo, Joe," coughed George, struggling against the grip of his two captors.

"'Tis sad, Georgie ol' chum," pondered Joe as he walked closer. "'Tis sad indeed the way you're turnin' out. We was chums once." Joe appeared to be on the verge of tears. "An' now, you've taken to stealin' off me lil brother 'ere," He patted the head of the pug-faced boy that George had encountered earlier.

"Wot's 'appened to you, Georgie?" Joe asked.

"I told you, Joe," puffed George, holding his side, "I'm done with you." He pulled himself to his full height. "There was no more than a few pennies in that lady's purse, anyway."

"Ah, so that's it, is it?" laughed Joe, "Did 'er pretty face turn yer 'ead?" With that, Joe landed a solid punch in George's stomach. George's knees buckled and he fell forward onto the ground. There was no escape. He'd probably wake up in a gutter, maybe unable to work for a week.

Suddenly, the sky exploded in a burst of sparkling lights followed by a loud bang as somebody nearby set off a firework. Still little more than children, the thugs turned in unison to enjoy the spectacle. George rolled over and smiled with relief as he recognised a friendly face. Seizing his opportunity the dark figure darted from the shadows. A hard right punch hit Joe in the stomach. A left to his jaw, and Joe was out cold. George leapt to his feet and grabbed the torch.

"Come on, then," he shouted, "which one of you lot wants to be the next Guy Fawkes to burn tonight?" The gang backed away, growling from a distance, dodging behind each other whenever the torch came too close. "Help me with Joe, boys," one called out, "we'll finish 'im later."

George stumbled and his friend helped him up again. They tossed the torch into a large puddle, and the area returned to darkness.

"Thanks, Tommy," said George. They did not stop until they reached the safety of 1A Britton Place.

George slumped against the door and slid to the ground. Tommy banged on the door and tugged him back on his feet.

"Come on, George, you don't wanna stay down there," he said.

A pretty girl with rust-coloured hair opened the door.

"George! What 'appened?" she said.

"It's nothing, Cissie," replied George.

"Merciful Jesus!" cried Martha Smith. "What've they done to you, George? Tommy, put 'im to bed and I'll bring some water."

"Yes, Mum," said Tommy.

He helped George down the long narrow hallway. Along one wall were three doors – the first led to their parents' room, the second to his sisters' room, and the third to the tiny kitchen. Tommy drew back the curtain to back storage space that concealed the three narrow cots where George and his brothers slept. Tommy eased him down on his bed and his mother rushed in and examined the cut on George's lip. The years had dulled Martha's once bright, red hair to striking roan and her face was lined from too many worries, but her eyes still sparkled with a simple faith and love of laughter.

" 'Ave you 'ad yer dinner, Tom?" she asked, as she cleaned the blood from the corner of his mouth.

"No, Mum."

"Well, yer certainly welcome to eat with us," she added, dipping the cloth into the water. "George's dad and brother'll be home soon."

"Cissie, fetch a plate for Tommy," called her mother. Reassured that her son not seriously injured she rose, gave him a kiss on the forehead, hurried off. "Change yer shirt for dinner, George."

Tommy grinned. He loved the smell of the Smiths' flat. Fresh bread and good soup were always ready to be set before you on a clean table. George slowly sat on the edge of the bed and then tried his legs.

"George?"

"Yeah?"

"Why don't you do them nice drawings anymore?" asked Tommy.

The wall over George's bed was covered with graphite sketches of his family and friends, including one of Tommy from a few years back.

"Wish I 'ad the time, Tommy," said George. He poured more water into the chipped, washbasin, and splashed it on his face. The soap burned his cuts.

"What's this with the funny shapes?" Tommy said. He held up a paper that he'd found on the table. George limped over and peered down at his painstaking effort to copy some cuneiform characters.

"That's writing that the Assyrians used to do," he told Tommy. "I found 'em in 'ere." George picked up a worn copy of Layard's *Nineveh and Her Remains.*

"Writing? It don't look like no writing to me," scoffed Tommy.

"I know. It looks funny, don't it?" replied George.

They heard the front door open. George's brothers pushed the curtain back.

"Hurry up George, I wanna eat," grumbled Jimmy.

"Nearly ready," George replied. Jimmy went to the kitchen to wash.

"Can you read this stuff?" asked Tommy throwing the book back onto George's cot.

"Not yet, but I'm working on it." George put his hand on Tommy's broad shoulder.

Tommy helped George limp down the hall to the main living area. The evidence of William Smith's skill as a carpenter added an unexpected touch of elegance to small flat. He earned a decent wage and Martha saved as much as she could. There would be more, if not for the endless needs of growing children, the tithes paid to their church and the quality of the beer at the local pub. Yes, they were good people, and Tommy was proud to be George's best friend.

"Thanks for helpin' me back there," said George as they arrived to the dining table that was surrounded by hungry faces ready for their meal.

"I gotta take care of you, George," Tommy replied, "You're me best mate. If anyone gives you grief, Tommy'll take care of 'em. Don't you worry."

ↀ

CHAPTER 8

Order of the Bath

Monday, 4 February 1856
Westminster Abbey, London

Westminster Abbey loomed in splendour above the crowd. Its Gothic spires affirmed the true and impartial weight of justice dispensed by the ever-watchful Heavens to all men, regardless of their station in life.

"When will it start?" asked an impatient young man. The winter sun, struggling to warm the ice-blue sky, indicated that it was nearly noon. "We have to get back soon, George," he added.

"It won't be long now, Paul," George replied. The large woman in front of them leaned over to pick up her child, affording them a better view for a brief moment.

"Look! There's the Queen's guard," shouted Mary. The trio pushed their way through the crowd to the railing.

Her Majesty's yeomen, in their traditional red tabards, stiff white ruffs, stockings and black hats—marched in perfect unison, their long lances over their shoulders. They turned smartly toward the ogival doorway, and then vanished into the shadows beneath the abbey's magnificent stained-glass windows. The trio joined the crowd in an exuberant cheer. "God save the Queen! God save Prince Albert!"

At first, all that Mary saw was the sparkle of Queen's diamond tiara in the sunlight. Then her kind, gentle face came into view. Her Majesty, the Sovereign of the Order of the Bath, seemed to float by in her ermine-trimmed, crimson satin mantle. Gold thread shimmered in her white gown. Her gloved hand rested on the forearm of her gallant Consort.

Prince Albert thrilled the crowd in his splendid attire as the Grand Master of the Order of the Bath. The flowing crimson mantle was thrown over his left shoulder, revealing the elaborate 17th century costume beneath. He was wearing an intricately embroidered white satin doublet and paned trunk hose over white stockings, with red-cuffed white leather boots. Around his waist was a wide red sash from which dangled a large, golden tassel. His black velvet hat with its great plumes of white feathers was pulled down firmly over his dark blond hair. Awed by the spectacle, George and his friends waved their flat, felt caps and cheered as loudly as the crowd around them.

Behind the royal couple, the Officers and Knights passed in solemn procession, wearing white-lined crimson mantles, with the riband of the Order slanting across their chests. Only the Grand Master and Knights Grand Cross wore the embroidered, silver, star-shaped emblem depicting the crowns of England, Scotland, and Ireland surrounded by the motto *Tria juncta in uno*. They were also the only ones to wear the heavy gold insignia suspended from the linked clasp that held their mantles in place. A fanfare of trumpets could be heard from within as their Royal Majesties entered the nave of the cathedral.

"George, we must get back to work, or there'll be trouble," urged Paul.

"One minute... one *more* minute... There! There he is!" George cried, pointing towards the next group in the procession. "Can you see him? He's wearing his military uniform."

George waved his cap high in the air, shouting, "Hooray! Hooray for Colonel Rawlinson!"

Lieutenant Colonel Rawlinson marched by with perfect military aloofness, his medals brilliant in the sunlight. Among them was the Maltese cross of a military Companion of the Order sent to him while still in the East in recognition for his services during the Afghan War. George was oblivious to all except his hero. As the tail of the procession faded into the shadows of the Abbey, George reluctantly allowed his friends to pull him back to the ordinary world of a print-plate engraver apprentice.

ᘓᘐ

The invited guests and family of the Knights were still standing when Rawlinson entered the nave. He was awestruck by the splendour of Westminster Abbey. The repetitive, pointed, arches soared upward, lightening the burden of columns. They seemed to draw his soul closer to Heaven, alleviating the weight of mundane concerns from his mortal form. The high, stained glass windows blazed in variegated colours and thrilled his essence with empyrean sensibility.

The procession passed through the Nave and Rawlinson scanned the congregation for the faces of his family and friends. The Dean of the Order and the six Chapters greeted Her Majesty and Prince Albert. As the members of the Order took their seats in the Quire, the Cathedral choir sang a psalm. Their high, clear voices blended with the magnificent tone of the great organ. Then the Dean ascended to the altar and began reading the service, but Rawlinson's attention soon wandered.

He drifted back to the gentle Oxfordshire vale and the tall meadow grass that rippled in the breeze on the Chadlington farm of boyhood. Memories of skating on the pond in the winter, fishing in the spring, and hunting in the autumn, flickered before his eyes. Yet too many children, the hard economic times, and his education had been a heavy burden on his parents had darkened his early years. The worst had been bearing the mocking smirks and haughty looks of others when he accompanied Lord Normanton on shooting parties. His mount had always been some wretched hack, far inferior to the others', and his meagre wage was hardly worth the humiliation he had endured.

Rawlinson lifted his chin in defiance of his past. Today, on this splendid occasion, he was not only traversing the social rift that had always separated him, but was rising above most of them in social standing. This washed away the bitter gall of inferiority that he had tasted for as long as he could remember.

The Sovereign, Queen Victoria, and the Grand Master of the Order, Prince Albert, rose together and lead the procession past the shrine of Edward the Confessor to the entrance of the Henry VII Chapel, where the installation of the knights of the Bath would take place. The Prince escorted the Queen to her high-backed, dark oak stall, and permitted the Dean to conduct him to his place across from her. The Knights of the Grand Cross followed them down the ancient, worn stone steps into the chapel and assumed their places in the choir stalls on either side.

Rawlinson stood and waited his turn. The intricate golden ceiling rose above the coats of arms displayed on embroidered banners behind each current denizen of the stalls of the most senior Knights of the Order. Engraved stall-plates commemorated former occupants. Historic emblems in bronze, wood, and stone depicting dragons, portcullises, greyhounds, lions, fleurs-de-lis, and red-and-white roses danced about him.

The Bath King of Arms bowed to a Knight of the Grand Cross, who was to be installed in a stall recently vacated, due to the his predecessor's death. He moved to the altar, where he received the Book of Statutes from the Deputy Secretary. With the Dean carrying the Holy Scripture and the senior Canon holding the Scarlet Rod, they proceeded to the middle of the chapel. All bowed to the Grand Master. Descending from his stall, Prince Albert joined them as they escorted the Knight to the vacant stall. The Book of Statutes was conveyed to the Grand Master, and the Dean administered the oath to the knight being installed, who simultaneously repeated the words of the oath. The Grand Master led the knight to his stall, where he bowed in homage to the Prince Consort and took the seat that would be his for as long as God granted him life.

Once all had returned to their stalls and were seated, the Bath King of Arms moved to the middle of the chapel and bowed to the knights. As all rose to their feet, Her Majesty the Sovereign of Order approached the altar and kneeled down, before placing an offering of gold coins on the altar. The newly installed knight followed his *S*overeign to the altar and presented an offering of equal value. All Senior Knights then drew their swords, offering them to the Dean, who laid them upon the altar. They were then permitted to redeem their blades as he administered an admonition. When these were returned, the Knights of the Grand Cross stood with their swords half-drawn, symbolising their readiness to defend their Queen.

Those being inducted into the Order stood facing her. At last, Rawlinson's moment had arrived. When his name was called, he proudly stepped forward and bowed as the Queen placed the crimson ribbon holding the eight-pointed silver cross pattée of Civil Knight Commander around his neck. In unison, the senior knights sheathed their swords, concluding the ceremony.

To a fanfare of trumpets, the Sovereign and Grand Master headed the procession as they left the chapel and resumed their seats in the main body of the Abbey. All others remained standing as the choir sang, and the Dean gave thanks and blessings. The ceremony now was concluded. As the long procession emerged from the shadows of the Abbey into weak February sunshine, Sir Henry Creswick Rawlinson's mind was already racing ahead, formulating his next move.

☙❧

Following the most delightful afternoon that he could remember spending with those nearest and dearest to him, Rawlinson relaxed at the Athenaeum Club with his friends. Countless congratulatory handshakes and toasts to his continued good fortune punctuated the evening. As the hour grew late, they settled down to enjoy their last brandy and cigars.

"I always knew that one day you would receive the recognition that you so richly deserve, *Sir* Henry," said Norris.

"Thank you, Edwin," Rawlinson said with a modest smile.

"Now that you have rescued the lost Library of Ashurbanipal from the depths of oblivion, the world looks to you to reveal its secrets," said Vaux.

"Quite so, William," agreed Panizzi.

"The great Assyrian library was by far the most thrilling of my discoveries," Rawlinson said.

"The field of Assyriology is at a very early stage," Panizzi said to him. "You worked so long to establish it as a viable science and now it is desperately in need of your guidance. It is unfortunate that due to the current financial constraints, the Trustees could not offer you a permanent appointment at the Museum, Sir Henry. However, one might have supposed that the opportunity to have primary access to these treasures, not to mention the generous remuneration proposed, would have been sufficiently attractive to engage you."

"Why have you delayed accepting the Museum's offer, Sir Henry?" asked Vaux.

"Do not misunderstand me, gentlemen," Rawlinson replied. "I deeply appreciate both the honour and generosity of your offer. The primary cause of my hesitation is the lack of authority associated with the position."

"Authority, Sir Henry?" injected Samuel Birch, "I fail to understand what the problem could be, unless you have reservations about working under my superintendence?"

"Not at all, Dr. Birch," said Rawlinson. "We have always enjoyed the most congenial relationship, and I am confident that our future collaborations will be equally affable." He took another puff of his cigar. "It is simply that the offer does not state precisely what authority the position holds."

"What did you have in mind, Sir Henry?" asked Vaux.

"In my capacity as Her Majesty's consular to Turkish Arabia, I had extensive responsibility, the results of which have obviously met with Her Majesty's approval, as well as that of the trustees of the British Museum," Rawlinson said. "I must confess that, during those long years of duty, I became accustomed to managing the affairs under my jurisdiction with the freedom that comes with a position of high authority. If the trustees would convey upon me a status equal to my proven abilities, then I should be happy to accept their proposal."

"What authority do you feel would make the position more acceptable?" asked Panizzi.

"The museum is very fortunate to have a scholar of Dr. Birch's calibre, equally skilled in both Chinese and Egyptian hieroglyphics. On the other hand, my expertise is in cryptic Mesopotamian. The Antiquities Department is growing at an astonishing rate," Rawlinson said, extinguishing his cigar. "If I am to undertake the enormous task of reconstructing, translating, and publishing the multitude of Assyrian and Babylonian inscriptions, then I must have full authority over the artefacts." He paused to sip his brandy.

"That seems reasonable to me," stated Vaux.

"Sir Henry," Birch said, also extinguishing his cigar. "Let me make myself perfectly clear. I am the director of the Antiquities Department. I and I alone will decide who is permitted access to the artefacts."

"Might I remind you gentlemen that a substantial portion of those artefacts was donated from my own personal collection?" Rawlinson said.

"For which you were compensated most handsomely," replied Panizzi. "I must agree with Dr. Birch. The British Museum is our nation's great repository of wisdom. Its purpose of advancing scientific knowledge would be compromised if accessibility were denied to scholars."

"By what standard do you determine a scholar qualified?" asked Rawlinson. "Surely you do not propose that anyone be permitted to handle these delicate and friable relics?" Rawlinson leaned forward and, with an inflection of true concern, continued, "Dr. Birch, it would be impractical for you to disrupt your vital work whenever someone asked to see a tablet. Therefore, it stands to reason that this responsibility should be part of the position that I am to hold."

"As long as you remember, sir," Birch said, his eyes flashing, "who is the Director of the Antiquities Department."

"I would not consider questioning your authority, Dr. Birch, and I shall at all times follow the policies you have established," Rawlinson said.

"Good," said Vaux, nervous tension lifting his voice, "then we have an agreement?"

"I believe we do," stated Birch.

"There is another issue. I should need a reliable assistant who is familiar with the language to help copy the inscriptions for the lithographer, Mr. Bowler," said Rawlinson. "I would like the trustees to consider engaging Mr. Norris for this purpose. That is, if you are interested, Edwin?"

"Yes, indeed, Sir Henry," Norris replied. "But as you know, I am already engaged by the Foreign Office, as a translator."

"You could continue translating for them while working for me. Of course, the trustees must provide suitable remuneration."

"An excellent suggestion, Sir Henry," said Vaux, and Birch nodded his approval. "We are aware of Mr. Norris' linguistic talents, and he has already been an excellent editor and advisor on numerous translation projects."

"For my own part, I find your terms quite acceptable, Sir Henry," confirmed Panizzi, "and I shall present them with Mr. Norris' name for approval by the trustees at our next meeting. I am confident that the Board will find such an arrangement acceptable."

Rawlinson knew that he had made excellent progress. Vaux would be a useful ally, and Panizzi was also favourable. With Norris working directly for him, Birch could easily be circumvented. It may take time, but he was confident that he would eventually succeed in gaining full control over the Assyrian collection.

CHAPTER 9

An Historic Experiment

Tuesday, 28 April 1857
Killyleagh, Ireland

Undulating fields of soft green rolled towards the distant Mountains of Mourne, bridled by a crisscross lattice of low stonewalls. In every sheltered dip in the land, bright yellow marsh marigold flowers nodded above their broad, deep green leaves. The fields were garlanded with royal blue Wood Bells, feathery white bogbean, and pinkish-purple cuckooflowers.

"This has been a marvellous afternoon," said Talbot. "After such an excellent lunch, a walk through the beautiful Irish countryside is just what I needed." A nasal zee, zee, zee announced the arrival of a sooty brown-capped willow tit in a nearby cluster of birch and rowan trees.

"My wife and I are so pleased that you found time to visit us, Talbot," replied Reverend Hincks.

"It was fortunate that my business appointment in Belfast was postponed by a day," said Talbot. "By the way," he added gingerly, "I happened to meet Austen Layard at the House of Commons the other day. I was not aware that you were so closely acquainted. He mentioned that he visited you on his return from Nineveh."

"Yes, he stayed with us for two months that autumn," Hincks said, nodding.

"I understand that his last years in that inhospitable region ruined his health, resulting for a while in nervous exhaustion," Talbot said.

Hincks stiffened, but relaxed when he realised that Talbot did not expect him to reveal the troubles Layard had related to him in confidence.

"His constitution had been weakened by a severe fever, but otherwise he seems of sound mind. The purpose of his visit was to solicit my assistance in preparing for the publication of his *Discoveries in the Ruins of Nineveh and Babylon.*" They continued walking, inhaling the beauty of the day.

"I am gratified that there is a general agreement between your version and mine as to the meaning of the Bellino inscription," stated Hincks. "I prepared it with great labor under an agreement with the British Museum trustees. Though this was not stipulated, I certainly understood when I parted with the copyright to it and my other research that they would publish them. Had I not believed that it would be done, I would never have entered into the agreement with them. I even allowed the trustees to dictate the subject matter to me, and I was instructed to confine myself to the inscriptions of Sennacherib and those of the North West Palace. However, the all-important lexicon tablets, which would have enabled me to improve my translations, were kept from me."

"I find that very odd," said Talbot. "Why should they deny you access? The trustees permitted Jules Oppert to explore the cabinet on several occasions. Of course, he has the support of Bonaparte. While at the Museum, he was fortunate to re-assemble several broken pieces of the Assyrian cyclopedia."

"Is it true that Oppert has been appointed Professor of Sanskrit and Comparative Philology, and that he is now associated with the National Library of France?" asked Hincks.

"Yes, that is so," Talbot said. They walked in silence for a few paces, and then Hincks said, "I submitted my paper to the Museum in the summer of 1854, and I have been informed that it is now kept-locked up in the private repositories of the Principal Librarian! It has not even been put among the additional manuscripts, where it would be accessible to the public. By whom it has been seen, I know not, but Dr. Oppert recently published much of what was contained in my essay as his own work."

"I doubt that the trustees would have shown your paper to Dr. Oppert," reassured Talbot. "I asked Panizzi, and he stated that it has been seen only by Vaux."

"From Oppert's description, it seems to me that he must have seen it," Hincks said. "As it was delivered to a public body such as trustees of the British Museum, I consider that a form of publication, hence entitling me to claim priority. Oppert should have acknowledged this." Hincks paused for a moment to enjoy the tranquil, rustic scene.

"Perhaps my work was not suppressed in order to benefit Dr. Oppert," he continued. "but I am very sure that there is a determination in some influential quarters to that I must be kept out of the field of discovery, whatever may occupy it. I am now laid on the shelf, and I never expect to have the means again to pursue discoveries."

"Since control over the artefacts was granted to Sir Henry Rawlinson, all requests of access must be approved by him," said Talbot. "I fear that he took offence at your criticisms of his most recent work. Perhaps it was not prudent to oppose him openly before the Royal Institution and at the Glasgow meeting of the British Association for the Advancement of Science."

"Yes, you are probably right," Hincks agreed, "but you also considered his notions too fanciful. We may all be prone to an occasional flight of fancy, but we would never publish unsubstantiated claims such as his identification of the Birs Nimrûd as the Tower of Babel. As a clergyman, I have faith in the truth of the Holy Scriptures; but as a scholar, I would never claim that the House inscription contains an allusion to Nebuchadnezzar's madness. It is sensationalism, meant to excite the imagination of the masses. If this is the quality of his scholarship, is it not possible that he may bring forward something equally absurd in his translation of the Assyrian tablets?"

"Generally, his work has been good, though I often wonder how much of it should really be accredited to Norris," said Talbot.

"It would be ungracious to criticise a translation which is, on the whole, good," said Hincks, "although it can be said that it is not as good as it might have been. At any rate, he may make many minor mistakes, but what then? The public will fare worse, but he will have more credit. It is not my present intention to meddle with it. I may have a laugh in private over any mistakes that I notice, but I will not enlighten them. The public has given its voice in Sir Henry's exclusiveness, and then let it be so! I still think that the Trustees would have better served the public interest if they had allowed copies of the lithographs to be circulated among those scholars who are most likely to be translators, so that the translations might appear together. It would also have been better if they had encouraged a joint translation. It is quite evident that two or three scholars acting in concert and comparing and challenging their views would produce a better translation than any one of them would do singly."

"Quite so. By the way, my request for copies of the Tiglath-pileser inscription was finally answered." Talbot said.

"How was it resolved?" asked Hincks.

"After months of volleying letters with Panizzi, Sir Henry graciously gave his approval, but only on the condition that I agree to comply with his terms."

"I remember the time when a simple note to Birch was enough to gain access," lamented Hincks.

"I completed my translation from the lithographed pages," said Talbot.

"Even so, the lithographs were made under Rawlinson's directions, and we risk the possibility that they already contain his errors."

"What else is there? Either we accept what we are given, or we cancel our research," Talbot replied. "It still remains for us to put an end to the doubts which exist in the minds of many learned scholars as to the reality of what they term our 'alleged' translations of these ancient discoveries."

"How was the last meeting of the Royal Asiatic Society?" asked Hincks.

"I presented your suggestion as an historic experiment and offered my own translation of the octagon in a sealed packet, which I requested not be opened until Sir Henry had provided his translation," Talbot replied. "I fully explained my motive, namely to determine if our independent translations would be found to agree with the main one, as I confidently hoped would be the case. The Society accepted the deposit. It so happened that Dr. Oppert was present at this sitting, and he immediately asked for leave to deposit an independent translation of his own to the Society. He will not use the lithographs, but instead send in his version taken from a separate original copy found in the Louvre's collection. They, of course, consented to this. Dr. Oppert is the only continental scholar who has made any progress in cuneatics, as far as I am aware.

Under these circumstances, Rawlinson expressed his resolve to finish and present his own translation speedily, so that the comparison may be made during the present session of the Society. It was proposed that the packets be opened about the middle of May, and then all four will be published jointly.

"A few days later, Norris informed me that the Society had determined to invite you also to send a translation. It is disappointing that your copy of the lithograph has not arrived. Furnishing four concurring testimonies would be an unanswerable argument for the truth of the system."

As Talbot was speaking, a creaky old cart lumbered towards the two scholars. They had arrived at Killyleagh without noticing. The town was little more than two rows of shops with a road running between them. It was small and cosy, filled with good-natured locals who worked in the cotton mill, tilled the rocky fields, or fished the cold waters of Strangford Lough. There was a tavern, of course, where the town's men quenched their thirst after a long day's work.

"Reverend Hincks!" shouted the carter, whose face was almost hidden behind a mass of white beard and long, curly hair. "Reverend, there's a package for you." He reined in his pony and reached back under the tarpaulin, pulling out a large, brown paper package to which other letters were tied.

"Thank you, Patrick," said Hincks, "and how's your daughter? Feeling better, I pray."

"As well as can be expected, Reverend. Her mother is with her now, takin' care of the little ones."

"With the Lord's mercy, she'll be better than ever before you know it," said Hincks as he inspected the package.

"Well, I'd best be on my way," said Patrick, clicking to his pony.

"Thank you," Hincks called after him.

"It is from the Museum," stated Hincks. "At long last, it seems that my lithograph copy has arrived."

"I can think of no reasonable excuse for such a delay, Hincks," Talbot said. "Rawlinson, Norris, and Vaux were all present at the Society's meeting a full five weeks ago, when you were named as contributor. It should not have taken this long for the lithographer to print another copy."

"I shall begin work on it immediately," Hincks said. "It may be possible to turn this circumstance to a very useful account, and thus to produce good out of evil, which is always a great satisfaction. Clearly, the objective of the Society is to establish the truth of these discoveries in the minds of the many scholars who are, at present, hesitating whether to accept them or not, although many of them have conceived that something has been ascertained. However, at present they seem to think that no reliance can be placed on the deciphering system."

"My carriage has arrived. Permit me to drive you back to the rectory," said Talbot.

"No, no, that is not necessary," Hincks replied. "As you said earlier, it's a lovely day for a walk. Besides, you have a long road back to Belfast. You should begin the journey now if you intend to arrive by suppertime."

"Of course you are right. It is later than I had thought," said Talbot, as the driver jumped down and held the door for him. When he was seated, Talbot stuck his head out of the window and added, "I look forward to reading your translation. I only wish that you had more than a mere two weeks in which to complete it."

"As you so aptly put it, what else is there? Either we accept what we are given, or we cancel our research," replied Hincks. The men bade farewell to each other, and went their separate ways.

ଔଷ

CHAPTER 10

The Elusive Orientalist

Monday, 25 May 1857
British Museum, Great Russell Street, London

Mr. Talbot is here to see you, sir," stated Norris, closing the door.

"Tell him that I have just left for Leadenhall Street, and that I shall be occupied with the current crisis all week," Rawlinson returned, searching his desk drawer. "Where is that blasted file?"

As he waited for Rawlinson's attention, Norris amused himself by studying the top of Rawlinson's head. His hairline had receded to a line of perfect symmetry, bisecting his scalp from ear to ear. The front was smooth, but the back was still covered by thick, black hair.

"Aha! Here it is." He pulled out a large envelope addressed to Major-General Sir Henry Rawlinson, Director of the East India Company. His leather chair creaked as he pulled the document from its cover.

"He happens to be in London," continued Norris, "and hopes to have a word with you. Perhaps you could spare a few minutes?"

"It is impossible," Rawlinson replied. "I must draft my rebuttal to Layard's charge that we have mishandled the crises in India from the beginning."

"Of course, Sir Henry, but after all, the publication of your cuneiform work relies heavily upon Mr. Talbot's generosity."

"And you are concerned that Talbot might withhold the funds?"

"Well, yes. He might if he feels slighted."

"Without looking up, Rawlinson drawled, "Permit me to enlighten you on a very interesting facet of human nature. Rarity, my dear Norris, heightens the value of any object. The more difficult it is for Talbot and others to meet me, the more valuable my time appears to be and the greater their magnanimity when I request funding."

"I believe that this concept was aptly phrased by an American named Paine," agreed Norris, "'That which we obtain too easily, we tend to esteem too lightly.' On the other hand, what shall I say to Mr. Talbot?"

"Extend my regrets and schedule a meeting for next week," stated Rawlinson. "He already has the committee's official report on the decipherments, so I cannot imagine why I should disrupt my morning simply to exchange congratulations with him. Do you know of any pressing matter for which he may wish to see me?"

"Well, he appeared anxious and a little disturbed," Norris replied.

"Perhaps I should have a quick word with him. Here, walk with me." Rawlinson took his hat from the stand and draped his wide lapel cape over his shoulder. Norris opened the door for him.

"How is our work on the cuneiform inscriptions progressing?" Rawlinson asked, placing his hand affectionately on the bent shoulders of the meek little man.

"I must apologise for the rather slow progress." Norris admitted. "I have had to translate several documents from Persia and India for the Foreign Office this week. Also, precious hours had to be dedicated to explaining the finer points of Bornu grammar to a delegation destined for Africa. My duties at the Asiatic Society have added to the burden. I have been asked to edit two papers that are to appear in the next issue of the journal, but if you will kindly bear with me, I promise to complete the transcription of the tablet and begin the initial translation by the end of this week."

"Considering the current state of affairs, I suppose that must suffice," said Rawlinson. "Hopefully the situation will return to normal soon, and you will have the work ready for my inspection."

"I am so sorry to have disappointed you, Sir Henry," Norris said. His trusting expression reassured Rawlinson that he still held the man's blind devotion. This paradox always amazed him: it seemed that the more intelligent some men were, the more gullible and easily manipulated they were.

"Not at all," he said. "You know how much I appreciate your dedication to the advancement of scientific knowledge."

"I'll try to complete a little more this morning."

"Well, we seem to have found him," announced a familiar voice. Rawlinson turned to find William Henry Talbot approaching, while the two ladies who had accompanied him lingered discreetly behind, admiring the great bull sphinxes brought back ten years earlier by Layard.

"Ah, there you are old man," proclaimed Rawlinson. "We were just looking for you."

"Sir Henry, Mr. Norris," Talbot said. His round face tried to force a smile. He was obviously upset.

"You must excuse me, gentlemen," Wishing to avoid any confrontation, Norris sought to excuse himself. "I must finish my tasks, and then drop by the Foreign Office before returning to my office this afternoon."

"Certainly, Mr. Norris, we do not wish to detain you," responded Rawlinson.

"Sir Henry, Mr. Talbot," Norris said. He scampered off to the peaceful solitude of his workbench.

"What is the matter?" Rawlinson inquired.

"I have just received a letter from Dr. Hincks," Talbot replied. "He tells me that he compared the lithographs sent to him with the copies that he made himself from the original cylinder," said Talbot. "He claims that the lithographs are 'fearfully' inaccurate. Words essential to the sense of text were omitted, and the discrepancies are of such magnitude that he has no confidence in the lithographs."

"This is precisely the reason why access to the originals must be tightly controlled!" fumed Rawlinson. "Have you seen his lithograph and compared it with yours?"

"No, I haven't. I have only his letter."

Rawlinson began to relax.

"How old is the good Reverend Hincks now?"

"Sixty-five, I believe," Talbot said.

"There you have it. It is possible that his eyesight is failing. He probably miscopied the characters from the original clay cylinder."

"That seems unlikely," returned Talbot. "Rev. Hincks is a first-rate scholar. Besides, he is Mr. Norris' senior by only three years."

"As much as I admire the scholarly achievements of the good rector, I cannot help but wonder if he is not just a little jealous that you have surpassed him," suggested Rawlinson.

"What do you mean?"

"Your translation was closest to mine; this is obviously due to your greater proclivity for the work."

"And you think that Hincks is envious of my more successful handling of the material?"

"We are all only human. Even a man of the cloth is subject to the same afflictions as other men."

"I had not seen it in this light," Talbot admitted. "But then, Dr. Oppert made his translation from an original cylinder, and his version varied considerably from ours."

"Do not consider Oppert," said Rawlinson "No one of character would acknowledge a Jew as a gentleman and scholar, though several have bribed their way into positions of influence. I shall take care of 'Professor' Oppert."

Rawlinson walked with Talbot towards the Museum entrance.

"Ah, here they come now," Talbot said abruptly.

The two ladies approached them, fashionably dressed in wide layered skirts, with waists clinched as tight as could be tolerated without swooning. Rawlinson recognised the older woman as Talbot's wife, Constance. The other stately young lady was a stranger to him. The proud tilt of her head and confident look in her eyes suggested she was the product of a noble line.

"Did you enjoy the exhibit, my dear?" inquired Talbot as Constance and her young friend joined the two men.

"It is all so fascinating," she replied. "I only wish that we had time to see more."

"Constance, you must remember Sir Henry Rawlinson."

"Yes, of course, Sir Henry," Constance said. "It is good to see you again. Have you met Miss Seymour?"

"I have not had the honour until now," Rawlinson replied, removing his hat and bowing respectfully.

"Louisa, may I present Major-General Sir Henry Rawlinson."

"Sir Henry," The handsome young woman responded with a slight curtsey.

"I believe I am acquainted with Miss Seymour's father, Henry Seymour, from my days in Parliament?" Rawlinson enquired. Miss Seymour nodded slightly, and after a moment's pause he added, "Please excuse me; I must attend a meeting of the India Council this afternoon."

"As Director of the East India Company, Sir Henry is preoccupied with the current crisis," Talbot explained.

"Yes, of course. Is there hope of any progress?" asked Louisa Seymour.

"Layard has the entire Foreign Office in an uproar," Rawlinson replied. "He wants to visit India to investigate the causes of the mutiny."

"Layard is a man with strongly-held views," Talbot stated.

"Layard has no real expertise in this area," snorted Rawlinson. "Anyone with military experience in the region knows that this uprising is the result of our weak showing during the Afghan War."

"I understand that his party is suggesting that the Company be divested of power," added Louisa, "and that its holdings become nationalised."

Talbot signalled his wife with a raised eyebrow to intervene.

"Nationalisation would require a complete reorganisation of our operations, and would destabilise the whole region," Rawlinson responded, impressed with the young woman's grasp of the political situation.

Constance Talbot was becoming nervous. It seemed that the young would never learn the virtue of silence? She placed a warning hand on Louisa's forearm. It had difficult enough for her family and friends to find a proper match for the thirty-three year old spinster without her undermining their every effort by voicing inappropriate opinions.

"The latest reports have been most alarming," said Louisa. "It is said that the Sepoys have the advantage, since the native troops outnumber our forces five to one."

"My dear, perhaps now is not the best time for a political discussion," Constance gently rebuked her. "Sir Henry is a very busy government official."

"I have yet to meet a relative of the Duke of Somerset who lacks a keen interest in politics, Mrs. Talbot," smiled Rawlinson, "but I must say that rarely are they as charming as Miss Seymour." Rawlinson turned back to Louisa in time to witness her cheeks crimson slightly. 'What you need, young woman,' thought Rawlinson, 'is a gentle but firm hand on taunt rein.'

"If you will pardon my bluntness Miss Seymour," continued Rawlinson, "it is a bloody mess. But rest assured that victory is within our grasp. Bahadur Shah is not a charismatic leader, and he would never have had the nerve to instigate a revolt on his own. Also, keep in mind that their greatest weakness is in their diversity. The Hindus and Sikhs will not tolerate Muslim rule for long."

"So, we must fall back on the old Roman tactic of divide and conquer," suggested Louisa.

"Yes, Miss Seymour," grinned Rawlinson, "That seems the most likely approach."

Talbot could not remember seeing Rawlinson's attention so genuinely absorbed by another. Constance began to relax.

"Thank you for interrupting your business this morning to speak to us," Talbot said.

"It was my pleasure," said Rawlinson, glancing directly into Louisa's confident blue eyes. "Unfortunately, I must leave now or risk being late for the meeting." He replaced his hat. "However, if you would like to see more of our Near Eastern treasures, Miss Seymour, I should be more than happy to conduct a private viewing—once this Indian crisis has been resolved, of course."

"I should enjoy that very much. Thank you, Sir Henry," said Louisa formally, with feigned disinterest. She turned away, aware that her cheeks were burning again, and anxious not to appear eager.

"Well, I really must be on my way." Rawlinson turned to leave.

"Oh, Sir Henry," Constance called.

"Yes, Mrs. Talbot?"

"Miss Seymour has expressed an interest in seeing the renovations at the Zoological Gardens. Would you by any chance be free later this afternoon?"

"Possibly, Mrs. Talbot."

"Good. Then, if possible, you might join us there at, say, five-thirty?" she added.

"I hope to be free. Good day."

Rawlinson could not remember when it had been so difficult to walk away from a conversation with a woman in all his life.

ಡಖ

As it happened, Rawlinson did find the time, and he arrived promptly. It was a wonderful, clear spring day. He rationalised the unusual action as a much needed break from the pressures of his position. Constance Talbot was pleased with the turn of events. Miss Seymour was lovely and well-connected young woman, but her outspokenness and readiness to voice her opinions on issues in which women were not expected to take an interest had deterred many suitors. Her family was concerned at her inability to make a suitable match. Yet Louisa did not seem to mind, and she simply brushed their worries aside as if she had all the time in the world. Constance was pleasantly surprised to find that these two singular characters appeared attracted to each other. Besides, there was only fourteen years' difference in their ages.

The Talbots lingered before a cage of the monkeys, laughing at their antics. Louisa and Rawlinson seemed bored. They excused themselves and moved on in search of the great cat exhibit. After several minutes, Rawlinson managed to guide Louisa to the cage of a large, magnificent leopard.

"Please excuse me for a moment, Miss Seymour," he said. "Would you hold these for me?" He handed her his top hat and gloves.

"But of course, Sir Henry," laughed a bemused Louisa, as the items were thrust into her hands.

"Fahad! Fahad!" called Rawlinson, swinging his legs over the guard railing. The great beast rose from his nap on the concert floor.

From behind them came an alarmed cry, "Sir, sir, what are you doing?" It was the animal's keeper. "Take your hand out of the cage. This animal is very savage, and it will bite you!"

"Do you think so?" asked Rawlinson. The graceful animal walked across his cage towards Rawlinson, who put his hands between the stout iron bars to stroke the leopard's great, round head. "No, I don't think you'll bite me, will you, Fahad?"

The great feline answered with a loud purr.

"Are all wild beasts so enamoured of you, Sir Henry?" asked Louisa.

"Perhaps, Miss Seymour, but this is the only one that I would trust with my hand. I raised him from a cub while I was stationed in Baghdad."

"In that case, perhaps you would like to see his cubs, sir," the relieved keeper offered, wiping the perspiration from his brow with a great, white kerchief.

"Is this true, Fahad?" Rawlinson asked. "Have you sired a litter, now?" The leopard rubbed the side of his head against Rawlinson's hand as if to confirm the story.

"I would love to see his cubs," said Louisa. "Where are they?"

"Oh, they're with their mum, me lady, just over this way."

The keeper led the couple inside the animal house to another cage, where a young female leopard was affectionately licking two greyish, furry cubs that had only just begun to explore their new world.

"They're two weeks old today," announced the proud keeper.

"They are delightful!" exclaimed Louisa. "May I hold one?"

The keeper did not know what to say.

"I'm sure that would be possible," Rawlinson said. He admired the way that Louisa enjoyed ignoring the rules.

"But, that'll be against the Garden's policy, me lady," gasped the hapless keeper.

"Bring the lady the cubs," commanded the Major-General.

"But sir," moaned the keeper.

"The father is on loan from me to the zoo, and I wish to inspect his offspring," Rawlinson slapped his gloves against his palm impatiently.

"Uh, yes, sir," the keeper muttered.

Within a few minutes, a door sprung open at the back of the cage and the hungry mother smelled fresh meat. She stood up and padded through the opening that closed behind her. The keeper unlocked the door, stepped warily into the cage, and scooped up the cubs.

Miss Seymour was delighted as the keeper placed one of them in her arms. The cub's rough tongue rasped her skin tickling as it licked her hand.

Rawlinson noticed that her laugh had a most pleasing tone.

"Oh, how adorable!" said Louisa.

"Be careful, Miss Seymour," cautioned Rawlinson. "These are not domesticated cats."

Rawlinson took the other and holding it up, inspected its sex.

"It's a male, sir," the keeper said. "As a matter of fact, they are both males."

"Well, old Fahad has done a jolly good job here," said Rawlinson, beaming with pride. They could hear the mother growling behind the door.

"I'd better be putting 'em back," said the keeper. "Their mum's gettin' nervous, sir."

"Yes, I suppose that we should take the mother's feelings into consideration," said Rawlinson, handing his cub to the keeper.

"Oh, do you suppose, Sir Henry, that a mother's feelings are worthy of your consideration?" teased Louisa.

The mother growled menacingly at the keeper. The tiny predator alarmed by being passed about, scratched his hand. Its twin, reacting to dangerous situation, wriggled violently from Louisa's grasp and gripped the ruffle at her wrist with his claws. Desperately he scampered up the puffed, white muslin under-blouse into the dark, warm safety between it the flared sleeve of her redingote day dress.

"Sir Henry, help me!" she cried in alarm.

"Hold very still, Miss Seymour," he commanded. After the initial shock, Rawlinson rather enjoyed the role of rescuer. He lifted the wide, satin-trimmed sleeve and felt about her arm and back until he located the cub near her left shoulder, where the terrified creature was clinging for its life.

Louisa's cries alerted the Talbots to their companions' whereabouts. They came upon the scene to witness Rawlinson groping under Louisa's clothing while she made the oddest squeaking sounds.

"Well, things seem to advancing at an unexpected rate," commented Talbot. Constance did not share her husband's amusement.

Only with the greatest care of working the tiny leopard's sharp claws free was Rawlinson able to return the second cub to the keeper.

"Are you alright, Miss Seymour?" asked Rawlinson, trying not to laugh.

"Yes, of course I am," insisted Louisa, regaining her dignity.

"But, you are injured," he declared with alarm as tiny crimson drops appeared on the white muslin sleeve.

"I said that I am fine, Sir Henry," stated Louisa in a steely tone. Constance quickly lowered Louisa's dress sleeve and adjusted her small hat of silken spring flowers. Louisa turned to the worried keeper, who was struggling to control the cubs.

"Thank you, sir, for permitting us this rare opportunity to see your charges."

"Oh, thank you m'am," he replied, feeling a little less apprehensive of losing his job. "I mean, you are most welcome, me lady." He glanced nervously at the gentleman, but Rawlinson was only aware of the remarkable composure of his companion.

"Come Louisa," instructed Constance, "This is enough excitement for one day."

As the ladies moved towards the door of the animal house, Rawlinson caught up with them with a wide stride. He offered his arm to Louisa.

"Might I escort you to your carriage, Miss Seymour?"
Yes, you may, Sir Henry," she answered without the slightest expression betraying the burning pain caused by the scratches under her arm. She gratefully rested her left hand on his arm, and immediately turned the conversation to a controversial Bill recently presented for vote in Parliament.

ঔৣ

The day had turned into a pleasant clear night with a smiling crescent moon. George walked briskly down Belgrave Street. He turned down the narrow, cobbled mews that led behind the four-storey, cream-coloured homes of the London gentry. There was just enough light from the large windows above for him to find his way down the basement steps to the servants' entrance. A freckled faced boy answered his knock.

"How are you, James?" greeted George.

"I'm tired of polishin' boots!" stormed the boy. "That's how I am. The only fing that rain is good for is to muddy up the boots. Then they push 'em off on me. 'Here, James, my boots need cleaning.' That's all I hear, day and night!"

"Well, now that you mention it," said George, wiping his feet on the doormat.

"Oh no! Not you, too!"

"It was only a shower, James. Besides, it's cleared up now," George laughed and rustled the boy's rusty hair.

"Is Mary in?"

"She is entertaining some gent in the servant's hall," James grumbled, as he finished scraping the sole of a fancy black boot.

Two steps into the room, George stopped short. James was right. There, at the long table, sat Mary. She was transfixed by the tall, handsome man seated across from her. He had never seen her acting this silly and flirtatious.

"Oh, George," Mary started, seeming embarrassed by his presence. "Do come in. George, may I present Mr. Harris Richardson." Turning to her guest, she added, "Mr. Richardson, I would like you to meet my most promising student, George Smith." With a smile, Harris extended a soft hand.

"It is a pleasure, sir," George said. Without hesitation, he greeted Harris with his firmest grip. James entered the room and sat at his place.

"So you are a teacher, as well?" The gentleman asked in an amazed tone. "You are truly a young woman of many talents, Miss Clifton."

"Not in a formal sense, Mr. Richardson," Mary explained. "I have simply tutored him with the goal of improving his language skills. George is really very bright."

"I don't want to interrupt," said George, settling into the chair next to her.

"Oh, you are not interrupting," reassured Richardson, raising his eyebrows at Mary when George was not looking. She returned the gesture.

George didn't like him. His clothes were too fine, and his short beard was too well groomed. He had a useless, indolent air about him. A glimmer of gold caught George's eye.

"Is that a wedding ring, Mr. Richardson?" he asked.

"This? Most certainly not, young man," Harris spluttered. "I have never married. This was a gift from my beloved mother, may the good Lord give rest to her weary soul."

"Why, it's beautiful!" exclaimed Mary. "I don't think I've ever seen one like it."

"Yes, it is unique," he said with pride. "It's from faraway California. Notice how the native gold flakes embedded in the white stone form a perfect *R*. The ring casing is of the purest gold."

"Why, yes, they do form an *R*. Look, George. Look how lovely it is."

"Yes, it's very nice," glancing quickly at Richardson's smooth, manicured hands, George quickly hid his broken, stained nails from view.

"Can I see, too?" asked James.

"Certainly, lad," replied Harris.

"Wonder of wonders!" the boy exclaimed as he marvelled at the twinkling gold.

"Are those my boots, James?" Harris asked.

"Yes, sir. I got them as clean as I could."

"That's an excellent job, young man. Here's a nice shiny tuppence for your trouble." He said, tossing the boy a coin. He pulled the boots over his long toed stocking feet.

"Thank you, Mr. Richardson," James said. "I'd better get back to my dad's boots. He'll need 'em early tomorrow."

"Thank you, James, for helping out," Mary said.

"That's fine, Mary. I was glad to."

"What do you do, Mr. Richardson?" queried George.

"Mr. Richardson owns a brewery," answered Mary, obviously happy with her find.

"It is only a small concern left to me by my dear father," Harris said.

"A brewer…impressive. And where is this establishment?" asked George.

"George, don't be rude, now," Mary blushed.

"You appear a little young to be the lady's father, sir," quipped Richardson.

"I'm just curious," George responded. "I've never met a brewer before, and I was wondering where our London pubs get all of that good ale."

"The establishment, modest as it may be, is in Hertford," answered Richardson, "but if I do say so myself, we brew the best ale in England. And you, young man, what do you do?"

"Engraving's my trade, Mr. Richardson," George replied. "I make the plates that print all those fine notes that the pub owners give you for your ale."

"Really?" Richardson said. He glanced toward Mary. Her expression seemed to confirm the youth's story. "You seem rather young for such a heavy responsibility."

"Well, I'm still in my apprenticeship, but I'm assured a position when it's done," George said. He hadn't liked Richardson before, but when he saw that smirk, he started to hate the man.

"Mary, can you come here for a minute, dear?" came a voice from down the hall.

"Yes, Mrs. Pennyworth. Excuse me for a minute, please," Mary said.

"Is it still raining out, George?" Richardson asked. He was examining his fingernails, which seemed to be of far greater importance than anything else in the room.

"Not when I came in." George replied.

There was a long, uncomfortable silence until Mary returned.

"Mrs. Pennyworth is concerned about the late hour," she said.

"But of course. I must be going," Richardson said.

"I'll walk you to the door, Mr. Richardson," Mary sighed. "I would like to thank you again for your kindness."

"It was my pleasure. To aid a damsel in distress has always been one of my secret ambitions," Richardson said, retrieving his umbrella. "I enjoyed your company very much, Miss Clifton."

"And I yours, sir," she replied, holding the door for him.

"Perhaps you would permit me to call on you again, when I return to London."

"That would be lovely."

"Let's say in about a fortnight?" Richardson said, adding, "Hopefully the weather will be clement enough for a pleasant afternoon walk in the park."

"Yes, a walk in the park sounds delightful," Mary replied.

"Well, until then," he said, taking her hand in his. Mary directed Richardson to where he could find a cab, and they watched his dark silhouette ascend the steps and disappear into the darkness. Mary turned to George.

"What did you mean by all of *that*?" she said.

"All of *what*?" said George.

"Keep your voice down. You've caused me enough trouble for one night." She grabbed her shawl and pushed George out of the door.

"Where in the Heaven's name did you get the notion that you have any right to interrogate my friends?!"

"Well, someone has to watch out for you!" George fumed back. "You were acting like a scatterbrained flirt—'Oh, that would be just *lovely*, Mr. Richardson.'"

"How dare you mock me, George Smith?"

"So tell me, then—who is this man? How long have you known him?"

"There you go again. It's none of your business!" Mary said. She stamped her foot. "He, at least, is a gentleman."

"How do you know? 'Cause his clothes are a little nicer?"

"No! Because he saw me standing in the rain, and he—being the gentleman that he is—offered to share his cab with me. He brought me all the way home, he did not permit me to pay for half the fare, and he even escorted me to the door with his umbrella! *That* is the quality of a fine gentleman."

"And so what do you think will happen?" George shouted. "Do you think that a *fine gentleman* is going to want to marry a servant girl?"

At that, Mary's eyes filled with tears and one escaped down her cheek.

"Why? Is that such an impossibility?" her voice was huskier.

"I'm sorry," George entreated. "I didn't mean to say that. Please don't cry, Mary."

"You just don't understand, do you, George?" she sniffed, taking a handkerchief from her skirt pocket. "I want my own home, my own children, while I'm still young enough to have them." She dried her eyes. "If, by some miracle, Mr. Richardson should want me, I'd be a fool to turn him down."

"But, you don't know him, Mary," pleaded George.

"I don't even know if he'll come back after the way you behaved."

"The way *I* behaved?" he repeated. "Well, I think that you'd be better off if he didn't come back."

"That's it! Goodnight, George."

"Don't be angry, Mary."

"I said goodnight!" She stormed into the house and locked the door.

☙❧

CHAPTER 11

The Grand Tragédienne

Monday, 15 June 1857
7 rue Trudon, Paris

It was the most glorious morning—perfect for a leisurely stroll along the Seine or down the Champs-Élysées. The warmth was so pleasant against Jules' back that, for a moment, he was reluctant to knock on the door. He had walked all the way from the Louvre to Rachel's house, and the muscles in his thighs tingled from the exertion. He was spending too much time at his workbench and resolved to find time for more outings. His hand was sweaty as he grasped the door-knocker. He hesitated and took a deep breath.

"How are you, Maurice?" greeted Jules when the door swung open.

"Well, thank you, sir." A smile softened the butler's lined face. "It is good to see you again, Professor."

"I was pleased to hear that Mlle had returned from Egypt. Did you accompany her on the Nile?" Jules said.

"No, sir," Maurice replied. "Rose was with her. I remained to care for the house during the winter."

"Is she in the salon?"

"No, sir. Mlle is upstairs. I shall tell her that you have arrived. Would you care to take a seat?"

"Thank you, Maurice, but I shall just wait here."

A beam of blue filtered light slipped across Maurice's grey hair as he passed beneath the stained-glass panel. Jules heard a door open on the second floor. There were voices, but the words were too distant to discern. Heavy steps began their descent. Jules was expecting to see Nap's portly figure, but was astonished when the Lazare Isidor, the Chief Rabbi of Paris and his assistant stepped onto the landing above him.

"Rabbi Isidor," Jules greeted him, "this is a surprise."

"Professor Oppert, I am happy to see that you have returned safely from London," said the rabbi upon reaching the vestibule. "How is your research progressing?"

"Splendidly, sir," said Jules, adding, "I did not know that you were acquainted with Mlle Felix."

"It is true that Rachel's demanding schedule rarely allows time for Shabbat services, but for more than a decade, she has supported our schools and orphanage. Her generosity has benefited hundreds of less fortunate Jewish children."

"I didn't know," said Jules.

"She prefers to give anonymously," said Isidor. Accepting his hat from Maurice, the rabbi added, "I hope to see you at services soon, Jules."

"Yes, of course, Rabbi. I shall make an effort to attend more regularly."

"Excellent. We are all praying for her speedy recovery."

Jules shook hands with the two rabbis as they left.

"Mlle will see you now, Professor Oppert," stated Maurice.

Jules followed him up the stairs with slow and measured steps, remembering when he had raced up them to find Rachel, warm and vibrant, awaiting him with a thousand kisses.

He tried to suppress such memories, and to prepare his mind for the reality beyond the door that Maurice was now opening.

She was seated in a high-backed chair, watching a stonechat sun its rusty plumage on the balcony railing. Jules had not seen her since the previous autumn, and Rachel allowed him a few moments to adjust to the shock.

She was painfully thin, and so pale that he could hardly distinguish the her features against the white of the walls. Her luminous eyes seemed to have sunk into an abyss beneath her brow. The merciless morning sun revealed every line of suffering and scorned her attempt to conceal with cosmetics the dark shadows encircling her eyes.

"Jules, thank you for coming so quickly," Rachel said. She did not get up, nor did she extend her hand. When he approached, she placed a handkerchief to her pallid lips and pointed to a chair more than three metres away. Jules obediently occupied it. To see her like this caused an aching tightness in his throat. She was so frail—like a fragile porcelain doll that had somehow been granted animation.

"How was Egypt?" Jules asked, trying to sound cheerful.

"Majestically beautiful and pathetically filthy," Rachel replied. She peered outside the window, as if searching for some distant empyrean corridor. "However, it was pleasant to be rocked on the Nile, like the infant Moses of long ago." Her smile provided him with a small measure of comfort.

"But tell me about yourself, *Professor* Oppert," she said.

"Yes, well," Jules smiled at her emphasis. "The advancement is good, but I work too many hours. In the morning, I lecture on Sanskrit and gather material for a new grammar text on the subject. In the afternoon, I rework Fresnel's and my own notes, which hopefully will be published by this time next year as *Expédition Scientifique en Mésopo-*

tamie. If there are no pressing engagements, I spend my evenings deciphering cuneiform inscriptions or writing articles on Assyrian and Babylonian history and culture."

"We are too much alike, Jules," Rachel said. "Others have occupations. We have obsessions." She paused and gasped for breath. "What of this competition? It was in all of the papers."

"We prefer to call it 'the experiment,'" Jules replied. "It accomplished its purpose of validating our system of cuneiform translations." Rachel nodded, and he continued, "There were four translations of the same inscription submitted, all in sealed covers, which were opened simultaneously behind closed doors on the 20th May and compared by a select committee of scholars: Rev. Dr. Whewell, Sir Wilkinson, Mr. Grote, Rev. Cureton, and Professor Wilson."

"There were such conflicting reports," said Rachel.

"The conclusions were much as I had expected," said Jules. "Even though it was Hincks' idea; first suggested by Talbot, and enthusiastically seconded by myself, the credit was handed to Rawlinson for having 'requested' that they examine the translations from 'printed originals' prepared under his 'superintendence.' They deemed that only Rawlinson's translation was complete, but that Mr. Fox Talbot's was nearest to his. Rev. Hincks' was also very close, but unfortunately he *somehow* did not receive his copy in time to complete all of the text by the deadline. They outrageously pronounced that mine was made from a defective text, which was supposedly neither so complete nor so exact as the one used by the English translators. It was also lamented that I had chosen to translate into English instead of French. Still, they concluded that there was enough agreement between the translations to satisfy the committee that they were the result of a sound principle, and not of an arbitrary hypothesis."

"What is meant by 'imperfect copy?'" asked Rachel, her eyes flashing with indignation.

"It means that, so great is their confidence in Sir Henry Rawlinson, that lithographed copies prepared under his 'superintendence' are considered by the committee to be of greater authenticity than the original ancient inscriptions. Since the contents of my cylinder differ from his lithographs, mine must have been 'defective.' Thus, it follows that my translation, though 'cleverly given,' is flawed."

"That is..." Rachel began, but then she gasped and her fragile form shook with a racking cough. The onset of the fit caused Rose to set aside her knitting.

"Please move to the balcony, sir," she insisted as she closed the folding screen. Jules backed away, horrified by Rachel alternately choking and gasping for breath. At last, the spasms began to ease. Tears clouded Jules' vision as Rose wiped the dreadful crimson dribble from the corner of Rachel's mouth.

"You need to rest, Bubaley," cooed Rose, but Rachel shook her head and pointed to the bundle on the corner table, beside the bureau. Rose brought it to Jules and said, "She wants you to have these."

Jules recognised his letters, neatly tied with a blue ribbon. "She fears what might happen to them when..." Rose suppressed a sob. "Rachmones, rachmones..." with her eyes darting to heaven, Rose pleaded for divine mercy and slowly returned to the comfort of her knitting.

Jules sat down in his assigned seat. He felt empty and numb. All coherent thoughts were lost in mental fog. The tall, dark clock counted the seconds, accompanied by the clicking of Rose's needles. The ornate screen obscured much of Jules' view of her. Rachel was staring at a framed photograph of Louis-Napoléon standing beside Eugénie. He was holding his infant son, the Prince Impérial.

"Poor Louis," she whispered.

A small laugh escaped Jules lips.

"Why do you laugh?" inquired Rachel.

"It just seemed strange that you would call one of the most powerful and wealthiest men in the world *poor*."

"Wealth is not the only measure of fortune," she said. We are all poor in one way or another." They fell silent, while Jules pondered the paradox.

"Jules, didn't you say once that you are a descendant of great rabbis?" Rachel finally broke the silence.

"Yes, the Rabbi Abarbanel is my ancestor on my mother's side, thought there are several others who were not as famous."

"Do you believe in reincarnation, Jules?" she rasped.

"I don't know," Jules heard himself respond.

"I do," she said. She cleared her throat and added, "Not just because of this illness. I always have."

"I am familiar only with the basic concepts of traditional mysticism," said Jules. "I know that it is a central theme in the Kabala." A gentle breeze brought the scent of flowers from the garden below. "It is the conviction that God is too merciful to give us only one chance in life. We, therefore, are permitted to return until our errors are corrected, our sins forgiven, and we have each contributed our portion toward the *Tikkun Olam*, the 'repairing of the world,' and thus merited our portion in the world to come." The room fell silent except for the ticking of the clock and the clicking of Rose's needles.

"Do you remember my dream about you and I?" whispered Rachel.

"What dream?"

"Remember when you returned from Babylon? We were together, in my small bed. I…wept for Rebecca and you…for your children. I awoke that night frightened because of the dream."

"The one where we lived on a small farm?" he asked.

"Yes. It was such a quaint cottage. I was watching you return from the fields when I saw dark horsemen riding in from the north. One of them grabbed me as his horse galloped by. I saw you fall to the ground, the victim of their cruelty. I was screaming…and our home was burning…"

"I remember now," Jules said. With each rasping breath she took, his stomach clenched and his chest became tighter.

"I dreamed it again last night," Rachel said. "Do you think that we may have loved each other in previous lives, Jules? Does that explain our attraction to each other? And, if so, is there a chance that we shall be together again in the future?"

Jules could not determine if her dream was symbolic, prophetic, or fantasy. Powerless as he was to heal her, he desperately wanted to say something to comfort her—anything that might ease her suffering.

"Yes, Rachel, we must have, and I am certain that we shall again," he said. After a few moments, he added, "I often wonder what would have been if our ambitions had not driven us apart to distant shores. I often wonder what would have happened if I had stayed with you, and we had married."

"No, Jules do not talk such foolishness. You could not have saved me from this horrid illness any more than I could have prevented your tragic loss." Rachel took a sip of water with shaking hands. Rose stopped kitting and watched her, returning to her occupation only when the glass was safely back on the table.

"When we first met, I had experienced too much of life and you knew too little of it," Rachel said. "This life is what it is. We cannot alter our fate. Years ago, I had a premonition that I would die young. God grant that, in the next life, we find each other again." Another silence followed, and then Rachel continued.

"Earlier, you asked about Egypt. Something remarkable did occur there. Last October, on Yom Kippur, I attended the services in the Rambam's synagogue in Cairo. I was alone in the corner of the balcony. I prayed. During the *Vidduey*, I experienced something wonderful." she stared out into the bright day.

"It began with a sense of horror. I felt myself once again a child in the dark, evil alleyway. I relived the pain, the shame. Then in a flash, the sorrow was washed from my memory. Just as quickly the wounds were healed and my soul became light and unfettered. One by one I felt the destruction of all my burdens." she paused for a deep breath.

"Yet, I still do not know if I have fulfilled the true purpose of my life."

"You have touched so many, Rachel." Jules' voice was husky as he strained to control his tears. "If it were not for you, I would probably still be teaching rudimentary German." Jules had to stop to find his handkerchief.

"No, not you!" Rachel laughed. "It was your natural brilliance that.." Rachel coughed. Rose stood up, but Rachel motioned for her to sit.

"Will you do me a favour, Jules?" she asked.

"Of course, anything," he replied.

"Will you say kaddish for me when I am gone?"

"Do not say such a thing. Do not give up hope. You can recover, even from this." He could not bring himself to name her affliction. Both tuberculosis and consumption were synonymous with death.

"Please, Jules." The calm, pale resolve on Rachel's features transcended physical beauty.

"As you wish," he relented, "but may it be many, many years from now." Jules watched the wind toying with the leaves of the great oak. "I cannot imagine life without you," he choked, "You must recover my beloved."

Again, she began to cough, but not as violently as before. He moved towards her, but she raised a hand and motioned him back.

"Are you cold?" asked Rose. Rachel nodded. Rose placed a hand on her forehead and frowned. "The fever has returned," she noted, re-wrapping the shawl about Rachel's fragile shoulders and turned to Jules. "She really must rest, Dr. Oppert," the old nursemaid stated with finality.

"Ring for Maurice, Rose," Rachel managed to say.

"May I see you again later in the week, or perhaps early in the next?" Jules said. He was pulled between the desire to hold her once more and the restraining instinct of self-preservation.

"I leave for a resort in the country next week," wheezed Rachel as Rose helped her to her feet. "The house needs repairs and renovations. I shall be away all summer."

Rose supported her arm as she crossed the room. As, they neared Rachel's magnificent bed of gilded woodwork and crimson velvet pile, she stopped and rested for a moment against the grand rosewood cabinet.

"Rest well my beloved, my dearest Eliza-Rachel." There was a slight tremor in Jules' voice.

She turned, stepped into the beam of light that separated them, and transformed herself for an instant into the regal

Andromache. In Rachel's trademark deep, vibrant tones, she adapted the famous lines:

"Ah, Prince! You heard the sighs which feared refusal.

Forgive the fallen greatness, this
remnant of pride that fears to show itself importunate. You know my wish."

She paused, smiled, and in a sultry voice added, "Ah, with what memories you overwhelm my soul!"

Rose opened the door to Eliza's tiny inner sanctuary where her narrow, wood-framed bed waited. The covers were turned back and ready for her. In that austere solitude waited her worn copies of plays with which she had ignited the great theatres of the world.

Jules heard Maurice open the door behind him, but he could not move. He continued watching until Rose closed the door, parting him from his grande tragédienne.

ଓ଼

CHAPTER 12

Miracles Do Happen

Friday, 21 December 1860
British Museum, Great Russell Street, London

Flustered shoppers hurried down the street, desperately aware that Christmas Eve was near. Hidden under a large umbrella, George Smith breathed into the woollen scarf that Mary had given him the previous year. Beneath a brown bowler and heavy long coat, his heavy boots were distinctive social markers identifying him as working class. The rain turned to sleet as he turned onto Great Russell Street.

It did not matter that the umbrella blocked his view. His feet knew their way along the familiar street and the exact number of steps to be ascended. He ran between the giant pillars of the Museum and through the great doors, re-emerging into the icy downpour in the quadrangle courtyard. Reaching his destination, he shook his umbrella outside the door, cleaned his boots on the mat, and reverently entered the round reading room of the library. The racks were nearly empty, and his coat and hat found their familiar peg.

George glanced at the clock. He had made good time, despite the weather. The rain had prevented him from eating as he walked, but food could wait. His hunger for knowledge was much more acute. In thirty minutes, he would have to start back to work. He quickly found the book, page, and line.

Most of London's public buildings enjoyed the brilliance of gaslight, but fear of a devastating fire kept the Museum under the dimmer, but more trusted, glow of oil lamps. On such a day, the great windows provided little comfort for the eyes, so he pushed the book towards the oil lamp.

"Of course Dr. Oppert has made progress in the Assyrian studies. However, I fear the conclusions postulated in his *Chronologie des Assyriens et des Babyloniens* were rather pretentious. He is young, and in time I hope he will develop a greater propensity for the work," stated Rawlinson as he closed the door behind them.

"Reverend Hincks has also been very irritated about Oppert's failure to credit him for his discoveries. His publications seem to take those honours upon himself," said Talbot.

"But tell me, Sir Henry," continued Talbot, "what of this inscription that Oppert reportedly found here in 1855? He is of the opinion that it was probably the one previously viewed by Dr. Hincks, and has since been lost. Reverend Hincks rightly says that he cannot affirm if it is or is not the same without inspecting the inscription."

"I must say that I am confounded," Rawlinson said. "Since I accepted this mammoth task of organising the Museum's cuneiform collection, we have conducted a thorough search. To date, no one has succeeded in locating an inscription stating that the later Tiglath-pileser reigned until his forty-second year, or that he ascended the throne in the twentieth year of his predecessor's reign. We shall, of course, continue the search with diligence, but I truly do not know how to answer you."

"This is indeed a mystery," puzzled Talbot.

"You must bear in mind that, since the artefacts from my last expedition were added to the previous substantial collection of Layard, the shelves are overflowing with a multitude of yet-unexamined tablets," Rawlinson continued. "Mr. Norris is not getting any younger. Unless we can find qualified helpers to handle the cleaning and sorting, I cannot say how long it will be before this mountain of material will be accessible to serious scholars." There was genuine frustration in his voice. "However, you have my word that, if this inscription does exist, we shall eventually locate it." Rawlinson added, "Isn't that right, Dr. Birch?"

"Certainly, Sir Henry," Birch replied. "I assure you, Mr. Talbot that no stone will be left unturned. Excuse me for a moment gentlemen." Birch left them to speak with an assistant.

"Sir Henry," asked Talbot gingerly, "If you don't mind my asking, why did you resign from your Persian ambassadorship after such a short tenure?"

"When I accepted the appointment from Lord Stanley, I had served on the first India Council for nearly a year," Rawlinson replied. "The match seemed a good one, as Persia was under this Council's jurisdiction. I was dismayed when word arrived last January that the post had been moved from the Indian Ministry to the Foreign Affairs Office. In light of this change in administration, I knew that I could not continue."

"There was talk that Layard's advancement in the Foreign Affairs Office was an influential factor," added Talbot.

"Not at all! Those rumours are completely unfounded," said Rawlinson. "Layard and I are old acquaintances, and our relationship has always been most cordial. I was delighted by his appointment, and I sent him a congratulatory note at the time. To you I shall confess—but let it go no further—that I sorely missed the company of Miss Seymour."

"Here it is, Mr. Talbot," said Birch, concluding his search behind the counter. "I believe that this is the volume you requested." He handed him a thick, leather-bound book.

"Thank you, Dr. Birch," said Talbot. "I must hurry. My train for Edinburgh leaves soon."

"Then you will be away for Christmas?"

"Yes, Dr. Birch. We shall be in Scotland. My family has already arrived. I hope that the weather improves—they had a frightful snowstorm earlier in the week."

"Well, at least the sleet has stopped for now," said Rawlinson, offering his hand. "Have a safe trip."

Talbot shook Rawlinson's hand warmly.

"Happy Christmas, Sir Henry, and to you also, Dr. Birch." As Talbot closed the door, Birch caught sight of George turning quickly back to his book, pretending not to have been eavesdropping.

"Sir Henry, a word, if you have a moment."

"Yes, Dr. Birch, what is it?" Rawlinson replied.

"Well, it's the young fellow over there," Birch said, nodding slightly toward George.

"What about him? He appears rather ordinary to me."

"I do not quite know what to make of him. He has come in every day at this time for nearly a year now. He is always in a great hurry, shuffling through books and back issues of the *Athenaeum*."

"And?"

"Yesterday, I saw him copying cuneiform characters. Finding the sight amusing, I questioned him, and I found that he had a sound grasp of the fundamental system of decipherment. Only the rudiments, you understand, yet still a sound grasp. It seems that he has read all of your writings. I have never met a layman so well-versed on the Assyrian subject."

"Perhaps I should meet this young man," stated Rawlinson, and he followed Birch to the table where George sat.

"Mr. Smith," began Birch, and George jumped to his feet. "No reason for alarm, young man. How are your studies progressing?"

"Very well, sir," George said.

"Good, good. May I introduce you, Sir Henry Rawlinson?" Birch said. Turning to Rawlinson, he added, "Sir Henry, Mr. George Smith."

George grasped Rawlinson's extended hand with a firm, but rather sweaty, grip.

"Yes…yes…I know," babbled George. "Yes… we have already met."

"Have we?" asked Rawlinson, rescuing his hand from the young man who stood gazing upon a divine apparition.

"Of course you would not remember…there's really no reason why a man of your stature should remember. It was a very long time ago, back in 1851—August twenty-second, to be exact…at the Great Exhibition in the Crystal Palace. You gave me your pamphlet, and you didn't even charge us. You wrote in it: 'A gift to the young scholar, Master George Smith,' and you signed it 'Colonel Henry C. Rawlinson.' I still have it, sir. I could show it to you, if you want to see it."

"That will not be necessary, George," reassured Rawlinson. "I do remember a young boy. Were you with your mother?"

"Yes, sir! Yes, sir, That was me. You do remember!" George beamed.

"And how is your mother, George? I hope she is well."

"She's well, thank you, sir. We moved to Islington last year, and she's very happy there."

"George, Dr. Birch tells me that you have a keen interest in cuneiform," said Rawlinson in an uncharacteristically soft tone.

"Yes, sir, I have."

"As it happens, I was just on my way back to my work-room, where our cuneiform texts are sorted and cleaned. Would you like to see it?"

"Oh, yes, Your Worship!" exclaimed George.

"Just 'Sir Henry' will do," smiled Rawlinson as Birch suppressed a chuckle.

"Oh yes, sir—Sir Henry. Thank you so much, Sir Henry."

Once they passed beyond the entrance hall of the main building, George was completely lost. They walked down cold corridors and secluded stairs. The lamps became fewer and further apart, and they cast eerie shadows against the walls. At last, they opened the door to a large room. Several tables were piled high with thousands of pieces of broken clay tablets. The room was chaotic and dim, as well as cold and dusty. Most visitors agreed that it resembled a dungeon, but to George it was a paradise. He walked about the room, daring to touch the tiny bird-track inscriptions.

"Sir Henry, I am so glad that you made it in on such a nasty day," greeted Norris. "Here, sirs, take a look at this assemblage if you please. I think that we may have found another matching piece to your list of eponyms." Rawlinson rushed over to the table and peered at the group of tiny fragments. It was so small that it would fit in the palm of his hand.

"Very interesting," mused Rawlinson. "Yes, Edwin, I think you have found a very important piece," he said, examining the join with his magnifying glass.

"What do you have there, young man?" asked Norris. George was holding a small fragment and was pivoting it in different directions on the table near the assemblage.

"Mr. Norris, this is Mr. George Smith. Dr. Birch discovered him in the library. He is interested in our work."

"I was just wondering, sir, if this piece could possibly fit about here."

"You just might be right, my boy," exclaimed Rawlinson, scrutinising the fragment.

"Remarkable!" exclaimed Norris. "We have found two matching pieces in one day."

"You seem to have a prodigy here, Sir Henry," added Birch.

"Tell me, George," asked Rawlinson, "why did you choose that fragment?"

"Well, because of its shape and the direction of the characters. It just appeared to be a continuation of that one, there."

"What work do you do, George?" asked Rawlinson, "Do you have a steady job?"

"Yes, Sir Henry. I am with the publishing house of Bradbury and Evans," George announced with pride. "I have now entered the sixth year of my apprenticeship for the master engraver of print plates."

"Print plate engraving, you say? Fascinating! Such training must account for your keen eye," complimented Rawlinson. "Tell me, George, would you be interested in working here in the evenings?"

George was stunned into silence. His jaw dropped, and his eyes seemed a little glazed.

"Of course, you will need some time to think it over. I understand. The pay is not much and the hour is late."

"Time… Oh no, sir, I don't need no time. To work here…with you…why, that would be a dream come true. When would you want me to start? I could be here tonight if you want me to come."

"The Museum is closing early tonight, and it will not be open again until the day after Christmas. Could you be here by, let's say eight o'clock on Wednesday night?"

"Yes, sir—Sir Henry. I most certainly can. I will be here."

"Good, good. Would you be available to work until about ten or eleven in the evenings? Will that be a problem?"

"Oh no, sir. Not at all. That's fine with me," George said. He paused, looking round the room with an anxious expression, he asked "What time is it now, sir?"

"Umm, about one-fifty," said Norris, glancing at his watch.

"Why?" asked Birch, "Is there a problem, George?"

"Oh no, I'm late!" said George, shaking his head. "I must leave. How do I get back to Great Russell Street from here? I should have been on my way already—this is my dinner hour. I'll never make it back in time."

"You can walk with me, young man. I'm going that way," said Birch.

"I didn't realise, George. I feel responsible for this," Rawlinson said, reaching into his pocket. "Here, take this. It might help you to catch a cab back."

"But this is too much. You've given me a sovereign by mistake, sir."

"I am not prone to mistakes, George, and I have a feeling that you are more than worth it. Keep it, lad. Consider it a Christmas bonus. Now, be off with you."

"Thank you, sir, thank you." Grabbing his hat and umbrella, George fell into step beside Birch. "Merry Christmas to you, Sir Henry, Mr. Norris," he called before they disappeared down the hallway.

"Merry Christmas, George!" they called in return. "We'll see you next week."

"What do you think Edwin?"

"I think it's nothing short of a miracle, sir, to find someone so eager to do the dirty work just when our need for help is so great."

"Eager indeed," smiled Rawlinson. "He did not even ask what the salary will be."

cs80

The fog was heavier by the time George arrived at the Lindsey's basement steps. He knocked twice at the servants' entrance before the maid opened the door.

"Good evening, Annie," chirped George. "Here, help me with my overcoat."

"I don't think that Mary will be seeing you this evening, George." Annie could not look at him. Instead, she kept her eyes on the floor. "It's already too late. There's been enough going on today, and everybody's tired."

"Oh, no, princess," laughed George, "Nothing you can say will upset me this evening."

"Well, see for yourself, then," she sighed. "They're in there."

"Come on now, Annie. I've some great news to tell everyone," George said, ignoring her awkward manner. With a proud, long stride, he walked down the passage. He stopped before the kitchen doorway when he realised that Annie had lingered behind. He motioned enthusiastically for her to follow.

Mary, wearing her best Sunday dress, was laughing at Harris Richardson's ridiculous facial grimace. She did not even seem to notice when George took the chair across from them.

"Well, good evening, George," said Harris in a rather flat tone. "I swear that I shall never adjust to the way people just walk in at all hours in this house. When we're..." Mary kicked him under the table, and he stopped talking.

"Oh, George, you must see this," she said. "We were just discussing the royal family—the Princess Royal, in particular. She is expecting her second child! Imagine, she has not been married even two years, little Prince William is not yet a year old, and she is having another child this summer. And she is still so young...more than a year younger than you, George."

"A mere child," added Richard, smoothing his full, black moustache. Regardless of how many times he had met this man, George still did not like him. Perhaps it was his smile—it was the grin of someone with a dark secret. Something was just plain wrong about the man.

"Oh, and when I told Harris that the Germans call little Prince William 'Wilhelm,' he said 'Vill-hulmm.' Oh, I cannot do it right. Harris, do show him how it's done. It was so amusing."

Accompanied with a contemptuous scowl and sharp hand movements, Richard once again mimicked a deep, guttural German accent. To please her, George laughed.

"It's been a while since we saw you last, Mr. Richardson. We'd started to think that you were gone for good," noted George with a touch of sarcasm in his voice.

"My business concerns placed serious constraints on my leisure time. I am afraid that they forced a longer absence from my dear Mary than I had wished," Richardson replied.

"How is your brewery business?" George asked, noticing that Mary's gaze was fixed on her teacup.

"It couldn't be better, George. Actually, it's been quite profitable of late. And you, young man? How's the engraving apprenticeship coming along?"

"Well, I have just entered a new occupation, in addition to the engraving."

All waited for George to explain.

"I now work for Sir Henry Rawlinson at the British Museum's Department of Antiquities," he said.

"Now, George…" Mary said, starting to correct him, but George cut her statement short.

"That is, as of this afternoon," he said.

"Oh my goodness!" she gasped, pressing her palms to her cheeks. "Is it true?!"

"It's true," beamed George. "Sir Henry said that I should start on Wednesday."

"Oh, George, the miracle that you've waited so long for has finally happened," Mary said. This was the point at which she would have given him a friendly hug, and missing that made George resent Harris even more.

"Well congratulations, lad. I trust that the salary is good," said Richardson.

"It's handsome," said George, realising that he had not even asked the amount he would be paid. "But here," he added, "I've brought something with which to celebrate." George brought a bottle of wine from the floor near his chair.

"Jolly good!" exclaimed Harris.

"I'll bring some glasses," Mary said, removing their teacups.

"Where is the other young lady who was here earlier?" asked Harris.

"Annie?" said Mary, "Why are you standing in the doorway? Come on in and join us." She found a corkscrew.

"Here, let me do that. Such things require the experienced hands of a man," said Harris, picking up the bottle. Annie set the glasses down and settled into the chair next to George. She was stiff-backed, but she wore a polite smile. All glasses were raised.

"To George. I wish you much success in your new appointment," toasted Harris.

"Hear, hear," concurred Annie.

The wine lifted their spirits, and they quickly emptied their glasses.

"I owe it all to Mary," George said, pouring more wine. "Here's to Mary—the dearest, kindest, most patient teacher in London."

"To Mary!" they all shouted in unison, and drank it down.

"What is all this ruckus?!" shouted an elderly woman, standing in the doorway in her slippers and dressing gown. "You sound like a pack of young hooligans. Have you any idea of the time?!"

"Mrs. Pennyworth! Did we disturb you?" asked Mary, and then quickly added, "We apologise, madam, but you see, George just secured a new position…at the Museum."

"Congratulations, young man. Now, go home. It's late," she said.

"Thank you, Mrs. Pennyworth, I was just leaving."

"Of course you are right, madam," added Harris. "We seem to have forgotten the time, and I must get up early. I'm taking the train home in the morning." Mary looked concerned, and started to speak.

"A word with you, young woman," Mrs. Pennyworth demanded. George watched as Mary reluctantly followed the housekeeper down the hallway.

"Where did I leave my hat and coat?" asked Harris.

"They are near the door," explained Annie. "I'll show you."

When Mrs. Pennyworth returned to bed, Mary, her eyes round with worry, rushed past George without speaking, looking for Harris. Fortunately, Annie had delayed him.

"Harris?" Mary called. He looked up from pulling on his gloves.

"Yes, Mary?" he replied. There was a slight reluctance his tone, as if he knew what she was about to say.

"Perhaps I should speak to him. I feel certain that, with a little persuasion, we could soften his opposition," Mary said.

"I wish I had your optimistic nature, dearest," Harris said. He held her hands between his warm gloves and added, "But I am afraid my brother is much too stubborn to change his mind. He is much older than me, and set in his ways."

Mary bit her lower lip, and tears rolled down her cheeks. Annie grabbed George's arm as he stepped toward Mary, pulling him away from them.

"Don't interfere, George," Annie cautioned, standing in his way.

"Please don't look so glum, my love," said Richardson. He lifted her hands to his lips and kissed them tenderly. "But for now, we must part. It may be another month before I see you again. We shall be married, my sweet Mary, even if it must be without Ben's blessing."

"But how can we? You said that he controls the family finances," whispered Mary.

"When the time comes, we shall manage," he reassured her, but more tears welled in Mary's eyes. Harris took out his handkerchief and dabbed her pretty face. "Very well, I shall speak with him again, for your sake, but for now, goodnight." He kissed her on the forehead and was on his way. They watched as the fog swallowed him.

Annie closed the door, but Mary just stood there, stunned. She sat down on the bench next to the coat rack. The smell of boot polish was still strong, although James had gone to sleep hours earlier.

"I don't know what to do," she said.

"Don't you worry, Mary. He'll be back before you know it. He always does," comforted Annie.

"Mary, you don't need him," George said.

"Don't need him!" Mary fumed. "It's a miracle that Harris is still interested in me!"

"He's not good enough for you."

"Annie, what can I say? How can I make this dimwit understand how desperate my situation is?" Mary turned back to George. "Take Lucy, for instance. The man she married was thirty-five years old. She was just nineteen. *Nineteen*!"

"Silly Lucy! I could have had that simple scullery maid, if I'd wanted. She was lucky to catch him," George said.

"That's not the point. Why can't you understand? A man can wait until he's old and grey and still find a wife, but a woman must find someone while she's still young and attractive."

"Mary, not so loud, or Mrs. Pennyworth will be angry," urged Annie.

Mary grabbed her shawl and dragged George outside. He tried to put his hand on her shoulder, but she turned away.

"Can you blame me, George, if I don't want to spend the rest of my life cleaning someone else's house?"

"What about me, Mary?" George replied.

"You have all the time in the world to find a wife and raise a dozen children."

"But I only want you. He could never love you as much as me."

"Dear, sweet George, I'm six years older than you. As it is, it'll take you years to save enough to begin a family. But for you, that doesn't matter. You have time—I don't." Mary shivered from the damp and the cold. "I need to go back inside," she said.

As she started to turn, George took her by the arm. He pulled her near and wrapped his overcoat around her.

"You're freezing," he said.

He was so warm, and it was so good just to be held. Mary rested her cheek against his chest and listened to the pounding of his heart. She didn't want to move, though she knew she should go.

"Mary."

She looked up. The light coming through the window shone on his face—on the features that were so familiar, and yet in this light seemed so strange. She felt his lips touch hers, gently at first, and then harder. He pulled her deeper into his embrace. She felt dizzy. She suddenly wanted to bring him back into the house…down the hall to her room… Shocked by her own thoughts, Mary pushed herself free and slapped his face.

"Don't you ever do that again!" she said. Taking hold of the door handle, she whispered, "You are too young for me, George Smith!" Once inside, she bolted the door, feeling more confused than ever. She saw Annie scamper down the hall and disappear through the door to the servants' stairwell. Mary marched to the door and opened it.

"Mind your own business, Annie Thompson!" she shouted after her "or I won't be responsible for my actions!"

Mary listened in the doorway as Annie's steps grew slower as she ascended the five steep flights of stairs from the servants' area in the basement to the small, draughty attic room where they slept. She didn't want a confrontation any more than Annie. She decided to wait long enough for her friend to get ready for bed before she followed her. She returned to the table and sat down.

'How can I be so fickle?' she thought. Her lips still tingled from George's kiss. She tried to turn her thoughts instead to Harris, but to no avail. Of course, she cared for George, she rationalised. He was a good and kind friend. Harris, on the other hand, would make a better husband. He was...suddenly, her mind went blank. She tried to list his attributes. He was dependable...no, that wasn't true. He would disappear for weeks or months only to resurface seemingly from nowhere.

'Is George right?' Mary wondered. Am I only interested in him for his money? Her head started to ache. She cupped her hands over her eyes. It was just too confusing. She stood up, took the candle, and started up the dark back stairway. 'It doesn't matter,' she said to herself, 'Harris is the best prospect I have and he is the one I intend to marry.'

CHAPTER 13

Breach of Security

Thursday, 4 September 1862
The British Museum, Great Russell Street, London

The room echoed with a metallic clang as the tub of muddy water slipped into the large sink. George refilled it and once again straddled his short stool. With brush in hand, he began gently removing the thick layer of dirt from a large fragment.

"Why is Mr. Smith here during the day?" asked Birch. "He usually does not come in until the evening."

"He told his employer that he is ill and will not be in for a day or two," Norris replied.

"What ails him?"

"An affliction of the heart," whispered Norris. "The girl he loves is marrying another this morning. He's been sulking for weeks, but if this racket keeps up, I shall have to speak to him. I do hope he sorts things out on his own—you know how I hate confrontations. Ahhhhh…" A sharp pain stabbed Norris' face. He covered his left cheek. The violent twitching of the spasm was so severe that he could not open his eye. Birch helped him to sit down.

"Can I bring you something, Mr. Norris?" Birch asked. Norris motioned no with his hand. It was several minutes before the muscles relaxed enough for him to speak.

"I have been suffering from these fierce attacks of the *tic douloureux* for several months. It hardly allows me a moment's peace. If you do not mind, Dr. Birch, I shall go home now. It's the pressure—I have taken on too many responsibilities."

"Certainly, Mr. Norris. You should take a couple of days to relax. I'll help you gather your things." Birch looked over his shoulder. "Mr. Smith, Mr. Norris is not well and must go home. Will you be alright here alone?"

"Of course, sir," George said, shrugging. He was frowning over a stack of freshly washed fragments.

'My life is stupid!' George thought, clenching his teeth. 'All those years as apprentice were stupid. I've been stupid – so very, very stupid! Everything has just been a stupid dream. Mary could never have loved me. Why should she? I worked and worked for years and what do I have to show for it? The best can hope for is to be here, and spend the rest of my worthless existence cleaning and sorting these old pieces of junk. Who knows, perhaps when Sir Henry returns he'll tell me to leave.'

William Coxe entered and began straightening the room. George no longer cared. It had been a year since Coxe was appointed as Birch's assistant in the Antiquities Department. Eager to publish a discovery, he had joined George in sorting the cuneiform fragments in the evenings. Birch appreciated his daily reports on the amount of work accomplished, and on how frequently Sir Henry made an appearance. Coxe glanced at George, who was mutely brushing a fractured cylinder.

"George?"

There was no response.

"I was wondering if you would like to study the Assyrian with me for a few hours at the weekend," Cox continued. "I know you usually spend a few hours a week with Sir Henry, and I thought you might like to continue learning while he's away."

"That would be good. Thank you, Mr. Coxe," George replied. He didn't particularly like Coxe—he always felt that he was looking down his upper-class nose at him. However, now that Mary was out of his life, George was glad for the diversion. "Where would you like to meet?" he asked.

"Perhaps we could relax in a nice pub," Coxe offered. "It would be a fine change from here."

"Why are you here now?" George asked. "I thought Dr. Birch needed you to work on his project during the day."

"There's a visitor with Dr. Birch. I am to assist him with his research," Coxe said. They heard voices outside the door. "That's probably them now," he added.

"How is your good Queen Victoria?" Jules asked just before entering the workroom.

"Her Majesty remains in seclusion," Birch replied. "The shock of the Prince Consort's death was more than she could bear." Birch reached for the handle of the door.

"Prince Albert was a noble and magnanimous spirit. Having had the honour of meeting Their Royal Highnesses several years ago, this enormous tragedy has profoundly impacted on me."

"As it has on us all, sir," added Birch. "I trust that all is well with Emperor Louis-Napoléon and Empress Eugénie."

"The weight of the empire rest heavily upon his shoulders," replied Jules, "but in general his constitution is strong. I shall see them upon my return to France. After a brief stop at the Louvre, I shall join them at the Château de Compiègne." The door creaked as Birch opened it for him.

"How long before Sir Henry returns?" Jules asked.

"He will be away for at least two months," replied Birch. "He plans an extensive tour of Venice, Florence, Milan, Rome, and Naples with his bride."

"There is nothing better for a man than a good wife," Jules said.

"I rank among the first to agree with you on that, Professor Oppert. Charlotte and I have enjoyed twenty-eight wonderful years together." Birch permitted the door to swing closed behind Jules. "There have been a few changes since you were here last," he said, "but Mr. Coxe will be happy to assist you. He is a very capable young scholar, having graduated with honours from Oxford just last year."

Oppert! George could not believe his ears. Sir Henry had spoken of Oppert. What was Birch doing bring a *Jew* into the workroom? Had he lost his mind!?

"Thank you, Dr. Birch, you have been most helpful," said Jules. "I am certain that we shall manage quite well,"

"What's this?" shouted George. "Dr. Birch, no one is permitted in here without Sir Henry's permission, and he's away."

The unexpected outburst stunned Jules, and he looked to Birch for advice on how to handle the situation.

"Well, Mr. Smith, since Sir Henry is unavailable, I suppose that my authority will have to do," snapped Birch.

Coxe found the spectacle amusing. An unkempt hired worker without a single credential to his name was challenging the authority of a world-renowned professor. Still, he needed to maintain friendly terms with George, so Coxe gave him a solemn expression and a quick, slight shake of his head. George understood his error and felt even more isolated and out of place.

"I apologise, sir, for this rude outburst," Birch said to Jules. "This brazen young man is Mr. George Smith, Sir Henry's personal assistant, which accounts for his overt defensiveness." Turning to George, he added, "Mr. Smith, Professor Oppert is a guest of the Museum, and as such, I expect you to treat him with the respect due a scholar of great endeavours."

"My apologies, Dr. Oppert," conceded George.

"Now, if you will excuse me, gentlemen, I am late for an appointment," Birch said.

"Of course, Dr. Birch, thank you again," said Jules.

"My pleasure, Dr. Oppert. Good day."

With that, Birch left the room.

"Is there anything that you particularly want to see, Professor Oppert?" Coxe inquired.

"Yes, Mr. Coxe, there is," responded Jules, as he watched George begrudgingly return to his work. "Would you be so kind as to show me the Eponym Canon?"

"The Eponym Canon…are you sure, sir?" Coxe appeared very uncomfortable. Sir Henry Rawlinson, though not formally part of the Museum's staff, was a powerful figure in this field of study, and this was his pet project. The young man did not wish to alienate him. On the other hand, Dr. Birch was his immediate superior and had legitimate concerns about the slow progress being made in the Assyrian. Coxe saw George shaking his head with knitted brow.

"Yes, Mr. Coxe, I am sure," Jules said. It had taken him three long years to regain access to the British cuneiform collection. Multiple requests had been followed by endless delays and unreasonable refusals. Such treatment was inexcusable, especially considering the fact that Rassam had originally stolen the ancient Assyrian Library from the French sector at the Nineveh excavation. But at last he was here, and he knew that he must not waste this opportunity that Rawlinson's absence had provided him.

"Professor Oppert?"

"Yes, Mr. Coxe?" answered Jules politely.

"I just wanted to say that it is an honour to meet you, sir. Your *Grammaire Sanscrite* was most helpful in my studies."

"I am pleased that you found it useful."

"Are you by any chance related to the Sanskrit scholar, Dr. Gustav Oppert?"

"Yes, Gustav is my younger brother."

"I have had the privilege of attending his lectures on the subject. It was a most enlightening experience." Coxe began to relax and soon regained his confidence.

"Yes? Gustav and I use to write notes to each other in the Sanskrit characters as children."

George needed to do something to stop this man from seeing Sir Henry's work. He noticed that the cabinet in which the eponyms were stored was unlocked. Perhaps he could lock it and hide the key. He moved slowly toward it.

"Come this way if you will, sir," Coxe said. George froze. Coxe was looking directly at him, as if reading his mind. "Excuse me, Mr. Smith," he said, "but have you taken you dinner break today?"

"I'm alright, Mr. Coxe," George said. George could not think of food. He did not care if he ever ate another bite.

"Dr. Oppert, your brother, first came to Oxford a few years ago to examine the collection of rare Hebrew and Aramaic manuscripts that had been purchased from your family," Coxe said to Jules.

"How did you know of our family connection to the collection?" said Jules, stopping short as Coxe continued walking.

"My father, Henry Octavius Coxe, is the head librarian of the Bodleian collection. Father informed me of his visit."

"Yes, yes, of course. I have met your father as well. He is a brilliant scholar in his own right."

"The Eponym Canon is in this case," continued Coxe "I believe that we can set them over here, sir." He removed the board on which the tiny pieces had been assembled and nodded towards a table in the far corner.

"Excellent!" exclaimed Jules.

"If you will permit me, I shall light another lamp for you, sir." George watched in horror as this intruder took Sir Henry's seat and began examining the intricate little puzzle.

Jules was thankful to Birch for understanding that Rawlinson's senseless hoarding must end. Secretly, he felt a surge of triumph. He felt smug that he had managed to do what other scholars in the field of Assyriology could only dream of—he had breached the walls of Rawlinson's impregnable fortress. Now he would be able to see for himself if the evidence Rawlinson boasted of in his articles actually existed.

Taking out his notepad and pencil, he examined the tiny adjoined fragments on the table before him and jotted on his notepad: "Tablet K4329, 6.75 x 3.125 inches." Surrounded by the fragmented treasures, he picked up the magnifying glass and soon forgot about the two young assistants.

'Sir Henry will be very angry,' thought George, 'but there is nothing that I can do to stop it.'

Coxe returned to sorting the fragments. George sat limply in his chair like a discarded washcloth. First, he had lost Mary, and now he was powerless to protect Sir Henry's work. He had just resumed his mundane occupation when one of the Museum keepers entered the room.

"Mr. Smith should be in here," he said to the tall, red-headed youth behind him. "Mr. Smith, there is a young man here to see you." The keeper stood aside and James rushed over to George.

"What on earth are you doing here?" George asked. "I am working. I'm not allowed visitors." He was irritated; the last person he needed to see was a friend of Mary.

"George, I must talk to you," said James.

"Go away, I said."

The youth had come too far to be turned away.

"George, it's about Mary," he whispered. "Something terrible has happened."

"Mrs. Richardson's life is no business of mine," replied George, embarrassed by Coxe's curious stare. "Now get out of here."

"There is no Mrs. Richardson," James said. He took George by the arm and dragged him back to the sink. "That's what I need to tell you."

"So the scoundrel left her at the altar?" George smirked. "Serves her right for not listening to me. I told her from the beginning that he was no good."

"That's the problem, George—there was no altar, either."

"What are you babbling about?"

"It started out as a grand day. We all got dressed up this morning. Mary looked like a fairy princess. She was escorted by Mrs. Pennyworth, who rented a fine hansom just for her. Pa drove the rest of us in the Lindsey Hackney. We saw a few friends waiting outside the church, looking ever so confounded. Well, Mary started to get down…"

"Get on with it, James," George said. "The week will finish before your story does."

"I am!" James said. "Mrs. Pennyworth told her to stay inside the carriage until she discovered why the guests were just standing around and had not been seated. Mr. Watson went in with her, and you'll never believe it! I didn't, and I was there! All of this time, poor Mary was waiting outside in the carriage. I went over to her, and she asked me to go in and find out what was wrong."

George gave him a hard look and James finally added, "That Mr. Richardson was nowhere in sight and there was a christening going on in the church! What could we do? We had to wait for the service to end before we could speak to the vicar. When Mary saw that happy family leaving the church, she left her friends and all her dignity behind and rushed inside. At that very moment, the vicar was answering Mrs. Pennyworth's questions. You should have seen him, George! For a man of the cloth, he was in a fury. 'Why does this scoundrel keep using my church for his vile escapades?!' he shouted, just as our poor Mary entered the sanctuary.

"It turns out, he's pulled this same dirty trick four times before! Well, when Mary understood what had happened, she fainted dead away, right there on the spot where she had expected to be wed. When she came to herself, she was so pale, and then she started crying." James leaned over and whispered in George's ear, "She had given that man all of her money! Every penny of her life savings!"

George clenched his fists. His face flushed with hatred. James fell quiet, feeling as if he had done something wrong.

"Where is she?" George demanded.

"She's safe at home, George," answered James in a small, meek tone. "We took the best possible care of her. The doctor gave her a sedative, and she went right to sleep. Then I left to find you."

George threw off his heavy leather apron. It clashed against the empty tub. Without a word to the others, he stormed out of the workshop with James close on his heels.

"He certainly is an odd fellow," Jules commented.

"I really do not know him very well, sir," remarked Coxe. "However, Sir Henry seems to place a great deal of confidence in him."

ꕥ

Mrs. Pennyworth and Mr. Watson were standing at the top of the basement steps talking to a constable when George and James arrived.

"Well, rest assured that we will catch this thief," the constable was saying. "Though he is a slippery one, I must admit."

George stopped to listen.

"It's inconceivable that a man could be so heartless, preying on the loneliness of hard-working girls like your Miss Clifton," the constable continued, talking as he re-read his notes. "This time he has dishonoured the good name of Richardson. According to other witnesses, he has previously used Rushmore, Rollins, and Reynolds. It seems that we have a pattern, in that he always chooses a name beginning with an *R*. There must be some important connection here." He closed his notebook. "Yes, he's a slick one, but he'll make a mistake soon enough, and when he does, we'll lock him away for a very long time." The constable adjusted the chinstrap of his hat.

"It's the ring!" stated James, thoughtfully.

"What ring is that, young man?" the officer asked. He took out a pencil.

"Mr. Richardson's real name must begin with an *R,* because his mother gave him that ring."

"That's right," confirmed George, "I heard him say that too." James gave the constable a careful description of the ring.

"If you remember anything else, please come to the station, young man. I'll bid you a good day now Mrs. Pennyworth, gentlemen."

"I would like a word with you, Mr. Watson," said Mrs. Pennyworth. "Will you join me on my afternoon walk?" The butler walked solemnly with her towards the corner of the road.

"That's what I want to be, George," James said as he followed George into the house.

"What's that, James?"

"A policeman, that's what. I want to help keep people safe from the likes of men like that Richardson, or whatever his real name is."

"James, I need to see Mary." said George. The young man looked shocked. "It'll just be for a minute. Will you help?" George asked. James nodded.

"Follow me and pray that no one catches us."

He guided George to the back servant's staircase. Lighting the lamp, he put his finger to his lips. It was a winding, narrow stairway with bare stone steps and wooden stair rail that only permitted them to ascend in single file. By the time they reached the attic, the muscles in George's legs felt tight and tingled. He marvelled at the thought that Mary must climb them several times a day.

"Down there," whispered James. "Hers is the second door." James followed close behind, illuminating the dark corridor. The door creaked. There laid Mary, gold ringlets clustered on her pillow. Her eyes were swollen from crying. George pulled a chair to the side of her bed.

"I'll wait for you out here," whispered James. "Don't be long. If Mrs. Pennyworth catches us, it'll be my head."

George had been watching Mary sleep for only a few minutes when she half-opened her eyes. Her arm lifted in a wide arch as she reached out her hand to him. He took it, and it fell limp in his hand.

"Oh, George, you came back. I've missed you so much." Her eyes fluttered, and she was asleep again. There were voices in the corridor.

"What are you doing in here!?" came an indignant whisper from the doorway. Mrs. Watson had followed them. Her hand, still white with flour, she pushed James aside, pinched George's ear, and pulled him from Mary's room. "This is a respectable house, Mr. Smith!" she fumed. Closing the door, she added, "And that girl's been through enough for one day! Now be off with you, young man!" she added.

"Mrs. Watson, you won't tell Mrs. Pennyworth, will you?" begged James, "George just wanted to see that she was alright. I was here all the time. There weren't no harm done."

"I'll have a word with you later, James. Now off with you both 'fore I change my mind."

After leaving the Lindseys' house, George walked for hours, recalling every detail of the rogue who had called himself Richardson. For more than four years, this man had danced in and out of Mary's life, and all that time he had been wooing other girls like her. Obviously, it had taken him more time to convince Mary to trust him with her money than it had the others. It just wasn't right. Something had to be done, and George knew just the man to do it.

ঙ্ক

People were hurrying home to their families when George entered old Willie's pub and sat in his old, familiar place. He finally ate something while he and Willie caught up on old times and acquaintances.

"Wot's up with ol' Tommy Riggers? You 'ear much of 'im of late?"

"Tommy Riggers?" Willie scratched his gruff white beard. "Yeh, he's in and out of 'ere. He's got some really nice girls working for 'im." Willie winked, "Some really nice lookin ones."

"I'd like to see 'im." said George, breaking off another piece of Willie's good rye bread. "Maybe your grandson could run over an' get 'im for me?"

"You want ter see 'im tonight?" asked Willie, a little surprised. George nodded. "Well, all right, it ain't far. I'll send the boy now." With that, Willie got up and disappeared into the kitchen.

Time passed, and George was getting tired of waiting. He had just about decided to go home when the door opened and three rough-looking men entered. One sat down on each side of George, and the third took the seat across from him.

"Now, if this don't beat all," said the burly man facing him.

"Hello, Tommy," smiled George, extending his right hand. "How you been?"

"Me? Just fine, Georgie, just fine," laughed Tommy, grasping his forearm like in the old days. "Willie!" he shouted.

"Yes, Tommy?"

"Bring us your best bottle of rum. We'll have a drink with me ol' mate 'ere."

"You're lookin' good, Tommy," said George.

"Well, I see that no one's smashed your pretty nose yet, George, but then the night's still young." They laughed, and George began to relax.

Willie arrived with the glasses, poured the drinks, and quickly disappeared.

"What brings you back 'ere, Georgie?" asked Tommy.

"I need to find someone, and I can pay you for your time," George replied.

"Why? Did you lose someone?"

"It's a long story."

"I've got time. 'Ere, have another drink and tell Tommy yer story," Tommy said. He motioned for his brother to refill their glasses.

A sense of relief washed over George as he unburdened the frustrations of the past few years to his old friends. His contempt for Richardson was contagious and before the evening was over, Tommy and his brothers were just as anxious to find the rogue as George. They sat planning their moves for hours.

ᏣᏕᏈᏍ

CHAPTER 14

Vendetta

Monday, 5 January 1863
British Museum, Great Russell Street, London

As he unlocked his office, Rawlinson flipped through the bunch of letters in his hand. The room was musty and dark. He dropped them on his desk, and drew back the curtains. The window creaked as it opened, but the cold wind and warm sunlight did little to dispel the gloom. How dull it was here, and the silence was maddening.

The Christmas season was over, and with it, the parties. No new invitations were in the post. He had no appointments and, therefore, no excuse to be away. Their possessions were arranged in their new home. Louisa was spending the day with her sister, so he could not justify remaining home. There was no escape.

He shuddered at the thought of returning to that irksome, thankless labour. Each time he entered the workroom, he felt overwhelmed by the hopelessness of the task. The work was painstaking and progress depressingly slow. He never ceased to marvel at George Smith's buoyant enthusiasm. How could anyone enjoy such a tedious, boring job?

It was too late for regrets, but at times like this it was nearly impossible not to lament his misfortune. He could never have anticipated that the consequences would be so severe. If he had not been so impulsive and had remained a little longer in Tehran, he would have been rewarded with a pleasant government appointment.

He was proud of his successes. When Layard had left for London, he had taken command and brought discipline to the ranks of staff and workmen. When the French had moved into his territory, he had out-manoeuvred them by sending Hormuzd on night reconnaissance, and excavated under cover of darkness behind their lines. His well-planned tactics and daring raids had resulted in a resounding victory with the discovery of a cultural treasure trove. He had brought back to Britain the accumulated wisdom of that lost civilisation.

If only his subordinates had taken greater care. When commanding a battle on so many fronts, it was simply impossible to be in all places at all times. He had ordered them to harvest all artefacts with the greatest speed. Who could have foreseen that the idiots would throw and shovel them haphazardly into baskets? Now he must suffer for their oafishness by wasting hours sifting through mountains of debris.

The situation was further complicated by his orders that the field supervisors should send any interesting portions to him in Baghdad, while the remainder was to be boxed for direct shipment to London. Thus it happened that fragments were separated, and now it was nearly impossible to make sense of the inscriptions. The daunting task of re-assembling them was an affliction of mind and body.

Rawlinson ran his finger over the top of his desk and watched it trace a path through the layer of dust. This was totally unacceptable. He must speak with the custodian. It was then that he noticed a small, brown package on his desk.

He sat down, tore off the cover, and read: *Les Inscriptions Assyriennes des Sargonides et les Fastes de Ninive.* A note from Henry Fox Talbot encouraged him to read this pamphlet by Jules Oppert. Rawlinson settled back in his chair, but not for long. The more he read the more infuriated he became.

"What?!" he shouted and erupted from his office with the pamphlet clenched in his hand.

Edwin Norris sat at his bench with a magnifying glass in one hand and pencil in the other. Shortly after accepting this position, he had begun organising a list of new words. It was still rudimentary, but was slowly developing into a dictionary. He was especially pleased this morning, since he had discovered a new fragment of an Assyrian primer that was in exceptional condition. He was meticulously copying the tiny cuneiform characters into his notebook when the door slammed open against the wall.

"Mr. Norris!" shouted Rawlinson.

Norris jumped, causing a long pencil mark through the last two words that he had drawn. Staring in dismay at his ruined work, he failed to respond immediately. This apparent impertinence further agitated his superior's ill temper. Papers fell and were scattered about the floor as Rawlinson stormed into the room. Norris slid from his seat and cowered with his back to the cold wall. His frail arms were a poor shield as Rawlinson in his fury rained down blows on his head and shoulders with the offending booklet.

"What…is…the meaning…of…this?" growled Rawlinson with each blow.

"The meaning of what, Sir Henry?" whimpered Norris.

"Of this!" Regaining some control of himself, Rawlinson took several deep breaths. With great ceremony, he opened the badly battered booklet and read aloud the offending words:

"J'ai pu moi-même examiner les listes de Londres…" He paused, turned a few pages, and continued: "…le Canon des Eponymes Assyriennes que nous publions ici pour la première fois." In a furious voice, he repeated, smacking the pamphlet against the table's edge, "J'ai pu moi-même examiner les listes de Londres…le Canon des Eponymes Assyriennes que nous publions ici pour la première fois!"

With each blow, Norris flinched as if they had landed on his grey head. The little book was in pitiful shape when the abuse finally ended.

"I don't know who could have published such a fantasy, Sir Henry," he protested. "I swear, sir, that no one has examined your list, and the entire world knows that you have the sole rights to first publication of the Eponyms Canon."

"This is no fantasy, Mr. Norris!" Rawlinson shouted. "The names are all here and in order. Either the conniving, God-cursed Jew out-foxed you, or someone has sold the thief my work!"

Norris' face began to twitch. A stab of cruel pain pierced the old man's face and brought him to his knees. He could not speak; he could only rock back and forth.

At first George, who was absorbed in an article in *The Times*, had ignored Sir Henry's outburst. When he saw Norris crumple to the floor, however, he stepped forward without thinking.

"It weren't his fault, Sir Henry," called George. "He wasn't even here when Dr. Oppert came in."

Rawlinson froze.

"What do you know of this, young man?" he demanded, slapping the tattered booklet against his palm. "Were you here when this crime occurred?"

"Yes, sir."

Rawlinson stalked over to George, who stood his ground. "I was here when Dr. Birch brought him in and Mr. Coxe let him examine your work," he said.

There was something different about George—something Rawlinson found strangely familiar. He stepped nearer, close enough to look into his assistant's eyes. He was subtly different, like a battle worn soldier. Rawlinson could almost smell the aura of death.

"Be in my office at the half hour, Mr. Smith." Rawlinson barked, and, turning on his heels, he marched towards the door.

"Yes, sir," responded George.

"Don't just stand there, man," Rawlinson barked, "help Mr. Norris up."

The door slammed shut as the major-general left the workroom and turned down the corridor.

☙❧

The door to Birch's office was closed. Without slackening his pace, Rawlinson flung it open.

"What is the meaning of this, sir?" Birch shouted, as he sprang to his feet.

"What is the meaning of *this*, sir?" Rawlinson replied. He threw the booklet onto Birch's desk.

"How dare you barge into my office, Sir Henry."

"I demand an explanation, Dr. Birch."

"I owe you none. Need I remind you, sir, that this is my department, and not yours?"

"You permitted Oppert to steal my work!" Rawlinson's glare shifted from Birch to Coxe. The younger man seemed amused by the unexpected exchange of fire, which to Rawlinson only added insult to injury.

"Mr. Coxe, shouldn't you be reorganising the papyri collection?" Birch said.

"I have nearly finished, Dr. Birch."

"Nearly is nearly, sir. *Finished* is finished."

"Yes, sir. I understand, sir," Coxe replied.

Before the door closed, Birch called out, "Mr. Coxe."

"Yes, Dr. Birch?"

"Arrange some lamps for me. I'll work more on the Rhind papyrus this afternoon."

"Of course, sir," responded Coxe. Not another word was spoken until the young man had closed the door.

"Won't you sit down, Sir Henry?" Birch asked.

"I would prefer to stand, Dr. Birch," said Rawlinson.

"Very well, as you wish." Birch picked up the booklet and read the title page.

"You were commissioned by the trustees of the British Museum to organise and publish our cuneiform collection. The first volume of the *Cuneiform Inscriptions of Western Asia* has been successfully completed. Your commission does not convey exclusive rights to all texts at the expense of other scholars. Consequently, you have the privilege of first examination of the inscriptions. If you also want first publication rights, then I suggest that you work faster. Is this understood, Sir Henry?"

"We shall see about that," fumed Rawlinson. "Good day, Dr. Birch." He turned on his heels.

"Oh, don't forget your book, Sir Henry," Birch said, holding it out to him. Rawlinson snatched it and stormed from the room, slamming the door behind him.

"Come in," called Rawlinson in response to a knock at his door. He was busy looking over his cuneiform notes. "Have a seat George," he added. The young man sat quietly, squeezing his right forearm. His right hand was unevenly bandaged. After several minutes, Rawlinson addressed him again.

"What happened to your hand?"

"Nothing," he replied, placing it on the armrest. "A print plate slipped this morning and hit it. It'll be all right in a couple of days. I finished what I could and told them that I'd need a couple of days off."

"You didn't shave this morning," stated Rawlinson, still examining the text.

"No sir. I've decided to grow a beard," George said, then asked, "What'd you want to see me about, Sir Henry?"

Rawlinson picked up the battered booklet.

"A rebuttal to this outrage is necessary," he said. "The preparation for which will require many extra hours of work." He tossed the booklet on his desk. "By the time I have finished with him, Oppert will be lucky to find work teaching in a primary school."

Rawlinson glanced at George's hand again and took out a paper and pen.

"Your professional skills and dexterity will be needed to put Oppert in his place," he continued. "I want my personal physician to examine your hand." He finished the note and placed it in an envelope. "This is his address. Give the note to his assistant. I have instructed his office to send the bill to me. By the time it is healed, I shall have worked out the details."

"What is it that you want me to do?" George asked.

"The strength of Oppert's argument rests on a break in the continuity of the names between fragments. The connective pieces are certainly hidden somewhere in that mountain of debris. Finding the exact ones could take years, but this Judas must be dealt with immediately." Rawlinson scratched his ear. "Do you have access to the engraving tools at your daily job after hours?"

"Yes, sir," said George.

"If supplied with useless clay shards, would you be able to reproduce the cuneiform symbol on them?"

"It would take some practice, but yes, sir, I'm certain I could."

"Excellent. You'll begin practising with the name Tiglath-pileser."

Rawlinson leaned forward and slipped the note across the desk. Normally, this kindness alone would have so delighted George that his mind would have spun in a giddy swirl; but death had numbed all normal sensations. For the first time, George valued himself more than his idol.

"And what if I don't have the time to do this work for you, sir?" George asked.

"What do you mean?" Rawlinson asked, caught completely off guard.

"This is my eighth year with Bradbury and Evans. I'm now a master engraver. The demand for my skills is increasing."

"Are you saying that you plan to leave us, George?" Rawlinson said, sitting back in his chair.

"I have worked for you for more than two years, Sir Henry. Have I ever disappointed you?"

"Rarely, George. Overall, I have found your work most satisfactory."

"My time is more precious now, and I don't know how much there'll be for your new project."

"And just how valuable has your time become, George?"

"Let's say a hundred pounds, sir."

Rawlinson cleared his throat. His feeling about George had been right—he had changed.

"That is indeed precious; perhaps a little too precious."

"Of course, Sir Henry, it would take time to find and train another for my position," George continued, "perhaps as long as two or three years. But then, there's also the question of loyalty. I know how important both loyalty and discretion are to you, sir." George was examining his bandage. "Engraving skills, dexterity, loyalty, and discretion: that's what's important for a sensitive project like this."

"I see your point, George. In light of our long association and your proven dedication, I agree that you are deserving of a generous recompense. However, I feel that fifty pounds would be more than sufficient."

George sat across from the man he most admired in the world. Before he would have accepted the offer, but now he had a greater need, one that only money could solve. He started to leave his chair.

"Sit down, young man," Rawlinson said. When George was settled again, he continued, "Very well, consider this offer—for this project, you will receive fifty pounds today and another twenty-five when the work is completed to my satisfaction."

"Agreed," George smile for the first time in days.

"Good. Take care of that hand. If it does not heal well and the quality of your 'corrections' suffers, then our arrangement will be cancelled, so no more pub brawls until this project is completed," cautioned Rawlinson. Returning to his cuneiform copies, he concluded, "That will be all, Mr. Smith."

ઊ

14. Vendetta

The mew gate to the Lindseys' courtyard squeaked as George entered. It was a cold, clear night. The moon had just risen above the trees.

"What was that?" asked a familiar voice.

"The gate," answered Annie. "Someone is coming." The dark shape near the wall separated into two in the silky glow of the moon.

George froze, trying to make out the second figure. Thanks to the moonlight, he determined that it was not the constable. He started down the steps and approached them.

"Oh, it's you," Annie said. She sounded relieved. Timothy Collins greeted George with a warm smile and outstretched right hand. George gripped the long fingers with his left.

"Is Mary still up?" he asked Annie.

"She should be," she answered with a nervous tone in her voice. "We only just arrived. Come now, why are we standing out here freezing?" They entered the cosy warmth of the servants' quarters. Mrs. Watson stepped from the dining room.

"Timothy," she greeted them, "you and Annie just missed dinner."

"We've eaten, thank you, Mrs. Watson," answered Annie, finding pegs for their hats and coats.

Mrs. Watson stopped clearing the table for a closer look at the third young man. "George Smith! Look who is here, Mr. Watson!"

"Where have you been keeping yourself, young man?" asked Watson from behind his newspaper.

"Working long, hard hours, sir," George replied.

"Are you hungry, George?" asked the good-hearted Mrs. Watson. "But of course, you are. You look like you've not eaten or slept for a week, poor boy."

"Or shaved," added her husband. "It's a good thing Mrs. Pennyworth is away. She would close the door on you until you looked more presentable."

"I've decided to let it grow, Mr. Watson. I'm tired of shaving every morning."

"Now you just sit right down here, George, and I'll bring you a nice large portion of my steak and kidney pie."

"That's very kind of you, Mrs. Watson," George said.

"Just let me fetch a plate," she said, her round, red face beaming.

"Where's Mrs. Pennyworth off to?" asked George.

"She went along to care for Mrs. Lindsey," explained Mr. Watson. "They're visitin' the master's niece at the country estate."

"She's just had a son," said Mrs. Watson, placing a steaming plate before George. "The little lad will probably be declared their heir."

"Where's James?" George asked, turning to Collins.

"He's visiting my sister in Dover," replied the widower.

"Have you seen the paper, George?" asked Mr. Watson, peering over the edge of the page.

"This is delicious, Mrs. Watson. No, sir, I haven't."

"What happened to your hand, dear?" inquired Mrs. Watson.

"It's nothing, just a little accident at work," George replied, taking another mouthful. "Sir Henry sent me to his personal physician. He said that it'll be fine. Nothing's broken."

"You must be more careful, young man," she cautioned.

"There's an article here about that Mr. Richardson. You remember the man, I'm sure," said Watson, flipping the pages of Mr. Lindsey's *Times*. "Where was it? Ah, here it is," he folded the page in half. "It seems he was from Winchester, down in Hampshire."

"So?" asked George, steadily chewing.

"So," answered Annie, "they found him yesterday morning." In a lowered tone, she added, "He was dead." George stared at his plate and shook his head.

"Here," continued Watson, and he begin to read, "'The good citizens of Winchester were shocked Sunday morning to learn of the sudden demise of Mr. Harold Rickett, a clerk in the office of the prominent solicitors, Simpson & Simpson. Mr. Rickett, a bachelor who lived alone, was born in Winchester and was the only child of late Henrietta and Charles Rickett. By all accounts, he led a quiet, respectable life. Authorities believe that Mr. Rickett returned home Saturday night and surprised two burglars, and thus met his untimely death at their brutal hands. A long-time friend of the deceased, Mr. Ignacio Jones, who happened to enter as the intruders were leaving, was also accosted but is expected to recover. The police stated that they are investigating the incident and that their search will continue until the criminals have been apprehended.

"'A strange twist in the investigation occurred when evidence was discovered in his house linking Mr. Rickett to a series of crimes reported to London authorities over the past six years. It seems that a man fitting Mr. Rickett's description swindled naïve, lonely young women of their life savings through a false promise of marriage on at least five occasions. One such victim told this reporter that she plans to lay claim against Mr. Rickett's estate in the name of her young son, whom she claims is the natural child of the deceased. Articles of identification, indicating that Mr. Rickett had used various aliases—including Harry Rushmore, Harvey Rollins,

Hugh Reynolds, and Harris Richardson—were found, which link him to the thieveries.'"

"What do you make of that, George?" asked Annie as Mr. Watson carefully readjusted the paper to its original state.

"Such a cad!" declared Mrs. Watson. "If you ask me, he got what was coming to him."

"Does Mary know?" asked George.

"Yes, I know," Mary answered from the doorway. No one had heard her enter.

"There you are, my dear. Come on in here and warm yourself near the stove," said Mrs. Watson. Mary sat down next to George.

"What's wrong with your hand?" she asked. George did not answer. He seemed intent on finishing his meal.

"He injured it at his job, but, fortunately, it hasn't affected his appetite," Mrs. Watson said, smiling. She looked at her husband and tilted her head towards the door.

"My old bones are aching from this cold weather," complained Watson. "I think I'll retire to my nice warm bed and a good book," he held his back as he stood up, "so I'll bid you all a good night."

"Have a good night's rest," said Annie.

"And you, Timothy, take good care of Mr. Lindsey's gelding," Watson added.

"I most certainly will, sir. Good night."

"I'll be right in with a hot drink, Mr. Watson," reassured his wife.

"Timothy," asked Mary, turning to the tall, lanky fellow, "how is the gelding? Will his leg mend, or will he need to be put down?"

"That depends on whether or not an infection sets in," Collins replied. "We won't know for a couple more days."

"What happened to him?" asked George.

"It was Mr. Tatum's mare. She was in a particularly bad temper," Collins said. "Mr. Tatum's new groom and I were harnessing our teams in the courtyard when he let 'er get too close to the gelding. Well, you know that's a recipe for disaster," whistled Collins. Noting George's blank expression, he explained, "You don't let a high-strung mare near a gelding, George. She'll kick 'im to death, and, that was this one's full intent. It was a bit of good fortune that I was in the stables and able to get 'er under control."

"Poor creature. He is such a pretty horse," said Mrs. Watson as she added a nip of bandy to the bedtime drinks.

"A mare, you say," said George. "I would've expected it of a stallion but never thought of mares as so dangerous."

"Well, maybe that's what happened to Mr. Rickett. It might have been an angry female what done 'im in," suggested Collins. "Lord knows he'd made plenty of 'em mad enough."

Collin's comment brought a good round of laughter and lifted the gloom.

"Good night, all," called Mrs. Watson as she left the kitchen.

"Sleep well," replied Mary.

"Timothy is so marvellous with the horses," said Annie, and with a light, flirtatious tone, she added, "I would have been petrified."

"Oh, Annie, you just need to be around 'em for a while and get to know their personalities," said Collins.

"They have personalities? Like people?"

"Oh yes. Just come by when you're free and I'll show you."

"Perhaps we should go over to the stables now, Timothy, to check on the poor gelding?" asked Annie, toying with her ear.

"That sounds like a good idea," he said, jumping to his feet. "I want to make sure he has no signs of a fever," he added, going for their coats.

"Don't wait up, Mary. I have my key," called Annie as she closed the door.

"It looks like Annie has finally found her match," said George.

"Yes," Mary said, "Timothy's a good man."

The room was silent. Neither knew where to begin.

"Would you like a cup of tea?" asked Mary. "The water in the kettle has just boiled."

"That would be nice," George replied.

"I've missed having you around, George. We all have," said Mary as she placed the cups on the table. She lifted the heavy metal kettle and poured hot water into the teapot, then emptied it into the sink.

"I've been very busy, working late every night and all."

"On Sundays, too?" she asked, measuring two teaspoons of black tea leaves into the pot.

"I've been studying the cuneiform with William Coxe on Sundays," he said.

"I see." She poured enough water for two cups. "Well, I'm glad that you found time to stop by this evening. I wanted to talk to you." She set the tea on the table to steep.

"What about?" George asked.

"About all of that mess…" Mary began.

"There's nothing to say," cut in George.

"No, there is. I need to apologise to you," she said, watching his expression. "I've had time to think, and I now know how much I hurt you. My mind just keeps going over and over what happened, and I've realised how stupid and thoughtless I was towards you. I should've listened to you last summer, when Richardson suddenly reappeared after months without a word. I should've stayed with you and accepted your proposal, but he asked me first and…"

"And you thought you'd be better off married to a man of his fine manner than the son of a carpenter," George said. He stared at the bandage, his face like stone.

"I'm asking you to forgive me, George," Mary said. He did not answer. She managed to pour the tea with only a slight shake.

"Did you love him?" George asked, turning the cup's handle to the left side.

"I don't know," she whispered, adding the milk and stirring in a spoon of sugar. "It was all a lie, anyway. Everything he said was a lie. I was just another foolish girl to him. He never loved me."

"Did you love him?" he repeated, sipping his tea.

She was silent for a minute.

"One day last summer," she said, "after I told you our plans, he asked me why I was sad, and I told him that you'd stopped visiting. That made him happy. We were walking in the park, and I saw someone who looked like you from the back. I said, 'Oh look, there's George.' He was furious, and said he was going to call the wedding off if I didn't stop thinking about you. I begged him not to and promised to stop thinking about you, but I couldn't. I missed you so much." She paused for a sip and added, "Much more than I ever missed him. I knew then that I didn't really love him, but I thought to myself that he must truly love me, since he was so jealous of you." She studied the weave of the tablecloth for a moment.

"To answer your question, no, I didn't really love him. I just thought he was the only chance I'd ever have to get married."

George sat in sulking silence.

"Drink your tea, George. It's getting cold," Mary said, sipping hers.

George reached into his trousers pocket. He balanced an oval silver locket on the palm of his hand. It was a pretty trinket, of early Georgian workmanship with a pinchbeck finish around the textured, bevel edge.

"My grandmother's locket! Oh, George, where did you find it?"

"Where did you lose it, Mary?" George asked.

"In the park," she lied.

"Then that must be where I found it—in the park," he lied. Mary took the locket and examined it.

"What's this around the edge?" she said. "It looks like blood."

"It must be mud," he replied.

Mary shivered. Any woman can tell the difference between mud and blood.

"Where's the velvet ribbon that was on it?"

"It was too 'muddy,'" George replied. "I threw it."

She opened it. The black lock of Harris' hair was missing.

"Did you love him?" he asked again.

This time she understood what he really wanted to know. It was then that she noticed his left hand. The fingers and knuckles were dark with bruises. Mary took his swollen hands in hers, and kissed them. His breath caught in his throat. She looked up at him with determination.

"He's dead, and good riddance," she said. "It's time to bury the dead. If you can't do that, George, then go home and never walk through this door again."

There was a silence, and then George started to tremble. Tears were running down his face. He leaned his forehead on her shoulder.

"I didn't kill him, Mary," he whispered in her ear. She wove her fingers into his hair and he clung to her, shaking like a lost dog.

"We'd just found his money box, and I'd counted out what was yours when we heard him come in downstairs. I saw your locket, but Tommy closed the shutter on the lamp. We hid in the dark. When the door opened, Tommy jumped him from behind. He held him, and I hit him and hit him until my hands ached. He fell to the floor. I picked up the lantern and opened a tiny beam. Tommy had something in his hand, I don't know what. He kept hitting him with it. The sound was horrible. I can still hear his skull cracking. I was pulling on Tommy's arm, telling him over and over to stop. Then it was all still and the room stank. Oh, Mary, I could see his brains."

"Shush, shush, it's alright," she comforted him. He was shaking harder.

"Tommy's hands were dripping with blood," George continued. "He slipped the gold ring off Harris' hand, and put it on. I couldn't think, but I picked up the moneybox and your locket.

"Then there was a voice calling for Harris. Tommy took hold of my arm and whispered for me to stay quiet. He pushed me into the shadow and darkened the lantern. When the poor fellow stepped into the doorway and saw Harris on the floor, he screamed like a woman. Tommy jumped on 'im like a wild animal, beating 'im to the floor. Then he yelled for me to come on. I swear, Mary, his eyes were a glowin' in the dark like some kind of demon.

"We ran through the woods to where his brother waited. He told me to hide in the cart. All I could smell was Richardson's blood. It made me sick, and I threw up so hard I thought I'd die right there. I just want it to all go away, Mary."

"It's all my fault," she said, slowly shaking her head. "I was too afraid—afraid that one day you'd find a younger, prettier girl and leave, and I'd be alone forever. I thought he was my only chance, but God knows I missed you so very much. It was you I wanted, George; only you."

"Promise you'll never leave me Mary," George said holding her so tightly that she could hardly breathe. "I'd do anything for you, Mary," he said. His lips found hers. "Anything…"

This time she did not slap him. Her body throbbed with a longing that a kiss could never satisfy. She managed to push him back.

"What's wrong?" he asked.

"What do you want to do?" she answered.

"We'll be married." His voice was low and husky. "In the morning I'll make all the arrangements." He could barely speak. "We've got enough money now for a nice flat of our own." He leaned close to her ear. "You'll never have to work for others again. I swear to you, Mary. I'll give you everything."

She shivered, intoxicated by his warmth.

"I need you so much, Mary," he whispered, "I've got to be with you tonight."

She nodded and taking his hand, led him to the servants' staircase. Years of navigating the narrow ascent rendered a light unnecessary. He followed her, blinded more by passion than the lack of light, to a comfortable guest room on the second floor. Closing the door behind them, she silently counted the paces to the large canopy bed.

☙❧

CHAPTER 15

The Rebuttal

Thursday, 27 August 1863
65 rue de Grenelli, St. Germain, Paris

Did the mail arrive?" called Jules.

"Yes, of course. It's there on the table," Mathilde answered from the bedroom.

"I appreciate that you collected it for me while I was away, but it would be nice to know where you put it," he said.

Jules stood at his desk, trying to contain his irritation. Chaotic—there was no other term to describe his apartment. How could anyone create such mayhem in so short a time? Two or three pairs of her shoes, her jewellery, her silken petticoats, and an odd assortment of undergarments were scattered about the rooms. He stared in amazement at the monstrous, cone-shaped contraption hanging before him. Radiating vertical straps descended from its waistband, holding five successively wider hoops. Jules examined the cage crinoline and thanked God that he was not created a woman.

"Where is my shawl?" asked Mathilde.

"It's probably in the same hiding place as my mail," Jules replied.

She pranced into the study, dressed only in light cotton undergarments, and retrieved the silk shawl from behind the large, comfortable chair in the corner. The porcelain skin of her thighs was exposed above a lace garter supporting white stockings. Jules' irritation evaporated.

"Jules, do be pleasant and fasten my corset," said Mathilde. She adjusted her breasts in her bodice and gripped the back of his desk chair as he pulled the ties tight around her tiny waist.

"Here, help me with this too, my darling," she added. He lifted the hooped frame over her head and reluctantly caged his capricious companion.

"Just a few more moments and I shall free you," Mathilde said. Jules surrendered and followed her odd costume into the bedroom. A frilled petticoat preceded a skirt with blue trim and white lace. Mathilde slipped her arms into the matching bodice and was miraculously transformed into a prim and proper Parisian lady.

"I wish the maid had arrived sooner," Jules said as he fumbled with the last clasp. "There, it's done."

"Are you packed?" she asked, examining her hair in the mirror.

"I have not had time to unpack, my sweet Mathilde," he said. "When I opened my door last night, I found that the most adorable spider had spun an enchanted web in my room." He kissed her shoulder,

"Humm…" Mathilde sighed. She leaned back against him. "I must go. You too. There is too much to do if we are to arrive at the chateau before dark." Mathilde scanned the room for any forgotten belongings. "It will be wonderful. I love Compiègne."

"Before you leave, please, my love—the mail," Jules reminded her.

"Oh, Jules, it is there on the rosewood table, beside the miniature of Rachel."

"Are you certain?"

"Of course…I remember now. I put it in inside here." She opened the small drawer to the Louis XV-style table.

"Thank you, Princess Bonaparte," Jules said. He retrieved the stack of letters and small packages.

"Who will be at the chateau this weekend?" he asked, sorting through it.

"Louis, Eugénie, and Eugene left Paris on Monday. Nap and Clothilde, along with baby Victor, have also arrived early. Did you know that Clothilde is pregnant again?"

"No. When…?"

"I'm not sure. I think she's due around March."

"I remember when they arrived in Paris after the wedding," Jules said. "I was stunned. Her petite stature, graceful pose, and dark hair bore such a strong resemblance to Rachel from behind. I thought she was an apparition."

"Yes," added Mathilde, "but the illusion is quickly dispelled when one is confronted with her unpleasant features and dull expression." She put her reticule beside the parasol, on the sofa. "Oh, you must make a note—Nap's birthday is on the ninth. You must remember to return to Compiègne for the celebration."

"What day is that?"

"A Wednesday, I believe."

"Wednesdays are difficult. I shall have to check my appointments. Who else has arrived?"

"Alexandre is there, with Maria and the children." She noticed Jules' scowl and added, "He's bringing Alex, and I have arranged for Gabriel to join us. It was Rachel's wish to have the boys reunited whenever possible."

"I still cannot forgive Walewski for forbidding Alex to attend his mother's funeral," Jules said, ripping open a letter. "It was heartless."

"Yes, and Alexandre will never forgive Rachel's wretched mother for those nasty little rhymes that she taught the child." With an expression of total distain, Mathilde demanded, "Who teaches a grandson to demean his own father and benefactor?" Satisfied that she had gathered all that she needed, the princess inspected her companion.

"You are hopeless, Jules. Come here." Mathilde turned him around and redid his bow tie. "Now, Jules, please do not bring up unpleasant memories. The boys need this time together. Oh yes, and the de Rothschilds are also there with their children."

The morning sun illuminated the room, revealing the sparkle of silver threads in her dark hair and the deepening lines in her proud face.

"Good," Jules said, "I need to speak with Nat de Rothschild about sponsoring an important publication for one of our staff."

"Ah, yes, and an exciting announcement will be made during dinner. How do I look?"

"Perfect, as always," he said. He kissed her cheek. "Ah, here is the new issue of *The Athenaeum*. I must remember to take it."

"Am I so boring that you must bring a journal?" asked Mathilde.

"It is always possible that Émilien will appear from nowhere," Jules said. "If I am to be abandoned again, at least I should have something to read with me."

"I shall never speak to him again."

"Yes, yes, I know, *never again*. That is, until he apologises for whatever it was and you fall into his arms as always."

"No, it is over. From now on, I am all yours, my darling Jules," she said.

He loved her impish little smile.

"Why did you not marry him, Mathilde?" Jules asked, examining the contents of another letter.

"I married once," she said, pulling on delicate lace gloves. "It was such a horrid experience." She draped her shawl over the thin fabric covering her shoulders. "I swore never to repeat the mistake."

She pushed the letter aside and delivered a sweet, quick kiss to his lips. Jules pulled her near, savouring her perfume. "I really must go," she apologised. "I must call on the Lévys' and pick up Gabriel."

"Yes, I know. There is still too much to be done," he said. He released her. "I deliver a lecture at the Collège de France in one hour, and…"

"When do you plan to arrive?" she asked, retrieving her frilly parasol, but his attention was again distracted by the mail. He did not answer immediately, so she left the room.

"I should be there shortly before dinner," Jules called after her.

ଔଓ

The day was beginning to cool when the carriage stopped before the grand, gateway of the Château de Compiègne. The footman placed a card into the white-gloved hand of the Imperial guardsman. A refreshing breeze stirred the mountain of black fur on his head and cooled the tiny beads of sweat under his chin-strap. He stepped to the side of the carriage and opened the door.

"Sir?" inquired the guard.

Jules did not answer. He sat with arms and legs crossed, his copy of the Athenaeum open on his lap, staring ahead as if his arch-nemesis sat in the empty seat before him.

"Sir?"

Jules faced him with an annoyed expression.

"Of course it is you, Professor Oppert." The guard waved to his subordinate and the gate opened. The black hooves of four perfectly matched bay geldings clattered across the cobbled stone courtyard.

One footman opened the carriage door, lowered the step, and assisted Jules down while the other retrieved his luggage from the back. Stiff-backed servants escorted him through the golden, marbled halls. He was pleased to have his usual room. The sitting room was impeccable in comforting tones of blue and gold. The valet went directly into the bedroom and began unpacking Jules' bags.

"I shall have your evening suit pressed for you, sir," said the valet.

"Thank you, Jean," Jules replied.

The bedroom was as spacious as the adjacent sitting room, but it appeared smaller due to the central placement of the bed. The bedposts reached the full height of the room, and long golden curtains hung from the ceiling rails, gathered to the posts by matching tasselled sashes.

"Has Princess Mathilde arrived?" Jules inquired.

"Her Royal Highness was on the terrace earlier, sir," replied the valet.

Jules tossed *The Athenaeum* onto the bed and walked across to the enormous windows. Carriages continued to deposit dignitaries at the main entrance.

“There you are,” a melodious voice said from the doorway. Jules spun around to find Mathilde entering from the adjoining room.

“What is wrong, my darling?” she asked. “You seem distressed.” She kissed him on both cheeks. “Was your trip uncomfortable?”

“It was comfortable enough until I read a most disturbing article,” Jules replied. He glanced towards the *The Athenaeum* on his bed.

“You should have heeded my warning. What did it say?” inquired Mathilde.

“Perhaps I should not tell you,” Jules said. He pulled her near and admired the curve of her nose and dark brown eyes. “It was a very petty attack on my character.”

“Then I must read it,” Mathilde said. She raised her eyebrows. A movement beyond the window caught Jules’ eye. A large man with a full mane of grey hair was stepping out of a carriage below.

“Did you know that Émilien is here?” he asked, moving to the next window, in hope of seeing the woman whose hand Émilien was supporting.

“That is impossible.” Mathilde’s brow furrowed, and her eyes narrowed. “He was not invited. I made the list myself. His name was not included.”

Mathilde pulled Jules from the window, eager for a better view. He stepped back, bumping into her. By the time they regained their balance, only the backs of the couple were visible for a brief moment as the door closed behind them.

“Did you recognise the woman? Perhaps she invited him?” Mathilde suggested. Taking his arm, she added, “Come, this importunate incident will not be tolerated.” Jules rushed to keep pace with her as she sped along the ornate galleries and descended a grand staircase.

"Where are we going?" he asked.

"To find Louis, of course," she replied.

"But of course," Jules said. "This is a matter only the Emperor of France can resolve."

"He was in here earlier," said Mathilde, opening the door to the billiard room, but they found only Prince Napoléon and two youths: Gabriel Felix and Charles Walewski.

"Aunt Mathilde, why did you not tell me that Jules would be here?" Gabriel called, rushing over to his mother's dearest friend.

"My sweet Gabriel and Charles, how tall you boys are growing," Mathilde said to her nephews. She kissed their cheeks and Jules shook their hands.

"Won't you join us, sir?" asked Gabriel. "We are just racking them up. You can break."

"I accept your challenge, but the game must wait until later, Gabriel," Jules replied.

"We are searching for Louis," added Mathilde. Turning to her brother, she asked, "Have you seen him, Plon-Plon?" Prince Napoléon had lost more hair and gained more weight since Jules had last seen him.

"He and Alexandre left some time ago with Rothschild," said the prince. "The older de Rothschild boys are playing tennis."

Their luck did not improve at the tennis court. The two young contestants were tiring, but neither would give up and allow his brother to win. Their umpire, careful not to take his eyes from the game, informed her that the Emperor and his guest had left for the stables.

They arrived at the exercise ground just in time for the finale of a fine display of dressage. Alex Walewski looked very imperial mounted on a descendant of his grandfather's favourite war horse, Marengo, who was performing the less-difficult "air above the ground" exercises of *haute école* dressage movement. Marengo Lipica pranced, then paused, and rose to a perfect angled *pesade*, after which he executed a clean *ballotade*. Mayer Albert de Rothschild seemed less than comfortable on a bay mare. Elise Walewski waved happily to her parents as she trotted by on a white gelding. Arthur de Rothschild moved his mount into a gentle loop.

"Aunt Mathilde!" called the Prince Imperial, Eugene. "Aunt Mathilde, you must come see the new foal. He was born just last night." She could not refuse any request from her beloved Prince Impérial.

"First, let me see your teeth," teased Mathilde. "My rule is never to be seen with a toothless one."

The boy stretched his mouth into a huge grin, proudly displaying his new teeth.

"Well, some are only half there," said Mathilde, "but because it is you, I shall accept them." Then she was pulled away to the stables by Eugene and his young cousin, Eugénie Colonna-Walewski. Jules walked over to where the three middle-aged fathers were watching their children's performance.

"I heard from de Lesseps last week," said Alexandre. "His company is approaching the halfway point." With a glance in the direction of de Rothschild, he added, "However, they are in need of more funds to move the work forward."

"It cannot be an easy task," said the Emperor. "Still, we wish that the project would progress at a faster rate."

"It is a worthy investment," added de Rothschild. "When it is completed, this canal through the Suez will open an exciting new era in world trade."

"Jules! It is so good to see you again," Louis-Napoléon greeted.

Jules bowed to his emperor, and then to the other two dignitaries. All three were in high spirits. Even the aloof Alexandre seemed happy to see him. The men were soon joined by their spouses, who informed them that it was time for a rest before dinner. Mathilde and the younger children returned just as the group was leaving.

"I am afraid that we must leave for Paris in the morning, Your Imperial Majesty," said Charlotte de Rothschild.

"Why so soon?" asked Empress Eugénie. "We had hoped to enjoy your company for another week, at least."

"We have an appointment in the morning with the architect concerning who will transform our property on Rue du Faubourg, Saint-Henore into a more comfortable city residence," replied Charlotte.

It was then that Mathilde saw them. Émilien was strolling through the gardens with the delicate hand of the Countess di Castiglione curled affectionately under his arm. Mathilde stepped closer to Jules and laced her arm in his.

"There he is," she whispered. "He's with Nicchia!" They dropped a few paces behind the others.

"What do you intend to do?" Jules asked, watching as the pair paid homage to the Emperor and Empress.

"What can I do?" Mathilde said. "She was invited, but this is awkward. She was supposed to be with Louis tonight."

As they all continued toward the chateau, Nicchia flirted shamelessly with Louis. Only Eugénie seemed unaware of their body language.

"I never understood this about him," said Jules as they slowed their step even more. "Why would a man with a wife as beautiful and devoted as Eugénie keep mistresses?"

"He is just as devoted to her," Mathilde replied. Her tone was defensive. "Having a mistress is an unfortunate necessity."

"A necessity?" Jules was surprised. "Is it because of Eugénie's religious convictions?"

"Not really. She hides something much darker behind that veil of religious fervour." In a lower tone, Mathilde added, "She has an aversion to intimacy with Louis."

"So that is what Rachel meant."

"By what?"

"She was looking at their photograph and said 'poor Louis.' I did not understand at the time." said Jules. "To love a woman and not be permitted to embrace her is torment for a man," he added, remembering his anguish during the latter stages of Rachel's illness.

"Yes," Mathilde agreed. "Eugénie once told me that she found the act repulsive."

"Fortunately, she tried once," Jules said, smiling, "or the Empire would have no heir."

"So Rachel told you about that?" asked Mathilde with a mischievous smile. "Yes, Louis always thanked Rachel for that little miracle." She picked up the layers of her skirt so as not to catch the lace hem on a rose bush.

"After that first assassination attempt," she continued, "Louis became obsessed with having an heir. Fortunately, he was able to convince Rachel to stay with them at Tuileries for much of that summer."

"So that was why Louis was so eager to arrange for me to study the British Museum's collection," he said furiously. "I thought that she was working on another play. Now I understand that she was with Louis."

Mathilde was stunned.

"Jules, you are behaving like a jealous husband," she stated, staring at him incredulously.

"This explains a great deal," said Jules.

"You are jealous! Rachel has been dead for nearly six years, and you are still jealous about her." Her throat suddenly felt dry, almost dusty.

He started to walk away. Mathilde reached for his hand, but he walked on. She followed as fast as the cumbersome skirts allowed.

"Jules, please stop for a moment and let me explain," she called."

"There is nothing to explain, Mathilde," he said, but he did stop and let her catch up.

"It was Eugénie, not Louis," she added as she reached his side. "She was constantly fluttering about Rachel."

Jules stopped, but when Mathilde saw his expression, she blushed, which was a rare reaction for her.

"What do you mean?" he demanded.

"You didn't know?" she asked in amazement. "You've never guessed? I thought that Eugénie's infatuation for Rachel was embarrassingly obvious. Eugénie would have done anything to please her."

"But you said that Rachel was with Louis that summer?"

Mathilde diverted her eyes.

"No, Jules, Rachel's involvement with Louis ended when you returned from Babylon," she lied. Then she continued in a whisper. "Even though Eugénie understood that it was her duty to provide the Empire and her husband with an heir, the very thought of being with a man horrified her. So, Louis appealed to Rachel's dedication to the family and sense of patriotic duty to France to *be* with them," she said.

"No, such a thing never occurred to me." Jules stared at her with a dazed, disappointed expression.

"Rachel refused her advances for weeks, but Eugénie would not give up," she added, "even when she was pregnant. After her performance at the palace, she told Eugénie in no uncertain terms that she was not interested. You must remember the night. You left with her."

Jules nodded.

"Louis said that she made quite a scene. Eugénie cried for days. It was very stressful for all of us, especially since Queen Victoria and Prince Albert were visiting. I took her place at as many functions as possible, telling all that Eugénie did not feel well. Since it was her first child, they understood. I always felt that it was Eugénie's badgering that drove Rachel to embark on that disastrous American tour," concluded Mathilde.

Jules' gaze wandered over the distant treetops. His eyes reddened.

"If I had known that this would upset you," said Mathilde taking hold of his arm, "I would not have mentioned it." She leaned forward, past the boundary of her hoops, and kissed the stern line of Jules' lips. "Come, we shall retire to your room for a short rest. This corset is killing me!"

♣

Louis, how could you have allowed the appointment of Duruy to the Ministry of Education?" demanded Empress Eugénie.

"It was the most reasonable move, and one from which all of France will benefit," insisted Prince Napoléon. "Finally, we have a minister in place who is capable of curbing the superstitious indoctrination of our children by the Catholic clergy."

"The Church sustains the moral character of humanity, Nap," Eugénie responded. "These anti-clerical policies you promote will only serve to weaken the spirit of our people. I cannot believe that you have permitted yourself to be influenced by this laicism, Louis."

"And what of your policies, Eugénie?" snapped Prince Napoléon. "You pressured Louis into sending our troops to protect your precious Pope's sovereignty in Rome, when they are needed elsewhere." His face reddened as he continued. "That should be enough of your meddling. Women should attend to their children, gossip, needlepoint and little else."

"Throughout the centuries, kings and emperors have diligently sought the instruction of the Holy See," protested Eugénie. "The infallibility of His Holiness, Pope Pius IX, is…"

"Pius is a feeble old man!" interrupted the prince.

"Really, Nap, such heresy!" exclaimed Eugénie. "*Sensus fidelium!*"

"We govern real people, and we deal with real problems, Madame," Prince Napoléon responded. His voice was becoming much too loud for Louis-Napoléon to ignore for much longer. "Obsolete teachings concerning divine revelations and infallible proclamations of the Holy Spirit to the faithful have no place in public school curriculum."

"That is enough!" demanded Louis-Napoléon. "Stop this bickering! I have more peace in China than at my own table." Raising his voice to be heard by all present, Louis-Napoléon turned to a thoughtful young man with a bushy, rust-coloured beard.

"Maximilian," said Louis, "it has been four years since Jose Pablo Martinez del Rio and the Mexican aristocracy requested that you become their Emperor. General Forey has captured Mexico City and avenged last year's disaster at Puebla. The plebiscite contingencies have confirmed our proclamation of a second Mexican Empire. The situation is stable."

"Louis seems especially fond of Maximilian," whispered Jules.

"Of course, he is family," replied Mathilde.

"The time is right," continued Louis-Napoléon, "Will you, Prince Impérial, Archduke Ferdinand Maximilian Joseph of Austria, Prince of Hungary and Bohemia, now accept the throne of Mexico?"

"How could one refuse such a generous gift from the Emperor of France?" stated Max in a humbled tone, placing his hand over his wife's. "We accept this great honour," Louis-Napoléon lifted his glass.

"I give you, then, Emperor Maximilian and Empress Carlota of Mexico!"

The toast echoed down the table. When the cheers subsided the table was buzzing with a dozen different conversations.

"Of course, you know that Max is actually Franz's son," Mathilde whispered to Jules.

"Franz?" Jules was not certain that he had heard correctly.

"Dear Jules, do pay closer attention," whispered Mathilde from behind her fan. "Napoléon François Joseph Charles Bonaparte, Duke of Reichstadt and King of Rome," she raised an eyebrow, and continued, "is our glorious uncle's only legitimate son by his second wife, Empress Marie-Louise."

"Ah, yes, *that* Franz," teased Jules. Mathilde laughed and continued her explanation.

"Franz was Princess Sophie's lover. After all, what woman would not prefer our beautiful cousin to her feeble-minded husband, Karl? Sophia gave birth to Max only two weeks before Franz died. She has always insisted that he did not suffer from consumption at all, but was poisoned by Metternich. She mourns his death to this day."

Nieuwerkerke placed his arm across the back of Nicchia's chair and, with his other hand, moved her long, golden curls back to reveal the perfect arch of her neck. He followed its graceful lines with his finger. The countess swayed as if his touch would cause her to swoon.

Jules watched the tension mount in Mathilde's face. She rested her head momentarily on his shoulder, and then looked up with the most adorable flirtatious smile. It nearly convinced him that he was her greatest love. How pleasant it would have been to believe that smile, but the tension at the corners of her mouth and eyes declared it a sad ruse. He knew that she still loved Nieuwerkerke, but it did not matter—he was content to have her whenever he could.

Nicchia stole a quick glance at Louis-Napoléon, slipped her hand under the table, and placed it on Nieuwerkerke's leg. Louis-Napoléon pretended not to notice, but the twitching of his moustache gave him away. His irritation pleased Nicchia. Louis-Napoléon's gaze volleyed between the two couples. He understood this game, and he knew that he would win Nicchia. Poor Jules—he was bound to lose, and should be compensated for the inconvenience.

"Louis."

"Yes, Max?"

"You expanded French military control over Mexico in response to the Republic's refusal to pay its over-extended French loans," Max said. Louis-Napoléon nodded, and he added, "but the neighbouring countries, especially America to the north, continue their support of the Republicans. The creation of a French-backed monarchy in Mexico is a contravention of their Monroe Doctrine. How can my Regency be stable without the goodwill of so powerful a neighbour?"

"The American states are divided," Louis responded, "and are preoccupied with their own internal conflict. Your northern border adjoins the state of Texas and the territories of New Mexico and Arizona, which are part of the Confederacy. A smaller portion of your border to the far northwest is adjacent to the state of California, which is aligned with the northern Union forces.

"France has supported the Confederacy since the onset of the hostilities. You must remember that it was primarily due to French assistance that the initial revolt of the American colonists against the British was successful. When the Confederacy of Southern States has established its full independence from the Union of Northern States, an exchange of ambassadors between the Confederacy and the Empire of Mexico will be arranged, and peace and prosperity will follow," Louis assured Max.

Louis-Napoléon rose from the table. Dinner was over, and everyone followed the Emperor and Empress to the salon. As they walked, Prince Napoléon attempted to take his young wife's hand, but she pulled away.

"I must check on my dear little Victor and kiss him goodnight," she said to Carlota, ignoring her husband.

"May I come with you?" asked Carlota. "I have not seen your baby."

"Certainly," responded Clothilde. As they left, she whispered, "I do hope that better company arrives soon. All that we have so far are courtesans and Jews."

"Your husband seems very devoted to you," observed Carlota.

"My husband is an old, fat heretic!" spat Clothilde. "I never wanted to marry him, but my father sold me to him, so here I am. I detest him. I pray that this child will be a daughter. That is our agreement—I have given him a son, and the day that I give birth to a daughter will be the last that I shall have to tolerate him."

"That is very sad," said the delicate little Empress, as they passed Jules and Mathilde. "I could not live without my dear Max. We have not been blessed with children, but as long as I have him, my life is complete."

Jules watched the pair glide past in their wide satin skirts – one remarkably beautiful and the other painfully plain. Mathilde was eager to enter the salon and left him to follow. She surveyed the faces.

"Where are Nicchia and Émilien?" asked Mathilde.

"I have no idea," replied Jules, not attempting to hide his irritation. "They disappeared after dinner."

"I have decided to confront him and convince him to leave," she said, setting her glass down. "Do not look at me like that, Jules," she added, "I shall return in a few minutes."

Jules shook his head as he watched her go. A servant appeared from nowhere and refilled his glass with cognac.

Sounds of shrieks and laughter were coming from the grand ballroom. Mathilde took a moment to glance inside. The four younger children were running and sliding on the polished parquet floor. Three governesses sat at the side of the room, applauding their antics. It was a pleasure for all concerned, since the more exhausted the children became, the better everyone would sleep.

A powerful arm seized Mathilde from behind. The weight of the intruder's body pressed her into the shadow of a large golden pillar.

"Do not struggle, my sweet princess," Nieuwerkerke purred to his prey. "You know there is no escape."

"Émilien, release me!"

"Why?" he laughed, "so you can return to that little mousey man?"

"You were not invited! You must go!"

"Not without you, my love," said Nieuwerkerke. He kissed her as only he could, and she stopped struggling.

"Stop that and listen to me," she protested, pushing him away. "We must talk."

"As you wish, my love. Come, we shall find somewhere quiet where we can discuss this problem reasonably."

Louis-Napoléon saw Jules watching the door and knew exactly what was happening. He took a cigar offered by the butler, and the other men followed his example. The ladies soon excused themselves to find fresher air for their gossip.

"Jules," Louis called, "How is your work? Have you any new publications?"

"*Expédition Scientifique en Mésopotamie* and *Déchiffrement des inscriptions cunéiformes* have both been well-received," said Jules, "but a harsh rebuttal to *Les Inscriptions Assyriennes des Sargonides et les Fastes de Ninive* has appeared in the British journal, *The Athenæum.*"

"I find your labours among the ruins of that ancient empire fascinating," said the Emperor, examining his cigar. "Perhaps you will discover the secret of why some empires endure, while others crumble and vanish without a trace. Tell us—who has criticised you, and on what grounds?"

"It is a complicated issue; one that began ten years ago and involves numerous publications," Jules explained.

"Please, enlighten us," Louis-Napoléon said. He motioned with his hand for Jules to continue. All present followed the cue of the Emperor and fell silent.

"Ten years ago, our expedition at Nineveh was under the direction of Victor Place," Jules began. "Henry Rawlinson, the renowned British excavator, was also occupied in retrieving ancient artefacts from the dusty pits on the shores of the Tigris River. He sent his men into our areas under cover of night, and conducted illegal excavations there. Thus it was that a large portion of the artefacts that form the British collection were stolen from the French." Jules was pleased that all seemed interested in his story and continued.

"During this time, Dr. Edward Hincks was studying those texts previously deposited in the British Museum through the labours of Austen Layard. The great Irish scholar made several important discoveries, but one tablet was especially interesting. It recorded some details in connection with a list of certain great men, which we now call the 'eponym.' Unfortunately, this valuable inscription disappeared from its shelf.

"In 1855, Hincks requested of me to search for the tablets. I found one similar to the tablet he described. I was especially excited about this find, since it contained the name of an Assyrian king mentioned in the Bible, Tiglath-pileser. In addition, it gave the length of his rule as forty-two years, and stated that he ascended the throne in the twentieth year of his predecessor. I published the discovery as soon as possible, but this tablet suffered the same fate as the others—it disappeared and has not been seen since."

"Is this the same king whose inscription was the subject of competition among the top Assyrian scholars?" asked Alexandre.

"No, we translated from the inscriptions of an earlier Tiglath-pileser," answered Jules. "Ancient Assyrian royal houses favoured such names as Shalmaneser and Tiglath-pileser."

"Similar to the frequent use of regal French names, such as Louis and Phillipe?" asked Prince Napoléon.

"Yes, precisely," Jules replied and, after taking a sip from his cognac , he continued. "For the past two years, Rawlinson, Hincks and I have published several papers debating the significance of the eponym list, which Rawlinson calls the 'Assyrian Canon.' However, neither Hincks nor I were permitted to see the tablet. Sir Rawlinson hoards these artefacts as if they were his personal property."

"But this is in violation of the agreement of scholarly co-operation between our great institutions," stated Louis.

"And what exactly is an eponym?" asked de Rothschild.

"It was the practice of naming a year in honour of a dignitary. For example, the ancient historians identified years by the 'archon king' in Greece and the two 'consuls' in Rome. This is the importance of the names listed in the Roman Fasti. The eponym lists establish in which year an historic event occurred.

"Last year, Hincks published a lengthy criticism in *The Athenæum* of Rawlinson's chronological reconstruction. He declared that Rawlinson had not placed a single eponym in its proper year. I had come to the same conclusion, but neither of us could gain access to the artefacts, since Sir Henry Rawlinson was never available to be present during a visit.

"That was when I determined to out-manoeuvre the Major-General and penetrate the walls of his fortress. While Rawlinson toured Italy with his bride, I made an appointment with Dr. Birch, the director of the Department of Antiquities. As our Emperor has stated the British Museum and the Louvre have established policies concerning visiting scholars. Dr. Birch agreed that Sir Henry had not properly implemented the research policy and immediately escorted me to their Assyrian department. At long last, I sat before those treasures that we had lost so long ago.

"I copied as many texts as I could. Earlier this year, I published my findings. I knew that claiming first publication rights on the canon would anger Rawlinson. At the time, this only sweetened my victory. However, he has launched a vicious counter-attacks characterised by unpardonable, flagrant malice.

"A few months ago, a demeaning anonymous article, which I feel he encouraged, was published attempting to discredit my work in Assyrian and Sanskrit. I countered with a rebuttal in my latest edition of *Expédition Scientifique en Mésopotamie.*

"Today, I read a far more damaging attack in the *Athenæum.* Why he waited so long to publish his rebuttal, I cannot divine; but, he emphatically and vehemently denounces me as having 'no scruples.' He states that, in my anxiety to appropriate the results, I misrepresented the proper reconstruction of the canons. He deems my *Fastes de Assyriens* as 'untrustworthy,' 'invented,' 'garbled and unfaithful,' and therefore, 'worthless.'

"Then he throws the hungry public a bone. Through his 'tireless labours,' he has discovered the name of Tiglath-pileser—the latter one mentioned in the Bible—on a damaged cuneiform tablet. This new inscription states that this king 'ascended the throne on the thirteenth day of the second month, and immediately afterwards went down to 'the country between the rivers.' We use the term 'Mesopotamia,' which has that meaning in Greek. He also claims that this must be the missing tablet that Hincks had seen back in 1854, but I doubt that Hincks or any other scholar will ever be allowed to confirm or deny this."

"This is outrageous!" puffed Prince Napoléon.

"It is clear that Rawlinson aims to destroy the career of one of France's most respected intellectuals," stated Alexandre. "This cannot be tolerated."

"It is essential that we show our irrevocable support for Professor Oppert," added Prince Napoléon. "I would suggest advancing his position and status."

"I have often thought that the Collège de France should have a Professor of Assyrian philology and archaeology," suggested Louis-Napoléon.

"It would be an honour to fund a permanent chair for Professor Oppert at the Collège de France," offered de Rothschild.

"I am most grateful for your generous support," Jules asserted. "The opportunity to mould the next generation of Assyrian students would be most satisfying."

"Good, it is settled. Let the English know that France defends her own," announced the Prince.

ઉ෴ഊ

It was not until he reached the stairs that Jules thought of Mathilde. Perhaps she was waiting for him in her room. He stopped outside of her suite and opened the door. The salon was empty, but he wanted to be certain. His hand was on the handle to her bedroom door when he heard a giggle, followed by blissful roar of laughter. *Nieuwerkerke,* fumed Jules. He should have known. He hesitated a moment longer, trying to decide what to do. Suddenly, Jules felt like an intruder. He slipped out of the suite and crept down the corridor.

As he slowly dressed for bed, he pondered the enigma of marriage. If it is merely the enactment of a public ceremony, he speculated, then Mathilde and Nieuwerkerke were not married, but he and Dinah still were. If it is a lifelong commitment, then theirs was a true marriage, while his was not. As any rate, Mathilde was right. He still loved Rachel. He slipped his arms into his nightshirt. What of faithfulness? Is a monogamous relationship essential? He had enjoyed that comfort with Dinah but never with Rachel. What of children?

He had experienced that bond as well, yet still something had been missing. What was it?

Loneliness echoed the sound of the water filling his glass from every corner of the room. The conversation he had had with Mathilde that the morning whispered in his head. This solitude was precisely the outcome that he had foretold. He lifted his glass to the reflection in the tall dressing mirror.

"To Julius Jules Oppert, professor and prophet, *l'chaim*!"

ঔ

CHAPTER 16

Fealty

Thursday, 21 September 1865,
Regents Park, London

The red ball stopped next to the gnarled root of an ancient oak tree. Grasping it with both hands, the toddler jogged as fast as his chubby legs permitted back to his mother and deposited it in her lap. Mary smiled and brushed the golden curls back from his large blue eyes. She could not resist giving him a big kiss on his rosy cheek. He stepped back and held out his hands.

"Alright, Charlie, here goes the ball," she said. She threw it a short distance. "Go and get it."

"Ball," Charlie giggled, and was off after it.

Mary ran her hand over her stomach. It was still too early to be certain. She was debating if she should tell George that evening or wait another week. If it were true, then they would just have to make room in their small home for another.

"No…my ball!" screamed Charlie. Mary jumped to her feet. Charlie threw himself to the ground, kicking his legs and screaming at an ear shattering pitch. Head held high and fluffy ears flopping, a Blenheim spaniel bounced down the walk and delivered the ball to his master.

"Good boy, Rogue. Now we must return it to the nice lady." The dog sat while its owner attached the lead to its collar. Tapping his dark cane with each step, he sauntered over to Mary. gallantly presented the ball to the furious child. There was something calculative in the eyes of this gentleman in the brown tweed suit that disturbed her.

"Please forgive my small companion, Mrs…"

"Smith," inserted Mary.

Smith…thought the man, how deliciously common.

"Mrs Smith. Such a beautiful child, but then, beauty begets beauty." He handed the ball to her son. Charlie hugged the ball and watched the dog, which wriggled and whimpered to the boy.

"What is the young man's name, if I might ask?" the man inquired.

"Charles," Mary said. She made a slight curtsey. "Thank you, Mr…?"

"Blackmon, Madam," he said and bowed. "Ulysses Blackmon."

A sudden gust of wind picked up the falling leaves in a swirl of yellow and red. Mary held her lace bonnet until it passed.

"Well, it is time for us to leave." She sat Charlie in his perambulator and covered his legs with a light blanket. "Thank you again, Mr. Blackmon, and good day." As she made ready to move off, the stranger grasped her arm.

"It is a glorious day for a walk. Might I accompany you, Mrs Smith?"

Unseen nearby, Tommy stood watching them suspiciously. His shoulders were hunched under a long black coat and his right foot was perched on the edge of a wooden bench.

He had arrived in time to see the dog steal Charlie's ball. Now, curious to see how well Mary knew this man, he waited in the shadow of a tree.

"It's not safe for a beautiful young woman to walk alone. Ah, here is my carriage." He raised his cane to signal the driver. "It is nearly evening, Madam, surely the child is tired. Permit me to escort you home."

"Take your hand off of me!" Mary demanded. "I do not speak to strange men in the park, sir." She tried to wrench free, but Blackmon held her fast.

"Now, now, Mrs Smith, you misread my intentions."

"Free my arm immediately, sir," Mary repeated.

His question answered, the dark figure swooped across the grass towards them.

"You 'eard the lady. Let go of 'er." Tommy demanded.

Blackmon was shocked by this startling turn of events. The fellow's appearance was as uncouth as his speech—black hair straggled beneath a dark, shapeless cap, a heavy brow jutted over small black eyes, and coarse stubble half-hid his broad jaw.

"Do not fear, Madame," said Blackmon. "My driver and I shall protect you from this ruffian!"

The dog growled and barked a sharp warning.

"Tommy! Thank goodness you are here!" Mary exclaimed.

"You know this man?" The gentleman was surprised that the well-dressed young woman was acquainted with such an unsavoury person. He dropped his hand.

"He is an old friend of my husband," Mary replied, "and the answer is no. I do not wish to be escorted anywhere by you, sir."

"Is everything alright, Mr. Blackmon?" called the driver.

"Yes, Nibbins," Blackmon replied. "I seem to have misjudged the young woman." He jerked the dog to his side and stormed away. As he stepped into the carriage, he shouted as if to his driver, "A common tart should not be permitted to impersonate a lady!"

"Why, that bastard…" Tommy said. Mary pulled on his arm to restrain him.

"Don't think twice about his kind, Tommy," Mary said as she tied the bow on her bonnet. "Will you do me the honour of escorting us home, sir?"

"Yes, Madam, it would be a pleasure," Tommy replied.

Tommy took the handle of the carriage and walked with a proud stride across Albany Street. Mary glanced at his hands, and a glitter of gold caught her attention. Specks of gold formed a lopsided "R" against the white face of a smooth stone. It made her shudder.

"You alright, Mary?" Tommy asked.

"Yes, thank you, Tommy." She pulled her shawl tighter about her shoulders. "There is something I need to ask of you."

"What's that?"

"It's that ring."

"What about it?"

"Please don't wear it around me. It brings back bad memories," Mary said.

There was silence for a while.

"He was scum," Tommy said. "He deserved what he got." He took a deep breath to calm the anxiety welling up inside him. "I don't let anyone hurt my girls," he continued, "an' you and George mean more to me than any of 'em. No one's goin' to hurt you two and get away with it."

"I understand, Tommy," Mary said. It was better to have such a man as a friend than an enemy. "But please, take the ring off—as a favour to me."

"If it makes you feel better," Tommy said. He removed his trophy.

"It is getting late, and I must prepare dinner for George," Mary said.

The child pulled his blanket over his face.

"Where's Charlie?" she asked softly. Charlie pushed the blanket down and peeped out. "There's my Charlie!" she exclaimed. She reached inside the carriage and retrieved his stuffed lamb.

"Now that's a fine boy," remarked Tommy. "Yes sir. George's got himself a nice little family."

"You seem good with children, Tommy," remarked Mary.

"Oh, I have three little ones of my own, but not all with the same mother, if you know what I mean." He gave Mary a wink, and she blushed. "George's done alright for 'imself—a good wife, a son, and a nice little 'ouse. How old is the boy now?"

"He'll be two in another few weeks."

"I want you to know how proud I am of George," Tommy said. He looked off into the distance. "He's the only one of the old gang what's left the slums by other means than prison or worse. I want you to know," he continued, walking a little slower, "that I'll always be here for you. You, George, and little Charlie 'ere are like my own family. Anyone what gives you trouble, Tommy'll take care of 'em."

They walked on in silence.

"Thanks Tommy, but I'm sure we'll be fine," Mary said eventually.

"How's George's work? Is everyone treatin' him right?"

"Yes, it's good. George likes working for the museum."

"You don't sound like it's all that good," Tommy replied.

"It's just difficult for him to get on. George left school when he was fourteen and it matters," Mary explained.

"George is smarter than any of 'em."

"Yes, but Mr. Coxe went to Oxford, so will get any promotions. George works day and night; but, Coxe gets all the credit, and Mr. Norris always pokes fun at poor George."

"Why don't 'e complain to Sir 'enry?"

"Mr. Norris and Sir Henry are old friends, and he depends heavily on the old man," Mary sighed. She looked bewildered. "Sir Henry is kind, and teaches George, when he has time. However, he has to put up with his own rivals."

"Who could possibly go against 'im?"

"Oh, well, there's Edward Hincks from Ireland, and Jules Oppert from France," Mary said. "George is always telling me about their mistaken notions and how they cause so many problems for Sir Henry. It's a shame that they cannot respect his great genius."

They reached the modest house at forty-one Crowndale.

"Would you like to stay for dinner, Tommy?" Mary asked. "I'm sure that George would love to see you."

"No ta. I've got business to attend to."

"Well, if you change your mind, dinner's at eight."

"I'll keep that in mind, Mary. You give George my best, and tell 'im we'll talk later."

Tommy walked away, deep in thought.

"Coxe, Norris, Hincks, and Oppert," he kept repeating over and over.

ଓଃଃ

Robert Bowler measured twice and cut once. From the twenty-inch wide roll of heavy paper, he cut thirteen inches for each sheet. With that finished, he glanced at the handwritten notes from which he was expected to create the next lithograph plate.

How much simpler it would be, he thought, if Sir Henry would permit him to use the actual clay tablets instead of these scribbled notes. Bowler returned to cutting the sheets. He stacked them and meticulously aligned the corners.

"There. That should be enough for you, George. You can start coating these sheets tomorrow morning."

There was no answer. Bowler stood as straight as his bowed back would allow. "George?" he called, scratching the few hairs remaining on his head. "Now where is that lad?"

The workroom was quiet. Mr. Norris was not well, and was working from home again. Young Mr. Coxe had travelled to Oxford to visit his mother. Sir Henry was staying with friends in the country. In his absence, George had been instructed to help Bowler. There was still much to be done before the second volume of the *Cuneiform Inscriptions of Western Asia* would be complete.

Curiosity mounting, Bowler searched for George. "

Has he also taken it upon himself to leave left early," muttered the old lithographer. "Well at least he could have said 'good evening' before going?"

George's behaviour today had been mysterious. Every few minutes, he had disappeared, only to return with one excuse or another. Bowler gave up the search and was going back to his work when he heard the stairway door slam. He decided to investigate. He opened and closed the door quietly behind himself; he did not want to disturb anyone. He was not spying on George, he just wanted to tell him to prepare the new pages for printing. When he saw George carrying a large bundle of papers into the boiler room, he moved with greater caution. His heart beat faster, and there were beads of perspiration on his forehead. He steadied his step and descended into the dimly lit room. George was silhouetted against the glare from the boiler as its flames devoured the items from the open bundle at his feet.

"What are you burning there, young man?" Bowler asked.

"Nothing important, Mr. Bowler," replied George, stuffing more papers in the fiery mouth of the furnace. "Go on back up, sir. I'll be right there to help finish today's work."

"What are you doing?" shouted the old man. "Stop that immediately! You're destroying my work!"

"No, no, Mr. Bowler," said George, adding more sheets to the flames. "Sir Henry gave me exact instructions. He said that these lithographs are all useless, and that I should burn them." George never slacked in his pace, nor did he turn to see the horror on the old craftsman's face.

"Stop this minute, young man, or I'll call the warden!"

"It don't matter who you call, Mr. Bowler," George replied. "Sir Henry knows what's best, and nothing and no one'll stop me from following his orders."

"We'll see about that!" sputtered Bowler as he began snatching up as many of the copies of cuneiform as he could reach. George grabbed the remainder and tossed them into the flames.

"You really need to talk to Sir Henry first," he said.

"You know as well as I do, young man, that Sir Henry will be away fishing and hunting for at least two more months," Bowler said.

"Then write him a letter, Mr. Bowler. That's all I can say to you, sir. Write him a letter and you'll see what he answers." With that, George put his hand on Bowler's thin, bent shoulders and said consolingly, "Now you know me, Mr. Bowler. I'd give my life if Sir Henry asked it of me. You know I'd never do something like this on my own. Do I ever do anything but what Sir Henry tells me to do?"

"No, I suppose not, George," Bowler said. He rubbed his forehead with his palm. "But why would Sir Henry want to burn all this work? I worked so hard on each one of them."

"I really don't know, sir," George lied. "All I know is that Sir Henry said they were useless, and that I should burn them. I protect what he wants protected, and I burn what he says to burn."

"But I promised Mr. Talbot that I'd send the extra copies to him by the end of this week. What can I tell him now? This is terrible. I promised him, and now I can't do it. How can I explain to him? He will be very disappointed."

"I'm sure Sir Henry didn't know about Mr. Talbot's request, but a gentleman like him will understand."

George led Bowler back up the stairs. When they arrived at the workroom, George helped him into his favourite chair and poured him a glass of water. All the time, he was looking around to see if he had missed any of the papers earmarked for destruction.

"I fear that what remains will prove of little value to the great scholar," Bowler said, "but I shall send what can be found. I do not want him to suppose that I'm entirely forgetful of my promise. This is so vexing."

He shook his head and sipped the water.

ᴄᴂᴇ

CHAPTER 17

The Eclipse

Saturday, 31 March 1866
1 Hill Street, Berkeley Square, London

Usually, the clock ticking on the mantelpiece would lull Rawlinson into sleep, but for some inexplicable reason, it was having the opposite effect tonight. He sat on the side of the bed, listening with envy to the deep, regular breathing of his wife. Tomorrow would be a very long day. He dreaded the rising of the sun.

The previous day had been exhilarating. He had presented his maiden speech in Parliament as the new member for Frome. He and Louisa had dined with Lord Palmerston and Lord Stanley, and a possible appointment to the India Council had been mentioned.

Rawlinson rubbed his eyes. He knew what it was. His stomach had been too heavy, and his mind too active, when he had fallen asleep. Stepping into his slippers, he took his dressing gown and closed the door with care. Standing in the gloom of his dressing room, he puzzled over his next move.

There were just too many concerns. They would not have discussed the India Council appointment with him if the decision to offer it had not already been made. No one deserved it more than him—it was, after all, his area of expertise. He could manage both political positions, but that would leave precious little time for supervising the cuneiform research. With a fashionable wife, a young son whose education must be planned, a fully staffed house and a demanding social life, it would nevertheless be helpful to have all three salaries.

The Antiquities Department was to be reorganised. Rawlinson knew what Birch would do. He would promote William Coxe to Senior Assistant. That young man's loyalty was to Birch and his father's friends at Oxford. He was much too friendly with Layard and Hincks, and then there was that incident with Oppert. No, he could not trust Coxe. The only one loyal to him was George Smith.

Rawlinson walked over to the window and opened the curtains. The brightness of the moon lightened his mood. By its height, he estimated another couple of hours to sunrise. In the distant, a clock chimed the half-hour.

Norris' annoying tic complaints had increased and he was seriously considering retirement. If only Rawlinson could find some way to advance Smith to Norris' position, that would be the ideal solution. George also had to his credit the skills of a master engraver, a remarkable natural genius for organising and matching the fragments, relentless dedication to the work, and unshakable loyalty to his authority. These were the traits that Rawlinson needed in order to assure the continued progress of his work. With Smith managing the workroom, he could maintain his position at the British Museum and his control over the cuneiform collection.

However, his protégé lacked the necessary credentials. One might have the fastest horse in the world, but without a pedigree, it will never be permitted on the racecourse. Coxe was from a respected family of scholars and naval officers, while Smith was an uneducated nobody.

There were also Rawlinson's rivals, both political and professional. How could Smith handle them? Hincks had been writing to Norris for months now, insisting on seeing all cuneiform accounts of eclipses. From what Norris had said, he was working on a new chronological system based on Assyrian and Babylonian lunar observations. It seemed that, no matter what obstacles he threw in Hincks' way, the old man refused to give up on the Assyrian studies.

Norris had been instructed to respond to Hincks that, unfortunately, Rawlinson was out of town and thus unavailable to draw material from the collection. As usual, Hincks had recruited his friend, Talbot, to support his claims. He was already demanding copies of his new edition of the *Cuneiform Inscriptions of Western Asia,* even though the bookbinder had not begun his work.

To make matters worse, Layard had recently been appointed to the Board of Trustees, and he had told Norris to arrange for him to inspect the Assyrian collection. Poor Norris was crumbing under these pressures. Was it any wonder that retirement seemed so attractive to him?

However, with Coxe in control, all would be lost. Anyone who asked would be granted access to the collection. If the collection could only be protected for a little longer, there would be time to extract more evidence from the rubble. He knew that records supporting his true vision of ancient Near Eastern history would soon be discovered. Only unsullied science could purge those wretched Jewish fables from the hearts of the simple-minded.

Rawlinson watched, entranced, as the earth's shadow gradually engulfed the moon's brightness. Hincks was right. The chronology could only be settled by attaching it to the hard science of astronomy. The key was to be found in the mechanical repetitiveness of the Saros cycles. The moon's face gradually turned into a dim, rusty disc. Rawlinson mused that a solar eclipse was more dramatic. In that darkest moment, a brilliant solution flashed out from the shadowy recesses of his thoughts.

଼ꕥ

"Good morning, Sir Henry," called Norris. "You seem in good spirits this morning, sir."

"Yes, Edwin. It is a fine spring morning, isn't it?" returned Rawlinson cheerily.

"I should like to have a word with you if you have a moment, Sir Henry."

"Certainly, Edwin, and how are you feeling? Better, I trust?"

"That is at the heart of my concern."

It is so pathetic to witness the ruinous effect of aging, Rawlinson thought. Norris was fading daily. Until recently, he had led the field in linguistic research and could hunt down the meaning of the most elusive phrase. None could surpass him in faithfulness, and he never failed to lay at Rawlinson's feet the best of his discoveries. His movements were now slow and feeble, but at least he still had most of his hair.

"As you know, due to these annoying health issues, I retired from the Foreign Office at the beginning of this month. Also, Mr. Rost has already assumed my duties at the Royal Asiatic Society."

"Yes."

"I hate to let you down like this, sir, but I fear my eyesight is now deteriorating and must abandon text copying altogether."

"That is regrettable," Rawlinson said. He sincerely felt for the old chap.

"I would like to continue working from my office at home," Norris continued. "I could help with correcting sheets. I feel that at this point my greatest contribution would be to complete the first ever Assyrian Dictionary."

"Edwin, my dear friend," replied Rawlinson, "as much as we wish that things will remain the same, they never do. I shall always hold you in the highest esteem and value the innumerable contributions you have made, and will continue to make for many more years to come, to our noble science. Let us not consider this as a withdrawal from your position, but rather as a relocation of your official work and a lightening of your duties. Do not worry for a moment—there will be no change in your emolument for this year's contract."

"Thank you, Sir Henry," said Norris. "I appreciate your generosity, and I wish to say that it has been an honour to serve you." Tears gathered in Norris' eyes.

"Now, if you will, Edwin, I do have one or two more tasks that must be completed," Rawlinson said.

"Of course, Sir Henry, I shall do my best to achieve whatever you need." Norris was relieved that this painful transition was going so well.

"Send a note to Reverend Hincks informing him that the pages he requested from the new volume of *Cuneiform Inscriptions* are being prepared and will be sent to him within a few weeks. I am on my way now to speak to Mr. Bowler. When lithographed copies are ready, you are to pack them and send them immediately to Dr. Hincks."

"As you wish, sir," replied Norris.

"Oh, and have Mr. Coxe come to my office in about an hour. I should be finished with the lithographer by then." As the elderly linguist began to leave, Rawlinson called after him, "Also, Edwin, when George arrives, send him to my office. I wish to speak to him as well."

"Yes, of course, Sir Henry."

ര്യ

William Coxe felt uneasy as he knocked on Rawlinson's door. He wiped his damp palms on his handkerchief, straightened his coat, and adjusted his bowtie. What could he have done wrong now? Probably this would be another lecture on punctuality.

"Come in," called Rawlinson.

"You wanted to see me, Sir Henry?" asked Coxe, noting that there were only two cigar butts in the heavy, silver ashtray.

"Yes, yes. Prompt as usual, Mr. Coxe," praised Rawlinson. "Please have a seat, young man." Rawlinson leaned back in his chair. As soon as the door was closed, he asked, "How long have you been with us Coxe?"

"Four and a half years, Sir Henry."

"That is a substantial length of time, don't you agree?"

"Yes, sir, I believe it is."

"Are you aware that Mr. Norris would like to enter semi-retirement next year?"

"Yes, sir I have heard him speak of it more than once."

"In my annual report to the Trustees, I must recommend who should be engaged to assist in the cuneiform research. Formerly, Mr. Norris tendered much valuable aid in copying the tablets. However, the infirmities of age have so advanced on him that he can only continue by correcting proofs in his study at home. I am obliged to suggest another arrangement. Next February, when I must submit my recommendations for that year, I shall ask that the duties formerly entrusted to him be transferred to yourself."

"Thank you, Sir Henry!" Coxe exclaimed. Rawlinson held his hand up to forestall any further effusions of gratitude.

"In view of the aid that you have provided in the cleaning and joining together of the tablet fragments, I shall request that you be awarded an honorarium, specifically for devoting a period of your own time to a further study of the tablets to enable the preparation of facsimile copies for Mr. Bowler. In addition, I shall recommend that the other moiety of the allowance previously sanctioned for Mr. Norris should be granted to you for your ex officio services in connection with the publication of the third volume of the *Cuneiform Inscriptions of Western Asia*, which I plan to embark upon this next year. But perhaps I have been too candid—you must remember that this offer is conditional on your continued hard work throughout the remainder of this year."

"Oh, most certainly, Sir Henry. That is well understood."

"The other issue that I felt was important to discuss with you is the reorganisation of the Antiquities Department."

"I understand it will be renamed the Department of Oriental Antiquities," said Coxe. "I hope to apply for the position of Senior Assistant."

"You have touched so aptly on the very topic," said Rawlinson. "I can foresee only one minor obstacle to your advancement to Senior Assistant."

"Sir?"

"In my humble opinion, the position requires a man with a wider range of experience than you presently possess."

"I do not quite follow you, Sir Henry," Coxe said.

"At Oxford, you studied Near Eastern geography and archaeology, yet you have never visited those lands," Rawlinson explained.

"Well, no, sir, I cannot say that I have yet had that privilege."

"You might consider broadening your experience. It is, of course, only a suggestion. You are under no obligation to undertake such a long and difficult journey."

"A journey?" Coxe's eyes widened with excitement. "To where, sir?"

"A journey to experience those places that books can never adequately describe: Constantinople, Mosul, Baghdad, and Bombay."

"Such a wonderful suggestion!" Coxe enthused. "I must admit, I have often dreamed of travelling to those very places."

"I may be wrong," said Rawlinson, "but I would hazard that gaining first-hand knowledge of those peoples and places, not to mention visiting the excavation site during your journey down the Tigris, would be more than sufficient for you to secure the Trustees' approval." Rawlinson paused just long enough for his words to have maximum impact. "If you should decide to undertake such an adventuresome excursion, I shall be more than happy to provide you with ample letters of introduction to ease your way. I have many friends in Baghdad and Bombay. Personally, I always found the Indian tiger hunt most exhilarating."

"I am at a loss for words, Sir Henry," Coxe said. "How can I ever thank you, sir, for so generous an offer?"

Rawlinson stood up and extended his hand. Coxe jumped to his feet and shook it vigourously.

"It will be my pleasure, Coxe, to assist you in every manner at my disposal, and to ensure that you acquire every opportunity for recognition and reward that a young man of your talents deserves."

"Thank you, sir." Coxe did not know which way to turn. He turned to leave, paused, then moved to the door.

"Yes, yes, sir. There are so many arrangements to be made!" he added, walking to the door.

"William, you must not embark on the journey until after I have tendered my suggestions to the Trustees next February. If our conversation should become known, it might ruin our plans. Only discretion will ensure success."

"Of course, Sir Henry, I shall be most prudent. I will not repeat a word of our conversation. Good day, sir, and thank you."

Coxe closed the door. Rawlinson touched a flame to another cigar. A glimmer reflected off one of his canine teeth as he curled back into his chair with a large grin.

"Yes, Mr. Coxe, I shall see you richly rewarded for permitting Oppert access to my work," he said.

☙❧

George Smith sat stiff-backed, resisting the inviting comfort of the chair. The sky was grey and dark low clouds streaming closer on the wind gave promise of heavy showers to come. He worried how long the rain would last, and whether it would hamper his journey home that night.

"You look tired, George," observed Rawlinson as he offered him a cigar.

"Thank you, sir." George replied, sniffing the mellow tobacco. This was a treat. "Yes, sir, it is taxing, sir," he added. "My job at Bradbury and Evans begins at four a.m. and ends at noon. Then I work here from one until seven. But then, when a man has a family, he does all he can to provide for them."

"I remember that your Charles is only a few months older than our little Henry," noted Rawlinson.

"Yes, sir, and we're expecting another one."

"Well, congratulations," said Rawlinson, smiling. "'Sons are a man's immortality,' as Socrates said."

They enjoyed the fine Cuban tobacco for a few minutes.

"There are three important points that I wish to discuss with you today," Rawlinson said. He blew a perfect smoke ring. "Do you recall the special project on which we worked shortly after you were married?"

"Yes, sir, I do."

"Well, there is need for another, similar one."

"I could certainly use a nice bonus, what with another baby on the way," George said. This news lifted his spirits.

"Also, Mr. Norris has just informed me that he will be unable to continue copying the cuneiform text for Mr. Bowler. It seems that his eyesight is failing."

"I knew that he was struggling," George said.

"This will leave a great void—one not easily filled."

"I understand, sir. You rely heavily on Mr. Norris for many important tasks."

"Yes, I suppose that I do." Rawlinson blew a smoke ring and watched it float away. "Mr. Norris seems to favour Mr. Coxe for the position. What do you think of that arrangement?"

"Mr. Coxe is a very capable Assyrian student," George replied, the gloom returning to his voice, "but it really does not matter to me, sir. I'll be happy working for anyone you place over me."

"The truth is, George, that I would prefer to give the position to you," Rawlinson said.

George was stunned. Until now, a formal, full-time appointment as Sir Henry's personal assistant had been the stuff of dreams.

"Unfortunately, your lack of education is a heavy handicap," Rawlinson added.

"Yes, sir, I know that," said George.

"Before I say any more, you should understand that you must do exactly as I instruct you, and must tell no one of this conversation."

"Of course, sir."

"How much do you make as a banknote engraver?"

"I make five guineas a month there, plus another three crowns here in the evenings."

"That gives you seventy-two pounds a year."

"Yes, sir."

"Very well, consider this offer: for this project, you will receive fifty pounds today and another fifty when the work is completed to my satisfaction."

The offer was more than George had expected.

"In addition," Rawlinson continued, "I shall arrange with the Trustees for you to be contracted as a full-time assistant here at the Museum, beginning next year."

"But how can I do that, Sir Henry?"

"Each year, I must recommend to the Trustees who should be engaged to assist in the cuneiform research," Rawlinson explained. "Formerly, Mr. Norris tendered much valuable aid in copying the tablets. However, in my next report I must inform them that he cannot continue working here on a daily basis. He wishes to limit his assistance to correcting proofs at home, and thus I am obliged to suggest another arrangement. Next February, I shall submit my recommendations that the duties formerly entrusted to Mr. Norris should be divided between Mr. Coxe and yourself.

"I shall explain that you have devoted some years to the study of the Assyrian inscriptions. I shall also tell them that, since you are an engraver by profession, it would be very useful to employ you under my direction to make fair copies of the cylinder and tablet fragments. I shall recommend, therefore, that you be named a transcriber by the Trustees, with a compensation of a hundred pounds for the year."

"You are brilliant, Sir Henry," George said. He appreciated the connection between the two propositions.

"No need for flattery," Rawlinson responded with a pretence of modesty. "Since you have skills at transcribing the characters from the tablets to paper, I want you to refine your mastery of Mr. Norris' technique. You are to assume this portion of Mr. Norris duties. In the meantime, I shall purchase the necessary engraving tools for you begin practising for our new project. Is there adequate space in your home for the equipment?"

"Yes, sir!"

"The third issue concerns your future," Rawlinson continued. "The Trustees may decide to terminate your position after the one year. Your only hope is to impress them by publishing. You must write two articles concerning newly discovered material by the end of this summer. I shall see to it that they are published in appropriate forums. Then, you must present your findings before an audience of noted scholars. Don't look so worried, George," he added, "I shall be your guide through the entire process."

"What do you want me to do first, sir?" George asked.

"First, find the manufacturers of the engraving equipment—I'll provide you with the sum—then we'll go together to the storage room and examine our collection of squeezings."

"Squeezings?"

“Paper casts made by pressing dampened layers of paper over the monumental inscriptions that were too large to transport to London. These squeezings were made by Mr. Layard some sixteen years back,” Rawlinson explained. “I am afraid that they are beginning to deteriorate and need to be examined. Perhaps they will provide us with a couple of interesting topics.”

“Yes, Sir Henry. I’ll get right on it!”

“Good, good,” Rawlinson said. “There is just one very important thing that you must always remember, young man,” He paused for emphasis. “Never cross me.”

“Yes, sir,” George said. He felt a chill. “I would never consider it, Sir Henry.”

“Well, that will be all, George,” Rawlinson concluded. Extending his hand, he added, “and congratulations again on the anticipated birth. I hope it will be another fine son.”

଼

CHAPTER 18

This Temporal Veil

Monday, 3 December 1866
Killyleagh Rectory, Ireland

Good morning, Reverend Hincks." greeted Frederick Thorne as he opened the door to the rectory study.

"A good morning to you, Frederick, and a glorious day it is." replied the aged scholar.

Seizing his opportunity, the family cat pushed past the curate and scampered across the room to his master. He rubbed affectionately against his leg, purring profusely.

"Yes, yes, good morning to you too, Nebuchadnezzar." Hincks leaned over and rubbed the tabby's silky, arched back.

"Considering how late we worked last night, I thought that you might still be asleep, sir."

"The hour does not matter, Frederick, as long as the work is completed and one's argument is well constructed. But here, please join me in a nice cup of tea. It is still hot."

"From your good humour," observed Frederick, "I conclude that you have reread our corrections and are pleased that we have accomplished our goal."

"Yes, I am satisfied that we have achieved our objective."

"When will Mrs. Hincks and your daughters return from Belfast?" Frederick asked.

"They should be home by the end of this week," Hincks replied, bending over to pick up the cat, "but since I completed the corrections to my paper sooner than anticipated, I might surprise my family with a visit of my own."

"That is an excellent idea, sir," the curate replied as he gathered the cups and plates and put them on the tea tray. He carefully carried it to the kitchen. A few minutes later he was back, busy returning books to their proper places in the bookcase. Hincks applied sealing wax to the string around a carefully-wrapped parcel and examined it with a smile.

"There, my paper is finally ready to be sent for publication in the *Monatsbericht*. It should be well received," he said.

"Would you like for me to post it, Dr. Hincks?"

"No, no, thank you, Frederick. I have been indoors too much lately and need to stretch my legs." Seeing him reach for his coat and hat, the cat ran to the door.

"But it is bitter cold out, sir," Frederick warned.

"The sky is clear, and the sun will warm the way," Hincks replied. The cat followed him out, but was too wise to venture far from the comfort and security of the old rectory.

☙❧

The north wind numbed Hincks' face, and the ground crunched beneath his warm winter boots. The rector paused on his journey to marvel at his Creator's masterpiece. Above was the clear, pale blue sky, and below lay the dark waters of Strangford Lough. The fields were blanketed in a cold, white shroud. Icy trickles of water found their way through the jumbled cracks and crevices of the rough stonewalls to refresh the frozen earth. Withered grass and broken reeds, dark and humbled, patiently awaited their vernal resurrection.

The delight of the day danced about Hincks in a dazzling display of the Divine. His feet barely tread upon the frozen earth. A fragrance breeze, neither of winter nor of spring, permeated his senses, chilling his bones but quickening his essence.

'On a day like this, one can visualise the eternal order concealed behind this thin temporal veil,' thought the good reverend. 'How sad it is that the weak in spirit stumble about in senseless self-deception. This must be the theme of next Sunday's sermon.' He walked on occupied with this new composition.

Another man of his learning would have been given a bishopric long ago, but hidden hands had collaborated to block his every hope of a higher position. It caused him endless grief not to be able to provide a more comfortable life for his beloved Jane and their precious daughters. Yet long ago, they had resolved that there was no better place to live and no sweeter soil in which to find eternal rest.

By the time he reached the village of Killyleagh, Hincks was a little dizzy and short of breath. Small though it may be, this was his village; his home. For more than forty years, he and his wife had shared their joys and sorrows with these good souls. Its modest houses huddled in two parallel rows down the main street, bearing the brunt of the sharp north wind to provide their inhabitants some small comfort.

Hincks stopped short of his destination, catching a glimpse of a strange, burly figure. He was wearing a black Bollinger and ankle length greatcoat, and the rector could not help but sense that he was a harbinger of dark deeds. The young man stretched his stride and the distance between them shortened. Hincks' heart beat a little faster as the young man came into focus.

"Good day to you, sir." Tommy said.

"I don't believe that we have met, young man," Hincks said.

"Richardson, sir," he lied, "Harris Richardson. All the way from good ol' London town."

"The name is Hincks, Mr. Richardson," he replied. "Reverend Edward Hincks," They shook hands.

"Pleased to meet you, Reverend."

"And what brings you to our fair settlement, Mr. Richardson?"

"I've come to visit the land where me dear departed ma was born," said Tommy. "Seein' this pretty little place, I thought I might stop off here and 'ave a quick look round."

Hincks walked on, and Tommy accompanied him. A strong gust caused both men to reach for their hats. Tommy's broad hand took a firm grip on the door handle of the Post Office and generously held the door for the ancient clergyman.

"That's a nice size parcel, Reverend," noted Tommy.

"The fruits of many years' study, Mr. Richardson. A long labour brought to a happy conclusion."

"Good morning to you, Reverend," welcomed the brushy postmaster as Hincks placed the parcel on the counter.

"Patrick," Hincks said, "this parcel must be despatched immediately to Berlin, in Germany."

The postmaster stopped sorting the local letters and devoted himself to his important new task.

"To Berlin, in Germany," repeated Tommy, sounding duly impressed. Hincks walked over to the large, black pot-bellied stove. Tommy followed. The heat felt good against their hands and legs. A sharp gust of wind pushed the smoke back down the chimney and some escaped into the room, thickening the air.

"Do you think to make Killyleagh your home?" asked Hincks as they warmed their hands.

"My plans are not yet settled enough to speak of home," Tommy replied.

"I don't think you mentioned your trade. What line of work are you in?"

"A bit o' this and a bit o' that; I'm what you'd call a jack of all trades, but master of none."

"Well, you should put your mind to one and master it," Hincks said. "A man needs to be firmly grounded in order to make his mark on this world. Well, good day to you, Mr. Richardson. I hope to see you at church on Sunday."

Hincks knew that the best of the day would soon be gone, and the worsening weather would be a hard test for his body to endure, so he hurried back the comfort of his home.

ઉ෴ઈ

By the time Hincks settled into his favourite chair in the study and began to warm himself beside the fire, he was exhausted. He vowed to resume his daily walks. Too many hours at his desk were weakening him. With his cat purring in his lap, he soon dozed off. The clink of china pulled him back into this world. Frederick had just brought a tray from the kitchen.

"Pardon me, sir," he said, "I didn't realise that you were resting."

"That's alright, Frederick," Hincks replied.

"I brought us something to eat," said Frederick

"Excellent. Set it on my desk, if you will."

The cat jumped down and rubbed against Frederick's leg, insisting that his many merits were deserving of a tasty reward.

"Yes, Nebuchadnezzar, I saved some for you," Frederick reassured the cat. He gave a few scraps of mutton to the grey tabby.

"We'll break bread together," said Hincks, "and then I must write my sermon for next Sunday." The rector paused for a moment and said grace. After the simple meal was finished, the two men sat talking companionably of his inspirational walk.

"Why don't you let me take over this week's service?" Frederick said. "Then you could leave earlier and spend more time with your family."

"That's very thoughtful of you, Frederick." Hincks replied. "We could return next Monday, I suppose." Hincks reached for the letters that Patrick had given him earlier.

"This is interesting," Hincks said as he hastened to open one. "It's a letter from Dr. Oppert, in Paris."

Hincks' smile vanished as he read the letter. He buried his fingers in his thick, white hair.

"You seem upset, sir. What does Dr. Oppert say?"

Hincks seemed not to hear Frederick's question. He just sat there, staring at the second page for several minutes.

"He asks my opinion on plate fifty-two, published in Rawlinson's second volume of the *Cuneiform Inscriptions of Western Asia*," he final replied. Returning to the letter, he added, "He writes: 'This tablet, entitled 'Distribution of Officers under Tiglath-pileser,' is a record that is especially interesting in my opinion. The seventh line from the top contains a unique record of a solar eclipse. Since you are the only other Assyrian scholar besides me with sufficient knowledge of astronomic calculations, I would greatly value your opinion of its significance.'"

"A solar eclipse? But, that is impossible!" Frederick exclaimed. He could not believe his ears. "You scrutinised every page several times and found only a few lunar records."

Hincks did not reply.

"How does this affect the validity of your recent work?" Frederick asked.

"My paper, *On a Newly Discovered Record of Ancient Lunar Eclipses*, is still important." He continued, "Since eclipses follow well-established astronomical laws, scholars of history always become excited when new records of ancient sightings are discovered. They are essential in providing context for historic content. I must study this in greater depth. Please bring me the *Cuneiform Inscriptions.*"

Hincks moved to his desk and arranged a space. Frederick brought a box, two feet tall and more than a foot wide, and opened it.

"Last April, Mr. Norris provided me with these lithographed sheets," Hincks said. The elderly scholar tapped his knotted forefinger on a stack of enormous pages. "Plate fifty-two is not among them."

"Will there never be an end to Rawlinson's mistreatment of you?" Frederick asked. He shook his head. "For years, he has denied you access to vital materials, and when at last he is forthcoming, what does he do? He sends you a defective copy!"

"He has been a constant source of sorrow for more than ten years," Hincks agreed, "but I recall that Mr. Norris was ill at the time and delegated the task of posting my copy. Perhaps this was a simple oversight. When Fox Talbot wrote to me last June, saying that he had received his copy, I was confident that, except for the binding, the material was identical."

"Usually, Mr. Talbot is the first to consult you on this subject," Frederick murmured.

"He has been much occupied with refining his photographic process, and he has done little with the Assyrian this year," Hincks said. "I should be grateful to Dr. Oppert for having troubled to copy the cuneiform text for me." He glanced over the letter again. "It seems that my copy also lacks the annotated table of contents, which, according to Dr. Oppert, immediately calls the reader's attention to the plate on which this solar eclipse is recorded."

Hincks slowly rose from his seat.

"I would not be surprised if this were intentional," he said. "Rawlinson and I disagree on many points. He insists that the scriptural accounts are flawed, and that they are in need of correction. To me, he seems intent on discrediting the Holy Scriptures. Beyond this sentiment, I shall not venture to speculate on his motives for championing the superiority of Assyrian accounts while demeaning those of the Hebrew text." Hincks opened a bookcase and searched the shelves of his copies of the *Athenæum*.

"How could a rational man consider as reliable the accounts of a society that deemed the actions of anything that moved a portent for war and peace, whether it might be the appearance of a star, a shifting in the wind, the swarming of insects, or the entrails of a dead animal?" He mused, taking a few volumes of the journal and returning to his desk.

Hincks looked exhausted. Frederick was concerned how he was dealing with this new setback. Yet, he was still vigorous for his advanced age, and his mind had not lost its keen perception.

“The hour is late, and I should be on my way home,” Frederick said. He rose from his seat and wrapped himself in his warm winter coat. “Needless to say, if you decide to write another paper on this solar eclipse discovery, I shall be happy to help in any way that I can,” he added.

Hincks studied the pages from Jules again. He started to stand up, but then froze, the bones of his back forming a great question mark as he bent over the pages on his desk. He ran his finger down the columns and adjusted his glasses.

“I need to think about this for a while, Frederick.” Hincks said. He looked up and smiled at his curate. “I know you will take good care of our little flock while I am away.”

“Have a good night’s rest and a safe journey on the morrow, Reverend Hincks.”

“Good night, dear Fredrick.”

No sooner had his young friend departed than Hincks was again sitting at his desk, thumbing through volumes of cuneiform notes. Selecting an old, familiar notebook from the collection, he marvelled at how the binding had faded and the pages yellowed. When these pages were written, the hands that had held them were smooth and strong. Now they were gnarled and feeble. The ideas captured on these pages had flowed rapidly from his pen and this old house had been filled with the sounds of children and the hurried steps of a young mother. Time has a strange habit of slipping by unnoticed, like the beat of an aged heart.

Nebuchadnezzar forced his pink nose under the old scholar’s hand. He needed his fur stroked and his ears rubbed. Hincks’ response was automatic, programmed into him by countless household cats.

“Yes, Nebuchadnezzar, I believe you are right. We should reread Rawlinson’s letter to the *Athenæum*,” Hincks said and selected a volume on his desk. “Ah, this is it—

number 1869, published in August 1863. Here, on page 245, is footnote number sixteen. This is the reference we need. Let me read it to you, for you were just a tiny kitten when it was written."

The cat purred his approval and sniffed the journal.

"On a mutilated tablet, which seems to have been a sort of 'Royal Gazette' that noted all government appointments, it is stated that Tiglath-pileser ascended the throne on the thirteenth day of the second month, and immediately afterwards went down to Mesopotamia—'the country between the rivers' in Assyrian. As we know from his annals, he waged a successful war there against numerous petty chiefs." Picking up the sheet of text sent by Oppert, Hincks added, "This, then, is the tablet to which Rawlinson referred in several articles as the 'mutilated tablet.'

"Perhaps I have mentioned to you, my little friend, that Rawlinson used this as the final proof that his reconstruction of the Eponym Canon was correct and that Tiglath-pileser began his rule in 744BC; a date that Oppert and I consider to be too low.

"What do I mean by too low, you ask?" Hincks said to Nebuchadnezzar. "Well, as you know, the chronology in the margin of our Bible gives an interval of 164 years between the accession of Jehu and the capture of Samaria. On the other hand, Rawlinson's system, based as it is on the Assyrian Eponym Canon he discovered, allows only 120 years.

"Permit me to read to you from what Oppert has just provided us. The left column has 'Guzana, revolt in the citadel,' and the right column has 'in Sivan the sun eclipsed.' Now, what exactly does Oppert say?" Hincks scratched the tabby's head.

"He states: 'Immediately, I sat down to calculate the most probable dates for this astronomical event. Of course, we know that the third lunar month, Sivan, generally corresponds to the Julian month of June. I have found three candidates, which accordingly are the thirteenth of that month in 809BC, the twenty-fourth in 791BC and the fifteenth in 763BC. I favour 809BC, as it is the year that most conforms to our view. Please be so kind as to send me your opinion at your convenience.'"

Nebuchadnezzar rubbed the side of his face against Hincks' arm.

"I thought that you would concur with our French colleague," Hincks said, "but we must not be hasty. I ask you to examine this issue with the greatest care. Now, even Rawlinson agrees that Samaria was taken by Sargon in 721BC. I believe that I was the first to establish this, by combining the Babylonian kings' list with Ptolemy's canon of lunar eclipses."

The cat purred louder.

"Thank you for that kind acknowledgement," Hincks said. "You, Oppert, and I accept, while Rawlinson doubts, the biblical record that Shalmaneser is Sargon's predecessor, and we allow him a five year rule. That brings us to 726BC. The other important point on which we are in agreement is that each Assyrian official, honoured by having his name inscribed in these lists, held the position for one year. It is at this point that Sir Henry parts ways with us. In this same article, he insists that his lists of eponyms are complete, and that they indicate that Tiglath-pileser began his rule in the year 744BC. However, we maintain that his lists are fragmentary, and that more than forty years are missing. Thus, we hold that this particular king's rule began in about 788BC." Hincks stopped to count the lines.

"According to this plate fifty-two, there are nineteen lines, equalling nineteen years, from the solar eclipse and the first year of Tiglath-pileser," Hincks said. He thought for a long minute. "I now see what Rawlinson is aiming to achieve. Did you know, Nebuchadnezzar, that more than eighty years ago, a monk called Francois Clement raised the possibility of linking the brilliant eclipses of the fifteenth of June, 763BC with passages in the Book of Amos? That was in his *L'art de vérifier les dates des faits historiques.* Do you see, Nebuchadnezzar? To find such a connection would not only confirm Rawlinson's Canon, but it also would destroy the validity of the Scriptures as an historical source."

The cat rolled over on his back and rubbed his eyes with his paws.

"I am glad that you appreciate the seriousness of our situation," Hincks said, "but perhaps all is not lost." The cat jumped onto the desk as Hincks leaned forward to study the material again. "This is the first opportunity that the scholarly world has had to examine his new evidence, and I can already identify several oddities. First, it is anomalous. It combines different styles. References to eclipses are commonly found in Assyrian and Babylonian astronomical—or, more appropriately, astrological texts—I have never seen or read of one being found in an historical text. This aberration is compounded by the inclusion of the name of the month. Precise dates such as these are common in boastful monumental inscriptions and in regal annals, but not on eponym lists. It is a very queer fragment. We must also ask why only this eclipse is noted. According to Oppert's rendition, each side has forty-seven lines of inscriptions. Therefore, it covers a period of more than ninety years. During such a long period of time, there would have been many other lunar eclipses. Why were the others not included?

"There is another peculiarity. In this article," Hincks pointed to the open copy of the *Athenæum*, "Rawlinson states that this tablet is the one that I discovered in 1853, which was then 'misplaced'. But now that I see it, this cannot be true. The tablet I saw had three columns, with the left column intact. Notice here that the entire left column is broken off. The one I saw was inscribed with a list of names that included at least four kings. Tiglath-pileser's name was among them, but it was not in the centre column; it was in the one that is now missing. Also, I cannot for one second imagine missing this clear reference to a solar eclipse." The elderly scholar straightened up slowly with an audible pop in his back. He picked up Rawlinson's article, and a smile filled his face. The cat sat attentively on the desk.

"Yes, Nebuchadnezzar, I think we have a few questions that Rawlinson will find difficult, if not impossible, to answer. Considering the number of times he has referred to this 'mutilated' tablet in his publications and how careful he was in his description of it in this lengthy article in 1863, why did he not publish this evidence earlier? It is, after all, the perfect support to his theories and occurs on the same side of the tablet as Tiglath-pileser's name? I believe the truth to be that that this solar eclipse inscription did not exist 1863. This then begs the question: Was the inscription of Tiglath-pileser's name there before 1863? These irregularities seem to indicate substantial tampering with the original tablet." Hincks was satisfied that his suspicions were well founded.

"Well, it is late my little friend," he said, "and I am tired."

He closed his books and went to the kitchen to prepare bread and cheese for his supper, but when he sat down to eat, he had no appetite. Instead, he took out his diary and, placing Oppert's letter on the table beside him, he settled down to write an entry. The winter wind rattled the shutters and the timbers of the old house creaked under its onslaught. Suddenly, he heard a strange sound. His heart was pounding hard against the walls of his chest. He turned in time to see Nebuchadnezzar pounce on a hapless mouse. The dizziness returned, and his shoulder ached. It had been a long, tiring day.

Quickly he scribbled in his diary: 'Unwell. To bed at 9.15'.

Reverend Hincks settled in bed with his worn copy of the Bible and soon drifted off.

☙❧

Experience had taught Tommy always to check the doors of a building before bothering with a window. He was pleased to find the rectory door unlocked. The embers in the fire still cast an eerie glow over the great scholar's study.

Nebuchadnezzar opened one eye and lifted his head. The ends of Tommy's bootlaces flickered a few feet from his resting place under the desk. He wrinkled his nose at the strange odour. The heavy boots turned away from one door, when it proved to lead only to a cupboard. The cat crouched on padded paws, haunches up and head low, ready to pounce, but the bootlace moved away into the passageway. His eyes gleamed as he stalked the alien feet to his master's half-open door.

Tommy fingered the cold, smooth surface of his short metal club and peered into the room. The wick was burning low in the lamp beside the wooden-framed bed. There lay his intended victim, in peaceful repose. Without the slightest sound, Tommy stepped into the mellow glow of the lamp. The moment was perfect for his purpose. The bootlaces flicked once more. The cat pounced, sinking his teeth and claws into Tommy's boot and shin. He cursed and kicked out, loosening the cat's grip. Nebuchadnezzar hissed and dived for the safety of the door. Tommy spun round towards the bed, with his weapon raised, but the only sound was the pounding of his own heart. He was stunned.

"What are you goin' ter do, old man?" Tommy growled.

There was no reply.

Tommy walked over to the bed and poked Hincks' motionless, bony shoulder. There was no response.

"Well that was a lot easier than I thought," Tommy smirked to himself and turned his back on the corpse.

The cat hissed at him from the doorway. His shin still stinging from the fresh puncture wounds, Tommy, grabbed the lamp and chased the sleek shadow down the hallway. Nothing would have been more satisfying at that moment than to smash its head in. The cat darted into the kitchen and disappeared under the dresser.

Tommy soon tired of the search and set the lamp on the table beside Hincks' untouched supper. He tasted the cheese. It was good. Breaking open the hard-crusted loaf, he stuffed into it as much cheese as it would hold. This would help keep off his hunger on the cold walk back to his room. He wrapped the bread in two sheets of paper he found on the table and left the rectory the way he had entered.

"One down, three to go," he said, smiling as he pulled the door closed. "Now for Coxe, Norris, and Oppert."

CHAPTER 19

Keys to the Kingdom

Monday, 20 December 1869
Great Western Railway, Oxford to Paddington Station

Every bone in my body aches in this weather," Norris said. To avoid the draught from the window, he chose the seat by the compartment door, facing the back of the train.

"At least the rain held off until we reached the station," Talbot said, taking the window seat next to Norris.

"I am just glad that we did not miss the train," Birch said. He stowed their umbrellas under the seat.

"This weather suits the business of the day," added Layard as he sat down across from Talbot.

"He was such a promising young scholar, and only twenty-nine years of age," Norris said. He shook his head.

"He was a very pleasant young man, and I valued him as a personal friend," added Talbot.

"His death is a great loss to oriental studies and to the British Museum," sighed Norris. "We were so pleased when the trustees granted Sir Henry's request to give young Coxe greater authority and an extra allowance."

"That unfortunate journey to India was the cause of his illness," stated Birch.

"I tried to discourage him from accepting the position. He should have continued his Assyrian studies instead of going to Calcutta to teach Sanskrit," explained Norris.

"He once said that he hoped to impress the Trustees and encourage them to accept his application for a permanent senior assistant position," added Birch.

"But why go on a tiger hunt, of all things?" asked Talbot.

"Young men feel immune to the perils of life," observed Layard.

"A more competent guide would have foreseen the danger," added Norris.

"An accidental discharge of a rifle can happen during an English hunt as well," noted Birch. "Coxe told me that, had he not slipped on a wet stone at that very moment, he would have been killed on the spot."

"Considering how much the chap suffered, perhaps that would have been the better end," Layard mused.

"It was most unfortunate," Talbot said. "One did what one could to cheer him, sending him cuneiform materials. We all did what we could. But after they amputated his leg last year, he seemed to lose spirit."

"There was no choice—the inflammation had gone too far." Norris spoke in a low monotone as he watched the heavy, leaden, clouds hanging low over the countryside. "The leg was ulcerated. He had been laid up for four months, and his valiant attempts to return to work had all failed. A portion of the bone had died, and it was exfoliating. They hoped that his youthful vigour would return after the surgery. The doctor said that it had gone too far to save him by that time. The inflammation had so weakened his constitution that he finally succumbed to the malady."

"I don't understand it," said Talbot. "His leg was mending well. We exchanged a few letters concerning the cuneiform collection. Then his condition suddenly worsened, and the next thing I heard, he was forced to take a medical leave."

"Didn't you hear what happened?" asked Birch. "It was the first night after his return that Coxe worked late. The weather was cold and wet, and there were few people about. He was hit on the head from behind, pushed down the steps, and robbed. The fall re-opened his wound, and the infection was never again brought under control."

"Well, it's over now," said Norris, "and he has finally found relief after two long and painful years."

"The staffing situation in the Department has become more difficult since Sir Henry accepted the appointment to the India Council," rejoined Birch. "We were fortunate that he recognised George Smith's talents. I cannot imagine what would have happened if Smith had not been able to take over during Coxe's illness."

"I was happy to write a letter of recommendation in support of his application to be made a temporary assistant," added Norris.

"He has already done much," agreed Talbot, "and he appears to have a special aptitude for cuneiform literature. It will be my pleasure to recommend young Smith to the Trustees."

Layard watched the grey countryside sliding past the train. An old ache gripped him as the train raced alongside a swollen stream. In the weeping glass pane, the image of another lost face appeared, one whose peaceful smile he had covered with a wet blanket before they lowered her into a deep, soggy hole. He opened his pocket watch as if to check the time. Instead, he studied the likeness of the fair, noble face of his bride. He did not deserve her.

"Can we rely upon your support as well, Mr. Layard?" asked Birch. The sound of his name jolted Layard back to the present.

"I must admit that I am still most displeased about the loss of my squeezes of Assyrian monumental inscriptions," returned Layard.

"Be reasonable sir," soothed Birch. "You made them more than twenty years ago. Paper naturally deteriorates over time. You really cannot hold the Museum accountable for this."

"By Rats, Dr. Birch," corrected Layard glancing at Norris, who was studying his hands. "Years of hard work destroyed by rats making a nest out of my squeezes. One might assume that the British Museum was the one place on earth where irreplaceable artefacts would be safe from rats!"

"That is the report submitted by Mr. Smith," replied Birch shaking his head. "I cannot express how deeply we regret this loss."

"I suppose that you are right, Dr. Birch," sighed Layard. "If you consider Mr. Smith to be the best candidate, I shall write the letter directly."

"I find his knowledge of the Assyrian language and characters surprisingly good." Norris said. "Considering his limited means and deficient education, his progress has been wonderful. Often, his guesses are perhaps too bold, but then, that is better than timidity. I am afraid that he has been too sanguine at times, and has jumped too rashly at a tempting and plausible theory on which a more sober investigation would have thrown doubts. I fear that I am guilty of such things occasionally, but as I do not generally publish them, my faults are known only to a few friends."

At this, the other men chuckled, and Norris continued.

"Yet, if he is appointed, I for one shall be much gratified. I am sure that Smith will do good work. I only wish that he had a better education. He speaks only English, and even there, his grammar and literary style must be improved. He is ignorant of even the most basic Greek, Latin, or other Semitic languages. Despite these reservations, I have already submitted a very favourable letter in support of his current application."

"Over the past two and a half years," said Birch, "George Smith has made great progress. He read a paper on the annals of Tiglath-pileser before the Royal Society of Literature, and gave some very interesting historical notices about Egypt. He has supplied the 'missing link' caused by Mr. Coxe's illness. I hope his application will be accepted."

"I agree," said Talbot, "The successor to the late lamented William Coxe should be well acquainted with the Department's Assyrian antiquities, as well as understanding the difficulties of this important branch of archaeology. The British Museum contains a vast number of broken fragments that require a keen eye and delicate hand to be accurately reassembled, otherwise their meaning cannot be ascertained. I know of no one as skilled in this task as Mr. Smith. He is the one most suited to fill this great void."

"Will you be in London for long, Mr. Layard?" asked Norris.

"We leave in the morning for Madrid," Layard replied.

"How does your wife find Spain?" asked Talbot.

"Mary is entranced by the culture, and has made excellent progress with the language," Layard replied. He checked his watch. "We are staying with her brother, Lord Montague Guest."

"You are a fortunate man. Lady Mary is a most remarkable young woman."

"She is everything a man could hope for," said Layard, smiling, "and more than I deserve."

The train's guard tapped on the compartment door.

"Your tickets, please, gentlemen," he requested.

"What is your opinion of Livingston's new expedition?" asked Birch, taking out his ticket.

"One can only wish him the best of luck in his search for the source of the Nile," replied Layard presenting his ticket.

Having examined each in turn, the guard gave the tickets back to the four men and moved cheerfully on to the next compartment.

Tickets, please," the guard requested. This compartment had three French passengers.

"Yes, of course," the men replied, handing over their tickets for inspection.

"Thank you, gentlemen. Have a pleasant journey."

The guard closed the door and moved on.

"William was a fine scholar," stated Gustav Oppert. "He always received the highest marks, Jules."

"I saw him several times at meetings of the Asiatic Society, prior to his illness. He spoke fondly of you," replied his brother.

"I was a frequent guest at their house throughout my years at Oxford," commented Gustav. "This tragedy has devastated his parents. I did not recognise his father at first—he has aged so much in the past two years. When his mother collapsed at the graveside, I feared that she had joined him."

"I noticed that most of the people from the British Museum attended the funeral," added Jules.

"Sir Henry," noted his brother, "greeted you very cordially."

"Of course, Gustav. Protocol requires such public displays among gentlemen scholars," Jules replied. He raised his eyebrows. "However, my dear brother, if we met on a dark road, I would not turn my back to him."

"Neither would I," laughed Joachim Menant, shaking the rain from his hat.

"How is your research progressing? Are the two of you still collaborating?" asked Gustav.

"Joachim is progressing well with the first volume of *Le Syllabaire Assyrien*, while I have spent most of this year working on the more ancient Sumerian language," said Jules, adding, "but I believe that *La Chronologie Biblique Fixée par les Eclipses des Inscriptions Cunéiformes* is the best paper I have published this year."

"I agree," stated Menant. "The argument is well presented."

"It is my response to Rawlinson's work on the Near Eastern chronology," Jules said.

"What is the essence of the dispute?" asked Gustav.

"In the May edition of the *Athenæum*, he boasted of having settled the debate concerning Assyrian and Biblical history. Typically, he awarded the victory to his heroes, the Assyrians," Jules replied.

"How so?" asked Gustav.

"Rawlinson believes that the Biblical text is a corruption of Assyrian and Babylonian mythology and historical accounts. The debates have been quite heated in the past. Over the last few years, I have found myself increasingly isolated, with more scholars accepting Rawlinson's position, especially since the death of Dr. Hincks."

"Another great loss to Near Eastern studies," noted Menant.

"The timing of his death could not have been worse," observed Jules.

"Why is that?" asked Gustav.

"In the second volume of Rawlinson's Cuneiform Inscriptions is a transcription of a tablet on which a solar eclipse is recorded. Of course, I was the last to receive my copy. Knowing that he and I were the only scholars with the skills to read cuneiform and calculate the occurrence of eclipses, I wrote to him soliciting his opinion. Shortly afterwards, I received word of the great scholar's death. I am uncertain if he even read my letter. Afterwards, I read Hincks' article in the *Monatsbericht*, I found it odd that he did not discuss this important evidence.

"The following May, Rawlinson announced that his 'transcriber,' a M. George Smith, had noticed a resemblance between this tablet and the Eponym Canon. He very astutely connected the eclipse with one published eighty years earlier by Francois Clement in *L'art de vérifier les dates des faits historiques.* Rawlinson wrote that he remembered seeing a fragment of a canon that might complete the broken line of text. On examination, it proved to be so. According to him, this fragment was the missing link between his reconstruction of the Eponyms and a well-documented eclipse. The discovery just happened to validate all of his theories, including an alignment of the first Grecian Olympiad, the foundation of the city of Rome, and the beginning of the era of Nabonassar." Jules said. He paused.

"What argument did you offer against him?" asked Gustav.

"I have always maintained that he had misconstrued the fragments of the Canon, and that there is a forty-year hiatus in native Assyrian rule, during which time a Babylonian occupied the throne of the northern empire. I identify this eclipse with the one that occurred on June 13, 809BC."

"That seems reasonable," agreed Gustav.

"There is something that has disturbed me since I first read Rawlinson's article," added Menant.

"What is that, Joachim?" asked Jules.

"First, in his article, Rawlinson apologises profusely for not noticing this vital piece of evidence earlier. He states that the late Dr. Hincks had also failed to notice the importance of the solar eclipse inscription, even though the Irish scholar had had a copy of the transcription in his possession for twelve months. How could an astute and thorough scholar like Hincks have had a copy for so long and not noticed the eclipse? So, I searched through my past issues of the *Athenæum* and found that Rawlinson had described this tablet in at least three of his articles."

"In addition," added Jules, "prior to publication, Rawlinson must have transcribed the full text of this page for his lithographer, yet he wrote that he never noticed this remarkable solar eclipse, which is only a few lines above the name of Tiglath-pileser!

"In my letter to Hincks, I posed another question: why did the Assyrians record only this one eclipse on the tablet? The record covers roughly ninety years. I identified eight remarkable eclipses during that time. The entire inscription is anomalous, and therefore of questionable value."

"This is all very interesting," declared Gustav.

"Interesting, but futile," replied Jules. "Unfortunately, Rawlinson holds all the cards in this game."

"How is your work progressing in the Queen's Library at Windsor, Gustav?" asked Menant.

"Unbearably boring, especially since we lost M. Woodward," Gustav replied.

It pained Jules to see his brother look so miserable.

"Have you considered applying for the position left vacant by the sad death of Mr. Coxe?" asked Menant.

"That is a wonderful suggestion, Joachim," responded Jules.

"Do you think that I have a chance?" Gustav asked.

"Certainly," Jules replied. The British Museum is short staffed. Rawlinson is rarely there. You are a British citizen, so they must consider you."

"I am not as skilled in the Assyrian language as I am in Sanskrit."

"You have Hebrew and Aramaic to your credit. That forms a sound base. Besides, you are a published scholar."

"I shall be happy to give you a copy of my recent publication, *Exposé des éléments de la grammaire assyrienne*. You might find it useful as a primer," Jules offered.

"That would be very helpful. Thank you," Gustav said.

ঔ

Tickets, please," the guard said as he entered the last compartment. Taking the two tickets, he asked, "Excuse me, sir, but aren't you Sir Henry Rawlinson?"

"I have that pleasure," Rawlinson said.

"I saw your picture in the newspaper a while back. It's a pleasure to meet you, sir," said the guard. "May I wish you a pleasant journey."

"Thank you," Rawlinson replied. When the man closed their door, he resumed his conversation. "You must still pass the Civil Service Examinations," he said to George. "I shall arrange for it to be sent directly to me. When all of the letters of reference and the examination results have been reviewed, the appointment must be signed by the Lord Chancellor, the Speaker, and the Archbishop," explained Rawlinson.

"Do you still think that I can make it?" asked George, fiddling nervously with a button on his coat.

"Do you still want it?" Rawlinson asked.

"Yes, sir, more than anything in the world," George replied. His face clouded, and he continued. "Mr. Norris is very critical of my work. He finds fault with everything I say or do. I cannot believe that he gave me a letter of recommendation."

"Norris tendered his letters in your favour because he is not a fool," Rawlinson said. "His Assyrian dictionary is a project very close to his heart. He must have access to the cuneiform collection if he wants the work to advance."

"I always feel like he's laughing at me behind my back."

"Don't be so sensitive. Those who are important have been very impressed by the quality of your work." He did not want to say so, but George had done better than Rawlinson had imagined he would.

"All is progressing well. Your papers presented to the Royal Asiatic Society on the date of the payment of tribute by Jehu to Shalmaneser, and details of the war with Hazael were not only very well received, but have also been published in the *Athenæum*," Rawlinson said.

"If you hadn't insisted, Sir Henry, they wouldn't have given me the time of day," George said.

"It is only important that you have published," Rawlinson continued. "I have given you my full support, both publicly and privately, and credited you with discovering the link between the Eponym Canon and the solar eclipse. The academic world has now accepted my reconstruction of Near Eastern chronology, which is firmly founded upon this cornerstone." Rawlinson smiled reassuringly.

"Since then, you have amazed even me. This was followed by the 'discovery' of an otherwise unknown battle between Uzziah, King of Judah, and our famous Assyrian king, Tiglath-pileser. My personal favourite was the calendar proving that the Assyrians held the seventh day as sacred. However, the new portion of the Eponym Canon containing an otherwise unverified record of Shalmaneser was by far the more important discovery. This gives you four major discoveries that have endeared you to the religious masses."

"What can I say? It was an excellent year for discoveries," George said, smiling.

"You have my full backing because you are a talented cuneiformist and a skilled engraver," Rawlinson told him. "All that I ask in return is loyalty."

"You know that you have it, sir. I'm your man, and I'd walk through Hell for you, Sir Henry."

"I know you would, George, I know you would," Rawlinson said, smiling encouragingly at his young protégé. "Now, we must plan what will happen after your appointment is approved."

"It still seems like a dream. I'm so afraid that something will happen," George said.

"Stop worrying," reassured Rawlinson. "Now, I am planning a newspaper article. The masses love a success story, especially if it is an against-all-odds, rags-to-riches, penny-novel type. How about this? We discovered you studying in the Library, let's say in 1866. Similar to the Christ child teaching the Temple elders, you dazzled us with your unprecedented knowledge of Assyrian history and language. It may be a little melodramatic, but it really is not far from the truth. This also will serve to soften public criticism. If they accept that you are a natural, though uneducated, genius, then any critics will appear ungracious should they hold you to the same standard as a scholar who has the advantage of a formal academic education. At the same time, they will be mystified how you have advanced so far so quickly. This will cause them to fear you, which is an added advantage. You will need to produce a major publication. As you have already spent many years working with the material from the library of Assur-bani-pal, I suggest that you publish his annals, along with a transliteration and a translation."

"I can't do that, Sir Henry! It would take me a lifetime."

"I am confident that you can." Noting the expression of disbelief on George's face, Rawlinson added, "Let me put it this way: I am not asking *if* you would like to publish the annals of Assur-bani-pal; I am ordering you to do so as soon as possible. You will also do an excellent job, because, it might open the way for you to head your own excavation expedition to Kouyunjik."

Now that his dream was within his grasp, George's mind raced in a dozen directions. Rawlinson permitted the idea to take root. He needed George to be strong, self-confident, and totally subservient to him.

"Well, I see that we are nearing Paddington," Rawlinson observed. "Are you going back to the Museum?"

"Yes, I suppose so, sir."

"Good." Rawlinson paused, and then continued, "On second thoughts, take the remainder of the day off. Go home and enjoy some time with your family. As a matter of fact, take the entire week off. Let them see how much work you actually do. I shall inform Birch."

"Thank you, Sir Henry. Mary will be very pleased. She's always complaining that I spend too much time away from home."

"How are your wife and children, George?"

"They are doing just fine, sir," George was smiling, "Charlie's five years old now."

"That's right—he's the same age as our little Henry."

"Fred is three."

"Yes, he's a little older than our Toby."

"Elizabeth—we call her Cissie, is twenty months, and Mary's expecting another."

"Really? When?" asked Rawlinson.

"Sometime around next April."

"It sounds like you will be in need of a new house soon."

"Yes, sir. As soon as this appointment goes through, we're buying a new home," George replied.

"Good for you, make the most of this advancement. You deserve it." The train slowed and jerked to a stop. "Well, it seems that we have arrived." announced Rawlinson.

ଔଷ

Paddington Station was busy, even in the worst of weather. Steam shot from the engine as the porter opened the doors. Layard was the first off the train. He was eager to trade drizzly London for sunny Madrid. Talbot rushed off to make his connection with a train leaving for Chippenham. Jules and Menant took the first available cab with Gustav, intending to leave for Paris the next morning. They tipped their hat*s* to the British Museum contingent as they departed.

"Thank you again, Mr. Norris, for your kind letter of reference," said George, extending his hand.

"It was the least I could do," Norris said. He grasped George's hand with a firm grip. "I wish you the best of luck with your application." Norris was anxious that he had yet another task to complete before he could relax before his warm, cosy fire. He did not agree with Sir Henry's decision to promote George to senior assistant, and found it extremely irritating that such an important position was being given for political consideration to someone so unqualified. Still, he had kept his most serious reservations to himself.

"I just wanted you to know how much I appreciate it, especially considering our past disagreements," George added.

"Think nothing of it. Besides, a little friction between colleagues benefits true scholarship. It stimulates a higher quality of work."

"Dr. Birch," said Rawlinson.

"Yes, Sir Henry?"

"George is rather unsettled by the loss of his friend and colleague. I have given him the remainder of the week off."

"Very well," Birch agreed. "There is little that requires his attention this week."

"Thank you sir. There should be a train to Kentish Town soon. I must purchase my ticket. Good day, Sir Henry, Dr. Birch, and Mr. Norris," George said.

"We shall see you next week, George," said Birch.

"My carriage is waiting," announced Rawlinson. "May I offer you both a lift?"

"Thank you, Sir Henry." responded Birch, without a moment's hesitation. "That would be most welcome."

"I have an errand this afternoon that might take some time. I shall find a cab," said Norris. "An update to my dictionary will be ready for your inspection very soon, Sir Henry."

"Thank you, Edwin. I look forward to seeing it."

"Good day to you, Mr. Norris," said Birch.

Turning his collar up, Norris watched his two colleagues climb into Rawlinson's carriage and drive away. Spotting a cab approaching from the distance, he hailed it with his umbrella. The driver pulled in his horse and Norris stepped eagerly into the street. As the driver leaned forward, gold specks in the unusual ring on his hand reflected the station lights. The horse lunged forward as the driver violently lashed its hindquarters. Passers-by looked on in horror as the old man was crushed beneath the clatter of hooves and wheels. The cab did not slow down, but vanished into the murk of the wet London day.

"How brutal!" exclaimed a red-faced, middle-aged man, pausing in the act of climbing into his carriage. "This poor chap needs a doctor, quickly. Help me get him into the carriage."

"I am a medical student, sir." proclaimed a voice from the gathering crowd, "Perhaps, I can help."

"Do hurry then." The gentleman barked, "This poor fellow is badly injured."

Bleeding from multiple wounds, Norris was unable to move his leg. The kind strangers eased him into the carriage and remained with him until he was out of danger.

ઉଷ

CHAPTER 20

The Price of Success

Friday, 11 August 1871
Vine Pub, 86 Highgate Rd, London

You look like someone dug you up and warmed you over."

"I feel like it, too."

"Your hand's shaking so much, you're about to spill your ale."

"I've got to get away, Tommy. I've overworked myself," George said. He rubbed his forehead. "I'm sick of it. I can't do it anymore. I've been working for more than six months without a day's rest. I'm all broke down."

"Tell 'em you're staying home until you're better," Tommy suggested. "What good'll you be to 'em dead?" He had never seen George so thin. Dark shadows encircled his blood-shot eyes.

"I wrote to Mr. Talbot that I've small chance of getting the rest I need, as I have a large family and little means. He must have sent some extra funds, 'cause Dr. Birch gave me leave with a bonus for a vacation at the seaside. Whatever I do, it's never enough. The third volume of the *Cuneiform Inscriptions* is out. I finished the Assurbanipal and had copies of the sheets sent to Talbot. I got the syllabary set up in type, and had commenced to correcting it when I fell ill. I cannot bring myself to touch it anymore, so they probably will have to publish the Assurbanipal without it. Talbot and Bosanquet are paying for the publication, and it's not cheap, but just the thought of looking at another cuneiform makes me feel sick to my stomach." George finished half of his mug—it helped to calm the tremors.

"Mr. Birch is worried that this 'nervous debilitation,' as he calls it, might ruin my health all together. If he really wanted me to get better, he'd stop all the criticism." George buried his fingers in his thick chestnut hair. "There is always someone questioning my work and asking on what authority I've based my readings."

"Who's criticizing you?" Tommy's voice turned metallic. "Is it that Mr. Norris, what's saying things behind your back again?"

"No, no. He's been less of a bother since his accident," George said. "He suffers from some paralytic seizures and hardly ever gets out these days. Besides, he's so old that he probably won't be around much longer. Oppert's the main problem. He didn't like it that his brother's application was turned down. Birch told him that he was too old," George chuckled. "He's only two years older than me." Leaning forward, he added, "That shows you how powerful Sir Henry is."

"Oppert?" Tommy inquired.

"Yes, I told you about him before. He's the Jew working for the French museum."

"Right, I remember. Yeah…Oppert." Tommy said. His face was filled with pity. "So now he's taking his pound of flesh from your thin bones."

"I don't know, what I'll do, Tommy. These publications are important, but what I really need is a new discovery—something that'll really shake things up." George massaged his scalp. "If only my head would stop pounding." He looked sideways at his old friend. "Let's talk about something else," he said. "What's new with you, Tommy?"

"I'm doing alright. I've got some really nice girls working for me. There's this one—she's a beauty. The gents'll pay whatever she asks. But I've got worries too. I lost one to the pox last week. It's really bad right now. The pox is taking its toll in our part of London. Now I've another one that I'm worried about. I really hope she'll pull through without any scarring. She's really good."

"I guess there's always something to worry about, isn't there?"

"You're right there, George. Being a businessman, I have to agree with you on that one." Tommy said. He finished his drink. "So, who's the fella we're supposed to be meeting 'ere today?"

"Mr. Robert Hamilton Lang, Esquire and Her Majesty's Consul to Cyprus, wants to introduce a young scholar to me. He was so insistent that I found it impossible to put him off."

"Is that them?" Tommy asked.

"Yes. That's Lang," George replied.

"I'd best be going."

"Don't go far, Tommy," George requested. "I'm so exhausted, I'll probably need your help getting home tonight."

"I'll just be over here at the bar."

"Good. Here, they're coming over."

George stood up and forced a warm and cheerful smile. "Mr. Lang, good evening," He said.

"Mr. Smith, it is so good of you to meet with us this evening. May I introduce Demitris Yevani." The young man's palms were sweaty. His large, dark eyes were full of gratitude. "Demitris, this is Mr. George Smith of the British Museum's Department of Oriental Antiquities."

"Thank you, Mr. Smith, it is good meeting you," said Yevani with a heavy accent.

"It is my pleasure, Mr. Yevani," George said. As the two men took their seats, George noticed the box under Yevani's arm.

"Mr. Smith, I realize that you are leaving on a vacation in the morning," stated Lang, "and would I not have been so persistent if this were not a matter of the utmost importance."

"Would you gents like something to drink?" asked a shapely young woman with fiery red hair. At first, George thought that the waitress had a tulip in her mouth, but then he realized that it was just her bright lip rouge.

"Yes, I'll have a nice mug of your best ale, but my friend here would prefer red wine." Lang said. He glanced at his young friend, who nodded enthusiastically. An intense magnetism held Yevani's gaze until the girl disappeared behind the kitchen doors. This did not escape Tommy Rigger's hawkish eye. He slipped into the kitchen.

"Mable." He motioned for her to come over.

"What is it Tommy, luv?" she asked.

"The young stranger has a fancy for ya," Tommy said. He caressed her neck. "Be nice and give 'im a sweet smile."

"Sure, Tommy. I kind of fancy 'im meself, I must say."

"That's me girl," Tommy said. He returned to his place at the bar and waited for George.

"I do not wish to take too much of your time, Mr. Smith," Lang said. "You must have much to do in preparation for you journey. You did say that you were leaving for the seaside early tomorrow, didn't you?"

"Yes, Mr. Lang, quite early." George had reached the end of his patience and was on the verge of walking out. Lang nodded to Yevani, who opened the box, unwrapped an ancient tablet, and handed the precious object to George.

George's head was throbbing, and several times he had to force his eyes to focus. He was familiar with the Phoenician characters, but the others were strange. Then he remembered that Rawlinson had showed him a few samples of these enigmatic Cypriote symbols.

"Mr. Yevani," announced Lang, "claims to have decoded the ancient Cypriote script." Yevani nodded emphatically. "Of course, I am not an expert in ancient languages as you are, Mr. Smith," he added. Lang paused, watching every move that George made. "He is in need of your assistance in publishing his research. He has devoted many years of intense effort to this project."

"Yes, yes I understand. He wishes to publish his discovery."

"I…to be…help my family, my wife, my children," said Yevani, struggling with the English.

"At which university does Mr. Yevani study?" George asked.

"Well, that is the reason he was so eager to meet with you, Mr. Smith. Mr. Yevani, like yourself, lacked the resources for an advanced education."

"University, much money." Yevani shook his head with a woe-begotten expression.

"However, the young man is really quite clever. He is fluent in Greek, Turkish, Hebrew, Arabic, and other regional dialects. As a matter of fact, he was employed by our embassy as an interpreter. Last month, he brought this artifact to my office. He claims that this is a bilingual Phoenician and Cypriote inscription, and that this is the key."

"Yes, well, Mr. Lang, thank you for bringing this remarkable inscription and Mr. Yevani's interesting work to my attention," George said. "Has he completed a comprehensive dissertation on the subject?" Yevani looked confused, and Mr. Lang translated George's question. Yevani replied with enthusiastic hand motions.

The waitress arrived with their drinks. The young Cypriote again admired the finer qualities of the young woman.

"He has written it in his native language. I have agreed to assist with a translation into English, on the condition that you are interested in aiding with the final publication," said Lang.

"If his exposition is sound, I shall be most happy to assist Mr. Yevani in publishing his findings," said George. "How long will it take you to complete the translation?"

"Two or three weeks should be long enough. I do have other obligations, you understand."

"Yes, of course," George said. He was quiet for a few minutes. "Where is he staying while in London?" He motioned to Tommy, who walked cautiously over to them.

"Mr. Lang, may I introduce Mr. Rigger, an old acquaintance of mine," he said. The men exchanged greetings.

"He has rented a room; but, I must say that it is not very comfortable, and in my opinion a long stay is beyond his means.

"Mr. Yevani may stay in my home while we are away. It is a comfortable house in a pleasant and quiet neighborhood, very conducive to work. I'll return in a couple of weeks to check on your progress, and I will be happy to critique the work before publication." Lang translated the offer. Yevani appeared confused. He thanked George profusely, but indicated that he could not impose.

"Tommy, I would like for you to watch out for Mr. Yevani," said George. "Make sure that his needs are met. I'll settle any expenses with you when I return."

"No, no, Mr. Smith, really, you are too generous." Lang said. He paused to explain the magnanimity of their host to Yevani, who agreed completely.

"I really do insist, gentlemen," George said. "I consider this discovery to be of the utmost importance." George turned to Tommy and continued his instructions: "He is to be my guest until their business here is completed. Do you understand, Tommy?"

"Yes, Mr. Smith. I understand completely, sir," said Tommy.

"I look forward to reading your paper, Mr. Yevani," George said.

"Thank you, sir. This good you, Mr. Smith." Yevani's eyes filled with tears as he continued to praise George in his native tongue.

"My house is not far. Are you familiar with this area of London, Mr. Lang?"

"Somewhat, Mr. Smith."

"It's just down Kentish, west on Prince of Wales, and then south on Crogsland Road. The house is number fifty." George placed his hand on Tommy's shoulder. "Would you mind showing these gentlemen the way at, shall we say, noon tomorrow, Tommy?"

"It would be my pleasure, Mr. Smith."

"I shall see my family off early and show you about the property before joining them."

"Mr. Smith, we are at a complete loss for words to express our gratitude," said Lang.

"It is nothing more than a simple gesture of Christian charity, sirs," George said. His strength began to fade. "It has been a very long day, gentlemen," he said, "and if you don't mind, I think that I shall retire now. It was a pleasure to meet you both, Mr. Lang, Mr. Yevani."

"Good night, Mr. Smith and again, thank you," said Lang.

"God bless you, Mr. Smith," said Yevani.

"Tommy, if you would walk with me while I catch a cab," George requested.

"Certainly, Mr. Smith," said Tommy.

ঙ্ক

CHAPTER 21

Cypriote Inscriptions

Wednesday, 20 September 1871
Margate Beach, Kent

I am tired of washing sand out of the children's hair every night," said Mary. "When are we going home, George?"

A seagull screamed and circled around the beach.

"Not yet. Perhaps in another week," George replied.

"Laddie! Fetch it, boy!" shouted Fred. The ball bounced high, and the black and white collie twisted and jumped after it.

"You don't even know how to throw it. Look, it went over the edge," said Charlie.

"Laddie can find it. He's the smartest dog in England!" Fred shouted at his older brother and ran down the promenade after the dog.

"Charlie, go after him." called Mary to her eldest son. "We're turning back to the house in a minute." Noting that the wind had picked up and clouds were gathering, she turned again to her husband. "The summer is over, George," she said, "and it's turning colder. Charlie should be at school. He's nearly eight. His education is important."

Despite their growing family, Mary had not lost her slender figure. She was a striking sight strolling along in a bright green and grey seaside dress with elaborately draped overskirts supported by a stylish bustle.

"I know. I sent a letter to Talbot on Monday asking if he could suggest a good public school," George replied. "For now, he must continue with the tutor."

"Mrs. Smith," interrupted the maid, "See what our little Cissy can do." The tiny girl skipped a few steps.

"Wonderful, Cissy." Mary and George stopped walking to applaud their daughter. "You did that so well."

"You are adorable. Give Maria a big kiss." The young girl scooped the child into her arms and Cissy pressed her rose petal lips on her cheek. "Such a sweet kiss," Maria exclaimed. Little Cissy chattered on while Maria carried her and nodded approval to her countless observations.

"Madame," called the housekeeper from a few paces behind them, "little Tuppence is sound asleep in his carriage, and the wind is getting stronger. May I take him back to the house now?"

"Yes, Mrs. Barnard. That probably would be best. The baby is also asleep." Mary spread the extra blanket over the tiny form of the newest member of their family. "George, please call the boys. I'll take Bertie's perambulator. Those clouds are disturbing," she added nervously surveying the sky. "Maria, you go on ahead with Mrs. Barnard and see if Cissy is ready for a nap."

"Yes, mum."

The maid's long braids bobbed as she skipped after the prim and proper Mrs. Barnard.

George moved quickly to the sea wall and called his sons. They made an inspiring picture—strong, tanned limbs, rosy cheeks, and tousled brown hair flying before the teal grey sea. Sand scattered from their shoes as the boys ran to him. He held out his arms and the boys tackled him around the waist. George lost his footing and, laughing, all three tumbled over. With one under each arm, George started back to their rented house. They are worth it, thought George. There was nothing that he would not do to give them the life they deserved.

The boys raced into the house, slamming the door behind them. They were promptly shushed.

"Go upstairs and be quiet about it. Cissie's asleep," their mother demanded from the parlour door.

"Why are they always frowning and moaning about silly things?" complained Charlie as their mother smiled after them. "'Your faces are dirty.' 'Your shoes are full of sand.'"

"'You need another bath.' 'Pick up your toys.'" piped Fred.

"Then they don't understand why we stay outside as late as we can."

Charlie threw his hands in the air in dismay.

"Go on upstairs, boys, and wash before dinner," George said as he entered holding a package. Mary reappeared. "We have a guest for dinner, Mary," he added.

"Well, if it isn't Tommy. It's good to see you," greeted Mary.

"No, no, I couldn't impose. I'll get the next train back to London," Tommy said.

"Nonsense, Tommy. Seeing how far you've come, we insist that you stay. George, please take Tommy to the parlour. I'll tell the maid to set another place for dinner."

"You're a lucky man, George Smith, to 'ave found a fine wife like your Mary," Tommy said.

"Yes, but she can be hard-headed at times," said George. "And I can tell you now that she's not going to like this."

George patted Tommy on his back. "Come on, now, I'm sure that we can find a little whiskey around here somewhere." They had just sat down with the drinks when Mary entered and closed the doors behind her.

"So what's the news from London, Tommy?" she asked. She sat on the high-backed sofa with her hands crossed on her lap. George offered her his glass.

"What is this? I have a four month-old baby, and you're offering me whiskey?" Mary said. George knew that she did not drink when nursing.

"You might want that, Mrs. Smith," Tommy said. His face was solemn.

"Mary," George said gingerly, "Tommy's brought some very sad and rather disturbing news."

"What's happened?"

"I told you that a young scholar has been staying in our house while we are on holiday." George stared into his glass, searching for the best words.

"Well, don't stop now," Mary demanded. "I'm tired of all of this secrecy, George Smith. Tell me what's going on."

"He's dead," said Tommy.

"What? The man died in my house? When?" Mary asked.

"Last night at about ten o'clock, I believe."

"Tommy, you didn't!" Mary gasped. "Oh my God, not in my own home."

"I didn't do nothing, Missis!" He shouted back. George didn't like the look on Tommy's face.

"Tommy, it's alright," he said. "She didn't mean it the way it sounded."

"It was the pox what got him!" Tommy sat his glass down. "He died of the smallpox, he did." He put his fist on his hip and glared at Mary. "He first got the fever and chills around the first of the month. No one thought anything of it.

It weren't nothin' more than a bit of a headache and being sick. By the Wednesday, the fever was gone, but then the next day he said his tongue was hurtin. Mabel said his mouth was covered with big red spots. Come Friday, it'd started on his forehead, an' over the next couple of days, the spots were all over him—face, chest, arms and legs—was speckled red all over. He seemed strong enough, and we thought he'd get over it, but then, this pox weren't nothing like any I'd seen before. The sores didn't rise up all filled with pus, like most do. No, these was flat and soft, like a nice velvet cap. The whole time he was ranting and raving in his own funny language. This morning, he was dead. So you see, it was the pox, and nothing else, little lady." Tommy picked up his glass and took a deep swig of his drink.

It took a minute for Mary to take it in. She turned slowly to her husband.

"Are you telling me that you brought smallpox into the house where our babies sleep?!" she cried.

"Now, Mary, that's the reason I didn't say anything before. I didn't want to worry you. We'll have the house scrubbed top to bottom before you and the children get there."

"I can't believe this! My God...George Smith, what were you thinking? You brought a disease-ridden stranger into my home. And who's this Mabel?"

"She's just a housekeeper. She only came in once a week," George lied.

"You kept all of this from me 'cause you knew, yes, you knew what I'd say. Dear Lord, what a stupid thing! I thought you had more sense than that."

"Now Mary, calm down. It'll be fine. He was only in the guest room. I'll have the Public Disinfectors in. They only charge sixpence a hour."

"You'll have them burn everything that's in that room," she said, "and you…" she shook her finger in Tommy's face. "I know you're in on this, too. Don't you think for one minute that you'll fox your way out of it. You'll help replace the furniture out of your own pocket, you will."

"Yes, mum," muttered Tommy.

"And take that ring off," she added. "I told you before that I don't ever want to see it again. Don't you ever come around here wearing his ring again!" Mary stormed out of the room.

Tommy reached for the bottle and poured himself a large drink. He lifted his glass, but stopped, took off the ring and slipped it into his pocket.

"I told you she wouldn't like it," George said. He picked up the package and untied the string. He began to read the enclosed letter.

"What's it say?"

"It says that he found the 'Rosetta Stone' for the ancient Cypriote script on a bilingual Phoenician and Cypriote inscription, and that the script is based on a syllabary of about fifty characters, not a true alphabet. This is interesting—each consonant has about three forms."

"Now that's exactly what I always thought, only I never got round to putting it in writing," Tommy laughed, and drank a little more. Just then, the door opened and Mary stomped up to George.

"What's that?" she said, pointing to the package as she crossed the room. "It's his work, isn't it? You said that he was a scholar. That's his work. It's got the pox on it, too, and I'm going to burn it now." She tried to grab it, but George held her wrist.

"I can't let you do that, Mary," he said.

"Let me be, George. It's diseased, and I'll not have it making my babies sick."

"It's not in the Greek's handwriting," said Tommy.

"Cypriote," corrected George.

"Who cares!" shouted Tommy. "I know for a fact it was all written by that Mr. Lang. When he fell ill, Lang copied the bloke's work."

"I don't care," Mary said. "Maybe this Lang is sick right now. Let go of my arm, George. I'm burning it!"

"No you're not, Mary. This is going to pay for Charlie's school, or at least a good part it. We're going to squeeze every penny we can out of it."

She tried to break away, and he jerked her up hard against his body. "Go back to the kitchen, Mary, and mind the dinner," he said. She had seen that look before, long ago, when Harris died. It sent a chill down her spine. She relaxed her arms. "Go on, now," he said, more gently. "Nobody's going to get sick. It's all done now."

"They'd better not, George. That's all I've got to say. There's nothing that's worth one of them getting sick," Mary said. She backed away, turned sharply, and closed the doors behind her.

"Yes, that's a fine wife you've got there," Tommy said, looking over George's shoulder.

"When you go back to London in the morning, get the disinfectors in to clean the place," George said. "I'll give you a note for Lang." He stopped reading and asked, "Lang's not sick, is he?"

"No," answered Tommy. "We both stayed away during the worst of it. I did lose the girl, though. She was a sweet one, George. It'll be hard to find another so eager to please. That's a real shame."

The door opened again. A remorseful Mary walked slowly up to them.

"I probably should apologise for my outburst. This got me so upset. What do you intend to do, George?"

"I'll rewrite the paper in my own hand. Tommy's going to take care of the house, right Tommy?"

"That's right, Mary. I'll be up there early tomorrow. I'll go tonight, if you want."

"No," she said. "You have dinner and rest in the guest room tonight. Tomorrow will be fine."

"Lang and I will present the paper together at the next Society meeting," George replied, "but I get credit for the discovery and will have first publication rights."

"I don't like this, George. I don't like anything about it," Mary said. He put his arms around her, and she rested her head on his shoulder.

"The rest of this year is going to be busy," George said. "I've got this paper, and then a pamphlet on the reign of Sennacherib with a list of the characters of the Assyrian syllabary to publish. As soon as those are out, I'll start another on the early history of Babylonia."

"Now I wish that we could stay on here," she said. "At least we've had some time together this summer."

"We'll have plenty of good times together," George reassured her. "I promise to make more time for you and the children from now on."

ঙ৪ঌ

CHAPTER 22

An Epic Illusion

Thursday, 28 November 1872
British Museum, Great Russell Street, London

"Did you find the tablets you requested, Mr. Talbot? Was everything satisfactory?"

"Yes, George. They were excellent," Talbot replied. George's legs twitched with the effort of taking small steps as he escorted the elderly gentleman to the workroom. Talbot was moving more slowly than usual this morning,

"I commend you, young man," Talbot said. "You are like the magician in a children's story. As if by magic, you have transformed a mountain of rubble into a well-organised, catalogued collection and created order from chaos. It is so refreshing to request a tablet and actually have it located and made ready for inspection within a decent length of time."

"Thank you, sir, but if this was by magic, it was the world's most time-consuming magic," George replied. "It has taken me nearly twelve years to get this far. When I see how much still remains to be done, I wish I had a magician's wand."

"You should know that your hard work and dedication are appreciated by all scholars," Talbot told him.

"Have you examined my Assurbanipal?" George asked.

"Yes, indeed. It was very well done. Perhaps there are parts that I would have translated a little differently, but overall it is a most excellent and valuable publication."

"In the preface, I acknowledge that I am entirely indebted to you and Mr. Bosanquet for the means of publishing it, and my pamphlet on the syllabary," George said. He braced Talbot's hand as they slowly descended the stairs.

"Did you know that poor Mr. Norris' condition has worsened?" Talbot asked.

"I'm afraid that I have been so busy that I hardly find time for my own family," George said. He glanced back down the hall. There was still no sign of Ready. "I heard that his family had taken him for a brief holiday a couple of months back, but know little else."

"He has suffered from a curious affliction of the nervous system since his accident. He is downcast that his declining health has now brought about a complete halt to his dictionary."

"I find it difficult to imagine Mr. Norris idle."

"There comes a point in every man's life when his body can no longer bear its burden. After all, Mr. Norris is seventy-seven years old. But then, the years are advancing on me as well."

"You, sir? Nonsense. I wish I had your vigour and wit," George said.

Talbot chuckled at the flattery.

"How is your health, George?" he asked. "You seem very nervous today. You have not been over-working yourself again, I trust?"

"No, my health is generally good, but I am somewhat irritated by the delays caused by Mr. Ready."

"Who?"

"Mr. Robert Ready, sir, the Museum's sigillarist," George explained. "He makes copies of coins, medals, seals and gems in our collections. You must remember him. He worked closely with Mr. Vaux until he left us."

"Oh yes, yes, Ready. Good man," said Talbot.

"He has very cleverly developed a process for removing mineral deposits from my tablets," George said.

"Excellent."

"I found a very curious inscription, but could read only a few lines. Most of it is encrusted with a thick, lime-like deposit. My misfortune is that Mr. Ready was away on private business, and he only returned this morning. I am very anxious to see the results."

"Ah, I see. Is that all that is troubling you, George?"

"Not entirely, sir. My petition to the Trustees for a grant to reopen the excavations near Mosul was turned down."

"I can see how that would be disappointing for you."

"They are of the opinion that we have more than enough Assyrian and Babylonian artefacts. Of course, I lack the means to finance my own expedition."

"That is not the reason," Talbot remarked in a confidential tone. "It is because you have made yourself indispensible. Naturally, they would prefer that you remain safe at home instead of braving the dangers of a hostile land. As you see, you have only yourself to blame for this." Talbot was relieved to have finally reached the main floor.

"I am certain that that is Sir Henry's sentiment," George replied. "He will hear nothing of it. I had hoped that my recent publications and success at decoding the Cypriote syllabary would have convinced them." George checked the time and re-wound his watch. "But I shall not give up. I am still searching for something that will excite them and bring about a reversal of this decision."

"You are a young man and, understandably, yearn for the opportunity to test your mettle, but I must side with Sir Henry. You are much too valuable, George, for us to take such a risk." The two men shuffled across the polished tiles toward the Great Russell Street entrance.

"I could not have published the contents of either of my tablets without your assistance." Talbot's face shone with sincere affection as he continued. "Perhaps it was Dr. Oppert who first suggested that the solar eclipse of June of 661BC might match the one recorded in my historical tablet. However, it was you who contacted the Royal Observatory, obtained the confirmation, and thus established the chronology of the later kings of Assyria. Also, your remarkable talent for discovery provided us with a more perfect copy of my Sargon tablet. Without those lines, we would not have known of the amazing parallels between the birth of Sargon and the much later story of the infant Moses. I am deeply indebted to you for your invaluable assistance, George, and would be at a great disadvantage without it. Do you have any new projects under way?"

"I have a book on the early Babylonian inscriptions going to press now," George said. "I am considering giving up publishing. Our customary lithography is so expensive."

"May I recommend that future publications be executed by means of photography instead of lithography," Talbot suggested. "It is much cheaper. Also, the photo is less troublesome, as the treatment for photographic paper is less expensive than that of the lithographic paper."

"Are the photographed pages as clear?" George asked.

"I think that you will be pleased by our most recent improvements," Talbot replied.

"I shall discuss the possibility with Mr. Thompson."

"Who?"

"Stephen Thompson is the Museum's photographer. He did an impressive series of photographs of your Assyrian marbles."

"Did I hear my name being taken in vain?" said a new voice.

"Well, speak of the Devil, and he doth appear,'" George greeted his friend.

"You arrived just in time, Mr. Thompson," added Talbot. "I would like to discuss the creation of photo-lithographs for future cuneiform productions. I am certain that, together, we can resolve the major difficulties. But it is getting late. I must meet my solicitor about some mundane matter." Talbot placed his hat with care on his bald head. "Then, I am having dinner with Mr. Bosanquet," he continued. "He asked me to join him for a concert afterwards, but I am afraid that my gout is acting up again. Well, I must not be late."

"We shall speak later about the photo-lithography, sir," said Thompson as he held the door for Talbot.

"I look forward to it. Well, good day, Mr. Thompson, Mr. Smith."

"Good day, Mr. Talbot," George said. He waited until the door closed. His hand fluttered over his waistcoat until he found his watch. "Thank God," he said. "It took forever for him to leave." He turned on his heel and dashed up the stairs.

"Why the rush?" called Thompson, following him up the steps.

"I am about to go out of my mind waiting on Ready to remove the mineral deposits on that tablet," George explained.

☙❧

He opened the door to the second-floor workroom. Two students from Oxford were discussing a recent find. Sitting near them was a youth, about fifteen years old, who was painstakingly copying a cuneiform text with pen on paper.

"Who is the boy?" asked Thompson.

"He is my new apprentice, Ernest Budge," George said.

"Another prodigy like yourself?"

"We hope he will prove to be. The curious similarities of our backgrounds caused Birch to introduce him to me."

"Really?"

"Yes," George said. "It seems that Ernest also showed an early keen interest in ancient languages. He also was forced to abandon his education prematurely, but I was fourteen when this happened to me, while he was only twelve. Unlike me, though, he had the good fortune to find a tutor. A certain Mr. Charles Seeger has taught him the basics of Hebrew and Syriac for the past three years. About a week ago, Dr. Birch brought the tutor and the boy into my office."

George began to sort some fragments at the end of the table. Thompson watched him, amazed by his quick eye and agile hands. The door opened. Ready entered like a priest carrying a votive offering. George took the tablet from Ready and rushed to the window. Their eyes burned into his back. He leaned slightly forward into the light, surreptitiously removed a copy from inside his jacket, and slipped the original into his trousers' pocket. Lifting the "corrected" piece near the polished pane, he examined it in the afternoon light.

"I found it!" shouted George.

George filled the room with a loud, ecstatic cry. Placing the fragment on the table, he then shocked everyone by stripping off his jacket, waistcoat, and shirt. Racing about, he swung his garments over his head and then flung them about the room, all the while whooping at the top of his lungs. Everyone thought that he had gone quite mad.

"George. George, calm down, man!" called Thompson. Taking George by the arm, he managed to get him to stop and take in a few deep breaths. "What's wrong with you, man?" Thompson asked.

"I've found it!" George panted. "I found the Babylonian account of the Great Flood!" George broke the silence that followed with another exultant cry.

"What does it say? Read it to us," demanded Thompson. George's hands trembled and his voice cracked. He cleared his throat and began:

"For six days and nights,
The wind, the storm raged, and the cyclone overwhelmed the land.
When the seventh day came, the cyclone ceased, the storm and battle which had fought
like an army.
The sea became quiet, the grievous wind went down, the cyclone ceased.
I looked on the day and voices were stilled,
And all mankind was turned into mud,
The land had been laid flat like a terrace.
I opened the air-hole and the light fell upon my cheek,
I bowed myself, I sat down, I cried,
My tears poured down over my cheeks.
I looked over the quarters of the world, the limits of ocean.
At twelve points islands appeared.
The ship grounded on the mountain of Nisir.
The mountain of Nisir held the ship, it let it not move.

The first day, the second day, the mountain of Nisir held the ship and let it not move.

The third day, the fourth day, the mountain of Nisir held the ship and let it not move.

The fifth day, the sixth day, the mountain of Nisir held the ship and let it not move.

When the seventh day had come
I brought out a dove and let her go free.
The dove flew away and came back;
Because she had no place to alight she came back.
I brought out a swallow and let her go free.
The swallow flew away and came back;
Because she had no place to alight she came back.
I brought out a raven and let her go free.
The raven flew away, she saw the sinking waters.
She ate, she waded, she rose, and she came not back.

Then I brought all out to the four winds and made a sacrifice;

I set out an offering on the peak of the mountain.
Seven by seven I set out the vessels,
Under them I piled reeds, cedarwood and myrtle.
The gods smelt the savour,
The gods smelt the sweet savour.

The gods gathered together like flies over him that sacrificed."

"I am the first man to read this," George panted. "For more than two thousand years, this has lain in oblivion…until this moment."

He searched each face for the least hint of doubt, but found no unbelievers present.

"How amazing," marvelled Thompson.

"I have been collecting the fragments for several months in the hope of confirming my expectations," George added.

"Amazing!"

"Yet there are pieces still missing," George said, "and I shall find those fragments, even if I must journey to the ends of the earth."

☙❧

CHAPTER 23

Return to Nineveh

Wednesday, 14 May 1873
Tel Kouyunjik, Turkish Arabia (Iraq)

George discovered that the chill of the night burns away early in Mosul. The days were already as hot as August in London. Yet this morning the heat and flies were not his only annoyance. He must have all correspondences completed and properly addressed within an hour. The agent was anxious to leave for Constantinople and, of course, would expect his pay in advance. Since there was no direct post between Mesopotamia and England, this was the only means of communication with his beloved family.

He had dreamed of this journey for as long as he could remember. Layard and Rawlinson had written of the hardships, but like all dreamers, George had read the stories as adventures. The reality of saddle sores, vicious insects, and strange food was less romantic. Now he reread those worn copies of Layard's experiences with intense interest.

Birch had encouraged him, and Layard's advice had proven invaluable in dealing with the workmen and daily problems. Rawlinson, on the other hand, had objected to George's plan from the beginning. He had even tried to block permission for his leave of absence. Birch had tried to bypass Rawlinson and did not notify him of the meeting, but he showed up regardless and had presented a serious obstacle. Still, all had gone according to plan.

George paused to work out the wording of the next sentence. Thoughts of Mary overwhelmed him and for several precious moments he could not write a word. He forced himself to concentrate. He would be ready to leave within a few weeks, and by mid-July, he would be home with her and his darling family.

Contemplating his closing words, George reached for his small porcelain cup. He gazed at the expansive, pale blue sky beckoning to him through the window. Bringing the warm cup to his lips, he thought about the excavation and knew that he should have been there an hour ago. The workers were a lazy lot. George took a deep swig of the sweet brew. His mouth filled with the thick, bitter sediment that the locals called "mud." Brown droplets sprayed across the table. A stream of curses was drowned in hasty gulps of water. He'd never get used to Turkish coffee.

After the agent departed, George went to his trunk and removed his extra pair of boots. Reaching deep inside, he retrieved two small tablets. The first was of baked clay. The other was of stone. Smiling with satisfaction, George closed the trunk. He stood near the window, admiring the quality of his craftsmanship in the intense sunlight. George picked up his jacket and slipped the clay tablet into his right pocket. The heavier shield shaped was of stone, about the size of his hand, and roughly an inch thick. Mary had skilfully adjusted the inner jacket pocket for a perfect fit. He glanced again at the last two lines of the Assyrian kings' lists. These additions would provide support for Sir Henry's theories. George hoped it would soothe his benefactor's anger for having undertaken this expedition.

Though the gritty glass, he saw his foreman running towards him. At least, the poor man thought he was running.

Toma wheezed and coughed, and at last brought his mountain of flesh to a jiggling halt before George's door. This unfortunate fellow was one of the few amusements that this dismal place afforded him. Leaning against the wall, Toma gasped for air while dripping sweat on the tender vegetation.

"Yes, Toma, what is it?" George asked.

"A man…asking for you…" Toma puffed.

"A man? What man? Did you get his name?" George asked. "Well, speak up."

"Name…Kerr…Mr. Charles Kerr." Toma felt faint. "Water… Maybe water for Toma, sir?"

"Certainly," George said. He felt bad. He should have offered this simple hospitality to his worker before it was requested.

"Here." He plunged the dipper into the pail and filled a mug. Toma's hand was shaking so much that George brought him a chair. What could he do? The old man was practically useless, but it would be heartless to dismiss him.

"Where did you see Charles Kerr?" George asked.

"Near souq," Toma managed, between gulps of water.

George shook his head. How could a man let himself get so obese?

"I need to lock up now, Toma, but take the chair to the shade and catch your breath before returning to work. I can't pay you for work left undone." George locked the door. He gave Toma the customary reward of two coins for a bearer of good tidings and left him to search for Kerr.

ঙ্গ

Weaving through the narrow, crowded streets of Mosul was always a mixed experience for George. It was, in some ways, exhilarating to view firsthand the exotic customs of the East. On the other hand, there was the inescapable foulness of a hundred generations packed into a limited space. George had not gone far when he saw his former travelling companion and countryman strolling among the booths admiring the local wares.

"Charles," he called.

"There you are, George," said Kerr. "You're a difficult man to find." They shook hands and asked after each other's health.

"Shall we have a little something to eat?" asked George.

"A little something won't do. I'm famished," countered Charles. They sat at a small family café. The food was spicy and the stories brisk.

"Did you complete your business in Aleppo?" George asked.

"Yes," said Charles. He took another bite of his shawarma. "Don't you want some?" he asked.

"No, no, it doesn't sit well on my stomach," George explained.

"I placed the orders and telegraphed the details to my uncle in London," Kerr said. He finished his meal and added, "I also told him that I had had the good fortune of travelling with the world-renowned Assyriologist, Mr George Smith."

"World-renowned?" George blushed. "I was simply fortunate to find employment with our great museum."

"You are much too modest, George," said Kerr. "You are the only Englishman in history whose lecture was attended by a sitting Prime Minister."

"Mr. Gladstone has a keener interest in our work than most Prime Ministers. He has served three terms as Chancellor of the Exchequer, and the holder of that post also sits on the Board of Trustees for the British Museum," George said, smiling sheepishly. "If you only knew how tedious and boring my work really is, you would not be so impressed."

"Could you show it to me?" asked Kerr. "Your work, I mean."

"Of course, but I warn you that you will probably be bored stiff after a few minutes."

"All the better. I could use a good night's rest." Kerr finished his tea. "How are your excavations coming along?" he asked.

"Excellent," George replied. "We are making wonderful progress, considering the late start. I left London on the twentieth of January. Too much time was lost waiting for the firman. Even with the efforts of Lord Granville, it took ten weeks of bickering with thick-headed native officials before I actually obtained this essential travel authorisation and permission to begin my work."

"My uncle arranged mine," stated Kerr.

"The authorities are more suspicious of excavations than of business transactions. They worry that we are digging for gold." George looked exasperated. "We have very different definitions of treasure. So, we didn't start excavating at Nimrod until the ninth of April. Can you believe it? Ten full weeks! But since then, things have gone well. I spent a month there, closed it, and then started digging trenches here a week ago."

"I would love to see the excavation site; that is, if it is permitted."

"If I say it is permissible, then it is," said George with a cocky smile. "If we leave now, we should be able to make it to Kouyunjik and back before dark."

"I am ready as soon as I can leave my luggage," replied Kerr.

"Excellent. We'll go back to my lodging and arrange fresh horses." George took out his handkerchief and wiped his brow. The afternoon was pleasant by the locals' estimation, but hot for the Englishmen.

ଓଃଛ

After freeing themselves from the twist and turns of the narrow town, they crossed an ancient bridge to the east side of the Tigris. The fat, murky river, well fed by mountain streams, laughed beneath the ancient bridge. George pointed out the Assyrian slabs that had been pillaged from the excavation to fortify it.

"And there is Nineveh," announced George.

Kerr stood to his full height in his stirrups to better survey the great mound of Kouyunjik.

"My God, what an enormous plateau!"

"The embankment is roughly fifty feet high," informed George.

"What is that encampment?" Kerr asked pointing to the right.

"That's the shanty-town where the workers live," answered George, "We'll have to leave our horses there." They rode on.

"What is that mob of natives?" Kerr was pointing to a large, disorganised gathering of excited tribesmen racing about the plain to their left on sleek steeds. Women and children followed at a distance, carrying all their goods and driving cattle before them. "They look menacing. Are you sure it is safe to be out here?"

"They're not interested in us, Charles. War is raging among the Arab tribes on the west side of the Tigris," George explained. "The Aneiza tribe, which occupies the desert between Aleppo and the Tigris, plundered a tribe named Abu Mohammed. The Aneiza were defeated and put to death with great cruelty. In revenge, their relatives attacked the area of Hammum Ali and plundered the flocks and herds of the Sammer Arabs. I'm surprised that you managed to make it here without incident."

"They must have had a lighter war schedule on the day I was travelling," joked Kerr. They spurred the horses to a loop.

Soon they reached the shabby village where dark-skinned children ran naked in the dusty street. Wrinkled and worn beyond their years, three women squatted on irregular stone steps cleaning hulls from rice on large tin platters. They stopped gossiping as the two foreigners dismounted. Lida instructed her grandson to call his uncle.

"It is sad to think that these are the descendants of such a great civilisation," murmured George confidentially, leaning towards his friend. Soon a slender youth ran up and, taking the reins, led the horses to grassy area.

The Englishmen walked toward the remains of the earth ramp, down which Layard and Hormuzd had slid massive monuments. Years of neglect has rendered it almost useless. Rain had cut deep jagged trenches down the incline and made it too dangerous to ascend on horseback.

"I had the workers cut steps in these rougher places," informed George, as they made their way up. "Otherwise the poor fools would have slipped and broken their necks retrieving the artefacts for me." As they reached the summit, a boy spotted them and ran shouting at the top of his voice across the uneven ground and disappeared into the dark mouth of a tunnel. A few minutes a large figure emerged.

"O Great Bey, you have arrived so soon!" shouted Toma. Down below, his sons rushed about in a panic. Stumbling over each other, one pulled at a basket of looted artefacts while the other urgently tried to cover it with handfuls of dust and rubble. Toma shouted instructions and two other cohorts joined them.

"Who is that fellow climbing from the pit?" asked Kerr

"That's Toma Shishman, better known as 'Fat' Toma for obvious reasons." George explained. "He's an old hand at these digs. He had been reduced in fortune and was anxious to serve me in the same capacity as he had for Layard and Rassam, and I reluctantly agreed. After I closed the excavations at Nimrod and arrived at Mosul last week, I was astonished to find that he had done nothing. His excuse was that the donkey on which he rode from Nimrod had shaken him so much in a fall that he had been ill ever since. So, I set to work myself, gathering men and preparing to begin the excavation. When he saw that I had engaged men without his help, he began to fear I might exclude him from the work. He immediately collected a suitable body of men and set them to work."

"Is this shaft all that there is to the excavations?" asked Kerr sounding somewhat disappointed.

"All of this area was once open and hundreds of workers dragged the great monuments up an earthen ramp that remains buried over there." George pointed to the area he knew only from old maps.

"That great pioneer, Mr. Layard, closed up the opening as well as he could, in order to protect the remaining artefacts. Rassam, who was taught by Layard, followed the same procedure. Here is where the more important sculptures had been discovered. It contains the remains of the southwest palace of Sennacherib, where Layard discovered the famous Lachish inscriptions. This is where I initially instructed Toma to begin digging.

"But recovering great monuments is not the object of my mission." he added. "I was sent to recover inscribed terra-cotta tablets. So on the ninth, we opened some trenches over there," George pointed to another site a short distance to their north-east, "in what was the south-eastern corner of the north palace, which was built by Assurbanipal and where Rassam discovered the great library." A digger pushed a wicker basket out of the hole George was indicating.

"We have come upon the Library," George explained, "but its final excavation cannot take place until the autumn. My plan is to return, gather a much larger labour force, and work through the winter."

Another man dragged himself from the hole and the two carried a heavy basket of debris towards the Englishmen. Toma had made his way to them by now.

"I have already discovered some very early Babylonian inscribed tablets." stated George, appearing pre-occupied. "Charles, why don't you start down into the excavation with Toma? I want to examine this new find. I'll follow in moment."

"Certainly, we'll wait for you below." Kerr, eager to walk through the ancient chambers, hurried off with the foreman.

The workers set the basket at George's feet. He motioned for them to return to the excavation. As they obeyed, he kneeled down and examined a few of the contents. It all looks like rubbish to George. He glanced over his shoulder to be certain that no one was watching him.

Kerr was looking down into the pit. He hesitated and then cautiously lowered himself onto a large stone fragment that had been wedged into the gap caused by years of erosion of the upper portion of the steps. His hand appeared over the rim of the pit and waved at George.

When they had all vanished into the gaping hole, George took the terra-cotta piece from his right pocket, found a safe place for it in the basket, and covered it with a broken cylinder. He hurried over to where his friend had descended.

Extra lanterns were stored on that first platform. George seized one and lit it. He leaned cautiously against the wall and found the first of the uneven steps, hewn more than two decades before for Layard.

The temperature dropped remarkably in the thick darkness. George was ecstatic. His sense of exhilaration was comparable only to the predawn descent down the servants' staircase after his first night with Mary.

He paused at a junction of two tunnels and heard Kerr sneeze down the one to his right. Hiding in the tunnel to left, Toma's eldest son held his breathe and prayed that George would not find him with the basket of looted artefacts.

The light from George's lantern flashed over a pile of ancient rubble of a collapsed wall. He found a convenient crevice in which to hide his stone engraving. George pressed dirt around the edges of the stone. Before departing for London, he would 'discover' it.

"Who's back there?" called Kerr. "Is that you, George?"

"Over here, Charles," he answered hurrying carefully down the tunnel to his right in the direction of the voices.

"My apologies: I'm easily distracted down here," explained George, as he caught up with the others. Kerr was noticeably relieved.

"Toma, lead the way," ordered George. There was not much to see at first. Then they reached a break in a wall and entered a labyrinth of crumbling tunnels. The air was stale and left a heavy, musty taste in the mouth.

When George's light had moved out of range, Toma's son opened the shutter of his own lantern. He was curious. Why had the Englishman paused there? What was he doing? It did not take long for him to retrieve the engraved stone and replace it with a worthless shard. He continued bragging the heavy basket deeper into the tunnel until he was certain it would not be spotted. Moments later he also joined the tour.

They entered a large chamber where great monumental slabs still graced the walls. Like an expert guide, George told fanciful stories that transformed the dusty, broken remains into a magnificent throne room where ambassadors from conquered kingdoms brought tribute to the fearsome warrior-kings. Kerr was enchanted.

"It is getting late," announced George. "We must make our way back to the surface."

Kerr agreed and anxiously searched for some familiar marker to the way out. George patted him on the shoulder.

"It's this way." he said with a smile.

Soon they re-emerged into the intense sunlight and warm, welcome breeze. George paused to give instructions Toma. The old scoundrel smiled meekly to his face, but mocked him in his heart. Kerr walked to the edge of the mound to take in the view of the Tigris valley below. George followed his lead.

"Some say that this was the Garden of Eden," Kerr noted.

"The Hebrew concept of Paradise was heretical in Babylon," explained George, "where another version prevailed. Snakes were excluded. I plan to publish a Babylonian account of the legend soon. It will be interesting when it's worked out."

"I would love to read it. Please let me know when it is available," Kerr said.

The Englishmen left the ancient plateau in high spirits. They spoke of important matters as they walked to where their horses were staked.

"What are they doing today?" Kerr inquired.

"Who?" George asked.

"Those great early discoverers."

"Mr. Layard is Her Majesty's Ambassador to Spain," George said. "Sir Henry Rawlinson's hands are so full of political business that he seldom has time to attend to matters at the Museum. He has left all but the most important decisions to me. Of course, I must obtain his approval before beginning any future editions. Mr. Norris died last December."

"Mr. Norris?" Kerr asked.

"You wouldn't know of him. He was one of many who assisted us on more mundane tasks."

"What of the French? I once heard that a Dr. Oppert made some important discoveries here."

"Yes, but his work was mainly to south, at the Babylonian ruins. They do have an interesting collection at the Louvre," George admitted. "I visited it on my way here. They needed help deciphering an obscure text. Dr. Oppert is, I was told, getting very blind. His eyes are very bad. His student, Mr. François Lenormant, has done excellent work with the Assyrian studies."

"How much longer will you be here?"

"My six-month leave of absence from the Museum will end in mid-July. Besides, the hot season will begin then, making excavation impossible. I've found some good pieces at the excavations and purchased more from the local dealers.

The Trustees should be pleased." As they mounted their horses, George pointed to the south-east.

"Would you like to see the Great Gateway?" he asked. "It was the main entrance to Nineveh."

"Most certainly!" Kerr said.

"On second thought, perhaps we should wait until tomorrow," George said. "The sun will set soon, and it would be dangerous to remain here after dark. We can't get there from here anyway, because a deep trench, halving it, is cut into the mound by a stream called the Khosr River. Early in the morning, when we reach the village, we'll ride south-east. There's another embankment to climb after that, and then we can take time to explore Nebbi Yunab, the tomb of Jonah. From there, is a short ride across the top of the mound to the eastern gate. It's a difficult climb down and then back up. It'll be more interesting and less time-consuming than to ride around the mound."

"It sounds like a wonderful outing. I'm looking forward to it," Kerr said, as they reached the bridge to Mosul.

☙❧

The return trip was uneventful. They turned the horses over to the stable keepers and returned to George's lodgings. It was dark by the time they reached the door. George was grateful for the large, waning, egg-shaped moon, which gave enough light for him to fit the key in its hole. Three large baskets of terracotta fragments blocked the doorway.

"Good, the workmen brought today's gleanings," he said.

George opened the door. He felt his way to the oil lantern, lit it, and set it on the table. The smell of sulphur lingered as the light filled the room. The two men pulled the baskets inside.

"You said that you wanted to see what I do at the Museum, Charles," George said. "Here, help me place some of these onto the table, and I'll show you." He took a small brush from the shelf and began cleaning a decent sized fragment. He made a quick inspection of the lines of odd wedge-shaped markings. "This is an excellently preserved deed for the transfer of property." Taking another, he added, "Good. This is another part of the Assyrian astronomical text."

"What will become of these artefacts?" Kerr inquired.

"At this point, they are the property of the *Daily Telegraph*," George replied, "but that is only a formality.

"The day after I read my paper on the Deluge," George continued, "Edwin Arnold, its editor, offered me 1000 guineas to find the missing fragment. Of course, this sum must cover all expenses for the journey and excavation. As part of the agreement, I was to write letters home giving the details of my travels and adventures, which they have been publishing. You are mentioned in several of them."

Kerr was mesmerised by the quick hands and keen eye of his host.

"All discoveries that I make are to be presented in the name of the *Daily Telegraph* to the British Museum," George continued. "So ultimately, these fragments will become part of our permanent collection."

George picked up the terracotta tablet that earlier he had retrieved from his boot and secreted at the excavation site. He looked it over with moderate interest. He examined it.

"This is amazing!" he said.

"What?" Charles tried to get a better look at the fragment.

"We've found it!"

"What is it?"

"The missing piece to the Babylonian Deluge story," George said. He gave the tablet another thorough brushing and, holding it near the lantern, began to read:

Izdubar said unto him, to Uta-Napishtim the remote,
I am looking at thee, Uta-Napishtim.
Thy person is not altered; even as am I so art thou.
Verily, nothing about thee is changed; even as am I so art thou.
A heart to do battle doth make thee complete,
Yet at rest thou dost lie upon thy back.
How then hast thou stood the company of the gods and sought life?
Uta-Napishtim said unto him, to Izdubar:
I will reveal unto thee, O Izdubar, a hidden mystery,
And a secret matter of the gods I will declare unto thee.
Shurippak, a city which thou thyself knowest,
On the river Puratti is situated,
That city is old; and the gods are within it
Their hearts induced the great gods to make a great storm.
There was their father Anu,
Their counsellor, the warrior Enlil,
Their messenger, En-Urta.

"This is phenomenal!" exclaimed Kerr. "But please, explain what it means."

"Uta-Napishtim was the Babylonian Noah," George said. "The river Puratti is the Euphrates. The god Ea informed this devoted worshipper that the gods had decided to destroy all of mankind with a great flood. He instructed Uta-Napishtim to dismantle his house of reeds and build a great ship. Many of the details match those of the Biblical Flood, including his opening the window, releasing the birds, and sacrificing to his god afterwards. Yet, there are important differences between the two stories. Since the Babylonian version is much older, it is more authentic." George kissed the precious fragment. "But, unlike poor Noah, Uta-Napishtim was rewarded with immortality in the end."

George fetched a sheet of paper and a pen and sat down. "Why don't you go and wash up?" he said to Kerr. "I must copy this text first. Then we'll eat before retiring."

"Don't you want to telegraph them about your great discovery? The entire world is waiting for word on this, and only you and I know of it."

"I am concerned that they might close the excavation once they know. In a few days, I'll telegraph the circumstances to Mr. Arnold. I need another week to search for the other inscriptions." George involuntarily glanced at his trunk.

"Would it be possible for me to visit the mound at Nimrod, as well?" Kerr asked.

"I don't see why not. I'll send my dragoman with you for your protection."

With an expression of total rapture he began meticulously copying the tiny, wedged characters as if it were the first time he had seen. Kerr watched in awe.

ଔଷ

CHAPTER 24

Blindsided

Tuesday, 3 March 1874
Athenaeum Club, Pall Mall, London

Bowler had been waiting in the damp night air for more than an hour. He started coughing and his bones ached. This is not where he should be, but he simply could not tolerate the situation any longer. He had to speak his mind. Then he saw the round figure of a dignified elderly gentleman leaning heavily on his ornate silver-handled cane as a footman assisted him to descend from his carriage.

"Mr. Talbot, sir," Bowler greeted him.

"Mr. Bowler?" Talbot said.

"I came with the hope that I might have a word with you," Bowler explained. "When you were at the Museum today, I heard you say that you would be here this evening. I hope I'm not disturbing you, sir."

"Certainly not, my good man," said Talbot. "Please, come in with me out of this chill. We will be more comfortable in the Club."

"I've passed by many times, but I've never been inside," Bowler admitted. A beautiful young woman passed them, gracing the arm of a distinguished-looking gentleman. 'Probably not his wife!' thought Bowler with a smug sense of righteousness. He had heard rumours of the scandalous goings-on in these gentlemen's clubs.

As they entered the pillared lobby, with its polished marble floors and niches graced by classic sculptures, Bowler was overwhelmed. "Oh my goodness, how grand it is!" he exclaimed.

It gave Talbot immense pleasure to escort his old acquaintance up the stairs to the comforts of the wood-panelled lounge. They found a quiet, discreet corner. No sooner had they relaxed into the comfortable, brass-studded leather chairs than a waiter appeared. Talbot requested two brandies. Cuban cigars were offered and accepted. Mr. Talbot had such an easy manner that Bowler almost forgot their differences of class and means. They agreed that the weather was moderate for the time of year, and that the government was doing the best that could be expected, considering the circumstances. Talbot, aware that Dr. Oppert would arrive soon, decided to hurry the older man along.

"You seem worried, Mr. Bowler," he said. "What is troubling you?"

Bowler took a deep breath and looked at his hands. "As you know, Sir Henry has left the whole direction of our work in Mr. Smith's hands," Bowler said. "He is too wrapped up in India Office concerns to do anything. I rarely see him anymore. So it occurred to me to speak to you, if you don't mind, sir."

"Of course, but what of Dr. Birch? Shouldn't you first talk to him?"

"Oh, I have, sir, but to no avail. I know how much he respects your opinion, and I hoped that you might have a word with him."

"Very well, then. Please continue, Mr. Bowler."

"The crux of the problem is how poorly I am being treated under Mr. Smith. I am subjected to such a strict surveillance that I am only allowed to make copies in the presence of an attendant!"

Talbot's surprise was genuine.

"Formerly, I could have sent you at least my original rough copy," Bowler explained, "but now I am expected to give it up to the Museum as soon as I am done with it. It has been an unfortunate thing for me and for the work that it was ever committed to Mr. Smith's authority. When Mr. Norris was there, they disagreed so much as to readings and interpretations that their words were often very heated. Nowadays, Mr. Smith sometimes leaves me without any communication for weeks at a time. With him, it's always 'tomorrow! tomorrow!'" Bowler felt his face flush. He was unusually warm. He started to cough again, but he brought it under control by finishing his drink.

Talbot looked sympathetically at his companion. He knew that Birch would soon ask Bowler to retire. Photography would soon completely replace stone-engraved lithographs, and besides, Bowler was eighty years old.

"Do you feel," Talbot asked, "that this behaviour has a negative effect on the progress of the work at the Museum?"

"I must say that it is a burden on me and other staff as well," said Mr. Bowler. "The truth is that you real learned gentlemen have so petted and flattered and fondled Mr. Smith that it appears to me to have entirely unsettled his brain. Now, that that is combined with the false and fulsome adulation of the *Daily Telegraph,* he has become unbearable. He has made himself as difficult to access as the prime minister, and thinks his time is just as precious. Prior to the unfortunate discovery of the so-called 'Diluvial Tablet,'" he was a modest, unassuming student, glad to get any information he could obtain from anybody. Now his answers are as sure as if he, and he only, were the repository of all cuneiform knowledge! But this cannot be so! I only know that I cannot follow his readings. But then, I am nobody, and my doubts count for nothing! I can't make out why he is being sent to Asia again. Personally, I don't think he knows either."

Talbot's silence made Bowler nervous.

"I hope you aren't offended at my expressing myself so freely," Bowler added. "I rather fear that I offended Sir Henry on more than one occasion."

"No, no, certainly not," said Talbot. "I appreciate your candour, and I am pleased that you have such confidence in me that you feel you can bring your concerns to my attention." He extinguished his cigar. "I shall need some time to think about this, you understand," he added.

"Of course, sir," Bowler said. "I would not expect or want you to do otherwise."

"Ah, there you are, Mr. Talbot," Jules greeted his colleague.

"Dr. Oppert. It is so good to see you again."

Talbot struggled to lift his weight from the chair.

"Oh, do not rise, sir," protested Jules. "Here, I have found a comfortable chair."

"Dr. Oppert, have you met Mr. Bowler?"

"No, I don't believe that I have. Mr. Bowler."

"Dr. Oppert, a pleasure to finally meet the famous French Assyriologist," said Bowler.

"Mr. Bowler is the lithographer at our Museum," Talbot explained.

"I am a great admirer of your work, Mr. Bowler. You are a true artist," said Jules.

"Well, thank you." Bowler's fleshy face reddened to the roots of his white hair. "In my solitary station, I rarely receive such compliments."

"I can tell you with all honesty, sir, that your work is held in the highest regard at the Louvre," Jules said. "If you should ever wish to relocate, I am certain that you would be given many generous offers."

"I am flattered, Dr. Oppert, but I am too old and set in my ways to even dream of such a drastic move. But thank you for your kind remarks." Bowler said. His legs creaked as he pushed himself from the chair. "It is late," he continued, "and as my wife tends to worry, I must be on my way home. Good evening, Mr. Talbot, Dr. Oppert."

"Good night, Mr. Bowler. It has been a pleasure meeting you at last," Jules said.

"I shall give careful consideration to your concerns, Mr. Bowler," said Talbot. "Thank you for bringing them to my attention, and take care of that cough. Goodnight, sir."

"Thank you, Mr. Talbot. Thank you for a pleasant evening, sir," said Bowler.

"What brings you to London, Dr. Oppert?" Talbot inquired.

"My wife and I were visiting with our Emperor and Empress at Camden Place in Chislehurst," Jules replied.

"Tell me of His Excellency and Empress Eugénie. How are they adjusting to private life?"

"Quite happily, I think. The burdens of the State were bearing down too heavily on Louis during those last years, and it took a heavy toll on his health. After all, he will soon be sixty-six."

"Perhaps, it is better that France is once again a republic," Talbot said.

"I wish the transition could have been effected in a less painful manner," said Jules. "The defeat of his army and his capture at Sedan still haunts him."

"You said that your wife accompanied you on this visit," said Talbot. "I did not hear of your marriage. When did it take place?"

"It was four years ago, in February."

"May your life together be as congenial as the one that I have enjoyed with my dear Constance."

"Thank you for your good wishes."

"How is your eyesight? I did hear of your troubles, with much regret."

"Much improved," replied Jules, "though it was a burden for some time. I believe that it was the constant exposure to the fine dust from the fragments. Now the darkness has passed, and I have special lenses for various activities."

"I wanted to thank you for the invitation to the concert tonight," Talbot added, "but, having entered my seventh decade, late evening engagements have become less attractive."

"Caroline and I would have loved to have you join our other friends," said Jules. "Perhaps, when you are next in Paris, you might enjoy a matinée at the Comédie Française."

"I would enjoy that, thank you for the invitation. What do you think of this new actress, Sarah Bernhardt?" asked Talbot.

"She is excellent," Jules replied. "We saw her in Dumas' *Mademoiselle de Belle-Isle,* playing Gabrielle. I understand that she will do two of Racine's works next year."

"How does she compare to Mlle Rachel? Many say that she is even more talented."

"I am afraid that you have asked the wrong person. I am biased in favour of the grand tragedienne, since she was the brightest star of my youth," Jules said.

"Very understandable. I doubt that another could match the passion of her performance. Her light burned out much too soon." Talbot noticed that his words had an unusual impact on his companion, and he changed the subject. "I was so pleased when you contacted me," he said, "for it has afforded me the opportunity to thank you in person for suggesting the date for the solar eclipse on my tablet."

"Perusing your valuable paper on this eclipse, I remembered our old acquaintance," said Jules. "It has been a rather long time since our correspondence ceased. I feel it is very important to maintain a healthy scientific intercourse between colleagues."

"Yes, indeed," Talbot agreed. "The mutual exchange of ideas is essential for the advancement of science." He took a deep breath. "What do you think of our Mr. Smith?" he asked. "His work at organising the Museum has been nearly miraculous."

"In matters concerning cuneiform, Mr. Smith has some pretentions to papal infallibility, and would believe that he is right even when he knows he is not," Jules said. He noted that Talbot's mouth tightened and his brow set. "As you are one of the inventors of the great art of photography," Jules continued, "you will permit that I have some confidence in heliographic facsimiles, and my copy has none of the signs that Mr. Smith reads on the document. There are three incidences where the cuneiform on the stone and that in the photograph are not the same."

"I have noticed certain odd cases, Dr. Oppert, but I am certain there must be some logical explanation for the discrepancies," said Talbot.

"You are, sir, as capable as Mr. Smith or me of forming your own opinion after examining an inscription," Jules said robustly, "and I am quite sure that your eyes will see the same as mine." He sighed. "I do not know if you are aware that I have been Professor of Assyrian philology and archaeology for some years at the Collège de France."

"Yes, I am aware of your excellent credentials, Dr. Oppert," said Talbot.

"I suspect that if Mr. Smith had a more solid background in the science of linguistics, then he would not have presented to his readers the nonsense that he has," Jules said.

"Mr. Smith is, and I am certain that he will continue to be, the senior assistant in the British Museum's Department of Oriental Antiquities," Talbot said. "His appointment was the decision of the Board of Trustees."

"My concern is that as we have the photographed text, how can his statements be so erroneous?"

"It is a mystery, sir," Talbot agreed. "I am at a loss to explain it. But he is still young—only thirty-three years of age. In time, I am certain that his work will mature."

"I must be going," said Jules. He could see that this was going nowhere. "My wife is waiting. In parting, let me say that I shall not publish anything that might be not be accepted by you. As gentlemen and colleagues, we should always extend to each other the compliment of laying our ideas before the other for the mutual improvement of our science."

"Of course, Dr. Oppert," said Talbot. "I most heartily agree to a free exchange of ideas and discoveries. It has been a pleasure meeting you again."

"And, I look forward to your next visit to Paris," said Jules. "at which time I shall be pleased to show you several interesting—and, I think, important—tablets that are among our treasures at the Louvre."

ଔ

Jules was delighted to find a cab available just outside of the club. It was comfortable, and soon his mind began to drift. He and Caroline had stopped over in London on their way back to Paris following a visit to her brother in Belfast. The previous day had been Purim, the festival in honour of the Biblical Queen Esther's victory over the wicked vizier Haman. Jules was remembering the adorable costumes the children were wearing when the carriage stopped, and he descended without taking immediate notice of his surroundings. The driver cracked his whip and the cab disappeared rapidly down the road. Jules stood bewildered.. Where was the theatre?

"Wait! Wait!" he called to the vanishing cab. "This is not the street!" In the bright moonlight, he saw a woman and a man walking ahead of him. He called to them, but they ignored him and turned into the next building. Curls of fog silently gathered and thickened, bringing with them a sense of foreboding. Jules thought he saw a policeman further down the street, but this apparition vanished as quickly as the others. He heard footsteps approaching from behind and turned to greet them.

"Pardon me, sir, but my cab driver seems to have misunderstood my directions," he said. "What is this area?"

"You're in Southwark, sir," came the reply.

"That is strange," said Jules. "I cannot imagine how he came to bring me here. Would you be so kind as to direct me to where I can catch another cab?"

"Certainly, my good gent. Do you see that light?"

"Which one? That one?"

In the moonlight, the glitter of gold specks against a white stone caught Jules attention as he followed the man's finger, trying to judge the distance in the fog. He needed to leave this place before it became any denser.

"Yes, that one just there," said the man.

The force of the blow propelled Jules forward. The tip of his cane caught in a crack between the paving stones, breaking his fall. His neck stiffened. The back of his head felt strangely numb. Kneeling in the filth of the street, he swung the cane round, landing the solid handle hard against his assailant's knee. A surprised shout of pain echoed down the street. Something metallic clanged on the pavement next to him.

"Bastard," muttered his assailant, "I'll teach you."

The dark figure arose, looming over Jules, silhouetted against the bright fog. He felt the cane jerked from his hand and land hard on his chest. He lay flat on the slippery paving stones. He saw the shadow of the man's legs straddling him. His head throbbed. He had no weapon. In one last, desperate move, Jules kicked with both feet towards the man's groin. Then all went dark.

Amused spectators jeered from a dirty window. A woman opened the door of the closest house and three ragged children rushed into the street. Suddenly, whistles shrilled through the fog and several pairs of heavy boots could be heard pounding towards them.

"Hurry up!" The mother demanded. Expert fingers searched Jules pockets, relieving him of his pocket book and watch. The nimble young thieves rushed back into the loving arms of their grateful family.

When the constables arrived, they found two men lying motionless on the street. One knelt next to each, while ragged curtains were hurriedly pulled over the watching windows. A third policeman arrived, pushed back his helmet, and scratched his head.

"He tried to kill me," groaned the burly fellow, who was cupping his hands between his legs.

"This one is out cold, sir," said one of the constables, indicating Jules.

"What's your name?" the sergeant asked the burly man.

"Tommy…Rigger…sir," Tommy gasped, rocking slowly back and forth.

"This one's bleeding from the back of his head, sir."

The constable picked up the solid metal cosh. "Here's the probable weapon. It's bloody," he said. He handed the weapon to his superior and stood aside.

"And you say that this fellow attacked you?" asked the sergeant.

"Yes, sir," Tommy said. He pointed at Jules. "He's crazy."

"'Cuff him until we straighten this out."

"But I've done nothin' wrong!" Tommy protested.

"What's this?" asked the constable, grabbing Tommy's hand. "Sir, come look at this."

"What is it?"

"This ring, sir, I recognise it."

"You're daft," Tommy said. He tried to pull his hand back. He still could not stand.

"No…I'd know it anywhere," the young policeman said.

"What's so special about it, James?"

"Sir, when I was a boy, a man I knew was murdered. He was bludgeoned to death. They said it was with a solid metal object to the head. He always used to wear a unique ring and the murderer stole it. *This* was his ring."

"Get the wagon," demanded the sergeant, and the constable who had been tending to Jules ran off down the street.

"Don't be daft, I bought it years ago," Tommy snarled.

"We could take him in on suspicion, but we'll need more evidence to hold him," said the sergeant.

"There was another victim, Ignacio Jones—an artist. He survived the attack and made a sketch of the assailant. I'm certain it could be found, sir."

Tommy could hear the hooves of horses and the wagon wheels as it approached from the distance. He panicked. The pain was still intense, but his legs might make a short dash to the door of a friend. He head-butted the sergeant in the stomach and started to run. James was too fast for him. He caught the collar of Tommy's overcoat and several hard blows from James's truncheon settled Tommy Rigger on the path to the gallows.

ᴓᴥᴓ

CHAPTER 25

A Sad Farewell

Friday, 15 October 1875
50 Crogsland Road, NW London

Mary heard the door open and knew that her husband was home. He would be angry, but she lacked any will to move. In a vain attempt to avoid the inevitable, she pulled the blanket over her head.

George was surprised. The usual order of the house had given way to chaos. From the sitting room, he heard shrieks of laughter as five children with gold and copper curls scattered to their favourite hiding places, leaving the nurse holding two month-old Ethel alone in the centre of the mess.

"Charles, Frederick, Elizabeth, George and Arthur, come back here this instant!" shouted their father. The children froze. They knew they were in real trouble when their father used their given names instead of his pet ones. Slowly, one by one, the children returned and took their familiar positions in a line. One glance into those large, innocent eyes was enough to melt any heart, but a father must be firm.

"What is the meaning of this!" demanded George. "I leave the house for a few hours, and look at the mess you have made. What is this? Instead of eating your breakfast, did you have a food fight?!" All eyes were downcast. "Charles," George said, "you are eleven yet you're behaving like a baby!"

"It was Freddie's fault," complained Charlie. "He started it."

"That is enough, Charlie. A mess like this could not have been made by Fred alone. Fred, you know better. Nine year-olds do not engage in such antics. Not in this house, they don't. You all know that papa is leaving tomorrow for a very long and dangerous journey." George stroked his long, reddish-brown beard. "Must I spend my time worrying if my children are misbehaving and creating havoc for their mother while I am away? This is not what I expect from my children. Now, quickly clean up this mess and dress yourselves properly for the day."

"Yes, Papa," chimed the children.

"Mrs Wilson, why are the children not dressed?" George asked, addressing the nurse.

"I left my daughter ill at home," Mrs. Wilson replied. "That's why I was late. Mrs. Barnard isn't expected back until tomorrow morning. I had to prepare breakfast for the children. I was only hired to care of the infant, who's been colicky all morning, not the entire household, sir."

"Yes, I understand, we are short-handed today. Where is my wife?"

"She is in *bed*, sir," replied the matron. "I could not persuade her to get up."

The curtains were drawn. The room was dark. Mary Smith lay on her side, with her back to the door. The bedroom was in total disarray. His clothes should have been packed. Instead, they were scattered about the room, and few had found their way into the trunk.

"What is wrong with you?" he demanded, throwing open the curtains. He pulled back the blanket, revealing only a tangle of blonde curls. Mary's face was buried in the pillow. "Mary, get up! There is too much to do for you to laze in bed all day."

Mary did not move. She turned onto her stomach and hugged the pillow tighter.

"Get up, now!" shouted George. Still, she did not move.

"If you are so eager to leave, pack your clothes yourself," came her muffled response.

"I am not eager to leave you, Mary," George said. He sat down on the edge of the bed and rubbed his wife's back. "I would never leave you if it were not truly important. You know that."

"All I know is that tomorrow you're going, and that I need you here with me. I cannot do this again. I just cannot."

"We have been over this," George said. "I have committed myself to this expedition, and I must go." He gently turned his wife over and pulled her into his arms. "This will be the last time, I promise you, Mary. I'll never leave you again."

"You could tell them that you have changed your mind. You have a new baby. Your family needs you here. Tell them anything. Just, please, do not go."

"It will be the last time," George repeated. He smoothed her hair.

"But you must bear all the expense of digging and the Turks will only allow you to keep a third of the artefacts that you find this time. It is not worth making the trip," Mary said.

"I know. They placed twenty or more conditions on me. The government is to have one third, and the proprietors of the land one third—for damage done to their crops, of all things. The land where the excavations are is mostly wasteland occupied by shepherds. I have no doubt that the proprietors will accept cash instead of antiquities. I'll make them a liberal offer. The government also is open to a compromise. They only want to take the largest sum possible."

"How was your meeting with Mr. Talbot?" Mary asked. She leaned her head on his shoulder and stroked his long, soft beard.

"He still expresses surprise that I'm going to Mesopotamia," George replied. "He's concerned about the animus shown by the Turkish Government during my second expedition, and thought they would have refused to renew the firman. He wants the Trustees to give a handsome douceur to the Pasha of Mosul to ease my way. So you see, I still have friends."

"Mr. Talbot has always been kind to us," said Mary.

"He hopes that I'll soon 'favour the world' with the cuneiform text on the Creation and Fall of Man," George said. "So, you see, I must go. How else can I effect a greater sensation with the announcement of that new discovery?"

"Did you see Sayce today?" she asked.

"Briefly," replied George.

"You're still worried about him. I can tell."

"I'm certain that he suspects something. He keeps asking questions about the tablets I published in the third edition of the *Cuneiform Inscriptions.* I seem to have made the corrections a little too perfect."

"I wish you had never started that. I am so afraid that, one day, it'll all come back to haunt us."

"If he had anything substantial, he would already have told Dr. Birch," George said. "Ever since that blasted lady and gent stopped us at the Museum, Sayce's been giving me these odd looks, like he's trying to figure something out. All was going well—I answered their questions. They were about to walk away when Sayce called me by my name, and them two turned back around. I don't know why, maybe it was because of the way she called me 'the *great* Mr. Smith' with such innocence, like a blasted child. I suddenly felt so ashamed of the deception. I could feel the blood rushing through my face to the roots of my hair. From that moment, I could see it in Sayce's eyes—he suspects I've been up to something, but I'm certain that he doesn't know exactly what."

"Let's not talk about it," Mary said. "Mr. Talbot praised your last publication on the Assyrian Canon, and he said that it was very important."

"Yes, but things are changing in Assyriology. The French, led of course by Oppert, are creating more confusion. They've started to say that we're misreading the cuneiform characters. Ever since Oppert's work on the Sumerian and early Babylonian texts came out, there have been whispers that Sumerian had a greater impact on the Assyrian than was previously thought. The other day, someone actually suggested that the name Izdubar should be pronounced 'Gilgamesh.'" George shook his head. "I don't know what to expect next."

"Have you heard from Sir Henry?" asked Mary.

"I believe that we are past that obstacle," George replied. "He has been very cordial to me the last few times that we met."

"That's good. So he's no longer angry with you for pressing to go on the first two expeditions?"

"Apparently not, as a matter of fact, he is being very helpful with this one. He seems to have softened since I dedicated my book, *The Chaldean Account of Genesis*, to him.

"I remember, you wrote it to 'my teacher and predecessor in my present line of research, in remembrance of many favours.' Those were very touching words."

"If only that king's list had not disappeared. I was so certain of where I hid it. Sir Henry would have been pleased by it." George signed and then continued, "The strangest thing is that he seems to spend an unusual amount of time with McAllister Jones.

"The Museum's secretary?"

"Yes. I just can't figure out why. We have finished volume four of the *Cuneiform Inscriptions*. I find it somewhat disturbing that he is conferring more with Jones than he is with me." George didn't want to admit it, even to himself, but in the deep recesses of his mind, Rawlinson's behaviour toward Jones reminded him of how he befriended him before Coxe's unfortunate journey to India. If only he could shake that stabbing sensation in the pit of his stomach.

"Mary, I am very optimistic about this new expedition," he said. "It's just the officials who are so slow. You'll see—when I am there in person, all will work out well. I'll have a capable assistant, Peter Matthewson, and Karl Eneberg, a very pleasant Scandinavian archaeologist, with me. Eneberg and I are two of a kind: enthusiastic and optimistic, which will make the travel more pleasant. I picked up a little Arabic on my previous journeys, and Eneberg has classical Arabic and is familiar with their Quran, so we shall be just fine."

"I know you will be. I just worry too much. Ever since the baby died, I've been so nervous. And this birth was so difficult. One just followed so closely to the other."

George held his wife tighter against his chest, trying to keep her from crying. It didn't work. Tears fell from four eyes and mingled on their cheeks.

"I will see about our little pet's tombstone as soon as I return. We'll never forget him. I often dream of him, sad dreams about that bitter day when he died." George's voice broke, and it was a few moments before he could continue. "But let's mourn him softly, my love, and be grateful that our Blessed Saviour has given us this beautiful little daughter as a comfort."

"I should feel grateful," said Mary. "I know that it's wicked of me. I've been neglecting our beautiful children."

"Mary, I am doing this for you and for our children," George said. He pressed her back, holding her shoulder firmly. "I know exactly what I am doing. This is the last trip I shall ever make." He spoke slowly and comfortingly.

"You do not even have the firman," she said. "Why not wait here until the Turks issue the permit before leaving?"

"If I am there, I can put more pressure on the officials to issue one for me," said George. The earlier I arrive, the sooner I can begin the dig." He kissed her cheek. "If I leave now, I will arrive in Constantinople by November. I have better contacts now, and it should take about a month to obtain a firman. I'll arrive in Mosul by January. This will give me time, weather permitting, to hire workers and make all arrangements for the dig. By March at the latest, we will begin. During that time, I'll buy other artefacts on the black market, like before. I know exactly where I'll have them dig. Within two or three weeks, I will announce the discovery. By June, I'll be ready to close down, and I'll begin the journey home in July, just like before."

Mary began to relax. It all sounded so simple. This still meant that it would be at least nine months before he returned home.

"You know that I must make these discoveries," George continued. "They will provide evidence that will close all the remaining gaps in our theory, and end all criticism. Besides, Sir Henry told me something wonderful."

Mary wiped her tears on the cuff of her gown.

"When I return triumphant," George continued, his face bright with a new vision of the future, "He will encourage *The Daily Telegraph* to begin a campaign demanding that I be appointed a Civil Knight of the Order of the Bath, just the commendation that he received for his archeological discoveries. He will petition the Queen himself."

Mary smiled for the first time in weeks.

"I shall be assured of a lifetime position at the Museum, and leave a great legacy for future generations of our family. Just think of what this would mean for our children and grandchildren."

There was a knock at their door. They could hear baby Ethel crying.

"Yes?" called Mary.

"The baby is hungry, Mrs. Smith," called Mrs. Wilson through the door. "May I bring her in?"

"Yes, Mrs. Wilson," replied Mary, sitting up straight in bed. George helped to arrange the pillows behind her. Mrs. Wilson carefully transferred the infant to her mother, and then returned to supervise the other children. The large, trusting eyes looked grateful to have found their mother.

"Oh, my sweet little Effie, you are so hungry," Mary said.

"Nurse the child, and I'll get the others ready for an outing," George said. "A nice walk in the fresh autumn air is what you need." George walked to the door, turned for another glimpse at his precious wife and child. "I am doing this for you, Mary, and for our children. I told you long ago that I would do anything to give you the best that life has to offer."

"George, you're all that I desire. All that I could ever want is to have you here, home with us," Mary said.☙❧

CHAPTER 26

The Telegram

Monday, 4 September 1876
19 rue Mazarine, Paris

Smith is dead."

Jules' announcement jolted Caroline from the fantasy of her frivolous romantic novel. She frowned and quickly read the remaining lines of the paragraph. She made a mental note of the page number.

"What did you say, dear?" she asked.

"The knock at the door was a telegram. It says that George Smith has died." Jules stood in the doorway, rereading the telegram.

"How? When?" Caroline hoped that her voice reflected sufficient concern. She held her finger on the next line in the drama.

"August the nineteenth," Jules replied. He shook his head in disbelief and closed their bedroom door. "There will be a memorial in London. No date is provided, but there is a reminder that they are still awaiting my Sargon paper." The soft lamplight deepened the lines etched around his eyes.

"Who sent the message?" Caroline said. She stole a swift peek at the tender exchange taking place in her novel.

"Birch," said Jules.

"His poor wife," she replied in a softened tone, "to be left to rear so many young children alone."

"Yes," he muttered, "it is a tragedy." Smoothing his dark moustache, he poured water into his glass and envied the carefree repose of the rustic Alpine youths depicted on the pitcher. "Still, he was neither qualified nor suited for the position they gave him."

"Jules!" she rebuked. "You must not speak ill of the dead."

"Of course you are right, Caroline," said Jules. He slowly removed his robe and laid it across the back of the chair.

"A memorial? Not a funeral?" Caroline inquired.

"It said that he died in Aleppo. Obviously, he did not return from his last expedition."

Jules sat on the edge of the bed, staring at the opposite wall. The patterned paper darkened, swirled, and danced like a blinding sandstorm. The sound of men cursing in Arabic echoed in his ears.

"Then there is nothing more to say," she mumbled, returning to her book.

"On this subject, I suppose not," Jules agreed, as the wallpaper regained its usual peaceful appearance.

"Does it say when his memorial will be held?" Caroline's voice trailed off as she wandered down the torchlight corridors of a mysterious medieval castle. She turned to the next page.

"No."

Jules was irritated. He suddenly appreciated the Oriental cultures that wisely refused to teach women to read.

"Everyone at the University is speculating on this new invention," Jules said, making a play for Caroline's attention. "They say that it might replace the telegraph one day." The highlights of her warm, brown hair gleamed against the cloud-white yoke of her pale blue nightgown.

"The telephone?" Caroline's almond eyes sparkled as her lips regained their characteristic curve. "Yes, it sounds wonderful."

Jules slipped back into bed, but just sat there. Caroline stole a quick glance at his troubled face. There it was again—his eyes had that strange, fixed look, as if focusing on some distant, perplexing object. The news of Smith's death was more disturbing to him than he was willing to admit.

"Jules," she said softly.

He did not respond.

"Jules," she demanded.

"Yes dear?"

"I know that Smith was often problematic," she began. Her husband gave her one of his 'that's an understatement' looks.

"And often he behaved disrespectfully toward you," she continued, combing a stray, steel-grey strand back from his brow with her fingertips, "but he is gone now, and those issues must be forgiven and forgotten."

"I know you are right, Caroline," Jules said. His brow was still knitted. "However…"

"It makes no difference, my love." she kissed him softly on the cheek.

"Of course," he said, smiling. "You are right." She was once again deeply involved in her novel, so he extinguished his light. Soon, the weariness of the day took its toll and he drifted off to sleep.

ঙ্ঙ

26. The Telegram

Distant whispers disturbed Jules' slumber. He sat up in bed and listened more intently. It was annoying that he could not make out the language. The house was quiet. Then he heard them again—they were coming from the direction of the children's rooms. Not wishing to alarm his wife, he slipped out of bed, only to sink knee-deep into sand. The short walk to the door seemed to take forever. He struggled to free each foot, only to have it sink deeper with the next step. A cruel, mocking laughter filtered in through the door. He heard the voice of a young girl calling his name. She sounded familiar, but remote. She was asking him for something, but he still did not recognise the language. When he finally opened the door, he found himself standing under the stark light of a desert moon. The girl was crying and calling his name from within a dark house—their house. He had to find her before it was too late. Trying to form her name in reply, he opened the door. A dark, thick liquid oozed toward his feet. He jumped back. Blood covered the floor.

Jules forced his eyes open. He was suffocating. '*Breathe!*' *h*is brain commanded. At last, his lungs obeyed. He placed his hand on his chest to soothe the pounding of his heart. Sitting on the edge of the bed, he felt around for his slippers. The texture of the wool rug beneath his bare feet was comforting. Familiarity guided him to the door. It opened into the dim glow of hall light.

His throat tightened as he turned the doorknob of his son's room. The light behind him slowly gave structure to the room. Except for an awkward toy soldier guarding the bed, the floor was clear. Jules smiled at the boy's angelic face. One spindly leg dangled over the side of the bed. Careful not to block the light, he walked to the bed, straightened the boy, and gently covered him. He was growing so fast.

Backing out of his room, Jules whispered a prayer of thankfulness that someone had taught him long ago.

ଓଃ

CHAPTER 27

The Wooden Box

Thursday, 5 October 1876,
19 rue Mazarine, Paris

The final rewrite of Jules' paper was completed by the time the second telegram arrived. The day before his departure for London, a servant was sent to the attic to fetch his luggage. Caroline was in her daughter's room braiding her long, flaxen strands.

"Mama."

"Yes, Anita?"

"Do you ever think of our father?"

"Yes, of course I do," Caroline said. She paused.

"What do you remember about him?"

"Oh, about how handsome he was, and intelligent and brave…" she leaned over Anita's shoulder and spoke to their reflections in the mirror. "And how he loved mountain climbing."

"It was very foolish of him to climb that silly mountain and die," stated her younger daughter from behind the satin dress of her doll.

"He was not foolish, Alice," snapped Anita.

"Well, I love my father!" insisted Alice. "He is always good and kind to us."

"You do not even remember our real father, so just be quiet. I am talking to Mama!" said Anita.

"You don't remember him either!" retorted the younger sister.

"Now, girls, that's enough," Caroline said. She resumed braiding Anita's silken locks. "Alice is right—Jules is a wonderful father. He loves both of you very much, and he provides us with everything that we could need or want. And you, young lady, should be ashamed to be speaking poorly of him."

"I do not think poorly of him," the girl said. She puzzled over her emotions. "He just goes to work and comes home, goes to work and comes home. Sometimes he travels to give lectures, which are always too boring. The stories of our real father are more interesting."

Caroline was grappling for a reply when a crash and scream echoed down the hall.

"Mama, what was that!?" Anita cried. She jumped up and peeped over her shoulder. Alice dropped the doll and flung her arms around Caroline's waist.

"Alice, please, I cannot move. Girls, put on your slippers, both of you…now!" Without a pause, they obeyed as their mother rushed from the room.

"Jacob! Jacob!" Caroline called down the staircase, "Come quickly!"

The thump of Jacob's irregular gait pressed her into action. Gathering the skirts of her indigo dress, Caroline began to climb the narrow steps to the attic. The servant girl was huddled on the floor, moaning and holding her left shoulder, a crimson stream blood trickling over the back of her hand.

"Lea," Caroline comforted, "my sweet, dear Lea."

"Oh, Madame," the girl said, her lips trembling, "it hurts." Untying the girl's apron, Caroline wrapped it round her wounded arm as well as she could in order to stop the flow.

"Lea!" puffed Jacob, his stocky frame filling the doorway.

"Papa," Lea replied. Turning her eyes to the fallen shelf, she added, "I am so sorry. I was just curious about that box. Oh, please forgive me, Madame." Caroline and her father helped Lea to her feet. "I should not have reached for it. It was too high. The chair tilted over. I grabbed the shelf and everything fell!"

"No one is angry with you," Caroline reassured, "but you must be more careful, dear one." They eased the girl down the stairs to the servants' quarters, with Anita and Alice bouncing after them. Soon, comforting hands were inspecting the wound.

"What were you thinking, Lea?" her mother scolded. "You must apologize to Madame Oppert."

"That is not at all necessary, Freda."

"Excuse me, Madame, but it is most certainly necessary," Freda said. She secured the bandage, and to Lea, she added, "This is your punishment for snooping into things that are none of your business. Remember this lesson, and learn it well! Those things in the attic belong to Madame and Professor Oppert. You should have taken the luggage and come directly down."

"Yes, Mama," the girl whimpered. "Please forgive me, Madame Oppert."

"Of course, Lea, it is all forgiven," Caroline said. She smiled. "I'll have your father bring the luggage after lunch."

"Madame, you must change your dress. There are spots on the cuffs. I'll clean them before the stains set."

Caroline left her daughters with the servants and returned to her room to change. Pausing at her mirror, she smoothed a loose strand upward, tucked it back into place, and adjusted the curls at her hairline. How sad—more grey seemed to appear each day. It was then that she noticed that her bracelet was missing.

The search began in Anita's room, but it was not there. She scanned the narrow steps. Nothing. Taking the lantern from the trunk where Lea had left it, she examined the floor. A flash of colour near the fallen shelf caught her attention. As she retrieved the bracelet, she noticed that the old wooden box was still lying on its side. She had never seen it before. Its latch was rusted shut. Taking a pin from her hair, she prised it open. Dust tickled her nose and made her sneeze. The box held two bundles of letters—one tied with a faded, blue ribbon, and the other with a plain cord. Taking the box with her, she gingerly made her way down from the attic. She had just managed her descent when she heard a cough and whimper. Her son stood near her bedroom door.

"Edouard, what is wrong?" she said.

"I was looking for you, Mama. Where were you?" asked Edouard.

"In the attic, my darling."

"I do not feel well, Mama. My throat hurts," he said. His dark hair was damp with sweat, and his forehead was hot to the touch.

Caroline stashed the box in her armoire and returned to her son. The remainder of the day was hectic—the doctor was called. Edouard's prescription was fetched. The girls' piano lessons were endured. Dinner was prepared and eaten. It was late when her husband's bags were finally packed. As she laid in the dark that night, she again wondered about the letters. Soon, the rhythm of Jules' breathing lulled her to sleep.

ଓଃ

Jacob tucked the last bag in the back of the cab. The pre-dawn air was cool and veiled by a light, translucent fog. Only the distant sound of a dog barking disturbed the calm.

"Is that all, Professor Oppert?"

"Yes, Jacob, that is all. Thank you." Jules glanced back at the house. "I wish that I did not have to go," he said. "Edouard is still ill."

"The boy is young and strong, and the fever has broken. I am sure that he will be fine, sir." The old servant put his bag in the cab. "Is Madame up?" he asked.

"No, I did not want to wake her. I must attend, for my absence from the memorial would be misinterpreted, but she need not be disturbed so early in the morning."

"Certainly, sir."

Jules stepped into the carriage. The driver gave a snap of his whip, and the team surged forward, whirling down the street. Jules began to relax. Fortunately, he had had enough time to settle a few pressing matters at the Louvre and arrange for a replacement lecturer at the Collège de France. He glanced absentmindedly at the vacant seat beside him. For some reason, its emptiness caught his attention. For a moment, his breath stopped. He had forgotten it. His mind raced through the morning's events. There—the last time he had seen it, it was on his bedroom table next to the lamp.

"Pierre! Turn back to my house! I have forgotten my papers." The horses were reluctant, but with the urging of the cabbie, they complied.

“Wait, please!” Jules insisted, practically leaping from the door. “This will take only a moment.” The horses stomped impatiently, but the cabbie held the reins taut.

Leaving his hat and coat in the cab, Jules rushed in and up the stairs. The children still slept, and the house was quiet. A line of light escaped from under their door. As he burst in, Caroline jumped. She sat on the bed with a stack of papers on her lap. A pathetic sound squeezed out from deep in her throat as he entered. He was stunned. In six years of marriage, he had never seen such an expression. The color of her cheeks deepened, and she lowered her gaze. Jules walked to the edge of the bed.

The blue ribbon had reluctantly yielded to her inquisitiveness. Pinched and twisted, it lay vanquished and partially covered by the thin pages. Lingering in the dusty box was the other bundle of letters, awaiting its fate. Several envelopes, yellowed by time, were scattered over the lavender bedspread. The familiar script, browned and faded, seemed odd and out of place. ‘Mademoiselle Rachel Félix, Hôtel rue Trudon, Paris,’ it read. His letters. He had forgotten about them.

Lifting Caroline’s chin, he kissed her forehead. Leaning nearer, he whispered in her ear, “If they amuse you, read them.” The confidence returned to her brown eyes. “But if they distress you, burn them,” he added. Then, with his characteristic abruptness, he announced, “Time is short.” He turned on his heels “I must go.” Taking his papers, he rushed from the room, leaving the fading pages of his youth in her hands.

The horses, heads held high, trotted briskly through the melody of a perfect Parisian morning. It was still early. He would arrive at the station in time to catch the train for the coast. Jules settled back into the seat.

"Ah, Rachel," he muttered, "has it really been twenty years?"

☙❧

CHAPTER 28

The Memorial

Saturday, 7 October 1876
9 Conduit Street, London

Jules descended from the carriage and mused at the pale, waning moon. The last couple of years had been difficult. It seemed that each day another critic arose to contest his work. Tonight he worried if his career, like this ominous moon, might also be waning.

He turned his thoughts to George Smith, who had played such a pivotal role for so many years. He wondered how the British Museum would cope with his loss. The lecture hall was filling rapidly. A flurry of greetings and handshakes with colleagues and associates from three prestigious institutes—The Royal Asiatic Society, The Royal Society of Literature, and The Society of Biblical Archaeology—slowed his progress through the crowd.

"Guten Abend, Professor Oppert," called a familiar voice.

Jules turned to find one of his most ardent critics, Friederich Delitzsch, at his side. "Have you met my fellow student of Assyriology, Herr Archibald Sayce?"

"Yes, Herr Delitzsch," replied Jules, "I have had that pleasure. Good Evening Mr. Sayce."

"It is very good to see you again, Professor," responded the Englishman.

"I was just describing the latest exchange in the ongoing debate between you and Joseph Halévy," smiled Delitzsch.

Jules returned the smile with the same insincerity with which it had been offered. Delitzsch was sharp. Everything about him was sharp; his intellect, his nose, and, most of all, his tongue.

"For how long will you continue with this foolish notion that a Sumerian nation actually existed?" asked the German scholar.

"I maintain, sir," stated Jules, "that the evidence regarding Sumer is sound."

"But, Halévy has argued so well that Sumerian is not a language, but merely an ideographic writing method invented by Babylonians."

"I am aware of my esteemed colleague's unfortunate position, Herr Delitzsch," responded Jules with a forced coolness. "However, it seems that we shall not have long to wait for the verdict. Ernest de Sarzec, our Vice Consul at Basra, has requested to excavate the site at Tello, which recent evidence indicates might prove to be the ancient Sumerian city of Lagash.

"Jules." A solid, well-groomed man with a robust white beard motioned to him. "Jules, over here."

"If you will excuse me gentlemen," concluded Jules.

"Of course Professor," conceded Delitzsch, as Jules walked away.

"Why do you antagonise him?" asked Sayce. "Is this issue really so important to you?"

"Not at all," said Delitzsch coldly. "I just enjoy baiting rats to fight. If we cannot drive the Jews back into their sewer, at least we can have some fun with them." He watched with narrowed eyes as Jules joined Layard.

"Austen, how are you?" he greeted.

"Good... You look well, Jules," Layard responded, shaking his hand. "It's good to see you, even if it is on such an occasion."

"Are you still in Madrid?" asked Jules.

"I am still an envoy extraordinaire, but a change of appointment is in the works," smiled Layard. "Soon, I'll be off to Constantinople as Ambassador to the Turks."

"You and Lady Mary must come to Paris before you depart," said Jules. "Caroline will be delighted to see you again." Looking around the room, Jules asked, "Is Rawlinson here yet?"

A short man with a head of thick, grey hair slowly rose to his feet behind Layard. A dusky hand touched Layard's arm.

"I saw him a few minutes ago with Birch," the man said. Layard stepped aside, and Jules recognized the dark face and smiling black eyes.

"Hormuzd Rassam," greeted Jules, taking his hand. "How are you?"

"It's good to see you again, Professor Oppert."

"Mrs. Rassam." Jules bowed slightly to the fair Englishwoman seated next to him.

"Professor Oppert," she replied.

"Jules, please join us," Layard said. He motioned to the vacant chair next to him.

"Thank you. Do you know what happened?" asked Jules.

"I spoke with both Peter Matthewson, the assistant who accompanied Smith on the expedition, and Dr. Birch." Layard said. "He explained that it was chaotic from the beginning." Layard searched the room for Birch, but did not find him. “Birch kept mumbling that if he had known of the danger, he would have recalled them in June.”

“The press said that he died of dysentery.”

“Yes. It was not until Matthewson arrived last week that the full story was known.”

“Wasn’t it about this time last year that his party left for Constantinople?” asked Jules. “I heard that he encountered extraordinary difficulties obtaining a firman.”

“Yes, well, Smith had many talents, but protocol was not among them,” said Hormuzd.

“I am afraid I must agree,” Layard said. He checked his watch. “All attempts to explain Turkish, Persian, and Arab politics and the importance of respecting their customs fell on deaf ears.”

“The political terrain of the region is more difficult to navigate than the geographical,” Jules said. His voice lowered as his eyes met Hormuzd’s.

“I always thought it ludicrous of the British Museum to send someone as ill-prepared as Mr. Smith to head their expeditions,” stated Alice Rassam.

“The man could not speak a word of Turkish or Persian, and he knew very little Arabic,” added her husband, leaning back in his chair. “They refused to permit me to accompany him. His folly cost us valuable respect, time and artefacts.”

“Undoubtedly,” Layard said. He shook his head. “I warned the organisers of his first expedition that Smith would need the guidance that Hormuzd could provide, but they pig-headedly considered an Englishman more capable than a native.

“Anyway, the milder winter months were wasted in Constantinople, waiting for the Turks to issue an official travel permit, but this time the firman was not granted until March,” he added in an exasperated tone. “They cautioned him to avoid Mosul and Baghdad, since cholera had been reported in those regions. Consequently, the expedition first passed through Syria. If you believe the Museum's version, Smith fearlessly led the expedition along the banks of the Euphrates northward from Balis, without any previous knowledge of the region, and miraculously discovered the ancient Hittite capital of Carchemish."

"Such a tantalising discovery!" injected Jules, and Layard nodded.

"You know as well as I do that any party under his guidance would not have survived a day in those mountains," stated Hormuzd, looking smart in a stylish brown suit. "Doubtless, it was their guide, whose name we shall never know, who brought the ruins at Yerabolus to his attention."

"I blame the press," stated Jules, shaking his head. "They re-shape people and events to appeal to the fancy of the public."

"This is where the story takes a turn for the worse," continued Layard. "Instead of collecting valuable Hittite artefacts and returning home before the heat of summer became too unbearable, Smith insisted that they proceed to Mosul. Matthewson informed me that Smith ranted on and on about how the reports of a plague were either altogether false or exaggerated. He was convinced that the Turks were conspiring to undermine the success of his expedition. Unfortunately for everyone, he was wrong.

"When he reached Mosul, the officials tried to persuade him to return to Constantinople. Instead of listening, as any reasonable man would have done, he interpreted their warnings as a challenge to his power. He travelled south to Baghdad, where the plague was worst, for letters confirming his authority." Layard searched his jacket and pulled out his pipe. "By this time, it was late June." He filled the pipe from his tobacco pouch. The flick of a match released a pale cloud of smoke and the aroma of Layard's favourite blend.

"Even though this was Smith's third expedition to Turkish Arabia, he had never spent a full summer in the region," Hormuzd said. Turning to Jules, he added, "You must remember Baghdad in June."

"Yes," Jules said, shaking his head "All too well."

"Few know the region as well as we. How many years were you baking under that devastating desert sun?" asked Layard.

"Nearly three years," responded Jules.

"My tenure was nearly twice as long. For five consecutive years, I directed the excavations at Nimrud, Kouyunjik, and Khorsabad. Then, after only one year's absence, I added a sixth year."

"It is the land of my birth, and Mosul will always have my heart, but, London is my chosen home," Hormuzd noted pensively.

The crowd suddenly fell silent. Sir Henry Rawlinson entered, escorting a veiled woman dressed in black. The crowd rose to its feet as if it were a single body, in respect for the grieving widow. Rawlinson led her to a chair next to his wife, and took the seat next to her.

Samuel Birch stepped onto the podium. Old colleagues and old rivals sat together in reverent silence, waiting for the renowned Egyptologist and Director of the British Museum's Department of Oriental Antiquities to begin. He bore his decades with dignity, but with less hair than many. He smoothed his white hair and noted how much they all had aged.

"Ladies and gentlemen," Birch began, "we have gathered here tonight to remember our esteemed colleague, George Smith. We wish to thank his widow for consenting to join us."

Mary sat motionless, studying the textures and tones of her black lace gloves against the shimmer of her black sateen dress.

"The untimely loss of your husband is deeply felt by us all," Birch said. Mary lifted her head toward the speaker, and her veiled silhouette captured the hearts of all present.

"Special gratitude must be expressed for the tireless efforts of Mr. William Ricketts Cooper, Secretary of the Society of Biblical Archaeology," Birch continued, "who had hoped to attend this evening, but unfortunately was kept home due to ill-health.

"George Smith was, for many years, the British Museum's dedicated senior assistant in the Department of Oriental Antiquities. Prior to this, he served as a most able second in command during Sir Henry Rawlinson's periods of absence from the Museum. Few knew him as well as Sir Henry did, and he has requested to address a few words to you this evening."

Taking a firm grip of the podium, Rawlinson scanned the audience. His Assyrian Studies students were all accounted for—most were standing against the back wall, but Archibald H. Sayce and William St. Chad Boscawen had obviously made the wise effort to arrive early enough to obtain front-row seats. The odd trio of Oppert, Layard, and Rassam caught his eye. They, like the others, waited patiently for him to begin. William Henry Fox Talbot sat a row behind them. 'Good,' Rawlinson thought. 'The presence of a philanthropist of Talbot's stature would stimulate the generosity of others when the time came for the appeal.'

"Thank you, Dr. Birch," Rawlinson said. His voice was a little huskier than usual, and tiny beads of sweat made his smooth crown glisten above the band of white hair.

"Friends and colleagues—most of you knew George Smith, and some were also at the touching memorial given for him at his parish church last month." Rawlinson paused, cleared his throat, and continued.

"There are, in our midst tonight, others of that elite corps—others who have known the danger and toil of that inhospitable wilderness—Ambassador Austen Henry Layard and Professor Julius Jules Oppert. We are comrades-in-arms who have sacrificed years of our lives in the noble ranks of knowledge, combating the darkness of ignorance."

Hormuzd stiffened. His name had not been included. This slight was deeply offensive. He had worked so hard to please Rawlinson—it was he who had outsmarted the French and found the great Library of Assurbanipal, and yet Rawlinson took the credit while he was still treated like a common digger. He was painfully aware that his was the only dark face in this gathering of the British intelligentsia. His jaw tightened. His wife's long, ivory fingers laced together with his dark, leathery ones. Unions such as theirs, even between two Christians and sanctified by the Church of England, were still deemed unnatural by most in 'polite' society. Alice understood and gave his hand a reassuring squeeze.

"George was one of us—one of the selfless few who have laid the foundations of the new science of Assyriology. This small fraternity is based on unwavering devotion to honour and truth." With these words, Rawlinson stared directly at Jules.

Jules was disgusted. Rawlinson never missed an opportunity to remind the scholarly world of their old rivalry. He had never met a man so incapable of acknowledging his own faults.

Layard's eyes narrowed. The words—fraternity, honour and truth—cut deep, reopening old wounds. He tried to block Rawlinson's voice from his mind.

"This morning," Rawlinson continued, "I walked down the corridor of the British Museum leading to the workroom, where our Assyrian treasures are studied. Those usually busy chambers seemed cold and empty. Everything was in its place—the tables, the stools, and the files—but emptiness permeated the space, as if some essential part was missing. George Smith was that missing element. How I longed to see his bright smile and hear his familiar voice."

Talbot's eyes misted. He found his handkerchief and dried the tip of his nose. The news of George's death was a terrible blow. His hands had taken on a tremor that would not abate. How would he be able to continue his research without George?

Birch was surprised. Those were the very words that he had said to Rawlinson only an hour earlier. Yet if they aroused compassion for George's poor family, then he could not complain.

"With his tragic death," said Rawlinson, "Great Britain has lost a patriotic son, the British Museum has lost its most talented and dedicated Assyriologist, I have lost my loyal assistant and friend, his beloved Mary has lost her devoted husband, and his young children have lost the tender, guiding hands of their father."

A slight sound from Mary's sorrowful silhouette shifted the crowd's attention from the podium. A black gloved hand slipped a handkerchief beneath the silent veil. She had known it would be difficult, but it was becoming unbearable. Mary regretted that she had come, but they needed the money. George had always said that Sir Henry was a master at persuasion, but this was a terrible price to pay.

"When I was preparing to speak to you this evening," stated Rawlinson, "I struggled for the words most fitting to describe dear George. How should I describe our fallen comrade? Of the many noble descriptors available, only one word suffices—loyal. He was the personification of loyalty. When George sailed, he knew the perils of his mission and he accepted them without question. With the unwavering courage of a veteran soldier, even as he fell on the front lines, his last thought was the performance of his duty." Rawlinson gauged the effectiveness of his words, and continued. "I should like to read to you the final entry in his journal, which, fortunately, was returned with his other belongings by his assistant, Mr. Peter Matthewson." Rawlinson opened the tiny book and began to read.

"'My collection includes some important specimens, including the two earliest bronze statuettes known in Asia before the Semitic period. They are in my long boots in my trunk. There are about thirty-five tablets and fragments—about twenty are valuable, some unique, including the tablet of Labir-bari-Kurdu the Laborssoarchus of Berossus. There is a large field of study in my collection. I intended to work it out, but desire now that my antiquities and notes may be thrown open to all students. I have done my duty thoroughly.'

"This was the George Smith that I knew," Rawlinson said. "The diligent young man who, with his last breath, was true to his duty. This was the young man that I am proud to have mentored and called my friend. But rest assured, dear friends and colleagues, that the work of George Smith will be carried forward to fruition, and that his legacy will continue to enlighten the minds of countless future generations."

Silence lay heavily in the room. Rawlinson felt exhilarated and privately congratulated himself.

"That…that is all that I have to say…" he muttered. He appeared to the crowd as if he might collapse. Without hesitation, Birch stepped forward and supported his elbow.

"Are you alright, Sir Henry?" he whispered.

"Yes, of course. Thank you, Dr. Birch," Rawlinson said. He made his way to his seat. He sat down and straightened his waistcoat over an ever-expanding waist. Louisa Rawlinson sat stiff-backed in her chair next to him. An attendant stepped forward. He placed a fresh glass of water on the podium and handed another to Rawlinson, who nodded in gratitude and motioned for Birch to continue.

Mary studied Rawlinson's profile. This was her husband's hero. George would have done anything for Rawlinson. Why had he insisted that George go on that nightmarish last expedition?

"Ladies and gentlemen," Birch said, "we have one other speaker this evening. Mr. Archibald Sayce is a fellow of Queen's College Oxford. He is an outstanding scholar who had the privilege of working closely with George Smith over the past three years."

Sayce took the podium. He placed his papers neatly before him and adjusted his round, wire-rimmed glasses. After taking a sip of the water, he began:

"The untimely death of Mr. George Smith is a loss that can ill be repaired. Scholars can be reared and trained, but hardly more than once in a century can we expect a genius with the heaven-born gift of divining the meaning of a forgotten language and discovering the clue to an unknown alphabet. The marvellous instinct by which Mr. Smith ascertained the substantial sense of a passage in the Assyrian inscriptions without being always able to give a philological analysis of the words it contained, gave him a good right to the title of 'the intellectual picklock,' by which he was sometimes called."

Mary fixed her gaze on Sayce's face; he had a stern jaw, sharp, penetrating eyes, and a high brow. Her nerves were frayed. George had been worried about Sayce, but certainly, he would not say anything—not here, not now.

"Mr. Smith was not only a remarkably talented pioneer of Assyrian research, but he was also the decipherer of the Cypriote inscriptions, which had hitherto been such a stumbling-block and puzzle to scholars. Such sanguinity can all the less be spared at the present moment, when a key is needed to reading those Hamathite hieroglyphics, to which the last discoveries that he was destined to make have given such an unexpected importance," Sayce continued.

Sayce noted that Mary's shoulders had slumped and her head shook slightly from side to side. He knew that Smith was incapable of making this discovery, but could not resolve how he had accomplished it. Tears filled Mary's eyes and dropped silently onto her gloves. God had taken George from her because of his sins, because of his ambition, which all stemmed from his love for her. He had reached too high.

"Mr. Smith was born of poor parents, and his school education was, consequently, broken off at the tender age of fifteen, when he was apprenticed to Messrs. Bradbury and Evans to learn the art of engraving. While in this employment, he often stole half the time allowed for dinner for visits to the British Museum, and saved his earnings to buy the works of the leading writers on Assyrian subjects," Sayce said.

Jules' mind began to roam to his early career and Rachel. When all was said and done, the secret of success was to have the good fortune of being in the right place at the right time in order to make the right connection. One never knows when a casually-chosen turn down a seemingly insignificant street can alter one's entire life. He wondered if Caroline had read the letters. But of course—she must have done so by now. Jules tried to focus on the speaker.

Archibald Sayce paused in his eulogy of George Smith for a sip of water. A good lecturer should never rush through his material. He scanned the gathering to determine the effectiveness of his presentation, and decided to try varying his tone and inflection more frequently.

Layard took a deep breath and put on his diplomatic face. His mind raced, trying to focus on what needed to be done before leaving for Constantinople, but it was too late. The memories had already begun to surface. Sayce was speaking again, and he forced himself to listen.

"Sir Henry Rawlinson was struck by the young man's intelligence and enthusiasm. After furnishing him with various casts and squeezes, through which Mr. Smith was led to make his first discovery—that is, the date of the payment of tribute by Jehu to Shalmaneser—he proposed to the Trustees of the Museum that Mr. Smith should be associated with himself in the preparation of the third volume of the *Cuneiform Inscriptions of Western Asia*. This was in 1867, and in that year, Mr. Smith entered into his official life at the Museum and devoted himself to the study of the Assyrian monuments.

"The first fruits of his labours were the discovery of two inscriptions: one fixing the date of a total eclipse of the sun in the month Sivan, or May, in 763BC and the other the date of an invasion of Babylonia by the Elamites in 2280BC. In addition, he published a series of articles in the *Zeitschrift für Ægyptische Sprache*, which threw a flood of light upon later Assyrian history and the political relations between Assyria and Egypt.

"In 1871, he published *The Annals of Assur-bani-pal*, or Sardanapalus, transliterated and translated, which is a work that involved immense labour in the preparation of the text and the examination of various readings. This was followed by an excellent little pamphlet on the chronology of Sennacherib's reign, as well as a list of the characters of the Assyrian syllabary. About the same time, he contributed a very valuable paper on '*The Early History of Babylonia*' to the newly founded Society of Biblical Archaeology which has since been republished in *The Records of the Past*, as well as an account of the Cypriote syllabary as determined by him. This has been the basis of the later work of Birch, Brandis, Siegismund, Deecke, Schmidt, and Hall.

"It was in 1872, however, that Mr. Smith made the discovery that has caused his name to be a household word in England. His translation of *The Chaldean Account of the Deluge* was read before the Society of Biblical Archaeology on the third of December, and in the following January, he was sent to excavate at the site of Nineveh by the proprietors of the *Daily Telegraph*. After unearthing the missing fragment of the deluge story, Smith returned to England with a large and important collection of objects and inscriptions. Among these were fragments which recorded the succession and duration of the Babylonian dynasties, a paper on which Mr. Smith contributed to the Society of Biblical Archaeology. It was in connection with these chronological researches that Mr. Smith's invaluable volume on *The Assyrian Eponym Canon* was written in 1875.

"Shortly afterwards, he again left England to continue his excavations at Kouyunjik for the Trustees of the British Museum. In spite of the difficulties and annoyances thrown in his way by the Turks, he succeeded in bringing home a large number of fragmentary tablets, many of them belonging to the great Solar Epic, in twelve books, of which the episode of the deluge forms the eleventh lay. An account of his travels and researches was given in his *Assyrian Discoveries*, published at the beginning of 1875.

"The remainder of the year was occupied in piecing together and translating a number of fragments of the highest importance relating to the Creation, the Fall, and the Tower of Babel. The results of these labours were embodied in his book, *The Chaldean Account of Genesis*.

"The great value of these discoveries induced the Trustees of the Museum to dispatch Mr. Smith on another expedition in order to excavate the remainder of Assur-bani-pal's library at Kouyunjik, and so complete the collection of tablets in the British Museum. Mr. Smith accordingly went to Constantinople last October and, after some trouble, succeeded in obtaining a firman for excavating. He set out on his last and fatal journey to the East in March, taking with him Dr. Eneberg, a Finnish Assyriologue.

"While detained at Aleppo on account of the plague, Smith explored the banks of the Euphrates from the Balis northward, and at Yerabolus, he discovered the ancient Hittite capital, Carchemish—a discovery which bids fair to rival the importance of Nineveh itself. After visiting Devi, Thapsakus, and other places, he made his way to Baghdad, where he procured between two and three thousand tablets discovered by some Arabs in an ancient Babylonian library near Hillah.

"From Baghdad, he went to Kouyunjik, and found to his intense disappointment that, owing to the troubled state of the country, it was impossible to excavate. Meanwhile, Dr. Eneberg had died and Mr. Smith, worn out by fatigue and anxiety, broke down at Ikisji, a small village about sixty miles northeast of Aleppo. Here he was found by Mr. Parsons and

Mrs. Skene, the consul's wife at Aleppo. After sending for a doctor, they conveyed him by easy stages to Aleppo, where he died on August nineteenth.

"The pioneer of Assyrian research and the decipherer of the Cypriote inscriptions—he can be all the less spared at the present moment, when a key is needed to the reading of those Hamathite hieroglyphics to which the last discoveries he was destined to make have given such an unexpected importance.

"He has left behind him the manuscript of *A History of Babylonia*," Sayce continued, "intended to be a companion volume to his *History of Assyria*, published last year. His loss is an irreparable one to Assyriology, for even beyond his powers as a decipherer, his memory enabled him to remember the place and nature of each of the myriad clay fragments now in the Museum, while his keenness of vision made his copies of the minute characters of the tablets exceptionally trustworthy.

"Mr. Smith's obliging kindness was only equalled by his modesty. Shortly after his return from his first expedition, Smith was showing me some of the tablets he had found, when a lady and gentleman came up and asked various questions, to which he replied with his usual courtesy. They thanked him and were turning away when, hearing his name pronounced, the lady asked, 'Are you Mr. Smith?' On his replying, 'That is my name, Madame,' she exclaimed, 'What, not the great Mr. Smith!' and then, like the gentleman with her, she insisted upon having 'the honour' of shaking hands with the distinguished Assyriologist, while Mr. Smith crimsoned to the roots of his hair.

"It is distressing to think that he leaves behind him a wife and large family of small children," Sayce said, "the youngest of whom was born but a short time before Smith's last departure from England. It is my fondest hope that all gathered here tonight will support this worthy subscription in the true spirit of Christian charity."

Sayce was pleased with his lecture. It covered all of the important points of the deceased's accomplishments and, more importantly, it was brief. As Sayce stepped down, Enthusiastic whispers swept the audience.

Birch took the podium and held up his hand for quiet. The members were eager to socialise, and Birch sensed the tension.

"Ladies and gentlemen, I shall be brief," he said. "When word of Smith's tragic loss reached us, Sir Henry was preparing to depart for the Geographic Conference in Brussels, which was held at the request of King Leopold II of Belgium. Overwhelmed by this severe blow, he spoke of cancelling his trip, but since the plans were too far advanced, he insisted that a subscription be established during his absence. Since returning, Sir Henry has adjusted his schedule to champion this urgent cause. As I am sure you have read in the press, we petitioned the Government that a pension from the civil list be provided for Mrs. Smith and her young family. An answer has arrived. With Mrs. Smith's permission, I shall read it now."

Mary nodded her approval.

Birch cleared his throat, and raised the black-edged card. He read:

Madam,

The Queen, sympathising with you in your bereavement and with the loss of one whose interesting and devoted labours have shed fresh light on ancient history, has been pleased to confer on you a pension of one hundred and fifty pounds per annum.

I have given directions that Her Majesty's gracious intentions shall be carried forthwith into effect.

I have the honour to be, Madam,
your faithful servant,
Beaconsfield

"Mrs. Smith is eternally thankful to Her Imperial Majesty, The Queen Empress, and Prime Minister Disraeli for extending such comfort during this time of grief. Yet, as you can see, dear colleagues, this sum will barely cover the necessities of a widow with six young children," Birch said. We wish to thank those who have already extended a supportive hand to the family, and we encourage all generous-hearted people to send their subscriptions for the fund at their earliest convenience. Please note that the address—Messers Bosanquet, Salt & Co., 73 Lombard Street, London—is printed at the foot of your programmes. Again, let me thank each of you for having joined us tonight for this vital effort, and we wish you a good evening."

The momentary silence was followed by the buzz of a hundred conversations beginning simultaneously.

"Hormuzd," Layard said. He turned to his old friend, who sat stiffly upright and stony-faced. "Let me say that I am embarrassed at this moment to call myself an Englishman. There is no excuse for such a snub. You are as deserving of praise for your work as any man present."

"Thank you, Austen," said Hormuzd. "I feel confident about the future. When they compare the results of my excavations against those of Smith's, they will be forced to acknowledge my contributions."

"When do you leave?" Layard asked.

"In a fortnight," Hormuzd replied.

"Then I shall see you next in Constantinople." Layard stood up and bowed slightly to Hormuzd's wife.

"Do give my warmest regards to dear Lady Mary," stated Alice.

"I shall," Layard said. "She deeply regretted that she could not accompany me tonight, but this stay in London will be very brief and her brother, Lord Guest, insisted on her company for the evening."

"Of course that is understandable." stated Alice.

"If you will excuse me, I promised to return early."

Jules, who until now had been lost in his own memories, stood up and walked with Layard a few paces away from the Rassams.

"Jules, it was wonderful seeing you again," said Layard.

"Yes, Austen," Jules replied. "I hope that you will find time to visit us in Paris."

"Hormuzd, do not be hurt," whispered Alice in her husband's ear.

"They ignored not only my contributions to archaeology, but also my years of diplomatic service in Zanzibar. Nor did they even mention those two horrid years of imprisonment I suffered in Abyssinia."

"The fact that you will resume the excavation was printed by all the leading dailies. Besides, the object of this meeting was to benefit poor Mrs. Smith."

"I agree," Hormuzd whispered. "As you said earlier, I do know his character too well. Besides, you can tell a great deal about a man from his wife. Prior to her marriage, Lady Rawlinson possessed the charms of a wild gazelle. Take note, my love—fourteen years of his overbearing domination have transformed her into an iron elephant."

It was true that Louisa, like her famous husband, had long ago lost her slender form to society's innumerable dinner engagements. However, Alice felt a little embarrassed by her husband's bitter remark. For whatever her husband's failings might be, Lady Rawlinson was praised by all for her kind and generous nature.

Jules watched Layard pause for a brief word with Rawlinson and Smith's widow. He could not help but agree that it was extremely rude that the British scholar had not acknowledged Rassam. However, he also knew that among French scholars, his unethical excavation of the Assyrian library would never be forgiven. It had rendered him a pariah, whose accomplishments they could never praise. As Layard made slow progress through the enthusiastic crowd, Jules turned to the Rassams.

"Congratulations on your appointment to replace Mr. Smith," Jules managed, taking his hat and umbrella and preparing to leave.

"Thank you, Dr. Oppert." replied Hormuzd.

"Before you leave, Dr. Oppert," Jules turned towards the voice to find Birch approaching them. "I must have a word with you in private."

"But of course, Dr. Birch." To Hormuzd, Jules added, "Have a safe and prosperous expedition, Mr. Rassam."

"We shall meet early in the morning Mr. Rassam." reminded Birch.

"Yes, of course sir." he answered. "Good evening gentlemen."

Alice and Hormuzd Rassam slipped unnoticed through the thinning crowd. When they had gone Birch turned to Jules.

"Dr. Oppert, I have a letter from Baghdad that is addressed to you." Birch reached into his coat pocket. "It was given to Mr. Matthewson, Mr. Smith's assistant."

"If I might ask, Dr. Birch, why did you not call them back?" Jules asked.

"There was pressure from certain Trustees to keep Smith there until the project was completed," Dr. Birch replied. "Mr. Smith wanted to return home and to leave his assistant, Mr. Matthewson, in charge. But, it was determined that his efforts would not be equally efficient as George's. For unknown reasons, the Trustees did not deem the death of thousands from the plague as a case of absolute emergency. A letter was dispatched recommending that Smith and his party take every precaution to protect themselves until the danger passed."

"Is there any substance to the rumour that Sir Henry is being considered for election to the Board of Trustees?" asked Jules.

"It does seem so," stated Birch. "Sir David Dundas is in poor health. It has been decided that Sir Henry will fill his place when it becomes vacant."

"May he have a complete recovery," responded Jules. An election to the Board of Trustees was a life-time position. It would secure Rawlinson control over the Museum's cuneiform collection for the remainder of his life.

"And may Sir David enjoy many more years," added Birch, worrying about his position as department head. He and Rawlinson had locked horns too many times in the past, and Sir Henry never forgot an offense.

Birch handed a small envelop to Jules.

"Thank you Dr. Birch." Jules took the letter. "The memorial was a touching tribute, and I shall be happy to support the subscription benefiting Mrs. Smith."

"I knew that we could rely on your generosity, Professor Oppert." Birch glanced back at Talbot, "If you will excuse me, sir, Mr. Talbot is waiting for me."

"Certainly, if you will, please give him my warmest regards." answered Jules, eyeing the envelope. Jules sat down again to read the letter.

Birch struggle to assist Talbot to his feet. With a firm grip on the elderly gentleman's arm, Birch managed to brace him on his silver-handled cane and, thus, balanced Talbot's weight on his wobbly leg. The dear old gentleman was becoming so frail.

"I have completed my study of Mr. Smith's recently published Deluge tablet in the original Cuneiform characters," Talbot said. "I agree with him on all the essential points—the building of the ship, the deluge, the letting the birds out of the ark to see if the land was dry, and the sacrifice of thanksgiving on coming out of the ark…"

It worried Birch that Talbot spoke of George as if he were still alive.

"His discovery is indeed a most important one, and it is likely to excite universal attention, especially in the religious world," Talbot continued. "It appears that the Babylonians possessed writings handed down from great antiquity, relating the early history of the world, and that the Jews and other nations accepted these histories as more or less true, nevertheless adding traditions of their own which they thought equally trustworthy."

"The Arab diggers," said Birch, not wishing to cause the elderly gentleman greater distress than the loss of Smith had already inflicted upon him, "have discovered a Babylonian library, and documents of the later dynasty of Nebuchadnezzar are finding their way to England. However, I am afraid that they are all sale tablets, and therefore of inferior interest."

Talbot slowly shook his head, and straightened up as much as the heavy hand of age would permit him. Tears streamed down Talbot's face, and he fumbled for his handkerchief.

"Dr. Birch, we have lost too many good men," he said. "First Coxe, then Hincks, and now Smith." He wiped his eyes and blew his nose.

"I know. I shall also miss seeing his children about our neighbourhood," said Birch.

"Why do you say that?"

"When George was appointed senior assistant, he purchased a house near mine. I have just learned that his widow will be forced to sell it."

"I have already sent a donation for Mrs. Smith, but I think that I shall send a little more," said Talbot. "Perchance it will help. I must go now. It is late."

"That is most kind of you. Here, allow me to walk you to your carriage."

Birch took Talbot's trembling hand and led him through the crowd. They paused to express their sympathy to the widow Smith as Lady Rawlinson helped her to stand. When the area around her cleared for a moment, Mary turned to Rawlinson.

"Why did you send him there to die?" she asked. "He idolised you. You knew he was not fit for such a task. Why…would you…?" Mary broke down in tears. Louisa supported her with a comforting arm. Her eyes pleaded patience of her husband.

"Come, my dear," said Louisa. "let me help you home to your sweet children."

As the two black-clad women moved forward, the crowd parted, permitting them to pass through in silence.

Rawlinson now stood alone, grappling with an unfamiliar mix of remorse and uncertainty. Images of George Smith—the shy boy he had met long ago at the Crystal Palace, the cheerful young man in the Round Reading Room, the amenable assistant poring for hours over dirty fragments, the meticulous copyist with a keen eye and unerring hand, and the zealous disciple savouring his every utterance—flashed before Rawlinson. His hand shook as he wiped the mist from his eyes on his silk, monogrammed handkerchief.

"Sir Henry."

He turned to find one of his former students, Delitzsch, standing at his side.

"Yes, Mr. Delitzsch?"

"I hope that I am not disturbing you, sir."

"No, of course not. How can I help you, young man?"

"Please accept my heartfelt thanks for your kind letter, and for the favourable review of my Assyrian textbook," Delitzsch said.

"It is always my pleasure to be of assistance to our Assyrian students. What have you set your sights on for the future?" Rawlinson asked.

"The majority of my time during my present stay at the Museum has again been devoted to my favourite subject of study, the bilingual texts," Delitzsch replied. "This is partly in order to make the *Sumerische Grammatik*, which I have worked out more and more completely. It and the second volume of my *Assyrische Studien* will be published by this winter."

"Excellent. I look forward to reviewing them," Rawlinson responded.

"The collection acquired by George Smith in Baghdad will indeed, as I presume, satisfy the need for New Babylonian texts of various kinds," Delitzsch said. "Yet I do not know if I will still find the time to copy this or that important text for myself. The ship that brings these newest treasures has happily arrived, but to my regret, the six boxes in which they are packed have, as of today, not been delivered to the Museum,"

"I shall do what I can to speed the process along," Rawlinson assured.

"The need for an Assyrian dictionary, however, is from day to day becoming more tangible. I have worked one out that pretty much suffices for my own use."

"Have you seen the work of the late Mr. Norris?"

"Yes, sir. It is a wonderful beginning. Unfortunately, a comprehensive production is still beyond our grasp. You may perhaps have noticed my commentary to the German edition of Smith's *Chaldean Account of Genesis*?" Delitzsch inquired.

"I found it very impressive," Rawlinson said.

"In our science, every day sheds new light and illuminates all at once some mystery previously thought impenetrable," Delitzsch said. "Of course, your Cuneiform Inscriptions is and will remain the one source, the only foundation, from which our science derives its nourishment—on which it can raise itself to a strong structure. For that very reason, Mr. Smith's death is a nearly irreplaceable loss for our science, for who will now edit a fifth volume with the same perfection and conscientiousness as he did? With all due respect for Boscawen's scientific endeavour, and despite the friendship that binds me personally to him, I do not, at least for the moment, consider him capable of such heavy responsibilities. Of course, the matter lies in your hands, Sir Henry. You are the Father of Assyriology and our sole mentor."

"I shall announce soon who will take up the mantle of George Smith," said Rawlinson. "All that I am at liberty to say at present is that fidelity to our lofty goals, great science, and grand institution is paramount in this decision. But rest assured that the work will progress in a timely manner."

Rawlinson placed his hand on Delitzsch's shoulder and began walking towards the door. "Our science stands on the threshold of a new era," he continued. "Much work remains to be done, young man, before we liberate the minds of men from religious superstition and facilitate the supersession of modern enlightenment. We of the pure Aryan race must rise to meet these challenges."

Jules sat in stunned silence at the end of the row, his forehead resting in his hands. Considering the ill-tidings that he had just received, this was understandable. Rawlinson and Delitzsch glanced back at him. Jules wondered what they had been discussing. They walked out together. This new generation of German scholars worried Jules. Most were blatantly anti-Semitic, which was starkly evident in their harsh criticism of every word he had written.

☙❧

CHAPTER 29

The Letters

Saturday, 7 October 1876
19 rue Mazarine, Paris

Caroline slipped lower on the pillows until her chin was forced down against her chest in a strained and uncomfortable position, but she did not move to relieve the pressure. She laid there, toying with the satin bow on her nightgown. From this angle, her stomach was flabby and distinctly unattractive. She remembered how flat it had been, and how slender her hips were only a few years ago.

"Can he possibly love me as much as he loved her?" Caroline whispered as her throat tightened and tears filled her eyes. She took a deep breath.

"Oh, why am I doing this to myself?" She pushed herself up to a sitting position. The clock ticked in time with her heart. She readjusted the stack of pillows—his mingled with hers. But the nagging questions were still there. Did Jules still love Rachel? Did he still dream about her, long for her? Reaching for her glass, Caroline took a long sip of the sweet, red wine. "How can I resent Jules' love for Rachel?" she said to herself. "After all, he was not my first."

Slipping out of bed, she opened her armoire. The wooden box was there, but she reached further back and retrieved another. Bringing both to their bed, she smoothed a place on the bedcover. From the smaller box she removed a tarnished, silver picture frame. Written on the back were the words "Dr. Bernhard Cohn, 1867."

A single drop of self-pity fell on the frame of a handsome, smiling young man. Her two beautiful daughters were evidence of her love for Bernie. Setting the picture on the table beside Jules', Caroline reopened his wooden box.

She had only read a few of the letters before jealousy had slammed the lid on them. Now she wanted to understand what had happened. She poured a little more courage from the decanter and arranged both sets of letters according to their dates.

> My Beloved Rachel,
>
> I really must go. I have surrendered too many times to the pleading of my dark, enchanting Lilith for one more night. I never hated my work before we met, but now, how I loathe returning to it!
>
> Believe me,
>
> Jules

> Dear Jules,
>
> Will this winter never end? I think often of you—too often. Please come to my new performance this weekend. I have reserved for you the best seat in the theatre, and for later, my arms.
>
> Rachel

> March 1850
>
> Rachel,

Do not torment me! You know I cannot come to Paris now. Soon, though, I promise.

Believe me,
Jules

September, 1850
Dearest Rachel,

Are you still angry? Please understand that I had to leave the tour early. This is a new position, and I could not miss the opening days of classes. As you pointed out, the salary is meagre, but it assures me financial independence from Father. Though I love him and I know he means well, I cannot live off his generosity. By the way, my parents found you charming. I still feel that we should have told them that evening, but your instincts are usually so keen that I leave the timing of the announcement completely in your hands.

With all my love,
Jules

August 1851
Rachel,

The rumours were true! That for which I have dreamed and worked has happened. I still cannot believe it – I have been appointed as the linguist on the scientific and artistic expedition to Mesopotamia! M. Faucher's letter just arrived, assuring me of the position. We leave on October 1st. A note of congratulations from Louis arrived in the same post, which was also accompanied by an invitation for both of us to attend a dinner in honour of those selected for the expedition at the Palais des Tuileries. I am most eager to meet Fulgence Fresnel, the head of the excavation. I have a few more arrangements to settle before leaving Reims, but I should be in Paris by the end of this week. Are you feeling stronger? We have so much to discuss.

Yours,
Jules

December 1851
My Dear Jules,

You will not be pleased, but I have returned to the theatre. I have responsibilities. I realise that this disappoints you, but my family and my sons depend upon me, as I am their primary support. My retirement, thought short-lived, has revived my strength. I must confess my restiveness was agitated by the gloating of Mlle. George. She had the nerve to say: "What keeps Rachel in the public eye is the champagne she drinks, the life she leads, and the moneyed fools who flock round her. Let her lead a decent life for a couple of months, and nobody will remember that she exists." Since her glamour faded and her audience dwindled, her resentment for me has known no bounds. She has no right to demean my talents, nor does the press to publish such rubbish. I must prepare for tonight's performance.

Forgive me, my love.
Rachel

Caroline could bear no more. Of course Jules had loved Rachel more! How could she possibly compete with the memory of the world's greatest actress? She regretted the nights when she had refused his touch. She was certain that he had been dreaming of Rachel when he had turned his back to her and gone to sleep.

Too much wine had made her dizzy. She cleared her side of the bed, pushed the letters and box to his side, and extinguished the lamp. The memory of his lips on her neck sent a tingling shiver down her body. She had never desired him as much as she did this night.

ↄ℥℘ↄ

Sunday morning caught Caroline off guard. She opened one eye and closed it again.

"See? She's not dead!" stated Anita.

"Well, she wasn't breathing a minute ago," retorted Alice. There was blessed silence for a moment, and Caroline nearly drifted off again.

"Mama, who is Rachel?" asked Alice.

Caroline's eyes opened. She bounced to a sitting position.

"Oh, dear Alice, you must give me that letter."

Caroline quickly gathered the letters still scattered across the bed and pushed them back into the box. At last, she sat back and straightened her gown. Edouard was holding something behind his back.

"Edouard, please give Mama that letter, too," said Caroline.

"Mama, where is Mosul?" asked Anita. The voice came from the floor at the foot of the bed.

"What did you ask me, Anita?"

"Here, it says, 'Dearest Rachel, At last we have reached Mosul! Pardon, if you will, the sparseness of my previous letters. We have endured months of choppy seas, freezing mountains, and parched deserts since leaving Malta…'"

"Anita, I must have all of the letters," Caroline said.

"But why can't we read father's letters?"

"It is too early, Anita. We have not yet had breakfast."

"Mama, see, I found a picture!" shouted Edouard.

"Let me see, Edouard." He handed the aging photo to Caroline.

"Don't you think she is very beautiful, Mama?"

"Yes, Edouard, she was very beautiful."

"Who is she, Mama?" asked Anita. "Such an odd dress."

"She must be Rachel," stated Alice.

"Yes," confirmed Caroline, "this is a photograph of Mademoiselle Rachel Felix."

"Is she a queen?" asked Edouard.

"Where does she live?" asked Alice.

"Sadly, she died many years before you were born," said Caroline. "No, she was not a queen. She was France's greatest actress. She is wearing the costume of a queen here because that was the part she liked to play." Caroline paused for moment and added, "I think that this picture needs a nice new frame." The children nodded in agreement. She sat the picture on the end table.

"But first," she said, "we must straighten up this mess. A quick search satisfied Caroline that she had possession of the entire collection of letters.

"After we have eaten, I shall read some of the letters to you," she said. "Now run along. I must dress."

There was no escaping the children's curiosity. About mid-morning, Caroline ran out of excuses. She found their enthusiasm amusing. Searching through the letters, she identified parts that were appropriate for the children. They proved an excellent motivator.

"That is all for now," stated Caroline.

"No, please, one more," begged Anita.

"You have piano practice," insisted her mother, "but I promise that you will have two letters before bed tonight."

Later, when the children were bathed and ready for bed, they all snuggled under the blanket with their mother as she took out the next set of letters describing Jules' journey from Mosul to Baghdad. The children were enthralled and begged for another.

> 24 March 1852
> Rachel,
>
> As we sail this great river with its wealth of ruins, we assure ourselves that one day we will widen our goal and explore in depth this amazing country that promises such a rich archaeological harvest. That noble enterprise seems more remote now. We have encountered a serious misfortune that has cost us valuable time.
>
> Yesterday, in the late afternoon, we entered a point in the Tigris that few other rivers can match for majesty. Here, it is roughly four miles wide. Instead of a river, it seems more like a sea. The sunset was striking! The sky was completely calm and beautiful, with a waxing crescent moon rising. A storm suddenly appeared in the middle of the night. Thunder put an end to our dreams, and the boat was tossed from one side to the other. The wind blew our raft like a cradle in this great river/sea.
>
> So rough were the waters that M. Fresnel ordered the dismantling of the racks above the beds. After a few more shocks, we attempted to reach the shore. Just as we approached, a new gust of wind threw the raft into shrubs whose branches were hidden beneath the water. These plants punctured the

raw skins of the raft and twenty of them were promptly shredded. One of the watchmen fell into the water. Fortunately, I reached him in time to pull him to safety. The wind died down. It was a difficult job to free the raft from the hugging plants and to regain the deep water, but once this was accomplished, it relieved the weight borne on the damaged side of the kelek.

It grows late, and tomorrow we must work again on repairs.

Yours,
Jules

"My papa is a hero! My papa is a hero!" proclaimed Edouard, bouncing on the bed.

"Edouard, stop jumping!" scolded Caroline, but the boy pretended not to hear. "Alright, that is all," she added. It is past your bedtime. Off to bed, all of you. I'll be there shortly to tuck you in." Their complaints were to no avail. When the house was quiet again, Caroline sat until late in the night reading her husband's letters.

Then she opened and read those about Dinah.

1 October 1852
Jules,

I have just read your letters, and can only say that I think that you have gone quite mad! We knew that this separation would be for at least three years. I had no illusions that your promises of fidelity would survive such a great distance and time. But this! This has left me astonished. I read your letter and without thinking threw it in the fire. How could you entertain such a barbaric idea? Yes, you may try to disguise it with romantic phrases like dowry or bride's price. But it is what it is. Plainly and simply put, you have purchased a wife. Bought her like a sack of potatoes, and at such a ridiculously high price!

Jules, nothing can destroy my true affection for you, and I am certain that yours for me is equally intact, but this has shaken my estimate of your intelligence. I had never imagined that you, of all men, would consent to the demand that your children be baptised simply to secure access to a pretty girl's bed! Men are meant to think with what is between their ears, but this seems rarely to be the case.

Rachel

This did not sound at all like her quiet husband. Caroline felt as if he had in some odd way betrayed both Rachel and herself. She could not sleep until all of their secrets had been revealed. Finally, she came to the last letter Rachel had written.

20 December, 1857
My dearest Jules,

I am very ill in mind, as well as body. I am leaving Paris, not yet for the next world but for my villa at Le Cannet. It has a better climate, where I hope to find the warmth which is denied me here. Nap has kindly brought his yacht to transport my ailing body. All of me must be renewed, provided it is not too late. Sometimes, it seems as though it suddenly becomes night in me, that all is dark in my brain. Everything around me disappears, and annihilation threatens your Rachel. Alas, poor me! The me of which I was so proud, too proud perhaps, is so much reduced today that hardly anything remains. This letter, my friend, is to say goodbye; it is Rachel's farewell which you are too far away to seek, and Rachel is too weak to bring.

How much we have endured, dear friend, since that terrible voyage! I cannot write without tears of that terrible disappointment, which was the cause of my illness. How could I expect so sad an end to an enterprise which began so well, and which fell to pieces at the very hour when success appeared to dawn? And how easily could I have foreseen and forestalled the evil which now grips me relentlessly, that shirt of Nesses which I may never take off! Alas, I had too much confidence in my physical strength, too much confidence in my stardom, and without any kind of precaution or nursing of my strength in any way, I went straight ahead on that interminable road which stretches from New York to Havana – the last halting-place in my fatal Odyssey! Indeed, my dear friend, I do not know whether I shall live to return home, whether God will have pity on me for the sake of my poor dear children and my friends, or whether He will take me to Himself.

Farewell, my friend. This letter is perhaps my last. You who knew Rachel in the brilliance of her splendour and the riot of her glory, you who have so often heard the theatre ring with her triumphs—you would not believe that the gaunt spectre which now drags itself wearily over the earth is your

Rachel

It was after midnight and Caroline was emotionally exhausted. While preparing to return the letters to the box, she noticed a folded paper pressed in the base. Unfolding it, she stared in shock at the photograph inside.

☙

CHAPTER 30

The Homecoming

Wednesday, 11 October 1876
19 rue Mazarine, Paris

The sun was setting when Jacob unloaded the bags. As he turned the doorknob, Jules enumerated in his mind the tasks that he needed to complete within in the next couple of days. When the door opened, he was surprised to find his little family waiting for him in the vestibule.

"How was your trip, my dear?" Caroline asked. She kissed him on his cheek, lingering for a moment longer than usual. The fragrance of an expensive perfume enveloped her in a seductive aura. She had had her hair restyled, and Jules was certain that the dress was new. Jules peered into the adjacent room. Perhaps they had guests?

"Let me take your coat, Papa," pleaded the usually aloof Anita.

"Oh, Papa, I am so happy that you are home again!" exclaimed little Alice, flinging her arms around his waist.

"Papa, here is a picture that I drew for you," declared Edouard. Jules studied his son's artwork. Beneath an enormous round sun snaked a ribbon of blue. A stick figure of a man stood in the brown square above it. In the middle of the "river" was a circular head and extended line arms drowning in blue. Written above, in bold proud print, was "Mon Papa est un héro." Jules knelt down and hugged his son.

"It is a beautiful drawing, Edouard," he said.

"Come, Papa," announced Anita, "We have prepared a special dinner for you."

Jules followed Caroline into the dining room.

He was so glad that Eugénie had had the good sense to discard those monstrous hooped crinolines for the sleeker more reasonable fashions. However, he still found these great, padded bustles rather ridiculous. Women's fashion was beyond his comprehension.

The children, with impeccable table manners, listened politely to a brief description of Jules' trip. Then more time was spent on an update of their activities during his absence.

"Papa?"

"Yes, Edouard?"

"Will you tell us a story about when you were in Baghdad?"

"Of course, if you children would like to hear one," Jules said, smiling.

"Oh, yes. Please, Papa," begged Alice.

With the dinner of all his favourite dishes finished, the family moved to the salon. The children gathered around Jules, their eyes filled with wonder.

"Would you like to hear how we managed to leave Baghdad and begin our excavation of Babylon?"

"Yes, please," begged Anita, and the others' heads nodded in agreement.

"Well, the Pasha…" began Jules.

"Namik Pasha?"

"Do not interrupt, Anita," corrected Caroline gently, her hands busy with needlepoint.

"Yes, Namik Pasha," Jules said. He reminded himself that he must reread those letters. "He was still maintaining that the countryside was in revolt, and that he could not permit us to embark on such a dangerous journey. We had waited so long, and it was already July. Then, a peculiar incident showed that his excuses were false.

"A message arrived for M. Fresnel, under the seal of secrecy. It said that the famous golden statue of King Nebuchadnezzar had been found. We did not know what to think. M. Fresnel requested that the Pasha immediately provide us with an escort to take us to Hillah, which is the nearest village to the ruins of Babylon. When the Pasha heard the reason, he had two companies of troops ready by the next morning. We were very excited about this opportunity. However, while we were hurrying with the preparations, we learned the truth.

"A young man who lived in Hillah heard that we had arrived and planned to excavate the ruins of Babylon. His sister lived in Baghdad, and he wrote her a letter saying that this was good news, since the children played in the street with Babylonian cylinders as if they were marbles. He added that they had recently found the golden statue of Nebuchadnezzar. His sister understood that he meant this as a joke, but the letter was seen by a servant, who passed it secretly to an employee of the consulate, who, believing it all, ran breathlessly to tell the story to M. Fresnel. Despite the secrecy surrounding the letter, by the next day the entire city was buzzing with the news that we had discovered the golden statue of Nebuchadnezzar, even before we had gone there!"

The children giggled.

"Suddenly, everyone wanted to go to Babylon," Jules continued. "All sorts of people were getting ready to leave. One Jew made two calculations, in American dollars, of the exact value of the gold statue—one for if it were solid gold, and another if it were hollow. The Jews argued that it had been discovered first by a Jew, and the Armenians argued that it had been discovered first by an Armenian. In the cafés, the Muslims said that the gold belonged to the Sultan, and that it was not for the Jews, the Armenians, or the French. But the rumour did not stop in Baghdad. The caravans spread the story to Mosul, Aleppo, and Damascus. From there, it travelled to Beirut, and was even reported in the American newspapers! When this little joke reached Europe, the statue was said to be wearing a crown of diamonds!"

The children burst into laughter.

"Did you ever find the real golden statue, Papa?"

"Unfortunately, no, Edouard, it was only a silly rumour," replied his father. "But it was a good one, because it enabled us to begin the work that we were sent to do. The original golden statue was probably melted down and minted into coins by the Persian conqueror of Babylon, the Great King Cyrus. We did find many wonderful works of art, and some gold coins from the Persia Empire. I shall show you these, if you wish to see them."

"Yes, please, Papa, do show us."

"Soon, then, I shall take the three of you with me to the Louvre. For now, it is late, and you must go up to bed."

"Please, Papa, just one more little story and we shall go quickly to sleep."

Jules glanced at Caroline, who smiled but shook her head.

"We must save the next story for tomorrow night," Jules said.

Anita nudged the others. The children gave each parent a hug and a kiss. Alice gave her father the biggest hug and whispered in his ear, "You are so brave, Papa."

"We shall be up in a few minutes to tuck you in," Caroline said.

"I shall tuck them in for you, Mama," stated Anita. "We are not babies anymore," she added, kissing her mother goodnight.

The children whispered together as they climbed the stairs to their rooms. Once they were out of sight, Jules noticed that the photographs on the mantel had been rearranged. Now nestled among them was a framed photograph of Mademoiselle Rachel Félix. He walked over and picked it up.

"She was a most remarkable woman," he said. "She was a flash of lightning over a stormy sea. I wish that you had seen her perform."

"Why did you not marry her when you returned from the expedition?"

"Rachel was already married," Jules replied. He smiled and returned to Caroline's side. "To the theatre. Regardless of how arduous, or even abusive, that relationship was, she could never be separated from her audience for very long. Compared to it, the men in her life were mere passing infatuations. I blame her death on *la vie Parisienne*—the all night parties and absinthe ultimately weakened her constitution."

"Madame, will that be all?"

Caroline peered around Jules to see the servant standing in the dining room. "Yes, thank you. Have a pleasant evening, Freda."

"Perhaps we could have some wine?" asked Jules.

"Yes. That would be nice," said Caroline.

"Should I bring the wine, sir?" Freda asked.

"No, Freda, thank you. We shall take care of it," said Jules.

The Opperts entered the long narrow kitchen just as Freda left. Caroline found the wine glasses and sat them on the fleishig counter. Jules noticed an opened envelope lying near them.

"What is that?" he asked.

"You will never guess," she replied inspecting the crystal for spots.

Jules took a bottle of Bordeaux from the rack.

"It is from Princess Mathilde Bonaparte. She is giving a dinner party and requests that we attend. Should we go?"

"If you don't object," said Jules, he paused to read the label, "Château Mouton de Rothschild, 1872; this will do." Then he added, "I would prefer to spend more time with you and the children."

"I agree. Your travels keep you away too often. I shall send her our regrets," said Caroline.

"I am certain that she will understand," added Jules.

Caroline was pleased. Though the invitation had intrigued her at first, the more she thought about it, the less comfortable she was. After all, the woman did have a reputation for outrageous parties.

"Jules?" she said.

"Yes, dear." he answered, working the corkscrew.

"I can understand how an average young man might be dazzled by one as famous and attractive as Mademoiselle Rachel, but frankly, I am surprised that one like you would be attracted to a woman of low reputation."

The cork was freed with a gentle pop. Jules glanced at his wife. Her naïveté was usually charming, but it also made answering such questions problematic.

"When you were a child, your parents protected and shielded you from all harm and unpleasant situations," Jules said.

"Yes, of course," replied Caroline.

"When Rachel was a child, her parents travelled from city to city, peddling their simple wares. On one occasion, they were on their way to another town when Rachel, who was ill at the time, rolled out of the wagon into the muddy road. If her sister had not been woken by the movement and alerted their parents, she would have died of exposure during the night."

Jules filled Caroline's glass and continued, "When you stood under your wedding canopy with Bernhard, you entered married life as virgin." Caroline nodded.

"Rachel and her sister were left on street corners to sing and beg for coins while their parents were selling what they could to feed the family." Jules said. "Rachel was snatched by a stranger who forced himself on her in a dark, rat-infested alley." He filled his glass and added, "I am certain that, if she had had a safer childhood, she would have made wiser decisions and chosen a more moral lifestyle."

"I should not have judged her so harshly," said Caroline. They returned to the salon and considered their good fortune.

"*L'chaim*," Jules said, clinking his glass against hers.

"*L'chaim,*" Caroline said. She smiled and sipped her wine. "It seems from the letters that you loved Rachel very much," she added.

"Believe me, it was not easy to do. She was such a paradox—longing for stability, but at the same time abhorring the fetters that are inherent to it." Jules paused for a little more wine. "I was not with her when she died," he said. "The one who stayed with her until her last breath was Prince Napoleon. Of the Bonapartes, he loved Rachel with the deepest affection."

"What became of her sons?"

"A few years after Rachel's death, Walewski formally adopted Alex. Now the young man has entered the French diplomatic corps. Prince Napoleon promised Rachel he would watch over Gabriel, which he has done quite well. The boy has embarked on a promising naval career."

Jules refilled their glasses. Caroline set hers on the table and opened the small drawer of the Louis XV rosewood table. She took out a folded paper and handed it to Jules. He stared at it for a few moments.

"I cannot help thinking that this is connected to the nightmares that haunt your dreams. Please, tell me what happened." Caroline requested gently.

Jules stared at the paper. He knew what was inside, but he did not want to face it.

"Jules, dear, are you alright?" Caroline asked. She suddenly felt jealous. She was considering leaving the room when Jules slowly unfolded the paper. It held an old photograph. Considering its age, the image was remarkably clear.

There, smiling back at him was his own face—young and handsome, with a confident smile and untrimmed, wavy hair. He was holding a chubby-cheeked infant with large, dark eyes who stared curiously up at him. Seated next to him was an exotic young woman. Another infant snuggled shyly against her mother's arm.

"If I was given the chance to change anything in my life," Jules managed to begin, "this is the one thing that I would gladly undo." He reached for his glass and took a long sip of the red wine. "Fulgence Fresnel, Felix Thomas, Victor Place, and Rachel were the only ones who knew the entire story, and they are all dead now." He took Caroline's hand and kissed the palm. "It is a sorrowful tale, and I fear that, if you hear it, I shall lose your respect."

"At this point, you should fear more the damage that *not* telling me would cause," whispered Caroline.

He rubbed his fingers across the creases of his brow.

"Many of the details you must have gathered from the letters. My infatuation for Dinah—for now I know that was not true love—drove me to distraction. One day, our servant was bemoaning the fact that he lacked the funds to pay a bride price, and therefore could not marry the girl that he loved. I sympathised with his plight and gave him the amount. That was when I decided to use the same tactic to acquire Dinah. I was determined to have her at all costs.

"I went to her house that evening and announced that I had business with her father. When he heard my purpose, he shouted at me to leave. I was not moved. I stood firm. I wanted something, and I would not leave until it was mine. I made my offer. He was stunned by the amount. He knew that passion had blinded me, and that I had lost all business sense. Taking advantage of the situation, he set heavy conditions, and I agreed to all of them. Among them, the children would be reared in their mother's religion. Not even this dissuaded me. I agreed, and she was mine." Jules could not look at his Caroline. Such a betrayal of his culture, his religion, his very existence, was unconscionable. After a few moments of strained silence, he cleared his throat and continued.

"There were two priests involved. The younger, a Father Nathan insisted that I also convert. This I refused to do. He tried to persuade me. I still refused. We were married a week later by the elder priest." Jules' brow knitted as if the drama was being re-enacted before his eyes.

"I had seen her only two or three times. It was foolishly impulsive. Had I known her character better, I never would have married her. I found her unbearably childish.

"After the wedding, we stayed with her parents," Jules continued. "I bought them expensive gifts, and they treated me well enough. In July, I left with the others for Hillah.

When we were settled, I sent for her and she arrived in due course.

"During the day, I was busy sorting and translating our discoveries. Sometimes she would ask questions about the cuneiform inscriptions, and I would teach her how to read the ancient markings. When the sun set, our team would meet Fresnel for instructions." He paused to sip his wine.

"We began work at eight. It was dangerous, and painfully slow. From midnight until four in the morning, we returned to our lodgings for a rest. Dinah and I spent these hours on the roof of our small, brick house, beneath the protective branches of the tall palm trees. Before sunrise, I left and she prepared our meals for the day. Nothing is more beautiful than the morning sun ascending the height of the Athlon, illuminating the desolation of ruins, and reminding us that this was once the wondrous city of Babylon," he said.

Caroline listened impatiently. She knew that he was stalling.

"We moved monumental inscriptions and wondrous works of art until the mid-morning sun made it unbearable to continue. Returning to our quarters, I would bathe, eat, and sleep. Then the cycle began again." Jules stopped. His eyes begged for permission to end the story, but it was not granted. When he continued, his voice was tight with tension.

"Before we had time to really know each other, she was pregnant. She became so large, so quickly, that I was very alarmed. At about six months, she began crying for her mother. She was frightened, so I returned her to Baghdad. I secured for her the services of the best physician. As you saw, there were twins. It was a difficult birth. We had a son and a daughter—Daniel and Esther. She remained with her family in Baghdad until I could bear my loneliness no longer and demanded that she and the children come to Hillah. I paid for her servant to accompany them. This photograph was taken on the first of September in 1853, when the twins were six months old. But our happiness was short-lived." Jules seemed at a loss for words. He sat for a while with that same distant stare that had always puzzled Caroline.

"Jules?" she laid her hand on his. He nodded, but still could not continue for a minute.

"The story of the golden statue of Nebuchadnezzar was never far from the minds of the local tribesmen," he finally said. "Consequently, when we found several large urns, rumours concerning their contents spread quickly. It was said in the bazaars and cafés of the city that we had unearthed twenty-seven jars filled with gold and jewels.

"Fearing unwelcome visitors in the night, we increased the number of Arab guards for our protection. This only increased their suspicions. Another factor that fed the rumours was that the urns remained unopened. We did this to preserve the fragile urns, since without the earth inside holding them together, they would fall apart. The rumourmongers were convinced that we were hiding the treasure until it could be sent to France.

"Politics also played a role in the tragedy. There is an ancient hatred between the Sunni and Shi'ite sects of Islam. The owner of the houses that we rented, Hadji Abd-el-Kader Tchaderdji, was a Sunni, and one of the local leaders of that sect. The most respected of the Shi'ite leaders was a certain Hamzah, who had great influence with the Turkish Prefect of Hillah, Hadji Ahmed Agha. As Abd-el-Kader's tenants, we were regarded as his friends, and therefore, in the mind of Hamzah and his son, Ahmed, we were antagonists."

"Was this the same Ahmed who had attempted to abduct Dinah in the market?" Caroline asked.

“Yes, he was, and he still resented that I had deprived him of his prey,” Jules said. He took a deep breath.

“On the tenth of September, I was alone in the ruins at Babylon. Felix Thomas was at Djumdjumah, and M. Fresnel was on a trip to Baghdad. Just before sunset I was in the building where we stored our discoveries. At the door several Turks and Arabs appeared, led by Agha and his friend, Hamzah. I received these officials with great civility. They accepted the compliments that I paid them, and we talked for a long time on topics of East and West diplomacy. The Prefect said that he had come to Hillah especially to visit me and to discuss a very serious and very unpleasant matter. I knew then that they had been watching, and had chosen this time due to my vulnerability. The truth was that Hamzah was determined to remove the imagined treasures from Abd-el-Kader’s property.

“Agha arose, as if to leave, but then stopped. ‘By the way,’ he said, ‘I almost forgot to speak to you about the twenty-seven urns full of gold that you found. Are you not aware that it is His Majesty the Sultan who allows you to make excavations in the territory of the Ottomans, and that therefore, all objects of gold and silver belong to him? I beg you, therefore, to kindly give me the treasures you've found.’

I replied, ‘I am aware that all objects in gold and silver belong to the Sultan, but we found only a few objects in bronze and iron here. As for the urns, see for yourselves what they contain.’

“I brought a vase, which I emptied in the presence of the Prefect. It contained nothing but dust. I did the same with several others. The Turkish officer, thinking that I wanted to deceive him, made me cast out the contents of eight or ten more. Nothing of value was found. Then Agha rose and said to Hamzah, 'Why have you brought me here?' He departed with his retinue, very disappointed.

"Barely ten minutes after they left a captain, sent by Hamzah, arrived and notified me in the name of the Governor of Hillah that I was to suspend all work at the site until a military commission could rule on the case.

"I replied, 'Tell your master that I am working here by order of the French Republic and His Majesty the Padishah, and under the auspices of its leader, Namik Pasha of Baghdad. Tell him that, in their names, I will continue the excavations.'

"My published account of this encounter ends at this point, with him replying very politely, Although I did point out that certain facts of the story could not be related." Jules paused for another sip of his wine.

"Actually, Hamzah sent the captain and his son, Ahmed, to extract the truth from me by force. They thought I would give in if they beat me. The first blows took me completely by surprise. As I lay on the floor, Ahmed told the captain, 'Cut off the right hand of this thieving Jew, and then ask him again.' The captain unsheathed a long blade. I lunged for the desk drawer, intending to hold them at bay with my revolver until they agreed to leave peacefully. Ahmed pounced on me. In the struggle, the gun discharged and he was seriously injured. I stood my ground and with the gun pointing at the captain. I said, 'Take him and go.'

"Immediately, I sent a letter to Fresnel in Baghdad with the details of the encounter. Three days later, Hamzah's son died and most of our workers disappeared. Fresnel arrived with a dispatch of French troops from the Consul." Jules finished his wine, which gave him the strength he needed to finish the story.

"The work stoppage effected all excavations in the region. Colonel Rawlinson, the British emissary, demanded that I provide him with a full report in person, after which he insisted that I accompany him to examine some inscriptions. This delayed my return to the excavation. The earlier trouble seemed to have subsided, however, and our troops had returned to Baghdad.

"I arrived with an escort on the seventeenth of October. The night was cool, with an bright autumn moon that transformed night into day. Since the days were cooler, Fresnel had discontinued the night work. I saw his light on and found him studying the site maps. We heard a scream. Two men ran from my house. The escorts gave chase. We found Dinah on the floor in a puddle of blood, clutching little Esther. She had been stabbed in the back, and there was a long gaping slash across the back of her neck and her left cheek. The baby was bleeding from a deep gash on the back of her head. Thomas took Esther, and we pressed our shirts to their wounds to stop the bleeding. Rifle fire sounded in the distance. Others arrived. The physician took charge of Dinah.

"Then I remembered Daniel. I ran toward the other room, calling his name. Fresnel, his sleeves streaked with blood, blocked my way. I pushed him aside, enough to see inside the room. He pulled me back. Blood oozed across the floor and splattered the walls. The servant girl's throat gaped open and her head lay oddly to the side. A small bundle was beside her—it was my son's blood-soaked blanket.

The room sounded as if it was filled with bees. Muffled by this buzzing, I heard Fresnel say, 'He's dead. I cannot permit you to see him.' My legs collapsed. Fresnel eased me to the floor."

Jules stopped and shook his head as if he still could not believe what had happened.

Caroline squeezed his hand. He nodded and continued. "The heartless bastards had decapitated my infant son." Caroline waited, appalled, until he could continue.

"A wagon was brought to transport them to Baghdad. Dinah's and our daughter's injuries were not life threatening. Daniel's body was brought to our headquarters." Jules took several deep breaths before continuing.

"The old priest who had baptised the children had died and been succeeded by the younger one. This man still resented my refusal to convert and wished to punish me. When I asked him about the burial, he dared to question if the boy was baptised. I was stunned and asked what I should do. He callously replied, 'Cast the coffin in a dry well, or burn it.'

"I sat alone on the floor in the courtyard of our headquarters in a daze, with Daniel's tiny casket before me. I had a message sent to the leaders of the Jewish community. Several men arrived. They brought me tea and warm food, but, they could do nothing more. The mother was Christian, and everyone knew that the child had been baptised. They expressed sympathy, and added that my choice had tied their hands.

"Darkness filled every corner of my mind. Thankfully, M. Tavernier, the French Consul, and John of Aristarchus, the turdjeman bey, brought this stage of my suffering to an end. They approached the Muslim authority, Mohammed Rashid, and explained the plight. He engaged the leaders of the Syrian Catholic Church and convinced them to receive the poor child, repudiated by both his mother's and his father's peoples, at their cemetery.

"It was a heartrending affair. In revenge for the accidental shooting of Hamzah's son, four had died—the two assassins that he had sent as his agents of murder, an innocent servant girl, and my little son. In the end, four parties demonstrated great charity—two Greek Orthodox officials, a Muslim community leader, and a Syrian Catholic patriarch.

"The situation was still dangerous at Hillah. The Shi'ite's refusal to work also affected the British excavation near Mosul. We carried on with the few remaining Sunni and Jewish workers. I spent the winter months working myself to exhaustion to keep the nightmares at bay. Fresnel feared that my life was still in danger. He decided that, in the spring, we would load a mule with our most important smaller discoveries and notes. I would take them and leave by the overland route. My comrades would crate the larger objects and float them down the river, where they would be shipped to Paris."

"What became of Dinah and little Esther?" Caroline asked.

"She refused to see me or to speak to me. One day I forced my way into her house. I wanted to take her and the baby with me to Paris. Dawoud blocked her door. Through it, she shouted that she would never leave her family. She said that if I came again, she would tell the Muslims that I often blasphemed their Prophet, and that she did not care if they killed me. I never saw her or spoke with her again.

"For years," he added, "I blamed others for the tragedy. It was a very long time before I could admit my own fault." He studied the fine lines of his wife's face, and continued.

"We deceive ourselves into believing that because we desire something, we should have it. That which stands in the way of our passions and ambitions, we consider as evil. But, it's not so. As the Torah teaches us–there are no accidents."

Caroline lifted the photograph and admired the girl's beauty. She suddenly felt insignificant.

"I am confused. What, then, am I to you, Jules?" she asked.

"You, dearest Caroline, are my blessed wife," he said. He could see that she did not understand. "Let me tell you one more story, and you will understand my answer.

"While I was preparing to leave, my guides asked to speak to me. I told them that I had much to do and did not have the time. They told me that Rabbi Yosef Hayyim was with them. This sage had earned a reputation for wisdom at a very early age and actually was several years younger than I. Since they were to accompany me on a dangerous journey, I could not snub their most revered scholar. He had come to give us a blessing for a safe and successful journey. This made me nervous, since no one was supposed to know that I was leaving.

"We had tea. The rabbi expressed sympathy for the loss of my son. He conferred a blessing on me, that in time I would find a righteous wife of my own people, who would comfort me for this loss. You, Caroline, are that righteous wife. You have given me Edouard. You are my comforter and my dearest treasure."

Caroline reached into the tiny drawer and took out a small handkerchief. She unwrapped a pair of exquisitely worked gold earrings with small beads of lapis lazuli.

"These were in the corner of the box," she said in a small voice. "I believe they are the same ones that she is wearing in picture."

Jules took them and carefully threaded them through the tiny holes in his wife's earlobes.

"There, now they are where they should be."

He kissed her cheek. She blushed like shy bride.

"But what of Dinah, wasn't she still your wife when we married?" Caroline asked.

Jules shook his head. "I don't see how." He smiled at her. "The marriage should never have taken place, and it ended more than twenty years ago. But more importantly, it lacked the special element upon which our relationship is built – kedushah, sanctity."

Caroline was pleased.

"On the fifteenth of April, 1854, I left Mosul disguised as M. Pétiniaud's servant, with my hair and beard dyed black and a deep stain applied to my skin. He was on a government mission to take Arabian horses back to France. Mme. Tavernier, the wife of our Consul, travelled with us as far as Mosul. She informed Victor Place of my departure. The Pasha's men did not recognise me. They escorted us for two hours, and then we took our leave.

For more than a month, my guides and I crossed swollen rivers and treacherous mountains. On the eighteenth of May, on a treacherous mountain passage outside of Antioch, I almost lost all of my work and the contents of my packs when the mule carrying the load nearly fell into the abyss. The next morning, I saw the Mediterranean for the first time in years.

"Shortly before I was to board the ship that would take me to Malta and on to Europe, I asked a favour of the guides. I requested that when they returned to Baghdad, they should spread the story that, while struggling to save my mule, I was dragged over into the abyss with him and had died. As her priest would not permit a divorce without papal dispensation, I felt that this was the surest way to free Dinah to remarry. I paid them well, and we parted ways.

"From time to time, I exchanged letters with my friends in Baghdad. They provided me with scant information concerning them. I learned that about a year after I left, she remarried. I did not wish to interfere with her happiness, so I never broke our silence. Then, at the memorial for George Smith, Samuel Birch asked to speak to me. A contact in Baghdad had given Matthewson a letter for delivery; since he could not read the Arabic address, he passed it on to Birch. It was from one of my guides. He felt that I should know that Dinah and Esther were among the thousands who died of cholera this summer."

Caroline walked over to the fireplace and placed the photograph of between that of Bernie and Rachel. Jules joined her and slipped his arm around her waist.

"They have remained in that stuffy old box for long enough," she said. "It is time that they joined the family." She gathered the wine glasses and bottle from the table. "I shall only be a moment," she smiled.

Jules watched his wife walk gracefully from the room. He turned again to the image of Rachel – so young, proud and vibrant.

Rest well my beloved Eliza-Rachel. He glided his index finger over the edge of the silver frame. May we all merit a portion in the World-to-Come.

Caroline returned and took his hand in hers.

"It is late," she whispered. He extinguished the lights, and they climbed the stairs together.

THE END

CHARACTERS

Archeologists and Assyriologists:
Austen Henry Layard (1817-1894)
Sir Henry Creswicke Rawlinson (1810-1895)
Julius Jules Oppert (1825-1905)
Edward Hincks (1792–1866)
Edwin Norris, (1795-1872)
William Henry Fox Talbot (1800-1877)
George Smith (1839-1876)
Hormudz Rassam (1826–1910)
Fulgence Fresnel (1795-1855)
Victor Place, (1818-1875)
Felix Thomas (1815-1875)
Archibald Henry Sayce, (1845-1933)
Joachim Menant (1820-1899)
Conrad Gerhard Friederich Delitzsch (1850-1922)
Ernest Alfred Thompson Wallis Budge (1857-1934)
Toma Shishman, excavation foreman under Layard, Smith, and Rassam in 1876 and later.

Leading Ladies:
Eliza-Rachel Felix (1821-1858), classic French tragedienne
Mary Clifton Smith (1835-1883), wife of George Smith
Hadla, a girl mentioned in Layard's *Nineveh and Its Remains*
Caroline Jaffe Burnhard Oppert (1842-1931), wife of Jules Oppert.
Louisa Caroline Harcourt Seymour Rawlinson (1824-1889), wife of Sir Henry C. Rawlinson
Constance Talbot (1811-1880), wife of Fox Talbot
Anne Eliza Price Rassam, wife of Hormudz Rassam
Dinah, pseudonym for an unnamed girl mentioned by Oppert in *Expédition Scientifique en Mésopotamie*

CHARACTERS

Royals:

Emperor Louis-Napoléon Bonaparte (1808–1873), nephew of Emperor Napoleon I

Empress Dona Maria Eugénie de Montijo (1826-1920), wife of

Louis-Napoléon

Queen Victoria (1819-1901), British monarch

Prince Albert of Saxe-Coburg (1819-1861), Prince Consort

Prince Napoléon Joseph Charles Paul Bonaparte (1822–1891),

nephew of Emperor Napoleon I; nicknamed Nap and Plon-Plon

Princess Mathilde Laetitia Wilhelmine Bonaparte (1820–1904) sister of Prince Napoléon

Count Émilien O'Hara van Nieuwerkerke (1811-1892), sculptor & Princess Mathilde's lover

Arthur Bertrand (born on St. Helena island 1817), son of General Henri Gatien Comte Bertrand.

Alexandre Florian Joseph, Duke Colonna-Walewski (1810-1868), illegitimate son of Emperor Napoleon I

British Museum:

Samuel Birch, (1813-1885) Egyptologist

William Henry Coxe (1840-1869), Birch's assistant

Sir Antonio Genesio Maria Panizzi (1797–1879),

Keeper of Printed Books

William Sandys Wright Vaux (1818-1885), numismatist & antiquarian

Robert E. Bowler (1794-1874), lithographer of the cuneiform Texts

Robert C. Ready (1811–1901), modeler, sigillarist, and electrotypist

CHARACTERS

Minor Characters:

Frederick Thorne, curate to Rev. Edward Hincks
Gustav Oppert (1836-1908), brother of Jules Oppert
Maryam - pseudonym for Hadla's mother
Demitris Yevani - pseudonym for an unnamed person, who died of smallpox in Smith's house in 1871.
Lazare Isidor, (1818-1881), Chief Rabbi of Paris
Children of Rachel Felix:
Alex Colonna-Walewski (1844-1898), illegitimate son of Alexandre Colonna-Walewski
Gabriel-Victor Felix (1848-1889), illegitimate son of Arthur Bertrand
Children of George & Mary Smith:
Charles Smith, (b. 1863) – "Charley"
Frederick W. Smith, (b. 1866) – "Freddie"
Elizabeth Smith, about (b. 1868) – "Cissie"
George W. Smith, (b. 1870) – Twopenny – "Tuppence"
Arthur W. Smith, (b. 1871) – "Bertie"
Ethel Smith, about (b. 1875) – "Effie"
Children of Jules & Caroline Oppert:
Alice Burnhard Oppert (b. 1868)
Anita Burnhard Oppert (b. 1865)
Edouard Oppert (1871-1944)

Important Fictional characters:

Tommy Rigger, devoted friend of George Smith
Harris Richardson, Mary Clifton's suitor.
James Collins, son of the footman/groom
Dawoud Shallal, Dinah's brother

EPILOGUE

Novels do not usually contain a bibliography. However, I feel bound to express obligations to the following sources from which biographic material and character sketches were drawn. Most of the dialogue was inspired by the letters found in the online resources, *The Correspondence of William Henry Fox Talbot,* Kevin Cathcart's *Correspondence of Edward Hincks: Volume III 1857-1866*, George Rawlinson's *A Memoir of Major-General Henry Creswicke Rawlinson* and the eulogies by Archibald H. Sayce for George Smith, Carl Bezold and Gustav Oppert for Jules Oppert. Other sources used, in addition to those mentioned in the text, are James Agate's *Rachel*, Rachel Brownstein's *Tragic Muse: Rachel of the Comédie-Française*, David Damrosch's *The Buried Book*, and the National Geographic Society's *The Adventure of Archaeology*. For a full bibliography and additional notes, please see our website at cornerstonedeception.com.

As a novel, *The Cornerstone of Deception's* purpose is to entertain. I made no effort to pry into the intimate lives of the historic characters, outside of basic family data gleamed from official census records. Thus, the romance threads were composed as entertainment and, though some may be loosely based on actual events, they are not to be taken as factual.